OF BLOOD AND PASSION

A VAMP CITY NOVEL

PAMELA PALMER

This is a work of fiction. Names, characters, places, and incidents are products of the author's imagination or are used fictitiously and are not to be construed as real. Any resemblance to actual events, locales, organizations, or persons, living or dead, is entirely coincidental.

BOOKS BY PAMELA PALMER

Vamp City Novels

A Blood Seduction
A Kiss of Blood
Of Blood and Passion
A Forever Love novella (in the *Vampires Gone Wild* anthology)

Feral Warriors Novels

Desire Untamed
Obsession Untamed
Passion Untamed
Rapture Untamed
Hunger Untamed
Ecstasy Untamed
A Love Untamed
Wulfe Untamed
Hearts Untamed novella

The Esri Novels

The Dark Gate
Dark Deceiver
A Warrior's Desire
Warrior Rising

Jewels of Time Novels

Sapphire Dream
Amethyst Destiny

To Bud Palmer,
my brother and best friend,
and one of the finest men I've ever known.

Chapter One

The vampire rushed toward her with terrifying speed.

As he leaped at her, fangs bared, Quinn Lennox grabbed his arm and turned, using his own momentum to send him flying against the back wall. As plaster fell to the ground around him, Quinn felt a surge of satisfaction, but she had no time to revel in her newfound power. Another vampire was already flying at her. Though her strength was a match for theirs, thanks to the magic now roaring through her veins, her speed was not. But with the full awakening of her Blackstone magic, she'd acquired an ability to track and sense their movements almost before they made them. She might not be able to move as fast as they could, but she could see them coming.

Quinn grabbed the second vampire and threw him against the opposite wall, then lifted her hand as the third started toward her, slamming him into his companion with a blast of her magic alone.

With a quick grin, she bent her knees and raised her hands, preparing for another attack. "Bring it on, boys," she called to the three vampires now picking themselves up off the floor. As one, they began to circle her again.

"Did she just call us boys?" Micah asked with a chuckle.

"I believe she did." A smile lifted the corners of Kassius's mouth.

No smile breached Arturo's handsome face as he stalked her, leading this training session. His expression remained intent and focused, even as approval and worry did battle in his eyes. She was doing well against them and they both knew it. But she didn't have to be able to read his mind to know that her growing confidence in fighting vampires worried him.

As usual, Arturo Mazza was dressed all in black. His close-cropped dark brown hair framed a strong-boned face with high, pronounced cheekbones and even, attractive features. Despite having been a vampire for centuries, his skin still possessed a hint of Mediterranean gold, a gift from his Italian ancestors. With his broad shoulders and long, lean body he was a fine-looking male.

"Now," he said quietly.

The three vampires flew at her at once and while she managed to throw off Micah and Kassius, Arturo got through. Three against one turned out to be her undoing and the next thing she knew, she was on her back on the padded floor, Arturo's hard body pinning hers to the ground.

His hips pressed against hers, a familiar pleasure.

Heat ignited between them, but he ignored it, his eyes hard, his voice frustrated. "You lose."

Quinn pressed warm palms against his cool cheeks. "My death touch. I win."

He opened his mouth to argue, then closed it with a snap. Her death touch was just one of a number of powers she possessed, most of which she'd only recently found access to. While she'd never actually use this one on him, she had the skill. Technically, she could drain his strength, and life, with a touch of her hands.

Dark eyes watched her as if probing deep for the truth. "Could you use it?" he asked quietly. "On anyone?"

That was a question she didn't have the answer to. But now was not the time to admit it. "I'll do whatever I must to win," she said instead.

"You should not have let me drive you to the ground like this." His voice remained sharp, but his eyes were beginning to heat around the edges as his body settled comfortably into the welcoming curves of her own. "You might be able to kill me, but on your back, you're vulnerable to attack from others."

He'd been riding her hard, training her relentlessly all day. It was time he lightened up. Her hands still on his cheeks, she began to trace his lips with her thumbs.

Wry amusement lit those dark eyes. "You're not taking this seriously, *amore mio*."

"I'm taking this very seriously." But a smile tugged at her mouth as she ran her fingers into his hair and pushed her hips up against his. "I have you exactly where I want you."

Dark eyes turned obsidian. He resisted her for all of three seconds before he surrendered, taking her lips in a hot, claiming kiss. Heat exploded between them, tongues stroking, twining, mouths devouring.

"I believe the training is over," Kassius said dryly.

Arturo pulled back with a muttered, "Hell no," then jumped to his feet, pulling her up with him.

Quinn groaned. "No more. I need a break, Turo." She was hot, tired, and badly in need of food. "I haven't eaten in hours."

Arturo's expression turned suddenly concerned. "I'm working you too hard."

A quick smile broke through. "No, but we've been at this non-stop for nearly two hours. I'm human, remember? We need the occasional break every now and then."

He watched her, his hard-assed training coach mien falling away, finally, as he smiled at her with pride, and pulled her against him. "You are a very quick learner, *tesoro*. Your skills grow by the minute."

"Thanks." She found herself grinning, although heaven knew, she had little enough to be happy about with her brother's death racing at her like a red-eyed Ripper and this world—Vamp City—literally falling down around their ears. But newfound power was a head rush and she was still riding the high of besting three vampires, even if this particular trio would never actually hurt her.

"Great job, Quinn," Micah said with a smile as he and Kassius joined them. "If you get much stronger, there won't be a vampire in Vamp City you won't be able to take."

"An exaggeration," Arturo murmured.

"I'm not so sure." Micah winked at her.

When she'd first met Micah, she'd thought he was human, a new neighbor in her apartment building in D.C. He'd looked a bit disreputable with his untrimmed hair, unshaven jaw, and the three-inch scar running down one cheek, but the moment she'd looked into those laughing gray eyes, she'd known she'd found a friend.

"She cannot take Cristoff," Arturo said quietly, releasing her, his vampire master's name sending a chill down Quinn's spine. A chill that was mirrored in Arturo's eyes.

The sadistic Cristoff's determination to find her and make her pay for having escaped him...twice...bordered on obsession. He would torture her, making her wish for death long before he actually killed her.

Cristoff believed that Arturo, Kassius, and Micah remained his ever-loyal lieutenants and were busy searching for the cunning sorceress, when it was actually Arturo and Kassius who'd helped her escape Cristoff the second time. If their master ever discovered the truth, all of their lives would be forfeit.

The mention of Cristoff effectively doused Quinn's feelings of jubilation. Because, while everything inside of her screamed for her to stay as far from Cristoff as possible, the entire reason for her training was to prepare her to breach the monster's castle and steal his prized possession, the enchanted sword Escalla.

Her pulse accelerated, her body chilling, at the thought of what would happen if that sadistic vampire caught her. After her first escape, he's promised to cut off her feet if she ever tried it again. She had no doubt that losing her feet would only be the beginning.

But as terrified as she was of going, not going terrified her far more. Because unless she destroyed Escalla, her beloved brother Zack would die.

Kassius clasped her shoulder. "You did well, sorceress."

Quinn met his warm, serious gaze and smiled. The male, another of Arturo's best and oldest friends, was built like a tree—a huge, powerful oak. Born a werewolf, he'd been turned into a vampire, or more accurately, a werevamp since he still had access to his wolf form when he needed it. She'd come to know him as a quiet man with a big heart, especially when it came to humans.

"Thanks, Kass." Quinn turned back to Arturo. "I need to grab a sandwich, but I can be ready to leave in an hour. It's time we got that sword."

"You'll need glamour," Micah said. "I should probably glamour all of us for the trip to Gonzaga, just to be on the safe side. Meet me in the sitting room when you've eaten, Quinn."

"No," Arturo said, the word dropping like a five-pound brick. "We'll go tomorrow."

Quinn blinked. "The plan was to go today, Turo. We agreed to work on my skills, then leave. Today." She looked for support from the other two, but both Kassius and Micah took a step back as if wanting to distance themselves from the battle about to erupt. Her jaw tightened as her hard gaze swung back to Arturo. "I'm ready."

"You need another day."

"Like hell!"

Kassius and Micah made a full and hasty retreat, heading for the door, damn them both.

Quinn swung back to Arturo. "I'm never going to be ready in your eyes."

He lifted his hands, but his expression remained obstinate. "One more day."

"Zack may not have one more day," she snapped.

It was the wrong thing to say. Arturo's expression hardened, telling her without words that he still believed she cared more about her brother than anyone else, including herself. Especially herself. As much as she hated to admit it, that might have been true once, but it wasn't anymore. Not entirely. But it didn't alter the fact that the magic sickness playing havoc with Zack might kill him at any moment.

"I'm ready, Turo. You know that." If she came under attack, she'd be fine. As long as Cristoff wasn't the one attacking her. "Between Micah glamouring me to look like someone else, and my own magic, no one will even know I'm there."

He watched her, his eyes alive with a myriad of emotions. "What about the sword?" he asked quietly. "You've yet to master the control you will need to lift the sword from its case without drawing the attention of Cristoff's guards."

And that was the real kicker.

Quinn looked away, her mouth twisting with frustration because she really was having trouble with that part. Her being able to lift Escalla from its deadly, booby-trapped case with magic alone was crucial to their success. And while she couldn't practice with the real thing, she'd been working to develop the skill to lift heavy objects with precise control in hopes that she'd be able to pull the sword from a case that didn't want to let it go. Preferably without making a racket that would draw down half the castle's guards.

Unfortunately, this particular skill continued to elude her.

"I can do it," she hedged. She hadn't said she *had* done it. Sooner or later she'd manage it. The question was would it be today?

"Show me."

Dammit. "We don't have time. We both need something to eat before we meet Micah."

"Show me, *cara*." Arturo slid one hand gently into her hair as he stepped close, facing her. "You would rush into Gonzaga Castle unprepared. And I fear that in doing so, you will die." Traces of anguish wove through the rich sable of his eyes as his other hand rose to her hair, as his thumbs traced her temples with gentle strokes. "But I have grave doubts that I will be able to protect you adequately, even though I will do everything in my power to do so, *amore mio*." The breath that tore out of him sounded pained.

And she believed him. Mostly. Her gut told her he spoke the truth. Then again, she'd always believed in him, even when his soul had been compromised. And she'd paid for that. Badly.

He wasn't that man anymore. She knew that. His soul had been fully restored. She was positive. Mostly.

"Cristoff has always been the strongest among us," he continued. "And while that strength, until recently, was tempered by compassion and mercy, it is no more." His fingers caressed her skull. "Stay here, *amore mio*." His words were a plea. "Let us retrieve the sword."

Quinn pulled away with a frustrated sigh. She appreciated his concern for her, she really did. But they'd had this discussion too many times.

"You don't have any way to get the sword out of its case. My magic is our only option."

"We will think of something else."

"No. You won't. I can do this!" She turned away from him, because she wasn't sure that was true. And if she failed? God help them all, because Zack wasn't the only one in danger. She would lose many, many she now considered good friends. When Vamp City crumbled, hundreds of vampires, werewolves, fae, and immortal humans would die.

And it could happen at any moment.

Vamp City, or Washington, V.C., as the vampires called it, was a magical otherworld created in 1870 by a powerful wizard, Phineas Blackstone. Blackstone duplicated a large portion of Washington, D.C. at that time—though only buildings and land, nothing living—to create a vampire utopia, a place where the sun never shone, where humans, brought in as servants and slaves, were unable to escape, where vampires could live and play and hunt in the open, free of human reprisal.

The vampires had been able to travel freely between the worlds until two years ago when the magic began to fail, trapping all within V.C.'s boundary at that moment. Hidden deep within the illusion of Blackstone's utopia was the true purpose of Vamp City—a vampire death trap.

As possibly the last sorcerer left in the world, Quinn was the only one who could possibly renew the magic and save the city. But to do that, she had to break the Levenach curse that was still partially binding her magic. And to do that, she had to destroy the enchanted sword, Escalla.

A shiver of dread rippled through her at the thought of intentionally walking into Cristoff Gonzaga's castle. Not only was he the most powerful vampire in Vamp City with the ability to pulverize the brain of any victim with a mere touch of his hand, be he human, werewolf, or vampire, but he was a sadist who literally fed on the pain of others.

"Quinn," Arturo said quietly behind her. Neither he nor Micah had been in V.C. the night the magic failed and were, as far as Quinn knew, the only two vampires remaining who were still able to come and go as they wished. There were other vampires in the D.C. area, others who were not trapped, but the others stayed far away from the crumbling city that could no longer fully protect its inhabitants from the deadly sunlight. Only Arturo and Micah remained, determined to save their friends. And determined to help her save her brother.

Strong hands cupped her shoulders from behind, then gently turned her to face him.

"I cannot lose you, *amore mio*," he said, the depth of emotion in his dark eyes melting her. As she slid her arms around his waist, he covered her mouth in a drugging kiss and she pressed closer, needing his touch, his strength, the momentary forgetfulness she found in his arms. She loved the feel of his cool lips, loved the way they turned warm when he kissed her—the way his entire body turned warm. She reveled in the strength of his arms sliding around her, and sighed with pleasure as her senses once more drowned in the scent of almonds and moonlight.

He was coming to mean far too much to her, which had her pulling away in a schizophrenic chaos of joy and frustration, of warmth and uncertainty. Because while she believed Arturo was as concerned with her safety as he claimed to be, that hadn't always been true. And, try as she might, she couldn't forget that.

The first time she met him, she and Zack had only just stumbled into Vamp City while searching for Zack's missing best friend, Lily. Arturo had lied to her and betrayed her even as he'd saved her over and over. Ultimately, she'd learned that his soul had been compromised, his morals damaged by the poisonous magic of Vamp City, but the goodness inside of him, even then, had not been entirely suppressed.

It was the purity of her own magic, he said, that had saved him. And, for the most part, she did believe that he'd fully reclaimed his soul.

But the memories of those old betrayals whispered warnings, still, especially when she caught him withholding information from her, as she had yesterday. Important information about Zack. That he would do that to her even now, after all they'd been through together, continued to prey on her mind.

Quinn pulled away from him, refusing to let him soften her resolve. There were too many lives at stake.

"I'm not waiting another day, Turo."

He met her gaze, an obstinate gleam flaring in his eyes. "First show me that you have acquired the finesse you will need to free the sword."

Oh, stubborn, stubborn vampire. She intended to win this fight. But perhaps there didn't have to be a fight. Maybe she really could prove to both of them that she had that finesse in her. Knowing she did would add to her confidence immeasurably.

"All right." She crossed her arms over her chest. "What do you want me to lift?"

He looked at her with surprise, then pressed his lips together, considering. "The barbell in the gym."

Quinn gave a short nod, dropped her arms and started for the door. "No problem."

"With two hundred pounds."

Her jaw dropped and she whirled on him. "That's ridiculous! Escalla can't weigh more than twenty."

"But the enchanted case in which it lies will not so easily let it go," he replied reasonably with a lift of his brow. "Lift the barbell a few inches using magic alone, then set it carefully down again, and I will be satisfied."

Yeah, him and her both. She'd been trying to find that kind of control for the past couple of days, and so far, had failed miserably. Another failure like before would only solidify his argument that she needed another day's practice. But she'd told him she'd try and she might as well.

Turning on her heel, she left the sparring room and strode down the hall toward the weight room where Zack spent most of his time these days. Both rooms were part of the extensive underground complex beneath Neo's safe house deep in the Vamp City otherworld. Just a week ago, this place had been swarming with humans who'd escaped their vampire masters—humans who Neo and his team had ferried back to the real world through a well-organized underground railroad. But as Vamp City raced toward its end, everything was changing. Neo and his team no longer cared if they were caught. They'd been taking risks they'd never have taken before in order to free the humans quickly.

No one was certain what would happen to the humans when the magic crumbled.

As Quinn entered the weight room, she found Zack and Jason— the human ex-marine who'd been training her brother—in the midst of a pull-up competition. Both men were sweating, Jason a little flushed with exertion, Zack a bright crimson thanks to the illness that had spiked his fever well over 120 degrees Fahrenheit.

He should be dead. According to Dr. Morris, he would be soon unless they managed to free him from the magic's deadly grip.

The sickness raging through her brother's body might be killing him, but it was not making him weak. Just the opposite. Against all that was logical, he felt perfectly fine and had been growing stronger by the hour. Quinn stared at her little brother, at the layers upon layers of muscle in his arms and chest, and shook her head. Just a couple of weeks ago, he'd been a tall, skinny computer geek who'd never lifted anything much heavier than his laptop. The two of them could have almost passed for twins, despite being only half siblings, with their height, wide mouths and green eyes inherited from their dad. Only their hair was strikingly different—his a mass of red curls, her own straight and blonde. Now, while she remained slender, he looked as buff and built as Jason.

On the surface, Zack appeared to have become addicted to bodybuilding, but Quinn knew the real reason he worked out constantly. He was determined to become as strong as possible, as quickly as possible. Just as she had a one-track mind when it came to keeping Zack safe, his own thoughts were focused on finding, and saving, Lily.

Arturo walked over to the weight bench, adjusted the weights at the ends of the bar to suit him, then stepped back.

"Now, *cara*," Arturo said. "Six inches."

Quinn met his gaze, then turned to her brother and Jason. "I hate to interrupt the pull-up battle, but I need you two to leave for a few minutes in case things start flying." She was fairly certain she could lift the weights. The trouble was doing it with any measure of control.

Jason responded immediately, dropping to the ground, but Zack executed three more seemingly effortless pull-ups before doing the same. He turned to Jason with a grunt. "Beat you."

Jason laughed. "No way in hell. You ignored direct orders."

Zack smirked. "You were hurting, man. Admit it. The moment she asked us to stop, you dropped."

Jason punched him good-naturedly in the shoulder and turned toward the door, but Arturo blocked their path.

"Stay."

Quinn looked at him sharply, then rounded on him as understanding crashed. "You'd endanger them intentionally."

"It will give you the proper incentive, *tesoro*."

She just stared at him.

But he didn't budge, just continued to meet her gaze with that unflinching stubbornness. And while she longed to tell him no way in hell, she knew he was probably right. With a suitable incentive, she just might find the necessary control. Then again, she knew Arturo wouldn't actually let Jason or Zack get hurt.

What the hell. It was worth a try. With a huff, she turned toward the weights and shook out her hands.

"Find the control, Quinn." Arturo's words were part demand, part plea. "Find it quickly."

"I'm trying. God knows, I'm trying."

She could almost feel the weights smirking at her, and had to quell the sudden, fierce desire to slam them against the wall. *That* she could do. Force was easy. It was the subtle lifting that remained steadfastly out of her reach.

"*Tesoro,*" Arturo pressed.

"I know, I know." With a huff of frustration, she concentrated on the barbell, willing it to rise. Almost immediately, the weights began to rattle and shake, but the bar remained glued to the bench.

Come on, she urged silently, pushing a little more energy into it. The rattling increased, the weights clanking together, but still the thing refused to rise. Dammit. She thrust still more energy at it and this time felt a welling of anticipation inside her as if she could feel the barbell on the brink of movement. They were almost... *There!*

The barbell shot straight up into the air, crashing against the ceiling.

Quinn gasped. "Zack, move!"

Jason ran for the doorway, but Zack started moving toward the barbell as if planning to catch two hundred pounds of steel!

"Turo!" she cried, but though the infuriating vampire moved close to Zack, he took no steps to interfere. Was he expecting her to use her magic to push the bar out of the way? There wasn't time!

Even as she lifted her hands, Zack caught the barbell with both of his, one leg lunging forward, his entire body absorbing the weight with ease.

Quinn's jaw dropped.

"Jesus, Mary, and Joseph," Jason breathed behind her.

Holding the barbells as if they weighed nothing, Zack turned to her, green eyes glittering with challenge and temper. "When the fuck were you going to tell me that I'm a sorcerer, too?"

CHAPTER TWO

Quinn stared at her brother. "Who told you that you were a sorcerer?"

She turned an accusing glare on Arturo, but the vampire lifted his hands with an innocent shake of his head as the three of them, and Jason, stood in the weight room beneath Neo's safe house.

"I'm not a fucking idiot," Zack snapped, holding a two hundred pound barbell as easily as he might a broom. "It wasn't that hard to figure out. My sister's a sorceress. I've suddenly got super power. It doesn't take Einstein to do the math."

Quinn met his challenging gaze. "Zack…you've also got a magic sickness."

Arturo edged toward the door. "I will let you handle this, *cara*. I have things to see to."

"Coward," she muttered, adding, "Both of you!" as she saw that Jason was following Arturo out.

"People die from magic sickness," her brother snapped. "They don't turn into freaking Superman."

Quinn stared at him. "Apparently you have."

"Yeah. Why did you tell me you'd inherited all your magic from your mother?"

"Because until yesterday, I thought I had. Your mom always called mine 'the witch'. It made sense, especially in light of the fact that I always had weird magical things happen around me as a child, and you never did."

He set the barbell back in its rack. "What changed yesterday?" he asked, his voice still stiff with temper.

"Arturo told me what I believe is the truth, that I inherited my

Blackstone magic from my mom, but my Levenach magic...and curse...from our dad. Which makes you a Levenach heir, too. But not a sorcerer, Zack. Thanks to the curse, heirs of Levenach have no magic."

It had taken her a while to untangle her own magic heritage, but she'd finally come to believe she was descended from two powerful wizards—the Black Wizard, from whom she'd inherited her Blackstone magic, and Levenach. Millennia ago, the two had been mortal enemies, according to legend, until finally Levenach had created an enchanted blade—Escalla—to kill the Black Wizard. As the sword stole his life, the Black Wizard had cursed Levenach and all his heirs, forever stealing their magic.

"I might not have magic, Quinn, but I've gained almost fifty pounds of pure muscle in less than a week. That's not humanly possible."

"No. But I don't think it would have happened without the magic sickness. You've been a Levenach heir all your life, Zack. You didn't start to change until you got sick."

His eyes narrowed. "Why did Arturo wait until yesterday to tell you I was a Levenach heir?" His mouth twisted in disgust. "He's *still* lying to you."

"He didn't lie," she said, unaccountably annoyed at her brother's accusation even if she'd accused Arturo of the same thing. "He withheld his suspicions from me." Which...all right...was lying by omission. And it still made her mad. "I already knew your magic sickness was tied to the magic of Vamp City in some way. If I could have renewed V.C.'s magic, you'd be fine." But she'd tried to do that once and failed. And when she'd tried again, yesterday, she'd been determined to succeed even if it killed her. And it nearly had. The only way Arturo had convinced her to give up was by revealing his belief that saving the city wasn't the only way to save Zack. "When I failed to renew the magic, yesterday, Arturo admitted to me that there was another way to save you—by breaking the curse."

Zack scowled. "Why didn't he tell you that before?"

Her mouth compressed and twisted. "Because I wasn't always convinced that Vamp City needed to be saved." When she'd first arrived, she'd encountered virtually nothing but cruelty and evil in this place.

Understanding lit Zack's eyes. "He was afraid that if he told you that you could save me without saving Vamp City, you might do it."

"Yes."

"And you might have tried."

"At first...yes. Probably. But not now."

Zack studied her as if considering that, as if not sure he agreed. "How do you break the curse?"

Quinn hesitated. No one could know where they were going or for what reason. If word somehow leaked to Cristoff ahead of time...

"I can't tell you."

He scowled at her. "I'm sick of you treating me like I'm still a kid."

"I'm not." But, yes, she probably was, because barely a month ago, he'd still been one—a twenty-two year old college student who'd lived with her and spent all of his time in front of a computer screen with his best friend, Lily Wang. Not until Lily went missing, and Quinn and Zack accidentally stumbled into Vamp City while searching for her, had he been forced to grow up.

"It's too dangerous for anyone to know the details," she continued.

Zack just stared at her in disgust. "You know, forget it." He turned toward the door. "You do what you have to do and I'll do what I have to."

Quinn's heart lurched and she started forward. "Zack, don't even *think* about going after Lily."

"Why not?" he said, not slowing down.

This couldn't be happening. "You may be as strong as Superman, but you're still no match for vampires!"

He whirled on her. "How do you know? Did you *see* me catch that barbell?"

"Yes! I saw you. You're amazing and you scare the crap out of me because if you go after her—" Her breath tangled in her lungs, her voice dropping. "I'm terrified you won't come back."

"Quinn..." Zack tossed his head back as if she required more patience than he possessed. "I'm not stupid. I won't do anything reckless."

She snorted. "No? Then maybe you're not related to me after all."

"Says the queen of reckless," he muttered, but his expression softened and he pulled her against his nearly scalding hot body. "I won't go after her until the time is right, and I won't go alone. I promise."

It wasn't enough. His endangering himself was never going to be okay with her. But this was the best she was going to get and she knew it.

"Okay."

Zack pulled back and peered at her. "Where do you have to go to break the curse, Queen Reckless? I can tell you're getting ready to leave again."

"Don't ask, please?"

His frustration visibly returned making him look far older than his twenty-two years. In his eyes she saw dawning understanding…and disbelief. "You're *not* going back to Cristoff's." But she was and clearly he could see the truth in her eyes because he whirled away from her, digging a hand into his mop of red hair. "Dammit, Quinn. Why would you ever go back *there*?" But as he turned to face her, his features twisted into a mask of disgust. "To save me. You're always trying to save *me*."

"Not just you. It's the only chance we have of saving the city."

But his disgust didn't lessen one bit. "And I suppose *Arturo's* going with you?" She nodded, earning herself a look of raw disbelief.

"How many times are you going to let him turn you over to Cristoff?"

"He won't. He's not going to betray me, Zack. He's changed, you know that."

"*Do I?* My god, Quinn, all I know is he's the fucking vampire that almost got my sister killed. Twice."

He wasn't wrong about that. "He's also saved my life. Both of our lives. Besides, I don't have a choice. We have to break the curse and this is the only way to do it."

"Fuck the curse." Zack grabbed her shoulders with fiery hands. "You can leave this place, Quinn. Almost none of the rest of us can." In his eyes she saw the same fear for her safety that she'd always felt for his and it eased something deep inside her, this certainty that he loved her as much as she loved him. "Leave. Go somewhere far away and live your life. You don't need to save me. You don't need to save any of us. It's not your job."

As she stared into those green eyes so much like her own, she felt his love for her wrap around her heart and squeeze painfully. "I can't abandon you," she said quietly. "You know that. And as unlikely as it sounds, I can't abandon the others, either. I'm the last sorceress, their last hope. Hundreds will die if I don't save this world."

Zack released her with a grunt of disgust. "Most of them deserve to die."

"Kassius doesn't. Neither do Neo or Amanda or Sam or Rinaldo. There are good people here in addition to the monsters, Zack. Though I might be a little single-minded when it comes to you, this isn't only about you any longer."

His mouth compressed and he looked away, then turned back to her fully. "Then let me help you. I'm no longer a ninety-pound weakling, in case you hadn't noticed."

"You're also not a vampire." The moment the words came out of her mouth, she regretted them. The anger, the betrayal that leaped into his eyes, physically hurt her. While her words might have been true, her quick delivery had been a slap in the face to his pride. But there was no way in hell she was allowing him anywhere near Gonzaga Castle.

Zack scowled at her. "If you could, you'd wrap me in bubble wrap and pack me away someplace safe where nothing could ever hurt me."

She didn't answer because it was true. It was absolutely true.

"You risk your life over and over to protect mine. It's not fair, Quinn. It's not *right*. You're more important than I'll ever be and everyone knows it. You're the fucking savior of the world. This world, at least. I'm through being coddled, Quinn. Do what you have to do because I sure as hell can't stop you. But you're not stopping me from what I have to do, either. You need to know that."

Her gut clenched. "Zack, promise me..."

He waved a hand, cutting her off. "I've already made you all the promises I can. And I don't even know why I bothered. I'm dying. What fucking difference does any of it make?"

Quinn sucked in a breath at the harsh truth of his words.

Regret flashed in his eyes. "Look, Sis, like I said, I won't go after Lily until the time is right. But that decision is mine, Quinn. Mine." Without another word, he turned and walked away.

Chapter Three

With Zack's dismaying promise still ringing in her head, Quinn headed down the hallway deep beneath Neo's house in search of Arturo and the others. The hall was narrow, lit by lanterns attached to the walls at wide intervals, for there was no electricity down here. Life in Vamp City was one of darkness and shadows and she felt that keenly, now. She was terrified that she'd return from this mission to find Zack gone.

While it pleased her that her little brother was becoming so strong, she feared his growing confidence was quickly outpacing his abilities.

Jason stepped into the hallway from the main room a short distance ahead and stopped when he saw her, a large, unopened Gatorade bottle in each hand.

"Are you through with your discussion?" he asked carefully, his eyes friendly.

"Yes. He worries me," she admitted, stopping just in front of him.

"The fever or Lily?" the ex-Marine asked quietly.

"Both. Lily. See what you can do, please?"

"I can't talk him out of going after her," Jason said. "When he's ready, he'll go."

Her muscles tightened. "You have to stop him."

"No."

She gaped at him. "Jason…"

The look he gave her chastised. "I've been searching for my wife for over a year and a half, Quinn. I've let myself be captured by one vamp master after another in order to search their castles for any sign or memory of her. So far to no avail, but sooner or later I'll find her, or learn what happened to her. Or I'll die trying."

He looked away, peering into a distance she couldn't see. "I never meant to stay here after my latest injuries healed. The only reason I'm still here is that Zack's become a good friend, the best I've had since I arrived in this world."

He turned back and met her gaze. "I can't leave him like this, on the verge of..." His eyes flinched and she knew he'd stopped himself from saying the word *death.*

"I appreciate your loyalty to him, Jason. But Zack..."

"Zack is a man, Quinn, and a powerful one, as you saw today. Sometimes we have to risk all for the people we love. You know that better than most."

She stared at him, wanting to argue, wanting to rail at him. But the truth was, she did understand, all too well. There was nothing she wouldn't do, virtually nothing she hadn't already done, for her brother. And she knew Jason felt the same about his wife. Neo would have helped him get home, but Jason refused to leave without her even knowing she was probably already dead. Humans didn't live long in this place.

If he stayed here too long—more than two years—he'd turn Slava, essentially immortal, and never be able to leave. Still, he stayed and searched for the woman who meant everything to him.

Quinn had always known Lily was in love with Zack. She'd suspected Zack would eventually realize Lily was the love of his life in return. Finally, he had. Once he'd lost her.

"Don't let him do anything foolish, Jason. Please?"

Jason's eyes turned solemn. "If Zack goes after Lily, I'll go with him. That's all I can promise you." He started past her. "Worry about yourself, Quinn. That's the best gift you can give him." He met her gaze. "He loves you as much as you love him."

Quinn watched Jason's retreating back knowing she'd gotten all the reassurance she was going to get. Dammit.

She continued down the hall and into a spacious community room dotted with leather sofas and chairs and dominated by a huge oval conference table. But she saw no sign of Arturo, she was about to head for the stairs when she heard the sound of low voices down another of the hallways and turned that way instead.

As she neared a living area where the Slavas often read by the light of oil lamps, or played chess or checkers, she heard Micah distinctly. And he sounded frustrated.

"Ax…" Micah chided, using the nickname only he, Kassius, and one other used for Arturo.

"You needn't worry," Arturo replied in a tone that held an uncharacteristic terseness toward one of his closest friends.

"I'm not sure you'll be able to do it, Ax."

"I shall do what I must."

"If you can't…"

"I said I will do what I must!" Arturo snapped. "I know better than you the price of Cristoff's fury these days," he added in a calmer voice.

Quinn slowed, blinking, because if she didn't know better she might think they were discussing precisely what Zack had warned her about—Arturo's betraying her to Cristoff…yet again. He wouldn't, of course. She really did believe that. But damn if that wasn't exactly what it sounded like.

She was frowning as she rounded the corner to find the pair standing together, in deep discussion. They saw her at the same time, both jerking guiltily.

Cool disbelief slid down her spine and she chided herself for letting Zack's words affect her.

"What are we discussing?" she asked, telling herself they'd come up with a perfectly logical explanation, and quickly.

But as Arturo's dark gaze slid away from her, and Micah looked down at his feet, her breath caught. Trust had come slowly, but it *had* come. *She'd trusted them.*

As she watched their gazes slide away, the traitorous doubt that lived within the memories of Arturo's betrayals roared fully back to life.

He won't betray me again, her heart argued. He'd changed, reclaimed his soul.

But the memory of his first betrayal—how he'd led her into Gonzaga under the pretense of looking for her brother only to hand her over to his sadistic master, still had the power to make her ill. Cristoff hadn't looked much older than Zack, but with his shoulder-length fall of bleached-white hair and his contrasting jet-black eyebrows and small King Tut beard, he'd looked strange beyond measure. His thin, cruel mouth and blue eyes as pale and cold as a frozen lake would forever live in her nightmares.

"Master." She could still hear the clipped, matter-of-fact tone of

Arturo's voice as he'd bowed to that monster. *"I have found you a sorceress."*

Arturo pushed her forward.

Quinn's jaw dropped, her head suddenly ringing with his words. With his lie. "I'm not!" *She whirled on Arturo.* "Why would you say such a thing?" *What did he think he was doing?*

Out of the corner of her eye, she saw a flash of movement, then shrieked as Cristoff grabbed her and bit her neck with a razor-sharp stab of pain. Tears burned her eyes as she struggled against his impossible strength.

Cristoff lifted his head, a triumphant look on his face as he stared at her, his mouth bloody and smiling. "You've done well, my snake."

"I'm not a sorceress." *But the weirdness she'd lived with all her life lifted its ugly head and laughed at her denial.*

She turned to Arturo for help, saw the apology swimming in his dark eyes, and understanding crashed. This was why he'd brought her here. This. Not, as he'd told her, to search for Zack.

"You lied to me."

"I said what I must to keep you from trying to escape." *And this time she saw only truth in those hard eyes. This had been his intention all along. To bring her to his master.*

Cristoff laughed softly, a sound that formed ice crystals in her veins. "I call Arturo my snake for a reason."

On a burst of fury, she tried to get at the vampire who'd betrayed her, but Cristoff held her fast, binding her against him with an iron arm until she could barely breathe. She trembled with outrage and a deep, quaking terror.

"Go, now," *Cristoff ordered his snake.*

And Arturo had, walking away without a backward glance.

I will do what I must, he'd just told Micah. And what exactly did he mean by that?

The shadow of fear passed coldly through her body, the terror that he might actually be considering turning her over to his vicious master once again.

CHAPTER FOUR

"I asked what the hell you were discussing!" With as much hurt as anger, Quinn lifted her hands and, with her magic, threw both vampires hard against the wall, pinning them several feet above the ground.

Micah, damn him, tried to smile. "You're stronger every time I see you, Quinn." Quinn turned on Arturo. "You told me you were through lying to me."

"I do not betray you, *cara*." But he met her gaze with a hint of pain that had her stomach twisting. "I will never…"

Without warning, the floor beneath Quinn's feet lurched. She stumbled as the house began to shake with a violence far worse than any she'd felt before. As she righted herself with effort, plaster began to fall from the hallway ceiling.

Quinn released the two vampires, her hands flying up in mock-surrender. "This isn't my doing." At least, she hadn't done it intentionally. Her magic was unpredictable, especially when she was angry. But earthquakes had become all too common as the city slowly crumbled.

"It's getting worse," Micah muttered.

Quinn turned for the stairs. So far no sunbeams had broken through close to Neo's house, but the way they were multiplying, it was only a matter of time before one did. And the sunbeams that broke through from the real world during these episodes could, and would, kill any vampire in their direct path.

"Quinn," Arturo called.

Ignoring him, she strode through the community room, and the huge oval table, to the stairs. The vampires took cover during these episodes if they could, or stayed below stairs. While the windows in the house above had all been covered with blackout drapes, with the earthquakes intensifying, there was no telling what kind of damage the house might ultimately sustain.

This was all her fault. Even if she hadn't actually caused this particular earthquake with her anger, she was to blame for accidentally setting into motion the destruction of the Vamp City world.

It wasn't the first time Vamp City had been threatened. Blackstone had sprung the trap himself back in 1877, seven years after creating V.C., as had been his plan all along. He'd waited until the vampires had moved into their utopia in large enough numbers, then pulled the plug, trapping them, intending to slowly kill all those caught within. What Phineas Blackstone hadn't realized was that Cristoff Gonzaga hadn't fully trusted the sorcerer and had captured the wizard's two young sons—Grant and Sheridan—for insurance. Cristoff had used them to force Phineas to renew the magic. Once he had, Cristoff killed him so that he could never pull the plug on Vamp City again.

Unfortunately, Cristoff had never anticipated *her*.

When she moved into D.C. two years ago to share an apartment with Zack while he attended George Washington University, she unknowingly triggered the city's demise for a second time, apparently a result of the battling Blackstone and Levenach magics within her. But with Phineas Blackstone long dead, and neither of his sons, now immortal, possessing the power of their father, the vampires had no one to renew the magic.

For two years, they'd searched in vain for another sorcerer...until a month ago when she and Zack accidentally stumbled into the otherworld through a sunbeam. Arturo had saved her from certain death at the hands of another vampire and had recognized in her a great, if mostly latent, power. A power she'd been struggling ever since to fully free.

Quinn was halfway up the stairs when she heard Zack behind her.

"What did you do, sis?" he asked with wonder.

"This isn't my fault," she muttered. "Probably."

By the time the two of them reached the top of the stairs, the house had quit shaking. The earthquake was over. But as they entered the study through the hidden panel, Quinn's heart sank at the unmistakable gleam of sunlight shining along the edges of the curtains.

"Damn," Zack breathed behind her.

As the Vamp City otherworld died, more and more of the deadly sunbeams—the breaks between the worlds—appeared with each earthquake. They didn't last. The light would disappear again in a matter of minutes or, at worst, an hour. But with the next quake, the sunbeams would reappear again, right where they'd been before, and more besides.

Quinn heard a sound of distress, realized it was coming from the kitchen, and rushed through the ground floor rooms of the house, Zack close behind her. As she entered the kitchen, she found Mukdalla gripping the countertop, one arm tight around her wide middle, her expression stricken.

"Where's Rinaldo?" Quinn asked.

"Outside." The word came out choked. Mukdalla was of the Trader race—immortals that were born rather than turned, a race Quinn had disliked intensely until she met Mukdalla. While many Traders dealt in the human slave trade, Mukdalla worked with Neo to help the humans escape back into the real world. With their bright orange eyes and their heads and ears slightly too big for their human-like bodies, Quinn had always thought Traders unattractive. But Mukdalla radiated warmth and goodness, and when she smiled, she was nothing short of beautiful. Quinn understood how she'd won the heart of Rinaldo, her vampire husband of centuries.

But Mukdalla wasn't smiling. And Quinn was terrified she knew why.

Quinn reached for her, placing a hand on the woman's shoulder. "I'll find him."

"No." Mukdalla jerked and grabbed Quinn's hand. "If anyone's watching the house, they'll recognize you."

"I'll go," Zack said behind her. Only those within Neo's knew that Zack was her brother.

She gave him a nod, then turned to Mukdalla and wrapped her arm around the woman's wide shoulders, giving into an instinct that, for once, she didn't check.

Mukdalla turned into Quinn's embrace, burying her head against her shoulder. "He's not dead," she whispered. "After all we've been through together, I would sense it. I would sense his absence." But doubt rang with hollowness in her words.

Quinn wrapped her arms slowly around the Trader woman. She'd never been a hugger, had always kept others, except for Zack, at bay. But Mukdalla had made it clear she wished to be Quinn's friend. And despite her natural reticence, Quinn was beginning to realize she wanted that, too.

Before Zack reached the back door, the light at the edges of the kitchen curtains winked out as if someone had flicked off the switch. As quickly as the sunbeams had appeared, they were gone.

Slowly, Mukdalla pulled away from Quinn and turned toward the door, waiting either for her husband, or for the news that would shatter her world.

Vampires began to swarm the kitchen—Arturo, Micah, and Kassius, and Neo, a male turned in the 1970's who'd never ceased to identify with his human beginnings and had spent the years since helping other humans escape as he'd failed to do. Neo was a one-man melting pot—his skin as dark as an Indian's, his eye-shape Asian, and those eyes as blue as a clear summer sky.

"Who's outside?" Arturo demanded, heading for the back door.

"Rinaldo and Carlos were on duty," Neo said, his tone thick with concern as he joined Arturo.

Zack, already at the door, pulled it open just as a blur streaked inside and crossed the kitchen, heading straight for Mukdalla. The woman gave a glad cry as Rinaldo swept her into his arms.

Quinn began to breathe again as she watched the two embrace.

Mukdalla finally pulled back, hitting Rinaldo on the shoulder even as she began to cry. "You scared me…"

Quinn felt her own eyes burn.

"I know." Rinaldo pulled his wife tight against him and stroked her hair. The vampire wasn't handsome, not by any stretch of the imagination—his face was too long, his mouth too small. But he loved his wife with a devotion Quinn marveled at, and secretly envied. "I was on the other side of the house from the sunbeam." His gaze rose to meet the other vampires'. "Carlos was not. We lost him."

Sounds of dismay peppered the kitchen. Quinn hadn't known Carlos personally, but the others had, and she ached at her friends' grief. Her friends…a Trader and vampires. An hour ago, she would have said they were absolutely her friends, that she could trust them with her life. No question. Damn Arturo for making her doubt him again.

"Where did the sunbeam break through?" Neo asked.

"The yard, halfway between the house and stables," Rinaldo replied. "I'll mark it." He shook his head as if he was still in shock. "They're multiplying, faster and faster."

To Quinn, the sunbeams breaking through resembled a large sheet of black construction paper with a flashlight hanging over it in a dark room. At first, only a few holes had been punched in the paper. Each time the flashlight turned on, light would shine through those holes, tiny beams of light that would kill any vampire unlucky enough to be standing directly in their path. But as Vamp City's magic slowly deteriorated, more and more holes were being punched in the paper. Where a beam of light broke through once, it would continue to, each time the light came on. And just as the construction paper would eventually fall apart from too many holes, so too would the fabric of Vamp City.

"The less we can venture outside during daytime hours, the better," Neo said. "From now on, the humans and Traders will take guard duty during the day. Vampires only at night."

Micah turned to Arturo with a lift of one brow. "Many more quakes like this one and there won't be anything left to save. I understand your preferring to wait, Ax." Micah glanced at Quinn before turning back to Arturo. "But I don't think we can."

Arturo met her gaze, frustration and acceptance in his eyes. He knew Micah was right. But he'd damaged her trust in him and she could see that he knew that, too.

He was finally ready to give into her demand to head for Gonzaga Castle.

The problem was, he'd reminded her that as recently as two weeks ago he'd been a vampire utterly loyal to his master, Cristoff Gonazaga.

She was no longer one hundred percent certain he'd changed.

CHAPTER FIVE

Arturo bit down on his frustration as he watched Quinn standing beside her brother in Neo's kitchen, watching Mukdalla and Rinaldo. Quinn's beauty made him ache, but the look she gave him was cool and wary, in align with her emotions. The first time he fed from her, he'd inadvertently created a rare connection between them, one that allowed him to feel the strongest of her emotions and speak to her telepathically, though he could not hear her thoughts in return.

After all they'd been through, she still doubted him. She'd had cause to, initially. He'd betrayed her unforgivably more than once in those first days. But had he not proven himself over and over since then? She should know by now that he was not the man he'd been before!

He strode toward her and gripped her elbow. "We need to talk," he said tersely. She might throw him against the wall. He was half-prepared for it, and loosened his grip on her so as not to risk harming her if she did just that.

Instead, she just stared at him, her green eyes cool as frost. Finally, she jerked her arm free, turned, and walked away. Arturo followed her out of the kitchen and down the hall to the empty sitting room where she turned to him, arms crossed, expression hard and closed.

"I do not betray you, *cara*." If only she could feel his emotions as he felt hers, she would know the truth. A truth that would probably scare her more than his deception. "I will never betray you again." Unfortunately, he'd made a career out of lying and manipulating and she knew it well. Cristoff's snake. "If you cannot find it within yourself to trust me, then at least trust Micah. As much as it frustrates me at times, he is a great admirer of yours. He would never allow you to come to harm."

"I don't know what to believe anymore." Her words were terse, but she uncrossed her arms, lifting and dropping them at her sides, helplessly. He watched the weariness flood her eyes and weigh down the lines of her sleek body. "I want to believe you've changed, Vampire. I did believe it. But you've lied to me so many times in the past. And I've paid a terrible price for it every time."

He hated that she'd gone back to calling him 'Vampire'. And hated that he could feel her closing up, pulling the walls back up around her. For so long, she'd been utterly alone, isolated by her inability to trust anyone with the truth of who…and what…she really was. Even Zack hadn't known she was a sorceress until she'd been forced to reveal her abilities in order to save his life.

But slowly, Arturo had worked his way past her barriers. Slowly, she'd come to trust him. Or, at least, he'd thought she had. The swiftness in which she'd lost faith in him told him he'd made far less progress with her than he'd hoped. And the knowledge was a fist in his stomach.

"I cannot banish the memories of my betrayals," he said. "They are nightmares that replay over and over in my head. I have given you much reason to doubt me since we met, *amore mio,* but none since my soul reawakened. I do not wish to keep any more secrets from you, but this one…" He shook his head, his brow furrowing. "Cristoff cannot know."

"Is it a bigger secret than you being his traitor?"

His lips compressed and he nodded. "You know that I asked you not to accompany me to Gonzaga. I asked you to let me find a way to steal Escalla alone, but you have insisted on going."

"Because you can't do it without my magic!" she said heatedly. "We all know that."

"I do know that." He'd finally accepted that yesterday. Now he used her doubts against her.

He felt the burst of frustration within her. And, unfortunately, no lessening of her wariness. She watched him with eyes at once fierce and haunted. She wanted to believe in him. He could feel that longing within her, but it was being devoured by the gnawing fear that she was being deceived yet again. And her fear slew him.

"*Tesoro.*"

Quinn shook her head and turned for the doorway. "I need to think."

Arturo watched her leave, frustrated and unhappy. The last thing he wanted was for her to once more retreat behind the walls that had, for so long, isolated her. He wished for her to feel connected to those who would be her friends. He wanted her to be happy. And safe.

He simply wanted her. In so many ways—her smile, her sunshine, her trust.

Her heart.

Perhaps it was better this way, better for her to doubt him, better for her to refuse to accompany him to Gonzaga Castle, for he deeply doubted his ability to keep her safe there.

But without her magic, they would almost certainly fail to retrieve Escalla.

And unless they destroyed Escalla, Quinn would never be able to save his world.

Mio Dio, it was an impossible choice—his world and his friends, or the woman who had slowly, utterly, stolen his heart.

Quinn strode through the hallway beneath Neo's, uncertain where she was going. She needed to think, to find the trust within herself that it would take to accompany Arturo once more into Cristoff Gonzaga's house of horrors. The thought of going back there had her stomach twisting, her skin flushing damp with perspiration.

Less than an hour ago, she'd been certain Arturo would never betray her again. But, from the beginning, his betrayals had taken her by surprise. They shouldn't have—he was a vampire, after all—but despite that, she'd seen honor in him. Unfortunately, back then, his honor had manifested mostly as unwavering loyalty to his vampire master. And while Arturo had never actually hurt her himself, not physically, he'd told her he would never protect her against his master. And he hadn't.

Since his soul had fully returned, he'd assured her, over and over, that he *would* protect her, that he'd never allow Cristoff to hurt her again. But this was the first opportunity she'd had to test it. And she was no longer certain he wouldn't fail.

As she turned the corner to the hallway where her own tiny room was located, she nearly ran into Dr. Morris, a petite brunette with long, wavy hair that glowed with the phosphorescence that marked her as an immortal human, or Slava.

"Amanda."

"Quinn." The doctor frowned, concern in her eyes. "What's happened?"

Quinn tried to remember if she'd seen her upstairs. "Carlos..."

"I know." Sadness pulled at the doctor's pretty features even as she continued to study Quinn. Dr. Amanda Morris was far too perceptive. "Are you okay? Is it Zack?"

Quinn hesitated. Amanda was another women who'd made friendly overtures toward her. Friendship had never come easily to Quinn, but damn if she didn't need someone to talk to now.

"Do you have a minute?"

"Of course." Amanda nodded toward the opposite hallway with her head. "My examining room is larger than the bedrooms. And private."

Quinn followed, her stomach a mass of knots. An hour. The vampires wanted to leave in an hour. Fifteen minutes ago, it had been her pushing to go and Arturo holding back. Now they'd switched places and she felt utterly conflicted.

Amanda led the way into a sterile, modern-looking doctor's examination room, and lit one of the lamps. She motioned to the chair in the corner, then took a seat on her stool as Quinn sat down.

"What's going on, Quinn?" Amanda had been a family practitioner in the real world until five years ago when she was captured, enslaved, then rescued and brought to Neo's. Before Neo and Mukdalla could ferry her back to the real world, Amanda met Sam, one of the Slavas helping Neo, a human who could never leave Vamp City. Now the two were married, both trapped here, both working to help the escaped humans, each in his or her own way. Both would die when the magic failed.

If it failed. If Quinn couldn't free her magic. If she couldn't trust...

"How much faith do you have in Arturo Mazza?" Quinn hadn't intended to be so blunt, but the question burst from her, unwilling to be contained.

Amanda's expression turned wry. "What's he done this time?"

Quinn's mouth compressed. "I overheard him talking to Micah, assuring Micah that he would be able to do whatever he had to, something Micah had doubts about. When I confronted them, neither would meet my eye."

Amanda frowned. "You believe this is something significant?"

Raking tense fingers through her hair, Quinn relayed the missing, damning piece. "We're supposed to leave for Gonzaga Castle in an hour."

The doctor's eyes widened, then melted with understanding and sympathy. "Oh, Quinn."

"Yeah. Do you have any idea what kind of trust it requires for me to go back there with him? I had that trust. Until I caught the two of them whispering, I *had* it." Quinn stood and paced the room, wishing there was a window to look out. "I just keep wondering if I'm being a colossal fool. If he's been playing me all along."

Amanda took a deep breath and let it out slowly. "I can't give you a definitive answer, Quinn. He's a vampire whose soul was compromised, though never completely. Even at his worst, he brought escaped slaves to us and helped Neo hide our operation. He never entirely lost himself. But there's no denying that for a long time he couldn't see what Cristoff had become. While he might not have lost his own soul, he couldn't see how completely his master had lost his. He sees the truth, now, I think. Neo and Kassius were talking about this just last night, how different Arturo is. How much you've changed him."

Quinn watched her. "But what if it's all a lie? What if I haven't changed him enough? His loyalty to Cristoff was absolute."

"Was. It's not anymore, Quinn, you know that. Arturo made his choice between you and his master the day he found you in Cristoff's dungeon. He chose you. He risked everything to get you out of there." Amanda shrugged. "I can't promise you anything, of course. But I see a look in his eyes when he watches you, a look that tells me he'd sooner rip out his own heart than let Cristoff touch you again."

With a heavy sigh, Quinn nodded. "Somewhere inside, I believe that. But on some level, I've always believed that, even when it wasn't justified. I can't be that foolish again." She shook her head. "I can't."

"I know." Amanda smiled, a quiet smile that almost reached her eyes. "Sometimes all we can do is go with our gut. In the meantime…"

A fist pounded on the door, making both women jump.

"Amanda!"

Amanda jumped up and opened the door.

Rinaldo stood in the doorway. "You're needed upstairs. Quickly! It's Zack."

CHAPTER SIX

*Z*ack.

As Quinn ran for the door of Amanda's examining room, both Rinaldo and Amanda disappeared in a vampire flash. Since Amanda was no vampire, Rinaldo must have picked her up and carried her, which meant she was badly needed. *For Zack.*

Quinn's heart seized, her vision blurring with moisture, as she tore out of the room. She was halfway down the hall when Micah appeared suddenly, swept her into his arms, and then she, too, was flying up the stairs, vampire-fast.

Moments later, Micah deposited her in the middle of the kitchen where she turned to find Arturo on his knees, leaning over Zack's prone body, his fangs buried deep in her brother's neck.

"What happened?" Quinn and Amanda demanded simultaneously as the doctor knelt on Zack's other side, Quinn at his feet.

"We don't know," Mukdalla told them. "He was standing there asking if there was any leftover ham when his eyes suddenly rolled up in his head and he started to go down. Arturo caught him before he hit the floor and ordered us to fetch you two."

Arturo pulled back, his fangs retracting as he met her gaze with sorrowful eyes, then turned to Amanda. "I've initiated healing with my bite, but…" He shook his head. Quinn's heart began to race, fear a live wire in her chest. "What's the matter?"

"His blood tastes off, *cara mia*," he said, meeting her gaze with compassion. "Almost rancid."

She stared at him, wanting to deny his words, wanting to rail at the universe. "He's out of time." The words felt ripped from her throat and she grasped Zack's blazing hot bare feet as if she could somehow keep him tethered to life.

Suddenly his right foot twitched, then jerked out of her hold as her brother pushed himself up to a sitting position.

"Shit," he muttered as if he'd been caught asleep on the kitchen floor. He stood, scattering those gathered around him.

Quinn pushed to her feet. "Zack?"

Her brother shook his head, but refused to meet her gaze as he turned and strode out of the kitchen. "I'm fine," he tossed over his shoulder.

But he wasn't fine. Not even close.

Dammit, dammit, dammit.

Shaking, she turned to Arturo. "We leave in an hour." She didn't know how she was going to steal Escalla, and wasn't entirely certain Arturo wouldn't betray her, but none of that signified when Zack was dying. There was only one possible way to save him and she knew what she had to do.

The look in Arturo's eyes—frustration, resignation—told her he knew exactly what she was thinking. And that he was remembering their argument of yesterday shortly after she'd tried and tried to renew Vamp City's magic, even when it was clear the attempts were killing her.

"You put him first," Arturo said. "Always you put him first. Look me in the eye and tell me you would have stopped trying to renew the magic when the pain became too much. That you would have given up at some point even if I hadn't been there to try to stop you."

She wouldn't have. Of course not. She'd believed that renewing the magic was the only way to save Zack.

"You'd have committed suicide before you quit."

"He's my brother!"

"He is more than that, tesoro," Arturo said quietly. "He is your only reason for living."

The words were a slap. The pain fueled her anger. "I don't have to listen to this."

But when she reached for the door of her small bedroom, he spun her around, furious eyes staring into her own. "Zack is all you care about. Your focus is so damn narrow, Quinn, that if it does not involve Zack, it does not matter. Kassius, Amanda, Neo, Rinaldo—all have befriended you, and when the magic fails, they will die, as will dozens of others, hundreds, many of whom do not deserve to. Yet you give them no thought."

"What about the human captives who will be saved if Vamp City dies? You give them no thought!"

"There you are wrong, cara mia. I do give them thought. When you renew the magic, most of the vampires will reclaim their consciences and their souls. The barbarity will end. Some vampires will continue to feed and abuse humans—it has been so since the dawn of time. But the majority will not."

He gripped her chin, forcing her to meet his gaze. "You rail at me for lying to you, yet you lie to yourself. Your concern is not for the captives, Quinn. To some extent, yes. You are not without heart. But your primary concern is and has always been Zack, even at the cost of your own life. Have you ever stopped to ask yourself why?"

"He's my brother." She glared at him, the ache in her chest spreading.

"Have you considered what it would do to him if you died trying to save him? You protect yourself, Quinn, above all others, above anything and everything else. And everyone else be damned. Even Zack."

"Go to Hell." She jerked free of his hold, refusing to listen to this anymore. He was full of bullshit. "You're wrong. I'm protecting him. It's the one thing I can do, the one thing I can give him."

"Can you not simply love him?"

Zack had so many who loved him. She'd never been his whole world, but he was, and had always been, hers.

A gentle hand caressed her hair. "You protect yourself, Quinn. Understandably so. You have known too much betrayal in your life— the mother who abandoned you by dying, the father who brought a woman into your life who could not love you, then sided with that shrew against you. The friends who abandoned you at the first sign of your differentness. It is surprising, tesoro, that you are as capable of love as you are, and you are capable of great love. It shines within you every time you look at your brother."

Quinn squeezed her eyes closed, trying to shut out his words and failing.

"You are not alone anymore, Quinn. Within this safe house are many who have not shunned you despite your power. Who, in fact, care about you very much." His hand stroked her hair. "You are my

weakness, amore mio. *You may not put your own safety first, but I must. I cannot help my need to protect you any more than you can help your own to protect your brother.*"

As she watched Arturo now, she knew what he was thinking, knew that he saw in her quick turnabout just more willingness to sacrifice anything and everything for Zack. But how could she not? From the moment her dad and stepmother brought him home from the hospital, he'd been the only one in the world whose love she'd never doubted, the only one she'd always been able to count on. How many times had she been banished to her room as a child? Yet Zack had always come to check on her, and often to join her, even if it was only to lie on his stomach on the rug beside her bed and play his GameBoy while she did her homework.

"We leave in an hour," she repeated.

"Then let's meet in the sitting room in half an hour so I can do our glamour," Micah said.

Arturo's mouth compressed as he met Quinn's gaze. Without a word, he turned and walked away.

A half an hour later, Quinn entered the sitting room beneath Neo's, a room as Spartan as the bedrooms, if a bit larger. Two dark gray sofas sat at right angles to one another, an oil lamp glowing from the end table between them.

Arturo sat on one of the sofas while Micah stood facing a male she didn't know. *A Gonzaga guard.* Even as her heart skipped a beat, Micah turned to smile at her.

"Kass is done," he said casually.

It took her brain a moment to catch up. *Kass is done.* Kassius. Her gaze snapped to the unknown guard. In his eyes, she recognized her friend. The eyes were the one part of the body that could not be hidden behind glamour.

"Kassius," she breathed and the stranger smiled at her. Micah's gift was extraordinary.

"Ready?" Micah motioned her over.

Taking a deep breath to gather her scattered wits, Quinn shook her head. "Do Arturo first." It was Cristoff Gonzaga's guards who were scouring the city for her, under orders to capture her and bring her in. Believing one had breached Neo's sanctuary had unsettled her more than she cared to admit, more than she already was thanks to the furtive conversation she'd overheard earlier, one that continued to play havoc with her imagination in the worst possible way. And at the worst possible time.

For a moment, as she'd stared at the guard, she'd thought he'd already betrayed her.

Arturo watched her now with deep, fathomless eyes and she wondered if he'd felt that stab of fear, that moment's belief in his duplicity. If she didn't find a way to put aside her doubts, *if she couldn't trust him,* their mission was doomed.

Micah moved toward Arturo. "It looks like your up, Ax."

As Arturo rose from the sofa, he watched her, his expression shuttered in a way that made her think he didn't want her to know just how much her lack of faith in him cut.

The truth was, despite the doubts preying on her mind, she did, for the most part, trust him. They'd been through so much together over the past days and weeks—had risked their lives for one another over and over again. He cared about her, she knew he did. Just as she cared about him.

But trust had never come easily to her. It had always been a fragile thing, made even more so with the stakes so terrifyingly high.

Micah lifted his hands to Arturo's face and Arturo closed his eyes.

"Will Lukas have difficulty without your help tonight?" Arturo asked Micah.

"He won't be able to get the kids out of the city until I get there—I'm the only one he has working with him who can still move between the worlds—but he'll continue to round up all the kids he can find. I don't think there are too many of them left. With any luck, I'll be able to meet him at the rendezvous point before sunrise."

"Who's Lukas?" Quinn asked. Bringing children into this hell world had been a new low, even for vampires.

"A friend of mine. Lukas Olsson," Micah told her. "He's been rescuing the kids being brought in and has amassed a surprisingly large team of vampires to help him. More than fifteen, last count, from kovenas all over the city."

"Children do not belong in this place," Arturo said tersely. "It has always been the law."

"They're all trapped," she murmured, watching as Arturo's features began to waver beneath the magic in Micah's hands. "So they need you to get the kids back into the real world."

"Right-o," Micah said. "I feel for Lukas. He'd been living on the outside, had fallen in love with a human woman, when he got trapped here the night the trap sprung."

"Does she know what happened to him?"

Micah made a sound, a strangled groan. "She does now, though Elizabeth didn't have a clue until she walked into V.C. through a sunbeam not long ago. Lucky for both of them, Lukas found her before she could be enslaved. She's back in the real world, waiting for him to be free to come to her."

Which meant either Micah or Arturo had gotten her out. Probably. The Traders could still come and go as they pleased, but of the vampires, only Micah and Arturo could hand humans through the boundary circle.

"It's too bad you can't free the trapped vampires the way you can the humans."

"Yes," Arturo said. "But that would have defeated Phineas Blackstone's plan to destroy us."

Truth. "I'm surprised you're able to rescue so many kids," Quinn said, "considering it's the vampires who ordered them brought here in the first place." They'd been declared fodder for the next Games, essentially vampire gladiator contests.

"A reprehensible choice by the committee," Kassius said. "Though if there is an upside, the depths of depravity of this declaration appears to have awakened many a slumbering conscience."

"I think it's more than that," Micah said. "I think souls are beginning to reawaken. The magic of Vamp City is finally losing its hold on us."

They'd all begun to believe that the magic Blackstone had used to create and renew the city had been filled with such hatred that it had slowly poisoned the vampires' souls.

"So what do you do with the kids you free, Micah?" Quinn asked. "You don't just leave them on the streets of D.C., I hope."

Micah threw her a look that said she should know him better than that. "While Lukas and the others steal their memories of all they've seen, I slip into the real world and steal a vehicle. Last night, I found a school bus."

Quinn's brow rose.

Micah grinned. "I drove it to the boundary circle, then carried the kids out, two at a time, and loaded them on board, fast asleep. There were more than two dozen of them. I drove them to a residential street, enthralled the first passerby I saw to call the cops, then waited in the shadows until they arrived."

"That must have been a sight when they first realized who was on that bus."

Micah nodded. "I didn't wait around, but I'm sure it was chaos."

So many people within Washington, D.C. had gone missing of late. The return of so many of the children would have the city euphoric.

"Are kids still being brought in?" she asked.

"Not to my knowledge," Micah said. "Not since the Games were cancelled." He studied Arturo with satisfaction. "What do you think, Quinn? Kass?"

Arturo had disappeared beneath Micah's hands, replaced by another Gonzaga guard, this one with light brown hair and a wide, genial face.

Micah turned to her. "Ready, kiddo?"

Quinn nodded and walked over to him. He'd glamoured her before, multiple times, and it didn't hurt in the slightest. She was usually barely aware of the transformation occurring. Besides, she trusted Micah implicitly. It was his involvement in that whispered conversation that eased her mind the most. Because although Arturo had given her reason to doubt him in the past, Micah never had.

As Micah's hands slid lightly over her face, Arturo and Kassius discussed the plan for tonight—how the four of them would travel onto Gonzaga lands in pairs, each person glamoured to look like a different one of Cristoff's guards. The only real danger would be if they had the poor luck to stumble upon one of the actual guards they were glamoured to look like.

Quinn refused to entertain that possibility. They'd make it safely to their destination, she had to believe that. Of course, once inside Gonzaga Castle, any semblance of safety would be nothing but an illusion.

Micah closed his eyes as the pads of his fingers lightly grazed the surface of her skin and her flesh began to tingle. Slowly, the feeling spread over her scalp, then down her neck and body.

Finally Micah opened his eyes and frowned. "It's criminal to make you look like a man, Quinn."

She snorted. "Whatever it…" She stopped abruptly at the sound of the deep male voice that had just uttered her words. "This is too weird." The other times she'd been glamoured, she'd remained a woman. Neither time had her voice noticeably changed.

Arturo handed her a small mirror and she took it, then stared at the unattractive male peering back at her, one with her own green eyes.

"You look just like Egor," Kassius told her.

Micah grunted. "Thankfully she doesn't smell like Egor."

Quinn glanced at Arturo and found him watching her with those dark, enigmatic eyes.

"A word of warning," Micah said. As he reached for her, he overshot her shoulder, then smiled and dropped his hand to give her shoulder a squeeze. "You're not as tall as Egor, though you'll appear to be. Keep your mouth closed around others unless you have no choice. Someone paying close attention might notice that your voice isn't coming from your mouth but the area around your neck. And don't let anyone touch you. You may look and sound male, because I'm good at what I do, but it's all an illusion. If they reach for you, get out of the way. The moment they touch you they'll know you're female."

Micah turned his magic on himself and, minutes later, Quinn found herself surrounded by three strange Gonzaga guards. She knew who they were beneath the glamour, of course. But it brought back memories of the last time she'd faced Gonzaga guards, the night she'd been ripped off her horse by one. The night Zack had nearly been killed. Once more, she questioned how well she really knew these men, these vampires.

As nerves braided her insides, Arturo pulled something out of his pocket—a roll of SweetTarts—and handed it to her. When she glanced at him, she saw gentle understanding in those dark eyes. He knew the situation unnerved her. He could feel her emotions.

She took one of the candies. "Thanks, Vampire." Hearing that deep male voice come from her lips startled her all over again.

A stranger's smile creased his unfamiliar face, traveling lightly to eyes she knew exceedingly well. Arturo's hand rose to her shoulder unerringly, his mouth brushing her ear. "You know me, *cara mia.* You *know* me." Then he released her and turned toward the door, leading their foursome into the community room now empty but for Mukdalla.

"Be careful, all of you," the Trader woman said. "We need you back here, safe and sound. Which of you is Quinn?"

Quinn lifted a hand and glanced at her companions. "I'll meet you upstairs."

"We'll saddle the horses and have them ready," Arturo told her.

Quinn nodded, then turned and joined Mukdalla.

The Trader woman took firm hold of Quinn's hand. "You must be careful tonight, sorceress. For your sake and theirs. It's dangerous business to sneak into Cristoff Gonzaga's castle, especially for you."

Quinn made a face. "Believe me, I'm aware."

Mukdalla's eyes softened. "Yet you do not hesitate. I know your primary concern is for Zack, but I thank you anyway. Your terrible risk might just save my husband."

"I don't do this just for Zack." Not entirely. Quinn squeezed Mukdalla's hand. "And I won't fail."

But as she climbed the stairs to join the others, a hundred doubts crowded her mind, tearing at her courage.

Heart pounding in her throat, she prayed she wasn't being a fool for trusting Cristoff's snake, yet again.

CHAPTER SEVEN

The night was dark as the three vampires and Quinn rode away from Neo's, but then every night—and day for that matter—was dark in Vamp City. Stars dotted the sky in a way they never did the skies of Washington, D.C. It always twisted her scientist's mind how the moon and stars shone in V.C., just as they did the real world. But never the sun. As she'd been reminded more than once, magic was the predominant force in Vamp City, not science.

As she stared at the vastness of the night sky, the stars bright against the endless black canvas, she found herself mesmerized by the dark beauty of this place. There was no light pollution here, for there was very little electricity—only that created by a handful of generators. She'd always loved the dark. As a child, it had been her only real refuge from the stepmother who'd hated her.

At the feel of the cool breeze, Quinn was suddenly glad for the hooded sweatshirt Amanda had thrust into her hands at the last moment. It was late September and even the real D.C. would be embracing fall weather by now. Arturo had once told her that whatever weather the real world experienced—rain, snow, wind—Vamp City did as well, though V.C., with its lack of sun, was always cooler. Sometimes, as now, she could feel the warmer D.C. air trying to merge with this world's coolness. The scent of the horses filled her nostrils, along with the exotic spiciness unique to this world—the scent, she suspected, of magic.

As her eyes adjusted to the dark, she could just make out the twisted shapes of the trees that grew in abundance here, trees that appeared, for all the world, to be dead. As far as Quinn knew, the trees were the only living things that grew in this place other than a bit of mold and mildew.

Silhouetted against the trees were her three riding companions. And while she felt like herself in her jeans, boots, long-sleeve tee, and Amanda's hooded sweatshirt, anyone who saw her would see, instead, the apparently imposing Egor in his guard uniform. At least until her glamour wore off.

They rode in silence, the only sound that met her ears the steady hoofbeats of the horses. There were no natural night sounds since there were no insects or animals in V.C. except those brought in by the vampires. She'd never ridden a horse before arriving in this place, but she found she enjoyed the feel of the animal beneath her.

Vamp City was such an odd juxtaposition between the Washingtons of 1870 and today. Horses and carriages were by far the most common—and most practical—form of transportation, given that in 1870 the roads had not been paved, and the vampires certainly hadn't seen to that detail in later years. But there were modern vehicles here, as well. Arturo himself owned a yellow Jeep Wrangler, though it drew far too much attention for their present purposes.

In the distance, a man's bloodcurdling scream rent the night air, chilling her to the bone. Screams were a horrifyingly common sound in this place.

"Every time I think they're regaining their souls...," one of her companions muttered. With their voices glamoured, she couldn't be certain which one.

"I fear some are too far gone," another replied.

"They will reclaim them."

Quinn recognized the glamoured voice of Arturo in the last and she wondered who he was trying to convince—the rest of them, or himself. He'd told her over and over that he continued to hold out hope that his once beloved master would reclaim his soul, too. Apparently Cristoff had been a pretty decent guy for a powerful vampire master before he'd moved to Vamp City. She had a hard time believing it, given the monster he'd become.

The vampires she knew were of the Emora race, vampires who fed on blood and emotion and needed both to survive. Each vampire was slave to a different need—Arturo and Kassius fear, Micah pleasure, Cristoff pain. According to her friends, the Emoras were once actually quite humane, most shunning any desire to cause the emotion on which they fed. Arturo had told her stories of how they used to roam the human battlefields together, Cristoff feeding on the pain of the dying while Arturo drank of their fear. The American Civil War had lured hundreds of Emoras from Europe for just that purpose, and many of those had become the first inhabitants of Vamp City.

But slowly the poison of Blackstone's hatred had begun to corrode the vampires' consciences. While at first, humans were given the choice of whether or not to serve vampire masters, soon the Emoras began to capture humans against their will and enslave them. As their souls became further compromised, the once human Emoras turned cruel, brutally so, feeding their hunger for pain and fear through torture and murder. The coliseum built for vampire soccer matches became the arena for the Games—death matches between untrained humans.

In the past two years, as the magic of Vamp City began to dissolve, so too had the last of the vampires' restraint. Humans were captured and driven into the slave auctions like cattle—their wares displayed for all to see—then sold to the highest bidder to be enslaved, raped, or simply tortured to death.

Though the human world remained unaware of the vampires among them, they'd certainly noticed the scores of people disappearing off D.C. streets. The cops had no idea what was going on and couldn't stop it if they did. Now, though, it seemed that some of the vampires were starting to reclaim their souls. Just in time to lose their lives when the magic crumbled, destroying their world.

Quinn heard one of her companions pull up. As the others did the same, she followed. By her estimate, they'd traveled a couple of miles.

"We'll separate here into two teams and regroup at the rendezvous point," Arturo said. "Micah and Kass take the north route. Quinn and I will come in from the east."

"Ax…"

Quinn glanced warily between the voices, wishing she could see the men's expressions in the dark.

"Let one of us ride with Quinn. If you're caught with the sorceress…"

"I won't be. Once we reach the castle, Quinn will accompany Kassius while I discard my glamour and report to Cristoff as myself.

But for this short leg of the journey, she will ride with me." Arturo paused. "If she is in agreement."

Quinn wished she could see his expression in the darkness. All she could really do was listen to her gut as Amanda had suggested. And her gut said she was safe with him. Which had always been the case, right or wrong.

She nodded, which was enough of consent since the vampires had excellent night vision and could see her clearly.

Moments later, two forms moved away and she heard the pounding hooves of Micah and Kassius's retreating mounts. As the third form started forward again, she followed.

"I do not betray you, *amore,*" Arturo said quietly. "I know I have given you much reason to doubt me in the past, but I am not that man any longer. I had hoped you knew that."

She wished she could see his expression. "You're keeping secrets from me."

"Only because I must. For your own safety as well as mine."

For a long time, she didn't reply. But finally, she sighed. "I trust you. At least I trust you enough. Your actions will be the proof, won't they? Don't betray me, Vampire, and I'll trust you completely again."

"It will be done. Calm yourself, *tesoro.*"

"That's not going to happen." Even if Arturo was completely loyal to her, she had plenty to be worried about. Cristoff had put a price on her head that had most of the creatures in Vamp City hunting for her. "Calm isn't a possibility. We're lucky I haven't started to hyperventilate yet."

He was silent for a couple of moments before he said carefully, "A fear feeder will taste your nervousness."

"If you're trying to settle me down, that's not the way to go about it," she muttered, swiping at a low-hanging branch to keep it from hitting her face. A nervous Gonzaga guard might become quickly suspect and hauled before Cristoff.

"It was not my intent to make you more nervous, *cara,* merely to remind you to be calm."

"Right. I'll put that on my to-do list."

"You are stronger than you believe, Quinn. There is nothing you need fear. Your magic will come to your call when you need it, if you will simply believe it is so."

"You think it's that easy? Just believe?"

"I know it is. Your own doubts are all that stand in your way."

She grunted. "Until very recently, I didn't even believe in magic."

"Then believe in yourself, *cara*," Arturo said simply. "And believe in me."

"I'm trying, Vampire. I'm trying."

As they rode though the dark, they passed a house, windows lit by firelight. She wondered who lived there, whether they were friend or foe. The only thing she was fairly certain of was that they were not human. Humans, even the immortal Slavas, were hunted by too many in this place to ever feel safe on their own out in the open like this.

As they rode through another dark copse, the scent of diesel teased her nose. "Do you smell that?" she asked her companion.

"A truck. Yes."

He'd once told her that smells occasionally carried into Vamp City from the real world. But never sound.

They continued on in silence but for the clop of the horses' hooves in the dirt, leaving the trees behind for the shells of dark structures—the doppelgangers of buildings built before the Civil War and left to rot. The five hundred or so vampires who'd originally moved into Vamp City had not needed the housing the human residents of D.C. had, especially when most preferred the simplicity of living in their masters' castles. Throughout Vamp City, there were nine vampire masters, each the head of his own kovena, or vampire family. Gonzaga was just one kovena, though arguably the most powerful.

They'd seen no sign of other vampires, nor heard any. Only that one scream as they'd first set out. Vamp City was quiet tonight, its inhabitants undoubtedly sobered by the threat of their impending demise.

Ahead, something large loomed in the dark, a huge building of some sort. It had an odd shape, almost like an egg halfway tilting out of its cup.

"Where are we?" she asked.

"The corner of Independence and New Jersey."

"New Jersey…" Quinn's eyes widened with shock as realization slammed into her. "That's the U.S. Capitol building."

"Yes. Quite unlike its modern day counterpart, no?"

"What happened to it?"

"Age. Neglect. It was never occupied by the vampires. The dome slid off its base some forty years ago."

Damn. Just when she thought she'd seen it all—the White House sitting half-collapsed in swamp water, the Washington Monument still only a third built. Now this.

As her mount continued to follow Arturo's, she tried to make out the features of that ruined monstrosity, wishing for some light. Suddenly, Arturo's voice spoke telepathically in her head.

Two Gonzaga guards approach on our right, cara. *And they are the real thing.*

CHAPTER EIGHT

Pretend to be injured and keep your head down.

At Arturo's telepathic words, Quinn tensed. They'd discussed this earlier, that Egor, like almost all vampires who'd been around for more than a century, was an excellent rider. And while she might look like him, she certainly didn't ride like him. They'd decided she needed to pretend that she—or Egor—had been injured by a bolt of magical energy thrown at him by the sorceress.

Quinn curved around her arm as if she'd been slammed hard in the stomach. As the adrenaline pumped through her veins, she squeezed her eyes closed in case they began to glow as they often did when she felt threatened, triggering her magic. In the dark of Vamp City, glowing eyes would give her away in an instant.

Do not be afraid, cara. All will be fine.

Quinn scowled. Easy for him to say.

"The sorceress!" Arturo called in a voice belonging to the vampire whose face he wore. "We came upon her not five minutes ago. She attacked us and fled, but she cannot be far. That way!"

She couldn't see which way he pointed, couldn't see the vampires he spoke to, but she heard the pound of additional hoofbeats. Her heart thudded, her body tensing even as she told herself she was safe. Nothing bad would happen, no one would realize she was really the sorceress under glamour. But the words did little to calm her.

As the vampires' mounts began to retreat, the earth began to rumble—another earthquake, as strong as the one before. And suddenly noise burst all around her, a cacophony of sound that didn't exist in this world—traffic and electricity, rock music and laughter. The real world must have broken through nearby. If she weren't forced to keep her eyes closed, she'd be able to see it and, if she chose to, walk right back into the real world through the breaks.

Thanks to her Blackstone magic, she alone could travel both ways between the worlds in that manner. Although a number of humans had apparently walked into Vamp City that way, to her knowledge, she was the only one able to escape. If she wanted to. And she alone could hear and see the real world when the two worlds bled together.

The temptation to take a look was strong, but she forced herself to keep her eyes closed, her body hunched, and her head down. She was glad she had when she heard, once more, the sound of approaching hoofbeats.

"Any sign of her?" Arturo called to, apparently, the same pair of guards.

"None. She's disappeared again."

"Come, then. We will report the sighting to Cristoff together," Arturo told them.

Quinn tensed, wondering why he'd invite them to join him. But a moment later, she understood.

"*We?*" The other vampire's voice shot too high. "No, no, my friend. You were the ones who fought her. You must report the sighting."

From what Arturo had said, Cristoff was as likely to kill the messenger these days as listen to him.

A moment later, Quinn once more heard the sound of retreating horses.

"You did well, *cara*" Arturo said quietly. "Keep your eyes closed. I'll find some place to safely release your magic."

At one time, that release could only have occurred through an explosion that could have possibly brought the roof down on top of them, but with her Blackstone magic mostly free now, she'd discovered other avenues of release that wouldn't alert nearby vampires of her proximity.

She felt Arturo take the reins of her horse and begin to lead it. Several minutes later, he said, "You may open your eyes, *cara*."

She did and could tell from the odd light in front of her face that her eyes were still glowing with power. A quick look told her they were in a small, empty building of some kind, maybe an old storage shed. Dismounting, she put distance between herself and the animals, then closed her eyes, lifted her hands, and called on the magic pulsing in her blood to form a thick, dark bubble around herself—essentially another world. Slowly, she widened the bubble, expanding it to include Arturo and the horses.

The animals nickered with surprise, but a few words from Arturo and they quieted. Quinn continued, expanding her bubble to include the whole of the shed, draining off the excess power in the process.

"Your eyes have returned to normal, *tesoro*. The magic no longer rages."

"I'm burning it off." Slowly, she pulled the bubble back, contracting it, little by little, until it no longer encompassed the animals or Arturo, until she alone stood within its center. And then she contracted it more, dissolving it altogether.

She'd come far since she'd accidentally created that first bubble and nearly suffocated herself and her werewolf captor in it. No one could escape one of her creations unless she handed them out, or contracted it from around them. But she no longer lost control of the things as she had at first. She suspected that Phineas Blackstone's ability to create worlds had sprung from a similar gift.

"Ready to go?" Arturo asked.

"Sure, though you'll have to lead me to my horse. I'm blind as a bat in here."

Cool fingers closed around her own. But instead of leading her away, Arturo tugged her against his long, hard body. As his arms curled around her, she stiffened for only a moment before melting into him and wrapping her arms around his lean waist. He didn't try to kiss her, merely held her, one hand stroking her hair.

"You mean more to me than you know, *tesoro mio*," he said quietly. "So much more than you know."

His words were a balm to the agitation that had been riding her from the moment they'd hatched this plan to steal Escalla.

"I've trusted you so many times, Vampire. Please don't let me down this time."

He stroked her hair. "I promise I will not. Never again."

She believed him. Pulling back, she brushed his cheek with her lips, then found his mouth. The kiss was as careful and tender as any they'd shared, a promise, a gift of trust.

When they pulled apart, she felt stronger than she had before, more sure of her path.

"We need to get going, Turo. Kassius and Micah are going to wonder what happened to us."

Arturo helped her mount in the dark, then led her horse outside, and together, they took off.

They ran across no other vampires and finally reached the stables where they were to rendezvous with Kassius and Micah. These particular stables hid the entrance to a network of tunnels that ran beneath Gonzaga Castle—tunnels created with the help of Grant Blackstone's magic. A couple of weeks ago, Grant had helped her escape and led her to freedom through the tunnels. Up to that point, they'd been known only to the humans.

But Kassius had found out about them later when, after she'd been recaptured, Cristoff had ordered him to bite her, and through her memories, Kassius had learned the truth of her escape. That had been a weird experience for both of them because while Kassius had always been able to divine another's truth with a bite, he'd never before had his gift hijacked in return. She'd done so unintentionally, of course, but while he'd studied her memories, she'd been privy to his.

While she'd learned he was a werevamp during that exchange, Kassius had learned of the tunnels beneath Gonzaga, but he'd kept the information from Cristoff. Now they would use the tunnels to sneak into the castle.

Arturo dismounted and she did the same. Together, they led their mounts through the stable doors.

"Any trouble?" Micah asked, his voice emerging from the dark.

"Nothing to speak of," Arturo replied. "You may turn on your small flashlight, *cara*. Keep it pointed low, please."

Without hesitation, she pulled the light out of her boot and flicked it on, glad to finally be able to see clearly. Kassius was grooming his mount while Micah poured grain into one of the troughs.

Quinn looked around, remembering this place and the friends she'd made here as she'd helped a handful of escaped slaves. How had it come to this, that she was now stealing *into* the most terrifying place she'd ever encountered, instead of out?

As Arturo and Kassius took care of the horses, Micah joined her.

"Are you doing okay?" he asked, curving his arm around her shoulders and pulling her close.

She leaned against him and sighed. "I'm scared shitless, to be honest."

"We've got your back, you know that. If I thought Ax couldn't be trusted, I wouldn't have allowed this." He released her, then turned her to face him. "You and I might have met because Ax sent me to keep an eye on you, but you've become like a sister to me, Quinn." His eyes crinkled as a gleam of mischief erupted in their gray depths. "Of course, if you get tired of him, I might well audition for a different role."

A jealous rumble emitted from the direction of the men currying the horses, making Micah grin. But as he continued to watch her, his expression slowly sobered to the point of absolute gravity. "I'll kill whoever tries to hurt you. No matter who he is."

Quinn slipped her arms around Micah's waist, placed a kiss on his cheek, then laid her head on his shoulder as his strong arms gathered her close. Finally, with a quick kiss to her hair, he released her and they joined the others.

"Ready?" Kassius asked. When the rest of them nodded, he knelt on the floor in the middle of the stable, brushed aside the hay, then closed his fingers around a hidden iron handle and pulled. The hatch lifted, revealing a ladder leading down into the dark.

Kassius started down first. Quinn turned off her flashlight, tucked it back into her boot, then felt for the ladder and followed him down. Strong hands closed around her hips from behind, swinging her off the ladder and setting her on her feet out of the way. She felt more than heard the next one down, but knew it was Micah. She always knew Arturo's scent. Above she heard the creak of a hinge and the soft thud of wood that told her he'd closed the hatch.

Quinn waited in the pitch dark, the only one of them unable to see. Moments later, the warm scent of almonds enveloped her and cool fingers closed around her hand and gave a tug. Silently, she followed him down the pitch black tunnel, one she knew ran for a long, long way, maybe as much as a quarter mile.

They hadn't gone far when something hit her in the head, suddenly, with a dull thunk. Arturo's hand disappeared from around hers. Before she could fully register what she'd run into, it was around her neck, pulling tight.

Quinn's eyes went wide, her fingers clawing at the chain now digging into her windpipe, cutting off her air. Slowly the chain began to lift her off her feet.

Terror ripped through her with horrifying clarity.

She was about to be hanged.

CHAPTER NINE

Quinn clawed at the chain around her throat, fighting not to panic as she felt it lifting her off her feet. Dear God, dear God, dear God.

"*Help me*," she gasped.

Suddenly cool fingers joined with hers, fingernails scratching her neck in their desperation to dig beneath the noose and free it. Arturo's fingers.

She lifted onto the balls of her feet, then onto her toes as the chain rose, tightening. Panic exploded. Any moment, she'd be hanging by her neck!

An arm circled her waist from behind, and suddenly she was being lifted up. The chain around her neck slackened and she felt Arturo's cool fingers slip beneath it, but barely. She could breathe, but the chain wasn't coming loose! She could feel it trying to tighten around her neck as if it had a mind of its own.

All of a sudden she began to swing, though still caught tight against…was it Micah? Kassius? Why was he…?

Understanding crashed over her. They were all being hung. The vampires could survive without air for an indefinite period of time, so were struggling to keep the noose from tightening around her neck.

Silver, tesoro, Arturo said in her mind.

Silver. *The chains.* While silver couldn't burn or kill a vampire, it would absolutely steal his strength and any kind of power he possessed. The four of them were sitting ducks…well…hanging ducks. And she was the only one with a chance in hell of saving them.

Magic. She had magic, but what would work against a silver chain?

As the one around her neck contracted, Arturo's fingers dug into her windpipe, making her cough. Heaven help her, she didn't have much time. Reaching up, she tried yanking on her own chain, trying to dislodge it from whatever it was hanging from, but she only managed to send them all swaying harder.

She could think of only one thing to do. Calling up her power, she formed a tight bubble around herself and her companions. And suddenly they were falling.

Quinn came to a jarring halt, still tight against someone's chest as the clink of falling chains echoed all around her. She'd done it! Her bubble had disconnected them from whatever the chains were attached to.

"*Dio*, Quinn," Arturo gasped, pulling the chain carefully from around her neck. "Breathe, *bella*, breathe."

Her feet touched the ground, but the arm around her remained, holding her steady as she pulled in a deep, wheezing breath.

Cool, frantic fingers grasped her face. "Easy, *tesoro*."

She filled her lungs slowly, deeply, the panic easing away. Straightening, she pulled away, leaned down to pull out her flashlight, then turned it on.

Her three glamoured companions stared at her with angry, haunted eyes.

"They nearly killed you," Micah growled. From where he was standing, she knew it was Kassius who'd been holding her aloft.

"They set the trap for vampires," she said, then coughed. "Could you see them? Do you know who did this?"

Kassius grunted. "The magic smells like Grant's." Grant Blackstone might not have the power of his father, but he had magic enough to pull off such a trap with ease. "He knows that I know about his tunnels—I had to reveal that knowledge to try to force him to aid you once before. I suspect this trap was set for me, and anyone I brought with me."

"I sensed no one," Arturo said, his eyes pained as he reached for, and gently stroked, the scratches on her neck. "I tasted no fear, not the slightest nervousness."

"Nor did I," Kassius said.

"I wonder if the magic will alert Grant to the fact that he caught something,"

Micah said. "We need to get moving."

Quinn turned to Arturo. "Maybe you should get rid of your glamour."

He shook his head. "Not until we're certain these tunnels have not been discovered by Cristoff and his loyal ones. Release your bubble, *cara*."

She didn't want to. Within the bubble they were safe. But she could always call it again, if she needed to. She did as requested, then blinked at the suddenly light-filled tunnel. Half a dozen lanterns revealed more than a dozen men and women aiming guns at them. Many looked human, a few Slava. But, to Quinn's surprise, there were Gonzaga guards sprinkled among them, as well. At least, men who were dressed in the all-black guard uniforms. At their head, no surprise, stood Grant Blackstone, the eldest of Phineas Blackstone's sons, a man born just after the Civil War. His brother, Sheridan, had been turned into a vampire in his early twenties and had retained little of their father's power at all. Grant had stopped aging sometime in his thirties. He was dressed, now, in his usual ivory linen shirt, dark brown pants, and boots—what she thought of as 19th century landowner casual. His blond hair possessed the phosphorescent glow of a Slava, his beard short and trimmed, his eyes as cool as blue glass.

"The guns are filled with wooden bullets," Grant said evenly. "Though real bullets would likely work just as well on one of you, wouldn't they, sorceress? Who's with you?"

Their sudden disappearance...and reappearance...had given her away. But Grant wasn't necessarily an enemy. He hated Cristoff nearly as much as she did. Maybe more.

"We're on the same side, Grant," she called. "Put the guns down."

Another male emerged from the shadows behind Grant, a vampire she recognized as the third of Arturo's closest friends. In recent weeks, Bram's need to feed on the pain of others had driven him closer and closer to Cristoff—dangerously close. But Arturo had told her his story, that before he became trapped, he'd spent most of his time in the real world working as an emergency room surgeon at George Washington Hospital, healing humans even as he fed, unhappily, on their agony. The last time she saw him, he'd looked more like a drug addict than a surgeon, his eyes dark-rimmed and bloodshot as his need for pain spiraled out of control right along with his master's. She was glad to see that he looked better today. Much better.

"One of them is Micah," Bram said. "He's the only one I know with the power to glamour four of them at once. If I had to guess, Arturo and Kassius round out the foursome."

"Dissolve the glamour, please, Micah," Arturo said with a sigh.

"All of it?" Micah grumbled. "Dissolving it takes almost as much energy as creating it in the first place." But he did as requested and moments later the four of them once more looked like themselves.

Bram stepped forward, motioning to his associates. "Lower your weapons. They are no threat. I stake my life on this." When he reached them, his appraising gaze landed first on her, then Arturo. "It seems we've been keeping secrets from one another, Ax."

Arturo dipped his head. "A necessity, given the circumstances. I feared you'd become too close to him."

"I feared the same of you."

A glimmer of a smile breached Arturo's mouth. "And now we are both involved in things of which Cristoff would not approve."

Bram gave a low laugh that held no humor. "Cristoff approves of nothing these days unless it involves the mutilation or death of another. Why are you here?"

Arturo glanced at the small, armed throng behind Bram. "I will share that with you and Grant alone."

"Fair enough." Bram clasped Arturo on the shoulder and thrust out his other hand. As they shook, he said, "I had thought you lost to us, Ax."

Arturo clasped Bram's shoulder in turn, his mouth twisting. "I was, more than I realized. But no more. You look good."

An understatement. Now that he was close, Quinn could see that Bram was both clean-shaven and dressed in clothes that didn't look like they'd been slept in a dozen times, neither of which she'd seen from him before.

"I'm feeling a hundred percent better. Three hundred." He shook his head. "I'm not sure what's changed, but in the past twenty-four hours my need for pain has almost returned to normal. I no longer feel like I need a hit every twenty minutes." He turned to Quinn. "Is this your doing, sorceress? Are you and your magic somehow healing us?"

She was about to say no, that she didn't have that kind of power. But she suddenly remembered what the dying elf Vintry had called her. The Healer. He'd claimed that her coming had been foretold, as had her partnership with the Snake. Presumably Arturo. But he'd never gotten the chance to tell her more, and he was likely gone now.

"I have no idea, Bram." she replied instead.

"We believe Phineas Blackstone poisoned the magic of this place, whether intentionally or not," Arturo said. "With the magic's dying, the poison is losing its grip on us."

Bram's mouth twisted. "So that which frees us, kills us." He glanced at Quinn. "You're either the bravest person I've ever met, or the most foolish. You must know what Cristoff will do to you if he finds you." He grimaced. "No offense, Quinn. You'd think I was a fear feeder."

Quinn shrugged. "No offense taken. I know what he'll do. Or as much as I need to. I'll tell you more in private."

Bram nodded, shook hands with Kassius and Micah, then turned and led the way into the throng of onlookers.

As they passed those who'd moments before held guns on them, Quinn found herself the object of intense interest and surprising warmth. Several people patted her on the back or tried to shake her hand. The vampires, however, were far more attentive to her friends, greeting them with smiles and no small amount of relief, especially Arturo, Cristoff's most 'loyal'. It occurred to her that everyone down there was aligned against Cristoff. The other vampires must be hugely gratified to realize that even Arturo and his circle were traitors.

Once they'd passed through the reception line, they continued down the tunnel, Bram leading the way, Grant bringing up the rear.

"I take it you trust those guards?" she asked Bram.

"I do. All here work toward the same purpose."

"Which is?"

He glanced at her. "Freeing Cristoff's slaves before he murders them all. Especially the children."

The thought of children in Cristoff's clutches made her physically ill.

"He hasn't touched any of the kids, yet," Bram added quickly, reading her expression right. "Perhaps there's a line even Cristoff won't cross, though I wouldn't lay any bets on that these days."

Finally, after they'd walked for what felt like half a mile, they reached the low doorway into the cavern where Quinn had been before. One by one, they ducked into what was essentially a large cave cut out of the rock. The light from the lantern Bram carried illuminated the damp walls, casting shadows above the numerous natural shelves. Not for the first time, she wondered if there were really tunnels and caverns beneath the once swampy D.C., or if these were strictly Grant's creation.

Quinn took a seat on a stone that jutted from the wall, and Micah sat beside her. The others remained standing.

"Cristoff has gone completely off the rails," Bram told them. His expression was that of a man who'd seen things no man should see. And she knew he had. They all had in this place. "The male we used to know is gone. You've seen evidence of it, Ax, but he's getting worse by the day. By the hour. Many of the long-time Gonzaga vampires are starting to reclaim their souls. Those Cristoff hasn't killed have escaped."

"You're still here," Arturo said.

"Someone has to get the humans out."

Arturo nodded. "So there are fewer guards?"

"Not fewer, no. In the past forty-eight hours, alone, we've had more than two dozen vampires arrive at Gonzaga, pledging allegiance to Cristoff."

Micah frowned. "Why in the hell would they do that when he's killing his own?"

"They say their own masters are returning to older, softer ways, and they want nothing to do with it."

"Souls really are reawakening," Micah said. "Across the city."

"Many of them." Bram grunted. "The vampires being drawn to Cristoff have no souls. They probably never had them, even when they were human. They're as depraved as our master."

"So nothing's changed at Gonzaga Castle."

Bram's mouth tightened, but he shook his head. "Essentially, no."

"Has he attacked any of the new guards?" Kassius asked.

"Not so far, no. He embraces them, encourages them to torture and kill to their hearts' content. Hence the grave need to get the humans out of here."

Arturo frowned. "If he catches you…"

"I'm dead. But when the magic fails…" Bram shrugged. "I'm dead either way. Maybe I can do some good before that happens." He scratched his chin, then paused as if surprised to find his jaw clean-shaven. "Tell us why you're here, Ax."

Arturo took a deep breath and let it out slowly, as if weighing his words. "Quinn's not just the Black Wizard's heir, but Levenach's as well."

Quinn found a small measure of satisfaction as she watched Grant's eyes widen.

Bram whistled. "The curse..."

"Yes," Arturo said. "Not only has it bound her Levenach magic, but it's strangling her Blackstone."

"That's why being in the Focus hurts her," Grant murmured.

And it was true. Twice she'd stood in the center of the small energy dome they called the Focus—the very spot where Phineas Blackstone had stood to create Vamp City in 1870—and tried to renew the magic. The Focus only accepted those with Blackstone blood and while it had let her in, the energy had turned on her, attacking her, both times. The second time, she'd honestly feared it might kill her, which was why Arturo had been so angry with her for not coming out. He'd been unable to follow her in to rescue her when her stubborn determination to save her brother at all costs had nearly cost her life.

"The Focus recognized her as Blackstone." Grant's brows rose. "But it also recognized her as Levenach. It saw her as both friend and foe."

"What's the answer then?" Bram asked. "It will always attack her."

"Yes," Quinn said. "I can handle the pain. The trouble is, the curse is hampering my Blackstone magic and as long as it is, I can't save the city. We have to break the curse."

Grant frowned. "And how do we do that?"

Arturo hesitated, his gaze moving from Bram to Grant to Bram again.

"Destroy Escalla."

The cave went silent. Finally, Bram made a sound of disbelief. "You'll never get near it."

Arturo turned to Grant. "What do you know about the sword?"

Grant looked at him with surprise. "Very little. Cristoff keeps it hanging in that case. I certainly don't know how to destroy it."

"Then it's a good thing we already have a plan." Arturo's smile was grim as his gaze remained locked on Phineas Blackstone's eldest son. "And we need your help." Grant scowled, but Arturo just lifted his hand. "You needn't do anything but lend your likeness to Quinn for a time so that she can travel through the castle without drawing attention."

Grant's scowl deepened. "And if she's seen...if *I'm* seen...sneaking away from the site of the crime? I won't survive the day."

"Then leave. It's not safe here for you anymore, not for anyone. Besides, you owe Quinn this."

"How do you figure that?"

Arturo advanced on him slowly. "When Quinn attempted to renew the magic yesterday, you promised to have Sheridan send her the words she needed to perform the ritual. The words were garbage."

The expression that registered on Grant's face was fleeting, but unmistakable. A smirk.

Quinn caught her breath.

Arturo grabbed Grant and slammed him up against the nearest rock wall, leaving his feet dangling in the air. "You never asked Sheridan for the words, did you, you bastard? You intentionally fed Quinn false words so that she would fail to renew the magic. *Why?*"

Quinn shot to her feet as she, too, rounded on Grant. They'd never been friends, but she'd thought him at least a casual ally seeing as they were both Blackstone sorcerers and shared a common hatred for Cristoff.

Grant managed to croak out an answer. "Haven't you figured it out by now? I hate this city. I want it to die. And I want to die with it."

A heavy silence descended upon the small group. Micah and Kassius exchanged looks. One after another, they turned to Bram.

Bram was the one who'd brought Grant into their midst to hear all their secrets and their plans. Yet it was clear, now, that Grant Blackstone was no ally. And if he wasn't, what of the others who knew they were down here? What of Bram himself?

Their mission might well have been compromised before it ever started.

CHAPTER TEN

The tension in the cave deep below Gonzaga Castle was thick enough to choke them all as Kassius and Micah pulled knives on Bram while Arturo continued to hold Grant pinned against the cave wall.

Grant Blackstone had never been Quinn's favorite person. He'd helped her a few times, but she'd never gotten the sense that he particularly liked her. Maybe because she supposedly had so much more magic than he did, though she knew Grant could do things she could only dream of. Still, feeding her false words when she'd risked her life to renew the magic yesterday had been a nasty move.

Bram lifted his hands slowly, watching his friends. "There is no betrayal here. You know Grant hates vampires. He's never made any pretense of feeling otherwise. But he despises Cristoff more than he dislikes all the rest of us combined. He won't betray your mission."

"True," Grant choked out.

Quinn's hard gaze swung from Grant to Bram and back again. She'd always found Grant hard to read. Or maybe not, now that she thought about it. The first time she was Cristoff's captive, Grant had helped her escape in exchange for her assisting a handful of humans to leave Vamp City. She'd figured he was either setting a trap for her or he was being particularly self-sacrificing, given that he had every expectation that she'd leave Vamp City as well. And she was the only one with a chance of saving his world.

Now it all made far more sense. He hadn't wanted his world saved. She remembered him saying something to that effect at the time, but she hadn't realized he'd meant it quite so literally.

As she watched, Arturo slowly loosened his grip on the sorcerer's throat. "You almost killed her yesterday in the Focus," Arturo growled.

Grant glanced at Quinn. "Not...my intent. Just wanted...her...to fail."

"I found the words," Quinn told him. "They came to me eventually. If my magic had been free, I could have saved V.C." It gave her a measure of satisfaction to tell him that.

Slowly, Arturo released Grant, but he kept him pinned by his gaze. "And why should you help us, Blackstone, when our goal is to save this world and yours is to see it die?"

Grant straightened his shirt, meeting the vampires' gaze. "Because as much as I want Vamp City to die, I want Cristoff to suffer more. And watching his favorite sons conspire against him is the most fun I've had in one hundred forty years."

Arturo stared at him. "As I said, Quinn will use your likeness. You will remain hidden. If she is seen and your safety compromised, you may escape. Or die. I care not which."

Grant's expression turned bitter, but he didn't argue.

Arturo turned to Bram who was still being threatened by his friends' knives. "Kassius, too, will need a glamour that won't be compromised. Someone else who will remain out of sight."

"He's welcome to take my face." Bram nodded toward the closed door. "Or that of any of the vampires' with me."

Arturo studied Bram for several minutes more, then finally motioned Kassius and Micah to put their weapons away.

"How is it that Cristoff's snake now betrays him?" Grant asked, his tone challenging.

Arturo sent him a hard look even as he answered. "I do not betray the master I loved, only the monster who now wears his face."

Grant's expression turned thoughtful. "My father hated Cristoff above all others for forcing him to renew the magic in the way he did." Grant lifted his hand, waving the three fingers that remained. "I believe he tied the magic most tightly to Cristoff, separating him from his soul most completely."

"Your father did not separate us from our souls," Arturo snapped. "No matter how much he might have desired to. But he took many of our souls hostage to varying degrees. Cristoff's has been bound more tightly than most."

"That's putting it mildly," Bram muttered.

Quinn hated that Arturo continued to hold out hope that Cristoff, too, would return to the man he'd once been. Even if Cristoff did, she wouldn't be safe from him. Even when he supposedly had honor, he was ruthless to his enemies. Grant's missing fingers were testament to that. And, having escaped him twice, she had no illusions. She was number one on his hit list.

The thought did nothing to calm nerves already stretched tight at the knowledge that Cristoff's house of horrors lay virtually on top of her right now.

"It's time to get moving," Micah said, rising. "The night won't last forever."

Quinn's pulse shot straight to the ceiling. As one, Kassius and Arturo swung her way as if they'd felt that jolt of anxiety. And of course they had, fear feeders that they were.

"I need to feed," Micah continued. "My stores are depleted from all the glamouring and unglamouring." Unfortunately, it was pleasure Micah needed, not fear, or he'd be feeding just fine right now.

"I'm sure a couple of our number would be willing to pair off to accommodate you," Bram said.

It took Quinn a moment for his meaning to sink in. Pair off. When it did, her eyes widened.

"No need. I've got the best source I've found in a while right here, if they'll kiss and make up." Micah's gaze moved from her to Arturo and back again, a question in his eyes.

Quinn knew he meant the 'kiss' literally. When she and Arturo kissed in his presence...or anything more intimate...they apparently fed Micah thoroughly.

"But I will need blood," he added.

"One of the Slavas will accommodate you." Bram looked to Arturo. "Are we through here?"

At Arturo's nod, Bram turned and exited through the low door, Grant following behind him.

Kassius eyed her, Arturo, and Micah with a hint of amusement. "Is it safe to leave you three alone?"

Quinn grunted. "Are you worried about them or me?"

"Them."

A badly-needed laugh burst from her throat. "Go. I won't kill them, I promise."

With a chuckle, Kassius ducked out through the doorway after Grant.

Quinn rose, crossing her arms over her chest and turned to Arturo. She could refuse to kiss him, of course. And part of her wanted to do just that, even if it would be foolish when they needed Micah's glamour to proceed.

For several moments they just watched one another, neither making the first move. No, she realized. He watched her. The first move was hers to make.

Slowly she uncrossed her arms and walked to him, stopping a hand's breadth away.

"*Tesoro*." He lifted a hand and brushed back a lock of her hair, then slowly raised both hands to cup her cheeks. Deep within those cool, strong hands, she could feel the slightest tremor.

Quinn frowned and covered his hands with her own. "You're shaking."

A tiny scowl formed between his eyebrows. "I do not shake."

"Of course not." But he was. And his being this unsettled unnerved her even more. "Vampire…"

Still holding her face in his hands, he tilted his forehead against hers. "The thought of you walking through this castle without me…" A shudder tore through him. "If he catches you…"

"Turo," she said softly, moved by the depth of his concern, then slid her arms around him and brushed his lips with her own.

The kiss started out tender, a caress, a promise, before slowly catching fire. Within moments, his mouth was plundering hers, and hers his, flames bursting to life all down the length of her body and deep, deep inside. Her breath grew ragged, her flesh burning as his lips trailed across her cheek, and down to the base of her neck.

Tilting her head to the side, she gave him access, a thrill of anticipation leaping within her.

She felt his tongue tease the tender flesh between her neck and her shoulder, and her fingers reflexively fisted in his shirt. His lips turned warm as they brushed her neck. A moment later, she felt his fangs sink into her on a painless slide. As she shivered with expectation, he took one long, perfect pull of her blood. She gasped, her body reacting as it always did to his bite, and his bite alone—with a violent, glorious orgasm.

She cried out in pleasure, her legs turning weak beneath her. Arturo pulled her tight against him, burying one hand in her hair as his mouth returned to hers and he kissed her fiercely.

"Thanks, kids," Micah said somewhere behind her in a voice rough with arousal. "That did the trick. I'll be back after I've found a blood donor."

She'd completely forgotten Micah was there. The moment he was gone, Arturo pulled away from her, removed his shirt, then reached for hers. Within moments, he had her jeans and panties pushed down below her knees and was entering her from the front on one long, glorious stroke.

Quinn cried out and Arturo covered her mouth with his own, drinking her cries even as he gripped her buttocks and thrust into her, over and over, each stroke more perfect than the last. Within moments she was once again climbing, this time not alone.

Higher and higher they rose, Arturo driving into her, filling her with heat and passion, until she felt as if the sun caressed her face, drenching her in its perfect warmth. Suddenly, as one, they shattered, the sun bursting, blinding, healing.

They clung to one another as Quinn's heart rate slowly descended from the stratosphere, Arturo stroking her hair with the most gentle of hands. Within the curve of his strong arms, beneath his tender touch, the last of her doubts fell away. He would never let anything or anyone harm her. He'd die before he let that happen, which terrified her in an entirely different way. Because she couldn't bear the thought of losing him. With a kiss to her temple, he pulled away and began to adjust his clothes, and she did the same.

"Every pleasure feeder in the castle probably felt that," she murmured wryly.

Arturo threw her a knowing look, hot laughter in his eyes. "You can be sure Micah did. I suspect he waited outside the door and is only now going to look for that blood donor."

When they were both dressed, Arturo pulled her close once more. "I'm changing the plan. I shall accompany you to Cristoff's private study, not Kassius."

She looked at him, shaken by how rattled this mission had him. "Turo..."

"I do not want you out of my sight."

"I know." And that knowledge warmed her. "But we need you to keep an eye on Cristoff and to run interference if anything goes wrong. I'll be fine. I have power of my own and Kassius to watch my back. He won't let anything happen to me." She had no doubt of that.

Arturo took her hand and placed a kiss in her palm, watching her with dark, fathomless eyes, setting butterflies to flight in her chest. He'd always had this effect on her, this ability to send her careening off her axis. She wasn't entirely sure what she felt for him—heaven knew, her emotions had always been jumbled where he was concerned. But the one thing she was certain of was that he had far more of a claim on her mind, her emotions, her heart, than she was comfortable with. And as long as he remained her partner and companion, she feared he always would.

"Everything's going to go without a hitch," she promised him. Even though deep in her gut, she knew that was a lie.

CHAPTER ELEVEN

Micah joined them in the cave a short while later. He was smiling, his eyes bright even as shadows moved in their depths. He knew the dangers that faced them as well as anyone.

"Let's turn you into Grant Blackstone, Miss Quinn."

"If we must," Quinn replied. And, of course, they must. Her best defense was a good disguise even if it meant wearing the face of a man she held little love for.

As before, she stepped in front of Micah and let him run his fingers along the planes of her face, and felt the tingle of magic. She watched him as he worked, his expression sober, his eyes intent with focus. Finally, he stepped back with a satisfied nod.

Quinn turned to Arturo. "What do you think?" She even sounded like Grant.

"I do not care for your glamour, *tesoro*."

Micah scowled. "What's the matter with it? It's a perfect likeness."

"Precisely."

Quinn laughed.

As Micah rolled his eyes and turned to work his magic on Kassius, Arturo walked over to her, cupping the back of her neck with his hand.

A smile lit his gaze. "How I love the sound of your laughter," he said quietly. "Even if it sounds like Grant's."

"I'm kind of amazed I can laugh, under the circumstances."

He gathered her close and held her against him, as she wrapped her arms around his waist. They stood there, entwined, soaking up one another's warmth, for Arturo had yet to lose the unnatural warmth he always acquired when they kissed. He'd told her that he'd never heard of it happening before—a vampire growing warm. He called her his sunshine and there really did appear to be something in her magic that warmed him as if he stood in a healing sun, instead of the real one that would kill him in an instant.

"They're done," Arturo said, finally, kissing her hair.

Quinn pulled back and turned to find that Kassius now looked exactly like one of the vampires waiting for them in the tunnels outside, a stocky, blond-haired male.

Micah was staring at her as if he'd just bit into a lemon.

"What?" she asked him.

He made a funny sound, half choke, half laugh. "It's going to take me years to get that image out of my head."

Amusement pulled at her mouth. "What image?" But she thought she knew. "Arturo and Grant?"

"More like Arturo tenderly kissing Grant's hair."

Quinn smirked. "You're living in the wrong century, Micah."

The vampire lifted an eyebrow. "It's not the fact that Grant's male. It's that he's Grant."

She couldn't argue with that.

Kassius met her gaze. "Are you ready, sorceress?"

Quinn nodded. "As ready as I'll ever be."

One by one, they filed out of the cave and joined the others gathered further down the tunnel.

Bram stepped forward and Arturo shook his hand. "Cristoff must continue to believe me loyal, Bram. Word cannot get out that I am otherwise."

"Nor I. We're all in the same boat, Ax. All betraying him."

Arturo nodded, shook hands with a couple of the other vampires, then turned and met Quinn's gaze. "Be careful, *tesoro*."

"You, too."

She watched as he turned and disappeared back down the tunnel, the way they'd come. The plan was for him to walk into Gonzaga Castle through the front door, Cristoff's snake come to report on his hunt for the missing sorceress. As long as his cover hadn't been blown, he'd be fine. If it had, he'd soon be dead.

That was something she couldn't let herself think about.

Meanwhile, she and Kassius would make their way to the stairs directly below the castle and wait for Arturo to tell her, telepathically, that he was in place and it was time to move. The original plan was for Micah to keep to the shadows within the castle in case he was needed, but there was risk in that since he was supposed to be searching for the sorceress, too. Now that Bram was in on the plan, it would be he who would keep an ear out within the castle and report to those below.

"Ready, Quinn?" Bram asked. He motioned to the Slava female at his side, a friendly-looking young woman. "This is Deb. She'll be accompanying us."

Grant led the way down the tunnels in the opposite direction from Arturo, followed by Kassius, then Quinn. Micah, Bram, and Deb brought up the rear. As they walked, Quinn studied Grant. Her impersonation of him probably didn't have to be perfect—people tended to see what they expected to see. But it had to be good enough that she didn't attract attention. Mostly, she just needed to keep her head down and keep from being drawn into conversation because, while she would sound like Grant, she certainly didn't use the same words or terminology as a male born right after the Civil War.

Above all, she needed to avoid Grant's brother, Sheridan, because there'd be no fooling that vampire.

There were a hundred ways this could go wrong.

"Quinn," Kassius said quietly beside her. "You must remain calm. It will not do for Grant Blackstone to radiate fear. He, alone, shows and feels none."

Her eyes widened with dismay. She hadn't known that. Any fear feeder would feel her emotions and suspect something, even if it was only that Grant Blackstone was up to something. Which could have her hauled in front of Cristoff.

"Why in the hell did we glamour me to look like Grant, then?" she said, stopping in her tracks.

Micah grabbed her shoulders to keep from running into her. "What's the matter?"

"You need to make me look like someone else. Kass says Grant never feels emotion and I sure as hell can't mimic *that*." If they needed proof, her pulse was already racing, her palms damp with sweat. And she was still perfectly safe down in the tunnel.

"Come here, Quinn," Grant said. "I want to talk to you. Alone."

Her vampire companions glanced at one another, but none of the three offered up an objection when she continued on with Grant. It occurred to her that she and Grant must look like twins.

"Stay in sight," Micah called quietly.

Grant said nothing, but stopped some twenty feet from the others and turned his back on them. "There's a reason no vampire senses my fear."

"And what is that?" But she watched him, unable to hide her interest. "Magic?"

"Yes. My father's." He took a stone out of his pocket, a small clear crystal in the shape of a squat Washington Monument, and handed it to her. "Hold onto this. I'm going to want it back, but you need it more than I do at the moment."

She looked at the stone, then at Grant. "A magic talisman or Dumbo's feather?"

Grant frowned. "Who's Dumbo?"

Quinn's smile was quick and amused. "A Disney character. Never mind the reference. I was referring to the fact that sometimes simply believing will make it true. Whether or not the stone truly possesses magic, if I believe that no one will sense my fear, then perhaps I won't feel afraid. Although in this case, I'm not sure that's going to work."

He nodded, his brow slightly furrowed as if he only partially understood what she was trying to say. "You'll still feel afraid. The vampires simply won't be able to sense it. I used the stone to cast a temporary spell over my companions earlier, which is why neither of your fear feeders sensed our presence when you first arrived in the tunnels."

"How did you know we were coming?"

"I didn't. Not until you entered the stables. I set that trap soon after Kassius learned of the tunnels. I didn't trust that he wouldn't tell others."

"How did you know we'd entered?"

He shrugged. "Magic."

She eyed him curiously. "You have an awful lot of magic for a sorcerer too weak to renew Vamp City."

"I have magic. It's just not the right kind."

He was being awfully helpful all of a sudden. "Why give me your stone, Grant? Why help me at all?" But she realized she knew. "I'm wearing your face. If I screw up, you're toast."

"Something like that. I've never had anything against you personally, Quinn. I'd love to see this world crumble because I'm sick to death of living in it and I can't leave. But I'll happily put up with another hundred years in exchange for watching Cristoff taken down by his own vampires."

She looked at him curiously. "This isn't the time for this, but I've been wondering...do you have any idea how we're related?" When he lifted a brow, she continued. "I possess Blackstone magic, therefore I must also possess Blackstone blood."

Grant shrugged. "Daddy dearest only had two legitimate children that I know of, but he was old by the time Cristoff killed him, Quinn. A lot older than he looked. He rarely talked to us of the past and never told us when he was born or anything about his own childhood. But a couple of times, a couple of things he said, made me wonder if he'd turned immortal as some of the most powerful sorcerers do. He may have fathered many children in his lifetime. You're probably descended from one of them."

Quinn nodded. "Thanks for this," she said, pocketing the crystal.

"You're welcome."

Grant motioned the others to join them and the small group continued down the tunnel. Quinn felt the stone in her pocket. Now that she had her magic feather, what could go wrong?

Her gut cramped, because she knew the answer to that.

Everything.

Arturo parked his Jeep in front of the iron gates of Gonzaga Castle. After leaving the tunnels, he'd retrieved his mount and ridden it to his house, then switched to his Jeep. The yellow Wrangler drew far too much attention these days, when he needed to be stealthy, but today he had no need or desire to hide his movements. Arturo Mazza, Cristoff's most loyal, danced attendance on his master, and he was happy for all the kovena to know it.

The moment he turned off the ignition, the screams hit him like flying glass.

Dio. Cristoff must be torturing a dozen at once.

As he climbed out of the vehicle and strode up to the gates of what, for decades, had been his second home, his flesh chilled to ice. Because all he could think about was that within minutes Quinn would be walking those deadly halls without his protection.

And that Cristoff wanted to hurt her with a hunger bordering on madness.

CHAPTER TWELVE

It is time, cara. Arturo's voice sounded in Quinn's head as she and Kassius waited in the torch-lit tunnel at the base of the stairs that would lead directly into Gonzaga Castle, her back against the cool stone. *Cristoff is well occupied. Mio Dio, but he has grown depraved.*

As if he hadn't been utterly so before. Maybe Cristoff really had grown worse. Or maybe Arturo could just, finally, see him clearly.

"It's time," she told Kassius, her heart starting to race. They probably hadn't been in place and waiting for more than ten minutes, but her nerves were stretched almost to the breaking point. What kind of idiot was she for willingly going anywhere near that monster? Every couple of minutes, the question burst in her mind all over again.

Was she *really* going to do this? It wasn't too late. If she told them she'd changed her mind, there wasn't a one of them who would blame her. But all she had to do was think of Zack lying on the kitchen floor and her spine turned to steel.

"Ready?" Kassius asked.

Not in a million years. But she took a deep breath and nodded. "Let's go."

Respect lit the werevamp's eyes.

Bram stepped forward, the female Slava at his side. "Deb and I will climb the ladder first and let you know when the coast is clear." The ladder led to a small empty bedroom, one in an unused hall of dorm rooms originally intended for slaves. No one would question a vampire male leaving a small bedroom with a female slave. If they encountered anyone in the hallway as they left the room, Quinn had no doubt Bram would greet them loudly…assuming Bram was on their side, as he claimed, and not Cristoff's mole. Once, she might not have questioned the motives of everyone around her, human and vampire alike. But if there was one thing Arturo had taught her, it was that.

Even as a myriad of doubts preyed on her mind, she knew she had to trust. She couldn't carry out this mission alone, and they couldn't do it without her. They'd never get into Cristoff's private study without her magic.

Bram clambered up the ladder first and the rest of them held their collective breaths as he opened the hatch slowly, then disappeared into the room above. The distant sound of screams filtered down into the tunnel, making Quinn shiver. Bram motioned for Deb and the woman followed him. As soon as she was up, Kassius started to climb.

Quinn turned to Micah, who would remain behind. "Wish me luck," she whispered.

He gave her a bear hug. "You'll be fine, Quinn. I have complete faith in you."

She wished she could say the same.

When he released her, she turned to the ladder and followed the others up into the tiny, Spartan room. Bram replaced the hidden hatch, then motioned them back, but Kassius stopped him.

"The screams," Kassius said. "They're not coming from the throne room."

"No. He bit a dozen Slavas and left them in the foyer."

Bit? Quinn's eyes widened. "Dragon fire?"

Bram nodded, his expression filling with pity. "You've experienced that particular torture, haven't you, Quinn?"

A hard shiver ran through her at the memory of an agony so overwhelming, she'd been unable to move.

Kassius cupped her shoulder. "You'll have to walk through the foyer. Keep your head down and just keep moving. Trust me, Grant Blackstone would give the victims no thought." As he and Quinn moved behind the door, Bram opened it, took hold of Deb's arm and ushered her into the hallway.

The sound of the screams rushed in five times louder than before, flaying Quinn with horrific memories of the pain she'd already suffered in this place. And that was nothing...*nothing*...compared to what Cristoff would do to her if he caught her again.

She began to tremble deep inside, her heart pounding, a thin panic rising on her skin.

Take slow, even breaths, cara. Arturo's voice stroked her mind like a soft, warm hand. *You are powerful. You are in complete control of your magic. You have nothing to fear.*

She wasn't sure about any of that, but he was right. If she didn't start believing she'd succeed, she would absolutely fail.

"I can do this," she whispered.

Kassius glanced at her, perplexed.

"I'll get it under control," Quinn promised. She had to.

The vampire's frown deepened. "I sense no fear in you."

With dawning understanding, Quinn smiled. "Grant shared his secret…and a bit of magic."

Kassius's confusion cleared. "Amazing. Now all you have to do is *act* as fearless and unconcerned as Grant does."

Her mouth twisted ruefully. The vampires might not taste her fear, but they'd see it quickly enough if she wasn't very, very careful.

Kassius eyed her. "Ready?"

"Yes." Which was an out and out lie and they both knew it. As she stepped into the hallway, the screams had her drawing in a harsh breath.

"Keep your wits about you, Quinn," Kassius said quietly, then he left her in a vampire flash. He would remain close enough to hear her if she needed him, but it wouldn't do for Grant to be seen looking chummy with a vampire. Cristoff and the other vampires left Grant alone to wander the castle as he pleased.

Heart pounding in her chest, Quinn started down the long hallway that would lead to the foyer and the suffering Slavas, and finally the stairs. As everything inside her yelled for caution, she forced herself to walk at a brisk pace, struggling to mimic Grant's nonchalant stride, channeling a man who hated his life and everyone in it.

Upstairs was located both Grant's bedroom—where she was to meet up with Kassius again—and Cristoff's private study—their ultimate destination. Unfortunately, upstairs was also Cristoff's throne room where he often entertained himself by torturing people.

But first she had to walk through the foyer.

Her breath grew more and more shallow the closer to the screaming she came, but she set her jaw and forced herself to keep going. Her legs turned heavy, her survival instinct fighting her forward movement. Her heart thudded, sweat beading at the back of her neck. As she neared the foyer, her vision began to turn white at the edges.

Tesoro, Arturo said quietly in her head, a reminder that she wasn't alone. His voice helped quiet the rising panic, if only a little.

Head down, she reached the foyer, the pain of a dozen humans flaying her from all sides. *Don't look,* she told herself. *Just keep going.* But she barely knew Cristoff's castle, unlike the real Grant who'd lived here for decades, and she had no choice but to watch where she was going.

The marble and ivory foyer was huge, easily the size of a small ballroom. In the very center stood a black lacquer grand piano, while along the walls sat lines of red velvet benches. Scattered across the marble floor were a dozen humans writhing in pain, each with a swollen protrusion on his or her neck, or bare groin, the size and color of a ripe plum.

Quinn's breath hitched as she stared at the sickening protrusions. The need to help them was a living thing inside of her, but she had no idea how. And this was not the time. Belatedly, she realized she'd nearly quit walking altogether. Shit. She had to be Grant! He'd learned to ignore all of this decades ago. More than a century. *Be Grant.*

"Grant." At first the name barely registered over the screams of Cristoff's victims. "Grant!"

Quinn froze, then turned slowly to find Sheridan, Grant's brother, walking through the foyer toward her.

Dammit to hell.

CHAPTER THIRTEEN

"What?" Quinn asked Sheridan brusquely, not looking up. Her green eyes in Grant's face would be a dead giveaway, though it was unlikely she could fool the sorcerer's vampire sibling for long, regardless.

"You're going to tell me what's going on, brother. And you're going to do it now, or I'm going to tell Cristoff you're up to something."

"I'm busy." Quinn turned away, praying the bluff worked, but before she'd gone two steps, she felt his palm slam against her chin in a move that felt awkward. Even as her eyes stung with tears at the painful blow, she understood what had happened. She'd seen Sheridan lift his brother by the neck and suspected he'd attempted to do that now. But her neck was slightly lower than Grant's and he'd hit her chin instead.

Sheridan stared at her and she lifted her eyes, knowing the gig was up. With this male, at least.

Though born shortly after the Civil War, Sheridan Blackstone looked no older than twenty-five and dressed as he probably had back in the 1870's—his shirt white, his sleeves wide, his pants black. He looked a lot like Grant with his good bone structure and the dark blond hair. She'd never seen him without a scowl on his face. Until now.

He stared at her with confusion.

"Say nothing," she said quietly. "A lot of lives depend on it, including yours."

"Sorceress," he breathed. He reached for her arm, then seemed to think better of it. "Follow me or I *will* yell for Cristoff."

Hell and damn. But she did as he asked and followed him back out of the foyer and into a nearby room, one blessedly empty. The moment they were both inside, Sheridan closed the door and turned on her.

"Where's my brother?"

"Hiding so that no one sees two of us. I just left him. He's aware that I'm wearing his face."

"What are you up to?"

She honestly didn't think this Blackstone had any more use for Cristoff than his brother, but the fact that Grant hadn't shared his secrets with Sheridan made her especially cautious.

"I can't tell you the specifics, only that this is the only way to save Vamp City."

He moved closer, aggressively so, crowding her against the wall. Her hand clenched with the longing to throw him against the opposite wall, but turning this into a fight probably wasn't her best option.

"That's not how this is going to work, sorceress," the vampire said, his voice cold. "You *are* going to tell me the specifics, every last one of them."

Quinn glared at him, but quickly filled him in—how the Levenach curse was strangling her Blackstone magic. And how the only way to save Vamp City was to destroy the sword Escalla.

Sheridan's jaw dropped. A grin began to spread across his face and he actually laughed. "I love it. Do you have any idea how you're going to accomplish this?"

Quinn shrugged, not willing to tell him the entire plan. "Magic. And a lot of luck."

His laughter died, but he continued to grin. "Cristoff's going to be livid, if you break his toy."

"At least he'll still be alive. Something none of you will be if the city's magic fails. Don't give me away, Sheridan. I'm the only chance you have."

He peered at her, his eyes a bit too sharp. "Someone's helping you other than Grant. Who?"

She said nothing.

"You're going to tell me who, Quinn, or I will blow your cover."

"No," she said, her own voice cold. "I've told you the truth, but I won't endanger anyone else. Turn me over to Cristoff and risk Vamp City, or let me go, Sheridan. I have a small window of opportunity and I need to take it."

He eyed her speculatively. "I'll walk you up there."

"I'm not sure that's a good idea."

"Nevertheless, you're getting an escort. If anyone else approaches you, I can deflect them."

She didn't really trust this Blackstone brother any more than the other one. Still… "All right. I'm going to…my bed chambers."

He looked at her a little sharply, then nodded. "Come."

Since she had no choice, she followed him out of the room, walking beside him, not trying to hide the annoyance she felt since Grant almost always appeared annoyed at his brother. But as they crossed the foyer and climbed the stairs, she was glad she wasn't alone. With Sheridan by her side, no one would give her a second look.

I have told Cristoff a tale, tesoro, Arturo said, his voice sliding through her mind. *A tale of how the wily sorceress leads me on a miserable chase, disappearing at will. And how my fine friend Micah accompanies me, how we lay traps for her, how it is just a matter of time before we catch her. He believes we lost you in the Crux and were forced to back away from the wolves. He is not pleased, but still he trusts me as he does no other. It pains me,* amore mio. *When I look into his eyes, I can find no glimpse of the Cristoff I knew, yet he remembers our connection and cherishes it still.*

By the time Quinn and Sheridan reached the top of the stairs, Quinn was almost sick to her stomach from the combination of screams raking her ears and heart, and her own quaking fear. But they made it to Grant's bedroom without incident.

Kassius, who was waiting for her, as planned, frowned at the sight of Sheridan.

Sheridan looked at him with speculation. "Denard? Or another who has been glamoured?"

"The less you know," Quinn said, "the better. I suggest you get away from this part of the castle before anything happens. Make yourself visible in the billiards room. You don't need to be implicated in this."

"As my brother will."

"Only if we fail. And we don't intend to fail."

The sorcerer-turned-vampire scowled, but turned and left without another word. Whether to do as she suggested or to tell Cristoff he'd found her, she had no idea. She had to assume the former and press forward.

She turned to Kassius with a groan. "Not a perfect execution of phase one, but I'm here."

He nodded. "Cristoff has stationed two guards outside his study. He must suspect someone might go after that sword."

"As much as I hate to say it, the screaming will help cover a lot of sound." Small sounds, at least, which breaking the sword free of its case wasn't likely to be unless she suddenly managed to control the force of her magic. A crash in Cristoff's supposedly empty study would end up getting them killed.

Arturo stood at Cristoff's side in the castle's opulent throne room. Thick gilt pillars soared high to the ceiling from a marble floor heavily stained and splattered with blood. The walls, too, were now badly bloodstained, as were the weapons and tapestries that had once so proudly graced them. Cristoff himself, dressed head to toe in peacock blue satin, now splatter-stained with blood, sat upon the golden throne he'd ordered built for himself just two years ago, a throne upholstered in dark red velvet. The old Cristoff had had no need for a throne, Arturo realized. He'd sat amongst his people.

When had everything changed?

Hands clenched tight behind his back, Arturo kept his gaze fixed at the level of the ceiling at the far side of the room as the screams tore through his head. He knew the male pinned to the floor in front of him was a Slava, and immortals healed most injuries quickly. But even an immortal could die, and it was quite clear Cristoff intended to torture this one until he did just that.

Where had the master he'd so admired gone, and how had he not noticed? How long had it been since the two of them had fed simply by walking the streets of D.C. late at night? There used to be a women's hospital on L Street where women gave birth. It had been one of Cristoff's favorite places. They'd walk around the back and stand in the shadows as the screams and groans of a woman in labor carried through the windows. Cristoff would feed, simply, enjoying the sound of new life being brought into the world. Cristoff's words. How many times had Arturo heard him say, "Pain is a part of the human condition. They suffer enough for us to feed well. There is no need, and no justification, for us to cause them more."

Now Cristoff watched with malicious hunger as one of his guards cut off the toes of the male Slava lying on the floor in front of him.

The guard doing the cutting was a male Arturo did not know, a male whose eyes glittered with the same savagery as Cristoff's.

Arturo's muscles quivered so strongly with the need to stop this barbarity, he feared his facade as the loyal son would, at any moment, crack.

And perhaps it was time.

But, no, it was not. The only way to stop Cristoff was to attack and kill his master before Cristoff could kill him in return.

The growing certainty that it would come to that, and soon, tore something loose inside of him. But first he must help Quinn save the city. His death in an attempt to save three Slavas would serve no purpose and would only end up costing the Slavas, and most of those residing in Vamp City, their lives.

No, there was nothing to be done but pretend he was no more moved by the suffering in front of him than he had been a few short weeks ago, before Quinn had walked into his life and changed everything.

"You and you," Cristoff said, pointing to two of the guards standing at attention. "Grab a Slava and join us." Cristoff waved impatiently to two Slavas, one male, one female, who sat against the wall, shaking with terror.

The one guard grabbed the male and threw him down hard enough on the marble floor in front of Cristoff to break bone. Arturo's head began to throb. The second guard, though not gentle, merely pushed the woman to her knees in front of him. She began to cry with great hiccoughing sounds that ripped at Arturo's heart.

"Show me blood!" Cristoff yelled.

The first guard pulled his knife and began to hack at the man with gusto. But the second hesitated, and Arturo suspected that he'd begun to reclaim his soul as so many appeared to be doing. Under different circumstances, that would have been a good thing.

"Blood!" Cristoff roared.

The second guard pulled his knife, but the woman's misery had gotten to him, there was no doubt about it. His gaze rose to Cristoff.

"Surely you've had enough pain by now, my liege," the guard said, his eyes wide.

Arturo winced because he knew what came next.

Cristoff leaped from his throne, strode to the guard, and slammed his palm against the male's forehead. Almost immediately, the guard's scream joined those of the two Slava males. Blood began to seep from the male's nose and ears.

Cristoff was using his mind blast, the ability to pulverize another's brain with a simple touch of his hand.

Arturo clasped his own hands hard behind his back, fisting them, his breath shallow as he fought the impulse...the *need*...to stop this.

It was not the time, he reminded himself. It was not the time. Quinn needed him.

The guard's screams slowly went silent. The male fell, boneless, to the blood-slicked marble floor. As Cristoff walked back toward his throne, the guard exploded as all vampires did when they died.

Cristoff turned, as if to take his seat, but instead just stood there, and Arturo wondered what new horror his master had in mind. But instead of barking another heinous order, Cristoff turned to Arturo, his face a mask of confusion. For one startling moment, horror bloomed in eyes Arturo had once known well. But as quickly as the horror appeared, it was gone. Cristoff's expression cleared and he sat decisively and clapped his hands.

"Continue!"

Arturo's pulse began to race. Had he just imagined he'd glimpsed the old Cristoff? Or was his master, too, finally beginning to reclaim his soul? Arturo had never stopped hoping that he might, that Cristoff, too, would eventually emerge from the darkness.

The question was, how many more would die before that happened?

CHAPTER FOURTEEN

Quinn paced Grant's bedroom, shaking her hands, trying to get control of her runaway nerves.

"It is time, sorceress," Kassius said quietly.

"I know, I know." It was all up to her, now. Taking a deep breath, Quinn concentrated on what she needed to do—form a bubble around the two of them, then push it outward, toward Cristoff's study. The bubble would form a secret passage that would pass right through locked doors and walls, and everything in its path including random Gonzaga guards. Completely unseen and undetected, if all went as planned.

Her sense of direction had never been great, and once inside the bubble, she had no way to get her bearings. But Kassius had assured her that he had an excellent internal compass thanks to his wolf's blood. It was the main reason he was her partner for this part of the mission and not Micah.

Quinn closed her eyes and called up her magic. It rose through her body, and into her hands, like a painless electrical current just under her skin. When her hands began to tingle intensely, she threw the power up and out in an exhilarating rush, forming a bubble around them, casting the pair of them into darkness.

"Nicely done, sorceress."

"Thanks." Quinn reached down and lifted the flashlight out of her boot, flicking it on. The walls of the bubble glimmered faintly like black opal, but there was no seeing outside, no hearing anything, which was a blessing. They were completely enclosed.

"How far do you think it is from here to the study?" she asked Kassius. "Twenty feet?"

"Yes. Thirty should put us in the middle of the room."

She handed Kassius the flashlight. "Point me in the right direction, Kass."

With a nod, he illuminated the far side of the bubble, some ten feet in front of her.

Lifting her hands, she directed the magic still pulsing in her palms toward the spot of the flashlight beam, watching with satisfaction as the black opal wall flew backward an additional ten feet. Her elongating bubble would quickly begin to look like a peanut. Then, finally, a tunnel.

"More, Quinn," Kassius said. "The same direction, another ten."

With a nod, she pushed the magic with her palm, then again.

"Perfect, I believe," Kassius said. "But let me check." He reached for Quinn's hand, poked his head through the rubbery wall, then pulled back. "The coast is clear, we're exiting in the middle of the room, and there is nothing to trip over."

"Excellent."

"Not exactly."

Quinn looked at him uneasily. "What do you mean?"

"You'll have to see for yourself." With his hand still in hers, he stepped fully out of the bubble and she followed, leaving the bubble intact for their escape.

Cristoff's private study, a room she'd been in once before, was surprisingly warm and inviting considering the mercilessly cold male to whom it belonged. Bookshelves lined the walls, a large chess table in one corner of the room, a large mahogany desk in another. A worn leather recliner sat before the hearth on a thick Persian rug. And in what appeared to be a glass case against the back wall hung one brightly glowing sword. *Escalla.*

Her brows drew down in confusion. "Why's it glowing?"

She'd seen the sword once before, and had actually held it that time. After Arturo handed her over to his master that first time, Cristoff had brought her back here, removed the sword from its case and laid it across her outstretched palms. She'd been in awe of its beauty—the hilt solid gold, inlaid with sapphires, the blade etched in intricate vines.

It is the sword Escalla, Cristoff had told her. *An old wizard's sword that recognizes great power. Power you do not possess.*

It hadn't glowed that time. It hadn't done anything at all, which had greatly disappointed Cristoff.

But it was glowing now. And she suspected she knew why. At that time, her power, both Blackstone and Levenach, had still been almost entirely imprisoned by the Levenach curse. But in the past week, she and Arturo had managed to free the lion's share of her Blackstone magic. Escalla clearly recognized her newfound power. Great power, apparently, which she was still struggling to wrap her mind around. A month ago, she'd thought of herself as nothing more than a lab tech with the NIH in Bethesda. A scientist. A normal person around whom weird things occasionally happened.

Great power.

No, it didn't seem real. And yet... She glanced back at the opal walls of the bubble, the mini *world* she'd just created and shook her head in amazement.

"It glows because of me," she said, turning to Kassius.

"It was glowing even before you left the bubble, if only faintly. When you entered the room, it flared brightly."

"So it sensed me even in the bubble."

"It would seem so, yes."

Cara? *You can do it, Quinn. I have utmost faith in you. Believe and you will succeed.*

"Easy for you to say," she muttered.

"Sorceress?" Kassius asked.

"Nothing. Arturo is talking in my head, trying to give me confidence."

His brow lifted. "It is working?"

She snorted. "We'll see, won't we?"

Moving forward, Quinn studied the sword which appeared to be suspended in air within that glass case. Once before, she'd watched Cristoff press his palm against the glass, watched as the top sprung open and Cristoff reached inside to pull out the sword.

If only she could figure out how to do the same. But Arturo had watched a man—a vampire—push his hand right through the glass, without breaking it. And promptly die. Cristoff had long warned his vampires that to touch his sword meant death, but Quinn suspected it was only the case that was enchanted against theft, not the sword itself since she'd touched it without issue. Either that, or the sword only killed vampires and not sorcerers.

Since they weren't sure how it worked, and knew it could be deadly, they'd decided their only option was for Quinn to lift it out of its case with magic. And that was exactly what she had to do now. But as she stepped closer, something crawled over her skin—a harsh, clawing energy that made her catch her breath.

"Quinn? What is it, sorceress?"

"I'm not sure. I think it's the sword. I can feel its energy."

"Is that a good thing or bad?"

"I have no idea. Let's hope Cristoff can't sense it, or me through it, or we'll be out of time before we ever get started."

"Then we must hurry. Pull the sword from its case, sorceress."

"Roger that."

Quinn took another step forward, and another, approaching the sword as she might a cobra in a basket. The closer she got, the stronger the stinging sensation grew. Did it recognize in her the blood of the one who'd created it, the wizard Levenach? Or maybe the blood of the one it had killed, the Black Wizard. Closing her eyes, she took a deep breath and tried to center her focus, center her magic, turning all of her attention on the sword hanging, suspended, in that magical case.

"Come to me," she whispered, calling the magic into her hands, then pulling the sword with enough strength to lift it, if the case didn't interfere. Which it did, of course. While the sword's glow flared brighter, it didn't move.

The clawing energy intensified, racing all over her body like tiny pinpricks, like tiny hooks designed to pull her closer. Why? Was the sword telling her it wanted her to take it? If not for that deadly case, she might try.

"If you want me, come to me," she said quietly, attempting to lift it once more. As she pulled a little harder, then harder still, the sword began to quiver, but the case continued to hold it fast.

Quinn stepped closer and pulled hard. Still nothing.

She looked at Kassius. "Screw finesse. I'm going to have to give it all I have. It may go flying."

His mouth tightened. "If it does, grab it and get us back into your bubble."

With a nod, Quinn took a deep breath, grimaced, then threw everything she had into it, yanking on the sword with all her might.

Still nothing happened.

"Well...damn." Taking a deep breath, she closed her eyes and gathered all the magic she could, feeling her own energy colliding with Escalla's in a blinding rush of pain. Biting down on a whimper, she fought past it, yanking hard enough that she should have imploded the wall. But when she opened her eyes she found the sword still caught fast in its case, if glowing as brightly as the sun.

"Shit." She looked at Kassius, her body on fire. "I can't do more," she gasped.

"Are you okay?" he asked worriedly.

"I think so. I'm afraid it's time for Plan B."

The werevamp nodded and took over with startling speed. As Kassius worked, Quinn stepped back with the vague thought of moving to the other side of the room to put distance between her and that awful sword, but she couldn't quite get her feet to move. Pain continued to pummel her body as she watched Kassius dig through the pack he'd carried with him, then begin to press explosive charges to the wall around the box. He had to be careful not to touch the box itself or, like the guard Arturo had watched, Kassius might be the thing exploding. Plan B had not been their first choice for several obvious reasons, not the least of which was that it was a lot more likely to get one or both of them killed. Unfortunately, they'd been unable to come up with a viable Plan C.

She was starting to feel nauseous and told herself, again, to move away. But the part of her brain that controlled her limbs didn't seem to be working right. She could feel the pull of the sword growing, tendrils of stinging energy sliding around her arms, her legs, her torso.

Quinn. Arturo's voice sounded quietly in her head. *Something is not right. Be careful.*

She thought about replying, then remembered he couldn't hear her. Perhaps she should say something to Kassius. But her thoughts scattered, her mind overrun by fog as if the pain were separating her from her body.

With blurring vision, she watched Kassius, his fingers moving vampire-fast. The fog in her mind thickened, blacking out her sight. Pain exploded.

Quinn!

She stumbled, knocking into a hard shoulder, which gave slightly, shifting.

The explosion sent her flying across the room.

Quinn screamed, Grant's deep voice emerging from her throat, vibrating with the pain blazing through her body.

Beyond the wall, she heard shouts. "Someone's inside!"

Quinn!

Quinn pushed herself up, trying to think, trying to remember where she was and why the sound of that shout filled her with such terror. But as she blinked, as her vision cleared and she saw where she was...*Cristoff's study*...memory came flooding back. She'd failed to call the sword from the case. Kassius had been setting charges.

"Kassius?" Quinn called softly, trying to move, trying to breathe. What had happened? Had he set off the charge with them both right there?

But, no. There was no destruction.

Understanding dawned with a sick horror. Oh, God. Oh no. She vaguely remembered getting dizzy and falling against someone. Had she knocked him into that deadly case?

No, no, no. Quinn turned, her still wavering gaze searching for her companion. *Kassius, don't be dead. Don't be dead.* Her head pounded as she looked, but she saw no sign of him.

Quinn. Arturo's voice was filled with such sorrow. He knew she feared Kassius dead. He knew. And of course after the racket they'd made, Cristoff was probably already on his way.

God, God, God. She had to do something. *Think!*

But she knew what she had to do—she had to finish setting the charges herself. Back in the safe house, when they'd conceived of Plan B, she'd made Kassius walk her through the process in detail just in case, for some reason, he wasn't able to help. She hadn't expected that she'd get him killed.

Her breath caught, her eyes burning, but she turned and stumbled to the sword case. But as she neared, that sword's terrible energy once more tried to latch onto her, and she quickly backed away while she still could. A quick perusal told her Kassius had set most of the explosives already. They would have to be enough. All she needed now was the remote that would set off the charges.

Grabbing his backpack, she found the remote in the outside pocket, right where he'd promised it would be. Their original plan was to return to Grant's room and set the charges off from there. But there wasn't time. At least her bubble was still intact.

Clutching the remote carefully, she ran back to that black shimmer. But as she was about to enter it, something caught her eye, an arm sticking out from behind the desk in the corner. Her heart seized, then began to beat again as she realized the arm was still attached to a body. *Kassius.*

She lurched to him, feeling for his pulse. *There. Thank God.* But his skin was ice cold. He needed blood.

The door to the study began to rattle. *Cristoff.* She tried to lift Kassius, hoping she was strong enough to drag him to the bubble. But he was too big, and she was still dazed.

Panic tore through her. Those charges had to be detonated, the sword destroyed!

Calling up her magic, she formed a second bubble tight around them. Then, praying it would be enough to protect them, she shoved her hand and the detonator through the rubbery wall.

Squeezing her eyes closed and hoping for a miracle, she pushed the button.

CHAPTER FIFTEEN

Pain tore through Quinn's back as the force of the explosion threw her hard against the wall.

She couldn't breathe. Couldn't move. Shafts of agony arced up her spine into her skull and she tried to focus her eyes, but the air was too filled with debris to see anything clearly.

The ramifications of that penetrated slowly. The force of the explosion must have thrown her clear of the bubble. Or destroyed it.

Where was Kassius?

From what she could see, most of the back wall of Cristoff's study was gone, most of the furniture turned to dust. Clearly the explosives had detonated. The question was, had they destroyed the sword?

But even as the question entered her mind, an eerie orange-red glow caught her attention on the rug—what was left of the rug—six feet away. Quinn blinked, trying to make out what she was seeing. Her stomach sank, her mind reeling with disbelief.

Escalla lay in its case on the floor, apparently untouched.

Dammit to hell.

They'd accomplished nothing. And she didn't dare try to pry the sword loose with her hands. Just brushing against its case had nearly felled Kassius. Had he, too, been blown free of her hastily built second bubble, or was he still inside, trapped there?

She pushed to her feet, every part of her body aching. Peering through the fog of debris, she saw no sign of him, but caught sight of a pair of black shimmers—one stretching into the room from the front wall and a small one tucked back against the corner where the desk now stood on end. It was the second one she'd left him in, the second one she had to reach.

But as she took a step toward it, a violent wave of dizziness hit her, driving her to her knees.

The study door swung open, blocking her view of whoever stood in the doorway. With raw frustration, she pulled yet another bubble around her, the darkness once more swallowing her, shutting her off from all that happened outside.

She needed to reach Kass! Not only did he need blood, but without her help, he'd never escape the small world in which she'd trapped him.

Arturo stood in the doorway of Cristoff's study as his master strode into the middle of the destruction. The blast had leveled half the room and what was left was quickly being covered by the debris raining down, much of it tiny bits of what had once been books.

Every muscle in Arturo's body had tensed. His pulse raced because…where was Quinn? He knew she was alive. He could feel her pain, her distress. He just hoped to hell she was hidden.

The wall where the sword's case had hung was now gone, but he could see the sword and case lying on the floor as if untouched. The sword was glowing. *Dio.* Was there no way to destroy that thing?

"Find her!" Cristoff yelled. "The sorceress is nearby. I want her alive!"

Guards swarmed the room, Arturo joining them, hunting for Quinn. But there was no sign of her. With bone-melting relief he realized that she must have escaped back into her bubble.

Slowly, he began to breathe again. He turned to Cristoff. "Why do you think this is the sorceress's doing?"

Cristoff grinned. "Because Escalla glows."

Arturo frowned. "For her?"

Cristoff's eyes flared with excitement. "Escalla craves the blood of the Black Wizard's heir."

Arturo's brows lifted, his mouth tightening. He'd thought Cristoff only wanted her in order to force her to renew the magic, and to secure his revenge. But this was something entirely different. Something far bigger than he'd realized.

"The blood…? You'll kill her with it," he said with sudden understanding.

"Of course. Which is why she's here to take it from me."

Arturo stared at him, stunned. He hadn't thought it possible for

Cristoff to be of even more danger to Quinn than he already was. Arturo searched his master's eyes for any sign of the conscience Arturo had thought he'd seen flare to life briefly in the throne room. But he saw nothing but a frantic excitement, as if a treasure beyond imagining was finally within Cristoff's grasp.

And what would Cristoff gain if he managed to stab Quinn, if Escalla did drink her blood?

As if he were reading Arturo's unspoken thoughts, Cristoff said, "You've heard of Nerian."

Every vampire had heard of Nerian, the most powerful vampire ever to live. Understanding crashed over Arturo.

"He had Escalla?"

"He was the one who stabbed the Black Wizard. He was the one who held the hilt of the sword while Escalla drank of the Black Wizard's blood. And I shall do the same."

Arturo's own blood ran cold.

Quinn struggled to her feet within the confines of her small, dark world, her heart pounding, a bead of sweat rolling down the back of her neck. Thankfully, no dizziness hit her this time. She had to get to Kassius before she lost track of where he was.

You must escape, cara. *Escalla glows for you. It senses you. Cristoff knows you are near.*

Which meant the monster was probably standing somewhere in his ruined study waiting for her to show herself. Waiting for *her*. Not Grant.

Her pulse raced as a plan formed in her mind. Cristoff and his guards would be looking for a woman. And they were so used to Grant that they'd likely pay him no attention, assuming no one noticed him appear out of thin air. If they saw her disappear, it didn't really matter because by then she'd be back with Kassius. Once the werevamp was on his feet again, they could figure out the next move together.

All she had to do was be Grant again. But…dammit…which way was the desk? She'd lost her orientation again. That way? she wondered, glancing right. No, it was that way. Left. She was pretty sure.

Taking a deep breath, she reminded herself to walk slowly, head down. *Be Grant.*

With a mental *here goes nothing*, she pushed through the wall of the bubble.

The light blinded her. Noisy chaos assaulted her ears.

But she was turned the wrong way. It wasn't the desk straight ahead of her but Cristoff dressed all in blue. Their startled gazes collided. In those pale eyes, she saw the flare of recognition.

And triumph.

CHAPTER SIXTEEN

Arturo stared as Grant Blackstone suddenly appeared out of thin air near the door of Cristoff's ruined study.

No, not Grant. *Quinn.* She stared at Cristoff as if frozen.

Beside him, Cristoff chuckled, the sound sending a bolt of ice through the base of Arturo's skull. Because Cristoff knew it was her. The game was up. It was over.

No. It was not. There was one thing he could do to protect the woman who'd stolen his heart and given him back his soul. He could kill Cristoff before Cristoff killed Quinn. Or at least give her a chance to escape.

Stepping back out of Cristoff's physical reach, he called up the rare and deadly power that only three people in the world knew he possessed. The mind blast, one that might or might not be equal to his master's. He'd never tested it against Cristoff, for doing so would have meant a battle to the death with the only father he'd ever known.

Unlike Cristoff, Arturo didn't have to be touching his victim, but neither could he contain the blast to a single target.

As he threw the power at Cristoff, his master yelled, gripping his head and sinking to his knees. But so too did the other guards in the room. There was no containing his assault, which terrified him with Quinn in the room. But in disabling Cristoff, if only for a moment, he was giving her a chance.

Quinn stumbled.

Even as his heart lodged in his throat, his head exploded with a mind-numbing pain that felt as if someone had taken a cleaver to his skull. Arturo roared, his eyes clouding over, his head splitting apart.

How? Cristoff had to be touching his victims. But this...this attack had slammed back through his own, like a counterstrike that had ridden in on the backdraft of his blast. They were going to kill one another. After all these centuries, the moment had come.

"Get him!" Cristoff yelled, his voice tight and choked.

Arturo tried to rise, knowing he had only moments before he was caught, before he was killed unless he managed to fell his master first. But the pain crippled his ability to move. His vision went dark, the pressure behind his eyes growing until he thought his eyes would rupture.

"Get Grant Blackstone!" Cristoff roared. His voice softened. "My son! My loyal one. Get out of here. Save yourself!"

Cristoff's voice wavered through the pain ringing in Arturo's ears and at first Arturo didn't think he'd heard him right. *Save yourself.*

"She attacks us both," Cristoff said. "The sorceress wears the face of Grant Blackstone!"

As Arturo struggled to keep Cristoff from unwittingly pulverizing the brain of his 'loyal one', his snake, one realization crashed, a glorious relief. Quinn had gotten away.

Yet Cristoff believed it was her who attacked him, even now. Arturo had to cease the attack, but how to do that without dying in the process? Then again, if Cristoff had only managed to attack him by riding in through Arturo's own attack, ending one should end the other.

Praying he was right, Arturo ceased his own attack suddenly. The moment he did, the counterattack died, just as he'd hoped. But the pain continued to hammer him, as if it had become trapped within the bones of his skull. He still couldn't see!

"My snake." Arturo felt Cristoff's hand on his shoulder and tensed. "What has she done to you?"

Clearly he had no idea Arturo was his attacker. "Blinded me."

"You were too close without the ability to protect yourself. The sorceress has grown strong. I knew of sorcerers like her in the old days, ones able to steal the powers of those nearby. She's acquired glamour, the mind blast, invisibility." His voice turned rich with wonder. "She is truly the Black Wizard's heir."

Thankfully, it hadn't occurred to Cristoff that the sorceress might have been glamoured by one of his own. Micah wasn't the only one with such a skill, but he was the best.

"You believe that if you stab Quinn with Escalla, you'll become as powerful as Nerian," Arturo said.

Cristoff laughed. "Not believe, my son. *Know.*" Cristoff's grip on Arturo's shoulder changed, tightened. *"My loyal one."*

Arturo frowned at the sudden change in Cristoff's voice, at the sudden ache in it. "My liege?"

"You cannot let it happen. *Do not allow me to become as Nerian.*"

Arturo's pulse leaped. The words, the ache in them, belonged to the Cristoff of old, the soul that struggled to once more break free.

"Cristoff?"

But suddenly the hand left his shoulder, glass and debris crunching beneath his shoes as Cristoff moving away. "The sword's glow is fading," he shouted, his voice once more strong and utterly lacking compassion. "She's getting away!"

Arturo heard something else, a sound that made his blood run cold. The sound of steel clinking against glass.

He turned his attention to Quinn, felt her pain, and knew he must have hurt her with his mind blast. *He has the sword, amore. He's taken it from its case. It will lead him to you. Get out of the castle. Run!*

If only they had the means to attack Cristoff now, to wrest the sword from him while it was free from its protective case. But no vampire had the power to stand against Cristoff's mind blast. Including him.

So many things made sense, now. Why Cristoff had laid the sword in Quinn's hands. Why his excitement had grown as Arturo spun tales of the sorceress's increasing power.

The situation was far worse than he'd thought. If Cristoff acquired the power of Nerian...of the Black Wizard...with his soul still compromised...

God help them all.

CHAPTER SEVENTEEN

Quinn sank to her knees within the safety of the bubble, grasping her head as pain tore through it like a sword hacking her brains to pieces. She'd made it, barely, escaping certain capture. How, she still wasn't sure. If she had to guess, Cristoff had used his mind blast on her. But he'd appeared to be in agony, too. Had her magic interfered with it somehow? She had no idea, and didn't really care, as long as she was safe.

But for how long?

Slowly, the pain began to recede and, with shaking hands, she reached for her flashlight to illuminate the small dark space. As the light flicked on, she gasped at the sight of the enormous wolf lying prone across the small space. What the hell?

It took her mind a moment to catch up with her eyes. Not wolf. Werewolf.

"Kass." She crawled over to him and slid her hand into the fur of the great beast's chest. Beneath her palm, she felt a soft rise and fall and relief swept over her that he was at least still alive.

He needed blood. The question was how to get hers into him without accidentally becoming his dinner. Kassius would never hurt her…intentionally. But she wasn't sure about his wolf.

Still, she had to try.

Quinn reached for the small switchblade she kept in her pocket and opened it. Slowly, she sliced the knife through the heel of her hand, gritting her teeth against the fire. Dropping the knife to the floor, she slid her hand beneath the wolf's head and attempted to turn it up so she could get the blood down his throat, which was harder than she'd thought it would be. Most of the drips hit his teeth, or the floor beneath him. Finally, she managed to get a few onto his tongue and a few more into the back of his mouth.

"Swallow, Kass. It won't do a bit of good if you don't swallow."

Her hand hurt like a son of a bitch, but at least it continued to bleed and the drops continued to fall into his mouth.

At last, the massive animal jerked. A moment later, he rose to all fours and turned on her, snarling, his eyes glowing.

Primal terror shot through Quinn as her pulse leaped, her muscles preparing to fight...or run. Fortunately, she knew enough about wolves to know that running was the last thing she wanted to do. Which was a good thing, since she had nowhere to go within the tight confines in which they were trapped.

"Kassius, it's Quinn," she said as calmly as she could manage. "Shift back into human form."

The animal just snarled at her.

"Dammit, Kass, shift back. *Now*."

The wolf snapped his jaws shut. In his eyes, she saw recognition flare. But the animal continued to stare at her for several moments more before finally he began to shift.

Quinn crab-walked backward, careful to stop before she hit the wall of her bubble. Pressing a hand to her pounding chest, she watched as Kassius took shape, hunching over as he hit the low roof, as naked as the day he was born.

As he began to sway, Quinn lunged to her feet and grabbed him around the waist. "Sit down before you fall, Kassius."

With her help, he sank to the ground, then shook his head as if to clear it. He'd yet to acknowledge her and she wasn't sure he even knew where he was. It was clear he needed more blood. A lot more.

Without hesitation, she lifted her wrist to his mouth. "You have to feed. You're as weak as a kitten. Or puppy."

He ignored her arm and grabbed her as if she were a rag doll, pulling her against him, sinking his fangs painlessly into her neck. She might be strong, now, but he was a hundred times faster.

"Kassius!"

She pushed against him, worried that he was acting on instinct alone, an instinct that might have him drinking his fill, which would likely kill her. But the power of his hunger made him a lot stronger than her. Before she could fight her way free, her mind suddenly blanked out, then awakened again in another place, another time. Another body.

Kassius's.

The sky was a light steel gray, rain falling in a cold, stinging torrent as battle raged all around the open field, vampire against vampire, Emora against Ripper. Quinn watched the scene through Kassius's eyes, understood the language as Kassius had, though it sounded like some sort of Italian dialect to the part of her that remained Quinn. From the way they were all dressed—in tight-fitting pants and loose shirts, their hair long—she thought the time must be several hundred years ago.

How had she gotten here?

But she thought she knew. The last time Kassius bit her, they'd somehow exchanged memories. It seemed they were doing it again.

All the vampires around them carried swords and wielded them with the speed and accuracy one might expect from males with vampiric speed and centuries of skill. Kassius was engaged in fighting no fewer than three Rippers, all with those hungry red eyes that promised death to anyone they turned on.

She recognized only three people—Micah, Bram. And Arturo. She got only a glimpse of him when Kassius's gaze scanned the field, but it was enough. He was a handsome male in any century, but there was something particularly dashing about that long, dark hair. She might have to encourage him to grow it again.

A shout went up and one of the vampires fell, one of Arturo and Kassius's friends. Micah let out an anguished yell, his sword suddenly moving double time. Her friends were badly outnumbered. And while Quinn could feel Kassius's concern, she knew she was seeing the past. They'd all survived.

She sensed no anguish in Kassius over the fallen vampire, only a stunned determination to redouble his efforts to win the battle he himself was engaged in. Another shout went up. Kassius glanced to find Arturo pulling his sword from a Ripper he held by the throat. Moments later, another shout, another Ripper held by the throat by Arturo.

Kassius smiled grimly and finally managed to dispatch one of the vampires who attacked him. But two more only took his place.

Kassius was fighting for his life, his size and skill an asset, but there were too many of them.

Out of the corner of his eye, Kassius saw Arturo take off, racing away from the field of battle. No fewer than six Rippers took off after him.

"He would leave us?" Micah asked Kassius with raw disbelief.

"Not leave, no."

Quinn realized that Micah didn't know Arturo well, but Kassius did. Within Kassius's mind she saw that he, Arturo, and Bram had only just joined the Gonzaga kovena, traveling from another kovena after their previous master died. Micah had been sired by Cristoff Gonzaga, so would know the other Emoras far better. No wonder Micah was so much more distressed by the deaths of the others. He was losing long-time friends. To Kassius, the dead vampires had been mere acquaintances.

Quinn felt Kassius tense as if preparing for a blow, and seconds later, a pain slammed into his head, trying to hack at his mind much as she'd experienced in Cristoff's study minutes ago. The mind blast?

All around him, the Rippers faltered and stumbled as if they, too, had felt the pain. But they hadn't been prepared for it like Kassius was and he used their surprise to take advantage, slaying three of them in quick succession. Bram, too, had taken advantage of the opportunity to slay two of his own opponents.

"What the hell?" Micah exclaimed, even as he continued to fight.

Kassius stole a quick glance in Arturo's direction, which was enough for Quinn to realize that all six of the Rippers who'd followed him were now exploding on the ground. Arturo returned to dive back into the fray. He'd drawn them off to kill them, she realized.

Mentally, her eyes widened with surprise as she thought she was beginning to understand.

She watched as Arturo once more took off, as if running away. This time four Rippers followed.

Kassius managed to catch Micah's gaze, sending a silent, *prepare yourself.* And moments later, pain slammed into all of them. Kassius and Bram once more took advantage, but so did Micah this time. But another Gonzaga vamp was slain, the last of the ones Quinn didn't recognize.

With most of the Rippers gone, Kassius, Bram, Arturo, and Micah quickly dispatched the rest. Winded and sweating, they met in the middle of the battlefield. Micah alone appeared grief-stricken.

"I've known Berto and James almost my entire existence," Micah said, his voice harsh with loss.

Bram clasped his shoulder. "My condolences. We might all have perished this day if not for Ax."

Micah turned toward Arturo slowly, a dark wariness creeping into his eyes. "Does Cristoff know you have the mind blast?"

Quinn stared through Kassius's eyes, stunned.

Arturo shook his head. "I've not told him. I use it only when necessary."

From the expression on his face, Micah struggled with something. Finally, he said, "You cannot use it at all. Never again, not as long as you remain with Cristoff."

Arturo looked at Micah with surprise. "You fear he will consider it a threat? My old master knew of my abilities and trusted me not to use them against him. When Cristoff knows me better…"

"It will not matter. He can never know you have the ability, Arturo. Not if you want to live." His brow creased, his eyes turning suspicious. "Where were you born?"

Arturo stilled. "Why do you ask?"

"Because, to our master's knowledge, the only ones who have ever possessed that particular gift were of Cristoff's human bloodline."

Through Kassius's eyes, Quinn saw the slight flicker of a muscle in Arturo's jaw. Mentally, she frowned. What was Micah saying?

"Would it matter?" Bram asked, but he and Kassius exchanged a look that told Quinn they understood something Quinn had yet to figure out.

"Yes, it matters." Micah's voice was tinged with anger. "Centuries ago, Cristoff rounded up six of his seven bastard sons and attempted to turn them. Only two survived, but both possessed the mind blast. Cristoff once admitted to me that he'd enjoyed a fantasy of ruling with his sons at his side. But both quickly abused their great power, for unlike their father, the sons did not have to be touching anyone to hurt them. They could send the blast out wide." His gaze speared Arturo. "As you've done."

Quinn stared. *My God, was it true? Was Arturo Cristoff's seventh son? His true son.*

"One of them killed half of his father's kovena," Micah continued. "Just because he could. The other remained loyal for a time, but eventually challenged Cristoff. Though he lost, dozens more were killed in the ensuing battle."

Kassius and Bram both glanced at Arturo. Quinn could feel their questions. Did Arturo know Cristoff was his father?

"If Cristoff realizes you possess the mind blast, Arturo, he *will* kill you, whether or not it turns out you're his son. He'll not risk his kovena again."

"Ax has complete control over his gift," Bram argued.

Micah shrugged. "I'm telling you what Cristoff has sworn. I urge you not to risk it, Arturo. Do not use the mind blast again. If you must, then do not return to Cristoff's kovena."

Silence fell over the foursome, another unspoken question hanging heavy in the air. A question Micah heard and answered.

"I'll keep your secret. I've seen how you use the blast—with care and restraint. But I would not trust anyone else to give you the benefit of the doubt. Many within the kovena suffered great loss at the hands of Cristoff's other two sons."

At last, Arturo spoke. "I will not use it again. Nor will we ever again speak of my gift or my parentage."

It was clear to Quinn that Arturo had indeed known he was Cristoff's son.

Quinn came back to herself suddenly to realize that Kassius was still feeding from her neck.

"Kassius!" she gasped, pushing at his chest as hard as she could.

He released her suddenly and she scrambled out of his lap, then turned to face him, surprised that she felt neither weak nor dizzy. The memory must have played in triple-time or she'd have been sucked dry by now.

Kassius stared at her, his mouth blood-stained, his eyes wide and confused. "Quinn?" Distress darkened his eyes. "I attacked you."

"No. You drank from me, which I offered. But I don't think you were fully conscious."

"I don't remember. Are you all right?"

"Yes. I actually feel great." There was something in a vampire's saliva that initiated healing in humans. Fast healing.

"What happened?" he asked. His face was in partial shadow, the flashlight lying on the floor, illuminating his bare hip.

The memory of what she'd experienced through his eyes rolled through her head. "Arturo is Cristoff's son. And he has the mind blast."

Kassius's gaze narrowed, understanding dawning slowly. And with it, dismay. "You saw my past again."

"I saw a battle, the first time Arturo used his mind blast in front of Micah. I don't think you'd known Micah long at the time."

He stared at her for several moments, a frown between his brows. "We had not. We'd been with Cristoff only a few months. Micah's learning Ax's secret is what bound him to us. And taught us we could trust him completely."

"That's the secret the two of them wouldn't share with me, isn't it?"

Kassius nodded. "Cristoff can never know, especially now." He gripped his head as if he were still a bit dazed. "The last thing I remember, we were setting explosives around the sword case."

She filled him in quickly—how the sword had pulled at her, how she'd knocked him into the case, how she'd tried to reach him and come face to face with Cristoff.

"Cristoff used his mind blast," she said, then stopped. "Except, he didn't, did he?" she said with sudden understanding. "He never touched me, and he appeared to be in terrible pain, too."

Kassius's expression grew troubled. "It had to have been Ax." His big hand gripped hers, his expression suddenly haunted. "Have you heard from him since?"

She stared at him, slowly understanding. Arturo had attacked Cristoff. Which meant Cristoff should have retaliated.

"Yes. He told me Cristoff took the sword from the case and is using it to find me."

"Cristoff must not have realized it was Ax using the mind blast." He stared at her for a moment more, his features grim. "We have to get you out of here."

"Not without Turo."

As if reading her thoughts, Arturo spoke in her mind again. *Meet me back at Neo's, tesoro. I will get there as quickly as I can.*

Quinn let out a huff. "He just told me to meet him back at Neo's."

Meeting her gaze, Kassius nodded. "Then that's what we'll do."

"He might need our help."

"No. He should be safe enough since Cristoff doesn't know he was the one who attacked him." He grabbed her hand. "I know you care about him, sorceress, but don't fight me on this. As it is, it will be all I can do to get you out of here alive. If Cristoff catches you, all is lost."

She knew he was right. With a frustrated twist of her mouth, she nodded. Arturo would meet her at Neo's, as he promised. She had to believe that.

"All right." Rising to her feet, she expanded her bubble upward so that Kassius could stand without hunching over. "Cristoff knows that I look like Grant. And you've lost both your clothes and your glamour. At some point you shifted into a wolf."

"I heal better that way. Are we still in Cristoff's study?"

"Yes. In a different bubble than the one we came in on. I was trying to expand it toward Grant's room, but I lost my bearings." She scowled. "Which I've done again…" Her eyes snagged on her knife lying on the floor a few feet away. "Wait." She went to the knife, remembered how she'd been oriented when she set it down, how he'd been lying.

"There," she said, pointing. "About three feet from here is where the desk sat when we first walked into the study."

Kassius nodded. "I know where we are, then, but we'll not be going back to Grant's bedroom."

"Fine by me." She handed him the flashlight. "Lead the way."

He met her gaze. "Thank you, Quinn. For your blood, and for risking your life to return for me."

Quinn smiled. "You've risked plenty for me, Kass. I wouldn't leave you in here. But you're welcome. Now, which way?"

He turned and pointed the light's beam to the right. "That direction. About fifteen feet."

Nodding, Quinn called up her magic and did as he directed. "Where will this take us?"

"Egor's room. We are of a size, he and I."

"I can only create passages for us horizontally. At some point we're going to have to get off the second floor. Do you have a back stair?"

"Several. But Cristoff will be covering them. I have another plan."

Quinn didn't question him, just continued to expand their dark passage.

"Ax won't be happy that you've learned his secrets," Kassius murmured as she worked.

"He'll get over it. It's not like you had a choice."

"I have always had the gift of seeing another's truths when I bite them. But never has anyone turned it back on me, as you do."

Quinn realized what he was saying. Her eyes narrowed. "What truths of mine did you see?"

He glanced at her, his expression grim. "Childhood memories of you enduring your parents' emotional abuse. If I ever get out of Vamp City, I intend to pay them a visit."

"You'd terrify them without ever saying a word."

A hard smile lifted the corners of his mouth. "I might say a few words...and show a few teeth...as well. Your parents would deserve it."

"Only one of them is my parent."

"Which makes your father's failure to protect you all the more reprehensible. I will pay them a visit, sorceress. They'll not be harmed. But they will know I do not approve of the way you were raised."

"You're a good friend, Kass."

Moments later, he handed her the flashlight. "That's enough. Hand me through, but stay here until I know it's safe."

Quinn took his hand and he exited partway, then tugged her through after him into what appeared to be a bedroom. As Kassius grabbed a pair of jeans and a t-shirt out of a chest of drawers, Quinn turned back to the opalescent black bubble filling half the room. No one else could see it. No one could accidentally enter it. But she'd probably left enough of them around the castle, by now.

"I'll be just a moment," she told Kassius, then stepped back into her bubble and dissolved it around her. By the time she was through, mere moments later, Kassius was fully dressed and peering into the hallway.

He glanced at her, his look telling her something she already knew—if they were caught, they were both dead.

"You are my prisoner," he said.

"Okey-dokey." But the thought of leaving the relative safety of Egor's room had cold perspiration running down her chest.

Unfortunately, there was no disguising her to look like someone else, not when she was already glamoured to look like Grant. Kassius took her upper arm lightly and steered her into the hall, leading her in the direction of Cristoff's throne room. For one horrible moment, she wondered if Kassius would be the one to betray her this time, but then he turned at the wide front stair and began to lead her down.

This was his plan? To walk through the castle foyer, calm as you please, as if Cristoff didn't have every guard hunting Grant Blackstone? It was a damn good thing Grant had given her a magical emotion-tamping crystal, because her heart was about to explode from her chest.

They were halfway down the stairs when two vampires moved into sight and looked up at them with surprise.

Quinn's heart dropped to her boots and she began to slow, preparing to run, but Kassius only tugged her with him as he continued down the stairs.

The two vampires remained where they were, one on either side of the staircase, as if waiting to take them calmly into custody.

Three steps from the bottom, one of the guards moved forward, blocking their way.

"Kassius," he said formally, then turned to her. "Sorceress."

CHAPTER EIGHTEEN

Quinn's pulse was racing, her body awash in terror. *They'd been caught.* She felt Kassius's grip on her arm tighten and prepared herself to be thrown over his shoulder as he ran.

But the guard's urgent words stopped them cold. "Cristoff must not find you. Which direction shall we send the others, Kassius?"

For a moment, Kassius said nothing, clearly as stunned by this turn of events as she was.

"Out back. I thank you, Samuel."

The vampire's grin was as swift as it was fleeting. "The world is changing. Now, go. Godspeed, sorceress."

Quinn stared at him, then nodded. "Thank you, Samuel."

As the guards disappeared, Kassius led her down the last few steps, then around the corner to an empty alcove.

"Pull a bubble around us, Quinn. Quickly."

With a nod, she called up the power and did just that, then turned on her flashlight and doubled over, gasping for the air she'd forgotten to breathe in her terror.

"Holy shit," she muttered, then straightened and peered at him. "Did you know they were allies?"

Kassius shook his head, his eyes comically wide, making her laugh. "I did not. Both of them—in fact, many of the vampires within the Gonzaga kovena—were fine, honorable males at one time. I admit, I didn't think so many had returned to themselves. I'm glad to be wrong."

"They're reclaiming their souls."

"It would seem so. I had thought Ax an anomaly, at first. I thought that his return was thanks to you. But that's clearly not the case. Expand the bubble this way, Quinn," he said, taking the flashlight from her and motioning with it. Then he began to walk.

Kassius' sense of direction turned out to be extraordinary. Only a short time later, he asked her to hand him through and, when she followed she found herself standing in the small dorm room with the trapdoor that led to the tunnels.

"Nice job," she murmured. And within moments they were once more safely underground.

As Kassius pulled the latch closed over her head, Quinn began to breathe evenly again. But not freely. Arturo was still with Cristoff somewhere, and Cristoff hunted her with a beacon that would tell him whenever she was near. To add to that, Zack could die at any moment, as could Vamp City itself and all those trapped within it. And Lily was still missing.

Quinn wondered if she'd ever breathe freely again.

Quinn strode in through the back door of Neo's with Kassius and Micah close behind. They'd spoken little on the ride home, but one thing was certain. She couldn't stay here now. Not with Cristoff able to find her with that damned sword. All he had to do was ride close to Neo's, and he'd know she was in the vicinity. Her presence might compromise Neo's operation, or even destroy it.

Mukdalla turned as they walked into the kitchen, her hopeful expression dying as she took in their unhappy faces.

"Fail," Quinn said.

"Where's Arturo?" Neo asked, striding in.

"He just left Gonzaga," Quinn told him. He'd spoken to her telepathically on and off since she escaped. When he got to Neo's, they were going to have to talk about where she might go. There was nowhere within Vamp City where she'd be safe. Not unless it was deep within an enemy kovena's castle. But that would just be trading one dangerous vampire for another.

She might be able to live with the wolves. Savin's pack might take her in. Though even they might consider her too great a liability.

The only place Cristoff couldn't reach her was the real world. But that meant abandoning all hope of saving Vamp City and her brother, and that was not something she could ever do.

"What happened?" Neo asked.

Quinn had no desire to relive any of the past hours. Leaving the story for Kassius to relay, she headed downstairs to check on Zack. Glamoured as she still was, she didn't need him to see her in return, she just needed to know he was still okay. But all was quiet downstairs, the exercise room empty and dark. Walking to the hall where hers and Zack's rooms were, she found his bedroom door closed. It was all she could do not to walk in and check on him, but where she might not have hesitated a few weeks ago, she did now. He was a full-grown man who deserved his privacy, especially in the middle of the night.

With a sigh, she started back through the community room to find Mukdalla coming down the stairs.

"They went to bed a few hours ago."

Quinn nodded. "Any more…episodes?"

Mukdalla frowned. "One. It was much the same as the first. He passed out, then roused seconds later apparently fine." She walked over to the big table in the middle of the room and set down a tall glass of what looked like lemonade. "Fresh squeezed. I thought you could use a pick-me-up."

Quinn nodded, but she didn't move to take the glass, still reeling from Mukdalla's words that Zack had passed out yet again. They'd probably had to work just as hard to save him.

Mukdalla walked straight to her and opened her arms.

Quinn hesitated only a moment, then took the comfort offered as tears filled her eyes. "I can't lose him," she whispered as she felt herself enveloped in a strength few human women possessed, a band of warmth and caring which drew Quinn in even as it had her stiffening. She'd never been comfortable with hugs. Then again, when had anyone ever held her like this? The realization that she couldn't remember broke something inside of her and she found herself sinking into Mukdalla's undemanding warmth, pressing her cheek to a shoulder strong enough to carry any load.

As tears began to escape her eyes, she pulled away and dashed at them. "I keep trying to save him, I keep failing."

Mukdalla smiled a soft smile that was utterly beautiful, one Quinn felt all the way inside. "You haven't failed, Quinn," she said quietly. "You've tried a couple of things that haven't worked. You'll try something else. And eventually you'll succeed."

"But will it be in time?"

"Yes. It will." Mukdalla picked up the lemonade glass and

pressed it into Quinn's hands. "I choose to believe that. I must believe it. And you must, too."

Quinn nodded. "You're right. I won't give up."

"I know you won't. Now, can I get you something to eat while you wait for Arturo? Or do you wish to sleep? You must be tired."

She was exhausted, but she'd never sleep until she knew Arturo was back and safe. "I'll wait. Are the others upstairs?"

"They're outside keeping watch for any sign of Cristoff's guards. If you'd like some company, I'm about to bake cookies."

If you'd like some company. The words felt foreign to her. She'd never needed company, or particularly wanted it, other than Zack and Lily. Yet right now, she didn't want to be alone. And the truth was, she would enjoy Mukdalla's company, very much.

"Sure. What kind of cookies?"

Mukdalla grinned. "Chocolate chip." Together, they started up the stairs. "Your brother and Jason are both cookie hounds. But I've been sending the cookies with Micah, too, for the children. There's nothing that calms a scared little one like a chocolate chip cookie."

Quinn smiled at the image of vampires bearing chocolate chip cookies. Good vampires. "Anything I can do to help?"

Mukdalla smiled in reply. "Absolutely."

"Mukdalla...my glamour hasn't worn off, yet you don't seem the least bit bothered by it. Can you see through it?"

"No. I simply don't see what is not important. Your eyes haven't changed at all, Quinn. They shine now as they always do."

Quinn startled. "They're glowing?"

The other woman laughed. "Not glowing, no. Not with magic. Your eyes reflect the goodness in your heart, sorceress. That's the shine I see now, the shine I've always seen. It's why I know you will not fail."

Quinn hoped to heaven she was right.

They'd just put the first tray in the oven when Arturo walked in the back door looking too much like he had after his captivity in the wolves' feeding trough.

"*Turo.*" Quinn met him halfway across the kitchen, hugging him tight as he buried his face in her hair. "What happened? You look terrible. You need to feed."

"*Amore mio,*" he said against her neck. "All I need is this, to know you are safe."

A rush of warmth welled up inside of her, filling her chest, pressing against the walls of her heart until she feared that organ would be crushed beneath the pressure. She pulled back, pressing her hands to his cheeks. "I'm sorry I doubted you." When she'd appeared in front of Cristoff, Arturo had risked everything to save her.

He stroked her hair with a gentle hand, his eyes tender, yet concerned. "You are unharmed?"

"I'm fine." She frowned, thinking of all that had happened, of all she'd learned about him. "We need to talk."

Arturo tipped his forehead against hers even as his hand slid down to curve around the back of her neck. "We need to do more than talk, *amore mio*. Much more."

CHAPTER NINETEEN

"I need you," Arturo murmured, his forehead against Quinn's as he drank in the warm scent of sunshine on her skin. He needed her kiss, needed to sink into her body until her cries of pleasure pushed away the icy cold that had invaded his soul in that moment when she'd appeared, suddenly, in Cristoff's study. *Dio*, but his heart had nearly stopped.

He straightened to find Quinn watching him with heat in her eyes. "Let's go, then." She took his hand. "Goodnight, Mukdalla."

"Goodnight, Quinn. Sleep well."

Arturo smiled, squeezing Quinn's hand as he followed her out of the kitchen, for he had no intention of letting her sleep. Not yet, certainly. Not until every hard kernel of ice had melted from his veins.

Quinn threw him a smile that said she knew exactly what he was thinking, and thoroughly approved. Yet shadows moved through her eyes and he knew she needed to forget the past hours as badly as he did.

She led him downstairs to her room and was pulling off her shirt before he even got the door closed. He closed his eyes, blocking out the falseness of the glamour, and took her into his arms where she was all Quinn. He pushed her gently back against the door, and kissed her, her warm lips a balm, a fire to a man dying of cold. His tongue swept inside her mouth, tasting sweetness. Chocolate chip cookies, if he wasn't mistaken. His hands traced her precious head, her slender hips, her lovely breasts, as he reassured himself over and over that she was alive, that she was fine.

Love swept through him, at once fierce and achingly tender, yet he refused to say the words. He understood her well enough to be certain she was not ready to hear them, that she struggled not to care too deeply for him. And he knew this, because he felt her emotions, the swells of affection, and the small stabs of love that invariably sent her retreating from him. She could love him, if she let herself. And it was his greatest wish that she do so. Not only because he longed for her to return his feelings, but because she so badly needed to learn to open her heart, and to trust in that most vulnerable of emotions.

Until she was ready to do that, he would show her how he felt without words.

Quinn reached for him, curling her arms around his neck to pull him closer and deepen the kiss. As their mouths caressed and joined, heat built between them, a passion that quickly erupted into a blazing hot flame, one that threatened to consume them both. They tore at one another's clothes, tossing them onto the floor, then fell to the bed in a tangle of bare limbs, greedy mouths and desperate, seeking hands. Arturo slid his hand between her legs, his fingers into her welcoming heat, and he found her more than ready for him. An instant later, he slid into her body at the same moment his fangs pierced her neck.

As her sweet blood flowed over his tongue, she gasped and cried out in pleasure. With keen anticipation, he took a single hard pull of her blood and rejoiced as she screamed her passion, as her body contracted hard around him, over and over and over.

Releasing her neck, he lifted his head to watch her face, forgetting she was glamoured. But even as he caught a glimpse of Grant's face, it disappeared, the glamour dissolving. With joy, he drank in the play of passion over Quinn's own beautiful features, loving the look of joy in her eyes as her gaze met his as he drove into her, faster and faster and faster. Together they rode the storm into a sky filled with warmth and life, as if they flew right up into the sun.

His own release tore through him like a wild storm made all the more perfect by the scream of pleasure that escaped Quinn's throat, by the way her body pulled him deeper and deeper, contracting around him as if to milk every last drop of his essence from his body. In his mind, color exploded, the sun erupting into a brilliant, glorious fireball of powerful, benevolent heat.

Utterly sated, Arturo collapsed, burying his face against the satin of her neck. "*Bella,*" he murmured. "What you do to me."

"And you to me," she murmured, sounding delightfully like a

satisfied cat. She ran her palms up and down his back as if enjoying the feel of his warm flesh beneath her hands. "Are you recovered, yet?"

"Your sunshine was all I needed." And it was. He felt hale and hearty, hungry for blood, but not unduly so. And for nothing more. For a reason he didn't understand, Quinn's kiss, her touch, the warmth that seeped into him when they were together was physically changing him. Fear no longer fed him as it had for all of his long, long immortal life. He needed only blood and Quinn's touch to survive.

"We need to talk, Turo."

He lifted his head slowly, uncertain what she wished to discuss, but fairly certain it was not something he'd be happy to share. "You need to sleep."

Her soft hands stroked his back, holding him fast with their gentle touch. "This can't wait, Turo. I fed Kassius. We exchanged glimpses of one another's pasts again."

Inwardly, he grimaced. There were so many things he'd done in his long life, more than a few he was not proud of. "You have seen my misdeeds."

A smile tugged at the corner of her mouth. "No, fortunately. Nothing like that."

Arturo pulled out of her and rolled to her side. "Tell me what you saw, *tesoro*. I would not have secrets between us." At the lift of her brow, he added, "Any more secrets than necessary." But when he would have pulled her against him and nestled her in his arms, she resisted, sitting up, peering down at him instead.

"As it happens, there might be fewer secrets between us than you think," she said archly.

Arturo rolled onto his back, one hand behind his head, his other stroking her knee. "Tell me."

She watched him with green eyes dancing with fascination. "I saw the battle in which you used your mind blast in front of Micah for the first time."

He groaned, then thought back, recalling that day—his using the mind blast, Micah realizing he was Cristoff's...

He went still. "What did you learn?"

"That you're his son. For real. And that you inherited his mind blast."

He met her gaze with a wry one of his own. "You are correct, *amore,* there are far fewer secrets between us. Those are the ones I refused to share with you. I regret that you're burdened with this knowledge, now, too."

"You know I won't tell."

He squeezed her knee. "Not intentionally, no. I do know that."

Quinn compressed her mouth, watching him thoughtfully. "Have you used the mind blast much since that day?"

"Never."

"Until today."

"Yes."

"You risked everything for me."

Arturo sat up, facing her, then took her hands. "I always will."

She squeezed his hands, her lovely brow knitting. "He didn't know it was you."

"No. I cannot target my blast easily. Fortunately, he couldn't tell where it came from."

"Did you *know* that he wouldn't know it was you?"

Arturo shrugged. "No."

Quinn stared at him, her mouth dropping open. "You didn't simply give me a chance. You attacked him believing he'd attack you back, that you'd have to fight him to the death."

"Yes," he said quietly. "But though he possesses no ability to use his mind blast offensively against one he's not touching, he apparently has the ability to counterattack. He hit me so hard and fast, I stood no chance against him." Arturo released her hand to rake his own through his hair. "If he'd known it was me, I would be dead."

"But he knows someone has the mind blast."

"He believes it is you." He squeezed her knee. "He believes you can do anything."

"I wish. How did you get him to stop?"

He explained, then said, "There is one thing more, *cara.* Twice…" He hesitated. As much as he wanted to share his hope with her, he feared she'd not understand.

Quinn squeezed his hand. "Tell me."

Looking into soft green eyes, he did. "Twice I saw a flicker of humanity spring to life in his eyes. Neither lasted long, but I believe his soul is beginning to reawaken."

Quinn frowned. "Yet still you attacked him with the intent to kill him."

His palm cupped her cheek and he wondered if she'd ever completely trust him. "I told you, I will never let him harm you again."

Her breath left her on a hard exhale. "He's your father."

"Yes." He lay back on the bed, tugging her down with him, pulling her into his arms. "And you are my sunshine." His hand stroked her back. "You were not harmed unduly by my blast?"

"It hurt like hell, but no, I wasn't hurt. The pain went away quickly enough."

"I felt it, your pain. I am sorry for it."

"I'm fine." She ran her fingers along the plane of his chest. "You're really his son?"

"I am. My mother called me Little Cristoff."

"My mind is going to explode. And he doesn't know?"

"He does not."

"Did he ever know about you?"

Arturo lifted his hand and tucked a lock of hair behind her ear. "Yes, he did, *piccola*. Once upon a time."

Quinn snuggled against Arturo's chest, his arm warm around her, as he spoke of a time so far in the past.

"My mother was sixteen, Cristoff only a few years older, when he seduced her. This was in Pavia, in what is now called Italy, in the early fifteenth century. Cristoff was a distant relative of the royal Gonzagas and his family was wealthy and powerful. My mother was a poor orphan living with her grandmother. When Cristoff learned she was with child, he supported her for a number of years. My earliest memories are of my father visiting us, bringing me a piece of fruit and playing with me. I adored him. My mother used to tell me that her greatest wish was that I would be just like him when I was grown— honorable and good and fine." He sighed. "I know that does not describe the monster you know him to be, Quinn, but he was once all of those things."

"Yet he didn't marry your mother or, presumably, the other six girls/women he impregnated."

Arturo shrugged. "It was a different time. And he did end up partially raising six of his seven children—all boys."

"Tell me."

"When I was nine, Cristoff disappeared. I believe that was when he was turned into a vampire. A small kovena of Emora vampires had moved into the area and I suspect they thought it prudent to recruit one of the village lords for their own. They chose Cristoff. When I was sixteen, Cristoff sent vampires to collect his bastard sons to be raised in the kovena and turned when they were grown. But the vampire sent to retrieve me, Raul, decided to steal me away in hopes that I would use my gift for his own purposes. He wanted to sire me himself someday. When he tried to take me, my mother attacked him and he killed her."

It had happened so long ago, yet in his voice she heard a tiny break, an old, old pain. A wound that had never entirely healed.

"He took me to Venice and left me with a human male in need of an apprentice. I became a skilled blacksmith while Raul waited for me to grow up."

When he didn't continue, Quinn glanced at him. "You can't stop now."

"It is painful, *tesoro*."

She laid her cheek against his chest, her arm tight around him. "I'm sorry, Turo. I'm sorry for what you suffered."

His hand caressed her head. "I can regret nothing that has led me to this moment, *amore*. Nothing."

She kissed his jaw. "Did Raul come back for you?"

"Yes. By the time he did, I was a widower with a seven-year-old daughter." His voice caught. "Her name was Abrielle."

Quinn tensed, knowing she wasn't going to like what came next. But she kissed him, silently encouraging him to continue.

He did. "Raul informed me that it was time I came into my power and I refused. He overpowered me, drained me, fed me his own blood in order to turn me. Then he sat with me as I changed. I woke ravenous, as all new vampires do. The bloodlust was a fire within me. But there was only one human heart beating in my home."

Abrielle's. "Oh, Turo."

"Even through the bloodlust, I refused to harm her, *amore,* but Raul knew love ties would only hamper my acceptance of what I was. So he took her from her bed, ripped open her throat with his fangs, and brought her to me. I was crazed, desperate to save her. But she was already bleeding out. She was dying. And the bloodlust was too powerful. I took her from him, held her in my arms, and drank her blood until her heart stopped beating. I killed her."

Quinn lifted up, looking down into his face with a fierce tenderness. "You didn't kill her, you know that. He did."

"I killed her. And then I killed Raul. And I continued to kill vampires until I found another as desperate to destroy the blood-sucking race as I was. Bram and I nearly destroyed each other before we realized we were cut from the same cloth, both hating what we'd become. We traveled together, killed vampires together, until the day we faced a powerful werevamp who had been tracking the Vamp-slayers."

"Kassius?"

Arturo nodded. "He was startled to discover the vamp slayers were, in fact, vampires. When he realized it, he understood what drove us and he convinced us to join his kovena, which was run by a vampire worthy of both loyalty and admiration. We lived there for nearly three centuries in relative peace until another vampire challenged our master and killed him. Our new vamp master was of a darker spirit, so the three of us left. It was 1725 and I had heard Cristoff's name from time to time over the years and knew him to be a powerful, though fair, vampire master. I wanted to see him again, so decided to seek him out. Bram and Kassius, who knew my history by then, accompanied me. Cristoff was much as I remembered him and we hit it off at once. I had not yet found the time to tell him who I was when the incident occurred that you witnessed through Kassius's eyes. After that, I knew I never could. The three of us pledged fealty to Cristoff and stayed. Before long, I became Cristoff's favorite and one of his most trusted."

"This all took place in Italy?"

"In the lands that are now considered Italy, yes."

"Then Cristoff decided to move your kovena to D.C. during the Civil War."

"War is a great temptation for pain and fear feeders. The move was to have been only temporary, and many within the kovena remained behind, initially. But we liked America and when the war was over, we decided to stay. Phineas Blackstone offered to create Vamp City...for a hefty price, of course...and Cristoff was intrigued by the prospect of a world without sunlight. We all were. It was everything Blackstone had promised it would be. For a time."

Arturo fell silent, stroking her back. "Sleep, *amore*."

But too many thoughts fought for attention in her head. "Cristoff can find me with that sword. It's not safe for me to stay here."

He ran his fingers through her hair. "You are safe here."

"I think I should see if Savin will take me in."

"Absolutely not. Quinn...Cristoff is no longer looking for you."

"What? Why not?"

He sighed. "If you are not going to sleep, then let us find Micah and Kassius. I have something I need to share with all of you."

"That sounds ominous."

Arturo said nothing more as they quickly dressed. Minutes later, the four of them filed into the sitting room. Arturo closed the door and pulled a folded sheet of paper from his back pocket.

"Cristoff has called off the search for the sorceress," he told his friends. Turning to her, he said, "He's come to realize he'll never catch you by direct methods. He believes you able to disappear at will."

"Which she can," Micah said with a small smile.

"Then what's his plan?" Quinn asked, but a sick knot was already forming beneath her breastbone. "He's going after Zack."

"Not just Zack." Arturo handed her the paper.

Quinn unfolded the sheet to find a photograph taken a little over a year ago of the three of them—Quinn, Zack, and Lily. Zack and Lily had surprised her on her birthday with a cake laden with candles. Zack had taken the selfie of the three of them and posted it on-line. All three of them had been tagged.

She looked up sharply. "Where did you get this?"

"Cristoff."

Quinn felt as if she'd been gut-punched. Not only were hers and Zack's shared last name a dead giveaway that he was her brother, but the two of them looked so much alike as to be twins. Cristoff knew what her brother looked like. Zack and Lily, both.

"Where did he get this?" Quinn demanded.

"He sent Traders to hunt for any humans you might be close to."

"So he could use them against me."

"Yes. One of them is quite adept at computers and searched social media to find this picture. Over and over, he found pictures of you with Zack and Lily, and no others."

As the room began to spin around her, Kassius grabbed her arm. "Sit, Quinn."

She did, sinking onto the small sofa.

"I am sorry, *tesoro*. Sooner or later, he was bound to realize he could find the information he sought if he looked in the right place. The real world, as it turned out. But Zack is here and safe."

"Lily isn't."

"No."

Quinn paled. And now Cristoff hunted her. Dear God, if he found her... "We have to find her first."

"We are looking for her, Quinn. We will redouble our efforts. You realize she may no longer be alive."

The words were another blow. "I know that. But I need confirmation. I need to know where she is, one way or another. Because if Cristoff captures her..."

There was no need to finish the thought.

If Cristoff got his hands on either Zack or Lily, he'd order Quinn to surrender. And she would.

CHAPTER TWENTY

Lily Wang peeled potatoes, tossing them into the large cooking pot as several other humans worked around her in the cramped kitchen, chattering and arguing.

"That bitch is crazy, with all her woo-woo stuff," Veronica said, only partly under her breath.

Lamar grunted. "She takes good care of us. I have no complaints."

"Yeah, but she hurts me every time she feeds from me."

"Then don't offer up your arm, moron." Lamar wasn't the most patient of people, but he always said what Lily was thinking, and she liked him for that. "Octavia doesn't require you to feed her, you know that."

"But I feel so good afterwards."

Lamar made a sound of disgust and Lily suspected he was rolling his eyes. "Then quit complaining."

"Fuck off, Lamar."

Lily had barely been here two days and was already tired of Veronica's whining. The girl…and she was still a girl, barely seventeen…had never seen a vampire other than Octavia and her friends. Apparently, they'd snatched her out of the hands of a Trader right after she'd walked in through a sunbeam. Veronica didn't know how good she had it here.

Lily let the heatless argument roll over her, glad to be helping with the cooking for this crowd. There were thirteen humans living in this house somewhere in the middle of nowhere, two of which had turned Slava. But they weren't slaves. They were well-fed and well-treated. And they were completely free to leave if they wanted to. None of them did. Most knew what awaited them outside. Most knew that escape from Vamp City was impossible. No, not impossible. Anything was possible if you just figured out the key to the puzzle. And Lily fully intended to figure out that key. Eventually.

"It's time to practice the earth ritual," Octavia called, sweeping into the room with a clap of her hands.

Veronica groaned loudly, but the others dropped what they were doing and followed their hostess without complaint. Lily still couldn't believe her good fortune in stumbling across Octavia. She'd escaped Castle Smithson—a vampire kovena housed in the original Smithsonian Castle—a few days ago, determined to find her way home. But surviving in a place as dead and dangerous as Vamp City was a skill she hadn't mastered. She'd found shelter that first night, but the next morning, she'd quickly found herself surrounded by hungry werewolves. That would have been the end of her if Octavia hadn't appeared suddenly, her bow cocked, her arrow aimed at the skull of the lead wolf. Octavia had asked Lily to come with her. She'd *asked.*

And while Lily had, rightly, suspected she was a vampire, the decision had been an easy one. Vampires didn't need to kill to eat. Wolves did.

Never had she expected to be brought to a cramped, homey house filled with generally good-natured humans. Why they were here, no one seemed certain. Octavia fed from them, sure, and asked them to cook both for themselves and for the wolves so that the wolves wouldn't have to hunt people for food. But that was it. It was like they were her charity project. Except, that's not what she'd said to Lily when she found her. She'd told her she wanted her to join her army.

Her army.

Lily had expected to be handed a sword or bow, and taught to fight. Instead, Octavia taught them New Age-y, Wiccan-like rituals, making them practice for a few minutes every few hours. Which was okay with Lily.

As they followed Octavia into the other room, Lily caught several of her companions rolling their eyes as if they thought the whole thing was ridiculous. Maybe it was, maybe it wasn't. But it didn't hurt anything or anybody and, in Lily's experience, that was unusual enough for a vampire to be just short of miraculous.

Octavia was a tall woman with plain features, nondescript hair that she wore perpetually twisted into a knot at the nape of her neck, and an old-fashioned, Little House on the Prairie dress in a color that might be best described as summer mud. Despite that, there was something about her…a glow that permeated her skin, her body, her very being…that made her somehow beautiful. She was definitely the most intriguing person Lily had ever met.

The vampiress stood now in the center of the large main room of the house, one furnished rustically with wooden tables and benches that had been pushed against the walls. As the others took their places around the circle, Lily pressed in, too, squeezing between one of the taller young men and Heather.

Heather smiled and made room for her. "How are you hanging in?" Heather was older than most of them—probably over thirty—but slender and toned with curly blonde hair, and kind blue eyes. Not only was she smart and nice, but she had an air of competence and confidence about her that told Lily that if things went south Heather was the one to follow. It didn't hurt that Octavia had put Heather in charge of the rest of them, even though she wasn't one of the Slavas.

"I'm fine," Lily replied. "I like to cook."

"Good. If you need anything, let me know."

With an answering smile, Lily nodded, then turned back to the center of the circle where Octavia closed her eyes, lifted her arms, and began to sing what was more of a chant than a real tune. And in a language Lily didn't recognize, let alone understand.

All around the circle, the others did the same, closing their eyes, lifting their arms, attempting to mimic the words. Some of them were pretty good, but a couple of them, including Veronica and, unfortunately Lily, did an abysmal job of it. The word-mangling didn't appear to bother Octavia. She just continued to chant until Lily began to get the hang of the words and her arms felt like they were turning to lead.

"Now drop your arms," Octavia said finally. "And open your palms."

Arms came down to a smattering of groans and sighs.

"Now we call on the power of Mother Earth," Octavia said, sounding more like a yoga instructor than a centuries old vampire stuck in a vampire otherworld. "Imagine roots sprouting from the soles of your feet, roots that burrow down into the ground, down, down, down to the very center…the white core of energy…the soul of the earth. Feel your roots connect with the power. Now pull that power up into you! Feel the energy bursting into your feet and racing up your legs, your torso, your arms and head…glorious, incredible power!"

Lily tried, or imagined she tried. In truth, she couldn't get past the idea of roots growing from the soles of her feet, not to mention the time it would take for roots to burrow the nearly four thousand miles to the center of the earth, if such a thing were even possible.

"I think I felt something!" one of the girls crowed. "It kind of tingled on the way up my legs."

Octavia smiled and nodded. "Good, Jeanette. That's good. Whether or not you feel anything is unimportant. The important thing is that you know how to pull the energy." She clapped her hands. "That's all for now. You may return to your duties."

As the circle broke up, Lily turned to Heather. "Do you ever feel anything?"

A small smile breeched Heather's mouth. "No, not really. But that doesn't concern me too much. Before she was turned into a vampire, Octavia was a powerful sorceress. She knows things, Lily. She understands the earth and sun and the energies of people and plants and how all of it intertwines. Before she was turned, she had incredible power. She still has a little, which is why the wolves are afraid of her. But mostly, she just has the knowledge of what she used to be able to do."

"That must be frustrating for her."

"Perhaps. She's a good person, older and smarter than all of us combined. And if she's right about war coming to Vamp City, we want her on our side."

"What kind of war?"

"I'm not sure. All I know is that it has something to do with one of the vamp masters, Cristoff Gonzaga. Most fear him, Octavia included. He's incredibly dangerous. Octavia believes he's going to become far more dangerous before this is over."

The front door opened suddenly and two tall, powerful-looking males strode inside. Not Slavas. By their air of command, Lily knew they had to be vampires. She froze, her heart beginning to race. But no one else seemed alarmed and a calming hand curved over her shoulder.

"It's okay," Heather said quietly. "They're friends." To the men she said, "I'll get Octavia."

"Hi," Lamar said, greeting the two vamps. "What's happening out there, William?"

"Nothing good," one of them, presumably William, muttered. With his long hair, nasty-looking scar over his right eyebrow, and small gold hoop earring in one ear, he looked like a pirate. A pirate in jeans and cowboy boots. His companion was dressed similarly, though, looked more like a professor with his closely-trimmed red beard.

The pirate's gaze surveyed the room, landing hard and suddenly on Lily. "You're Lily Wang."

Her heart lurched, her muscles tensing to make a run for it even as her mind reminded her they were *vampires*. There would be no outrunning them.

"What's going on, William?" Heather demanded.

"She's a friend of the sorceress. Cristoff Gonzaga has his troops scouring the city looking for her."

His words penetrated slowly through the thudding in her ears, but when they did, Lily frowned. They had the wrong person. Maybe the woman they were looking for was Asian, but she certainly wasn't her. The only sorceress she knew was Octavia.

The man shoved a piece of paper at Heather. "They're also looking for the sorceress's brother. Have you seen him?"

Heather opened the paper, which appeared to be a copy of a photo, but shook her head. "He's not here." She handed the paper to Lily. "Do you know where he is?"

Lily glanced down...and froze. Her hands began to shake as she stared at the photo of her, Zack, and Quinn. Zack had made it his profile picture for a short time last year. *Oh, Zack.* Tears burned her eyes. Because she knew he'd been taken for the Games. She knew he must be dead.

Her gaze snapped up to meet Heather's. "I don't understand."

"That's you, right?"

"Yes. And my friends. But not..." She frowned, gazing back at the picture, at Quinn. "Quinn's not a sorceress. She's a scientist."

"I assure you," the vampire told her. "Quinn Lennox is indeed the sorceress, and Cristoff wants her badly. He's now turned his attention to capturing those closest to her in order to force her hand." The vampire met Lily's gaze, his eyes filled with determination and little patience. "If he captures you, you will suffer unspeakably. He is a pain feeder and has lost all touch with his soul. Max and I would not have that happen."

Octavia swept into the room. "What is this, William?"

"One of your charges is wanted by Cristoff Gonzaga. Her being here will endanger you all. We're taking her."

Lily backed up, her gaze flying to Octavia, then Heather. "I'd rather stay here."

But Octavia simply lifted her hand as if to say, 'Do whatever you please'.

In the next instant, the vampire had Lily's chin trapped in his hand. As his gaze bore into hers, her mind slipped away.

CHAPTER TWENTY-ONE

"We have to find Lily." Quinn was still reeling from the revelation that Cristoff knew what Zack and Lily looked like and that he was hunting Lily, now, too.

"She's not at Castle Smithson," Kassius told them. "My sources are sure of that. They're trying to figure out where she went."

Quinn, Arturo, Kassius, and Micah were still in the small sitting room downstairs, the door closed against intrusion, though there were few left within Neo's anymore who could possibly intrude.

"Do you think she was sent to the slave auction?" Quinn's stomach turned to stone.

"Sent there? No. But if she tried to escape, she may have been captured by Traders and taken there. I have two men keeping watch on the auction as well, sorceress, and have had for days now," Kassius assured her.

Quinn shook her head. "Everyone's looking for her. She'll never make it to the auction. The moment she's recognized, she'll be taken to Cristoff."

"We will not let that happen," Arturo said.

"You won't, if you can help it. You forget, I understand how things work around here. Rarely does anything go as planned."

"You can say that again," Micah muttered. "What happened, Ax? From what Quinn told us on the ride back, it sounds like you used your mind blast."

Arturo quickly filled them in.

"He's a powerful son of a bitch," Micah said. "I always wondered what would happen if you challenged him."

"There may be a way I can keep him from counterattacking. I

sensed...a door...in my mind," he said thoughtfully. "I felt that if I could somehow close it, I could douse the counterattack. By the time I figured it out, it was too late."

"How do you practice something like that?" Quinn asked.

Arturo shook his head. "I don't. I hope never to have to test that theory."

"So, what now?" Micah leaned forward, his forearms on his knees. "Am I wrong, or are we completely out of ideas at the moment? If only we could get Cristoff to take Escalla from the case and leave it behind."

"Bram will be watching for any such opportunity," Arturo told them. "He is fully aligned with our cause and understands our need. If he ever gets the chance, he'll snatch the sword. But we all know that's unlikely to happen."

"And he's unlikely to survive the attempt," Micah added.

Quinn rested her elbow on the sofa back behind her, pulling one knee up on the cushion. "Let's look at what we know. We have to break that curse. And so far we've identified two potential ways to do that. The first is to reverse it, but that can only be done by the one who created it in the first place—the Black Wizard—and he's long dead. The second is to destroy Escalla, which we attempted and failed rather spectacularly." Her mouth twisted. "It's too bad we can't bring the Black Wizard back from the dead for a day, or travel back in time and stop him from uttering the curse in the first place." She peered at her three companions sharply. "You don't know anyone with gifts like that, do you?"

Micah just snorted, but Kassius's expression lit with a rare excitement.

"I might," he said.

All heads swiveled his way.

"Who?" Arturo asked sharply.

"Tassard. At one time, he possessed the ability to create a glamour so complete that he literally changed one person into another for a short period of time. Perhaps enough that the person changed could retract the curse."

Micah frowned. "I've heard that legend, but never saw it substantiated. Besides, where would we ever find him?"

"Here. In Vamp City," Kassius said. "A few years ago he came to spend some time with an old friend. If he stayed too long..."

"He did." Arturo's tone held none of Kassius's enthusiasm. "He's here. I've seen him."

Micah's frown deepened. "Even if he could turn one person into another, he'd have to have something that belonged to that person. Or he'd have to have known them. He'd need something to go by."

"He has it," Kassius said. "Quinn's blood. She already has the Black Wizard's blood running through her veins."

Quinn looked from one of them to the other. "So, you want Tassard to turn me into the Black Wizard long enough for me to break the curse?"

"I do not care for this plan," Arturo said quietly. "Tassard is very old, very dangerous, and extremely unlikely to choose to aid us."

No wonder he hadn't sounded enthusiastic. Quinn glanced at him, saw the stubborn set of his jaw, and thought she recognized what was going on. "You think he might hurt me."

"He is a pain feeder, *tesoro mio*. I know he will hurt you, and he will enjoy doing so."

She lifted a brow. "Do we have another option?" A telling silence filled the small room. "Okay, then. It sounds like we need to find Tassard." The look Arturo turned on her was unhappy, but resigned, as she held his gaze. "Where did you see him?"

His mouth tightened before he finally answered. "Sakamoto's."

Now it was her turn to frown. "Isn't Sakamoto Cristoff's greatest rival, reputed to be as strong as Cristoff himself?"

Arturo nodded. "He is a dangerous vampire. While his gifts are more defensive than offensive, they're incredibly powerful and make him a deadly foe."

Quinn frowned. "What exactly are his gifts?"

"The two primary—he can deaden another's powers with a touch, much in the way a silver cord around the neck will do. And he can phase—move from one place to another instantly."

"Even a vampire can't see him coming," Quinn mused.

"That is correct."

"Well...if he hates Cristoff, maybe he'll help us."

Arturo shook his head. "He is a very dangerous male, one who is unlikely to allow three of Cristoff's seemingly most loyal anywhere near his castle."

"Let me go alone, Ax," Kassius said. "I'll convince him to help, or not. But I have little to lose either way." When Vamp City died, so would Kassius.

"No," Arturo said, "We all go."

"Ax," Kassius said quietly. "I at least ask that you remain here. Micah and I will keep Quinn safe. Sakamoto will have no reason to keep our arrival a secret. Cristoff cannot know you work against him."

For the first time, Quinn understood why his friends were so adamant that Arturo remain in Cristoff's good graces. With Arturo's mind blast, there was always the possibility that he could use it at an opportune moment to get the upper hand, although that was sounding less likely given Cristoff's ability to counterblast.

"Where Quinn goes, I go," Arturo said. "There is no discussion."

As much as she hated to admit it, the tension inside of her eased with his words.

His hand slid beneath her hair, his thumb stroking the side of her neck. "It would be best if we could leave immediately, *amore*, while the night is still upon us. But you have not slept."

"I'll sleep when this is over."

"I may know of a way into that castle," Micah said. "Lukas's kovena, York, is aligned with Sakamoto's. Lukas would be welcomed there, and can vouch for us. I know where he's working tonight. We can pick him up on the way."

Quinn glanced from one of them to the other. "If this works, if Tassard can, and will, turn me into the Black Wizard for a few minutes, how do I go about lifting the Levenach curse?"

Her question was met by silence and blank looks all the way around.

Quinn grunted. "So this is all one big Hail Mary."

Micah shrugged. "A Hail Mary is better than no Mary."

"True." Quinn stood. "If no one has a better plan, let's go."

CHAPTER TWENTY-TWO

"Keep an eye on me," Quinn said quietly to her companions. "If I fall off the horse, someone catch me."

She could hear a low chuckle, one she thought was Micah's, but she couldn't be certain. It was pitch-dark out here, a dark like she had never seen in the light-polluted city of home. She couldn't see the horse she was riding on, let alone anything else, which was making it harder and harder to keep her eyes open when she badly needed sleep.

The only plus was that her riding skills were poor enough that she still tended to bounce in her seat.

The vampires, of course, could see just fine. As could, apparently, the horses. Only she was blind in the dark.

Once more, Micah had glamoured her to look like a Slava female, the vampires' portable snack. She wished she still had Grant's magic crystal. Knowing no one could sense her fear had helped her keep calm. But after escaping the castle, she and Kassius had rejoined Grant, Micah, Bram, and the others in the tunnels and Grant had demanded its return. She'd given it to him, figuring it was the least she could do now that the entire Gonzaga kovena was trying to catch him. Grant had asked to come with them, but both Kassius and Micah had said no. None of them trusted Grant *that* much.

Beneath her, the ground suddenly began to shake. Moments later, the real world erupted not ten feet in front of her and she pulled up hard on the reins. Within the column illuminated by a street lamp, she could see a neighborhood street, a car parallel parking in front of a small, well-lit home. As always, the temptation to walk through that break and return home tugged at her. As always, she ignored it, though the desire to escape this night's escapades was sharp within her.

"Quinn?"

"A bleed-through. I'm going to have to ride around it." Otherwise she'd get sucked right out of Vamp City again.

They rode for Sakamoto's, the castle of yet another dangerous vampire, this one not only as powerful as Cristoff, but with a natural hatred and distrust of Cristoff's men. Which meant they were all swimming in perilous waters. Sakamoto's men might try to kill them on sight. Or they might invite them into the castle to find out why they were there, then attempt to torture the 'truth' out of them if Sakamoto didn't like what they said.

Her imagination had been running away with her since they'd left Neo's. She knew that, but after her harrowing experiences with other vamp masters, she could be excused for expecting the worst. The only good news was that Micah's friend, Lukas, had joined them, as Micah had said he would. Lukas was a friendly bear of a man, a blond Swede she'd taken an instant liking to. He'd been stunned to realize that Arturo and Kassius were in league with the sorceress. Apparently he knew them both, but had been wary, still believing Arturo to be Cristoff's snake. He'd laughed out loud at the revelation, then shaken her hand as he told her he was honored to meet her.

Lukas had been far less enthusiastic about their plan of visiting Sakamoto, but he was willing to try and that was all they asked.

As she rode around the break-through, Quinn could see others scattered about, at least six such places within thirty or forty feet of her and far more than that at a distance. If it had been day, if the break-throughs had been sunbeams, all of her companions would be smoking by now, racing to put distance between them and the columns of light. If any had been standing within one when it erupted, he'd be dead by now.

As quickly as the break-throughs appeared, they disappeared again.

Thunder cracked, a bolt of lightning illuminating the landscape. Thick clouds that had rolled in at some point, threatened a downpour. And she had no way to avoid it.

Not five minutes later, the first huge drops splashed on her scalp and her hand. Moments later, it began to pour. The rain ran in rivulets down her face and arms, soaking her clothes. The night was already cool, and she began to shiver.

"We're going through the Crux, Lukas," Micah said.

Quinn suspected Lukas had tried to turn away, but since she couldn't see a thing she couldn't be sure. The Crux was what they called the lands in the middle of the circle that was Vamp City, lands occupied by wolves, Rippers, and others seeking to avoid the vampire kovenas.

"Micah…" Lukas's tone said he thought Micah was nuts.

"Call your wolves, *amore,*" Arturo called softly.

Quinn did. "Savin!" She wondered if the werewolves would be out in this weather, then decided that was probably a silly question.

"Mind explaining?" Lukas asked.

"Quinn has an agreement with Savin's pack. They'll provide escort across the Crux."

"Remarkable," Lukas murmured.

"She's a remarkable woman," Micah replied, his voice rich with admiration.

"Thanks, Micah," she said softly, wishing she could see him. "Tell me when you see the wolves, Turo. I'm blind out here tonight."

They pulled up and waited and it was several minutes before he replied. "Two wolves have appeared on the ridge to our right."

She heard one of them howl. "What's he saying, Kass?"

"He requests back-up, sorceress."

"Why?"

"I have to ask the same question," Micah said. "Do they see something we don't? Or are they no longer friendly?"

"Two more have joined the first pair," Arturo said. A few minutes later, "Three more. And three more again."

"That's ten wolves."

"Yes, *tesoro mio*. It is. One has broken away and is running toward us. Hold fast to your reins, Quinn. Your mount may not be pleased."

A crack of thunder was quickly followed by another flash of lightning, one that briefly illuminated the male mid-shift between wolf and man. A moment later the lights went out again. And a moment after that, she heard the rough voice of the werewolf.

"The storm clouds gather as our world crumbles, sorceress. We are seeing more and more vampires in the Crux. Savin has decreed that you never be without an escort of at least a dozen. Others will join us shortly."

"Any Gonzaga vamps?" Arturo asked.

"One vampire looks much like another to me, I'm afraid. I have seen none but you in the past couple of hours."

"That's good news," Micah said.

The werewolf continued. "When the time comes for you to renew the magic, the entire pack will accompany and protect you, sorceress."

"Thank you. What of the Herewood pack? Are you still at war with them?"

"We have declared a truce. For now. But I would not count on their assistance. You may proceed across the Crux."

"Thank you," Quinn replied. They once more started forward.

"He has shifted back into wolf and returns to his pack mates," Arturo told her. "Four more have joined them."

Some minutes later, through the rain Quinn caught a glimpse of something, a light in the distance, one that flickered and moved with a rainbow of colors. The Focus. The exact spot where Phineas Blackstone had stood the night he created Vamp City all those years ago, sending the magic out several miles in all directions. It was within the Focus's small dome of concentrated energy that she would have to stand to renew the magic.

As they drew nearer, she could see the familiar dome of colored light that always reminded her of a small aurora borealis trapped on the ground. The brilliant colors—blue, fuchsia, and orange, writhed within that space that none but a sorcerer could ever enter.

The ground shook suddenly and moments later, Quinn once more saw within the silos of light, houses and cars with their windshield wipers swinging back and forth. Silhouetted against the shafts of light were the wolves who marched alongside them.

Finally, the glimpses of the real world disappeared, and the street lights with them. The Focus fell far behind them and Quinn was once more fully swallowed by the dark.

"The wolves turn back, *cara*," Arturo said some time later.

"How close are we to Sakamoto's?"

"Another ten minutes and we should be there."

Another ten minutes and another gallon of rain, at this rate. She was soaked to the bone, truly cold now.

"Tell me about Sakamoto," she said, needing something to take her mind off her wet misery. "What does he feed on?"

"He's a fear feeder," Arturo told her. "Like me."

"I doubt he's anything like you."

Arturo didn't reply for several minutes. When he did, it was to remind her to play the servant as well as she could manage until, and if, they felt it was safe to reveal her true identity. Playing the part of the servant meant doing as she was told and keeping quiet. She'd faked it before, and would do so again, if it meant keeping them all alive.

Lights appeared ahead, though only a few, and only up high. At first she thought the lights were coming from the real world, then she realized they flickered. Firelight. They rode upon another castle. Sakamoto's.

Lightning tore across the sky, revealing a fortress built of thick stone, its walls a good twenty feet high and lit by torches. Guards walked atop the ramparts with what appeared to be some kind of machine guns strapped to their backs. She wondered if the guns carried wooden bullets.

"Wait here," Lukas told them. She could hear the pounding of his hoofbeats on the wet ground as he rode forward alone.

"Lukas Olsson to see Sakamoto," he called out.

"And why do you travel with Gonzaga's snake?" one of the guards replied from the ramparts. Even from that distance, he'd recognized Arturo.

"Our world dies and we have need of his assistance in order to save it."

At least there was no arguing that point. Even as Lukas said the words, the earth shook violently. One of the torches tumbled off the wall and snuffed out in a puddle on the ground.

Minutes passed and nothing happened, long miserable minutes as the rain continued to fall in cold, endless sheets. Quinn's shivering intensified.

"You must be warmed, *cara*," Arturo said quietly. "But I cannot aid you, yet."

"I know." Her glamour was one of a slave, and an immortal who couldn't catch pneumonia and die. "I'll be f-fine." She was far more concerned with the tension running through her companions, a tension she knew meant they were prepared for battle.

Suddenly a light appeared low in the massive wall, and a door opened, revealing a guard standing in the doorway.

"Sakamoto will see you, Lukas. Bring Arturo and his Slava, but no others."

"No," Arturo said, riding to Lukas's side. "He will see all of us. The matter is of most urgency."

The door closed on them. And once more, they waited, minute after miserable minute. Quinn sneezed, struggling to separate her mind from the intense discomfort of her body. Finally, the door opened again.

"He will see you all, but you will leave your mounts and your weapons outside."

Quinn could hear her companions dismounting, so struggled to do the same, but she was so stiff with cold that she wound up sliding off the animal with little grace.

"Your weapons, *cara*," Arturo said, beside her all of a sudden.

"I have a gun and a stake. And a penknife."

"Place them in my hands, please."

Quinn did as directed, her fingers numb and awkward. She hated handing over her gun, but it was so wet it was probably no longer functioning anyway.

A moment later, Arturo took her by the upper arm and led her to the doorway and into a well-lit Japanese garden beyond which a huge staircase rose to the massive doors of the main building. The doors were flanked on either side by guards dressed in Samurai suits of armor.

It occurred to him that all the plants were in pots, for nothing but dead trees grew naturally in Vamp City. She wondered how they keep plants alive without sunlight.

You shiver uncontrollably, amore mio, Arturo said to her telepathically as they climbed the stairs. *I will see you warm as quickly as I am able.*

"I'll survive," she whispered through numb lips.

You must.

Finally, they stepped inside the main hall, out of the rain, at last. While the hall had Japanese accents and a red and black color scheme going, it was far more Western in appearance than the garden outside had led her to believe. Crystal chandeliers hung from the ceilings, plush lounges graced the walls.

The guard led them down a long hall and into a room alight with two huge hearths, both of which now boasted roaring fires. Quinn pulled free of Arturo's grip and made a beeline for the closest, turned her back to it, then sighed with relief as the heat hit her sodden body.

Her gaze slowly took in the rest of the room—the wood paneling decorated with paintings of Japanese landscapes and tigers, the low, beamed ceiling, and the man sitting cross-legged on a cushion on the floor before a low black lacquer table. He was clearly Asian, probably Sakamoto, his head bald and round, his eyes sharp as he surveyed his guests.

Standing behind him, one on either side, were a striking man and woman, their skin a rich, dark mahogany, their features almost identical. The woman was nearly as tall as the man, both close to six and a half feet tall. The man wore only a pair of red silk pants, his muscular chest gleaming in the firelight. The woman, as beautiful as he was handsome, wore a sleeveless red silk sheath that floated to just below her knees.

Against the opposite wall, another man sat indolently draped across a comfortable-looking black leather armchair. His light brown hair was in need of a trim, his expression bored as he held a brandy snifter in one hand and a cigar in the other. He barely appeared old enough to enjoy either legally. He couldn't be more than twenty.

Six other males of various races stood at attention around the room, all dressed in the armor of the Samurai. On second thought, they were almost certainly all of the same race. Emora vampire.

The male she assumed was Sakamoto motioned to the cushions on the other side of the table from him. "Sit. All of you." His gaze turned to her. "Except for you, sorceress. The weather is not to your liking, no?"

Quinn tensed. So he'd figured out who she was. Still, she was glad he wasn't insisting she leave the warmth of the fire, as yet. She was only just beginning to stop shivering.

The vamp master glanced back at the female standing behind him and gave a nod. The woman strode quickly from the room and Quinn wondered if it was to fetch a slave to feed them, to fetch several to torture in front of them. Or to send word to Cristoff that he had her.

Heaven only knew.

"Why do you believe she's the sorceress?" Arturo asked Sakamoto carefully, his tone deceptively mild.

"My cats." Sakamoto waved his hand as if to include the dark-skinned twins, one of whom remained behind him staring fixedly at her. "They are talented seers. I knew you were coming long before you arrived, Arturo Mazza. I knew you brought the sorceress with you. And I know why. What I am not certain about is why Cristoff's loyal snake betrays him." Once more, he motioned to the cushions in front of his table. "I bid you sit, my friends."

Arturo hesitated. Wariness traced along Quinn's shoulder blades as she watched him. In her experience, a solicitous vamp master was a lot like a friendly rattlesnake. Plus she felt as if she were under a microscope. The seer...the cat—and what did that mean?...kept watching her as if she were a fascinating puzzle he wanted to figure out. Across the room, the bored-looking cigar smoker eyed her as if he wanted to make her his dinner. Which meant he was likely not a twenty-year-old, but a vampire.

Finally, Arturo stepped forward and lowered himself, cross-legged, onto one of the cushions, and his friends moved to join him.

Suddenly, the cigar-smoker appeared in front of her. She'd been distracted by the others and hadn't seen him move. Without warning, he grabbed her, sinking his fangs into her neck on a river of fire.

Quinn screamed with pain and fury even as she ripped him off her and slammed the asshole to the ground, pinning him there with her magic. When she looked up, she found that her friends had risen, presumably to come to her aid, but were now surrounded, no fewer than two blades pressed against each of their throats.

Lifting her free hand, she pressed against the warmth flowing down her chest, then pulled it away to find her palm covered with blood. The asshole vampire had done more than bite her. He'd ripped her neck wide open.

CHAPTER TWENTY-THREE

"If she bleeds to death, Vamp City will die." Arturo's voice rang across the room, low and hard. "Let me go to her."

As the blood continued to run down her neck, Quinn glared at the vampire she'd pinned to the floor through will alone. The male met her gaze with a mix of amusement and anger.

"Go," Sakamoto said.

The two guards on either side of Arturo stepped back and a second later he was at her side, holding her.

"Tesoro," he groaned, dipping his head to the other side of her neck from the wound, and biting her. *The injury is not as bad as I had feared. My bite should be sufficient. I am sorry I could not stop him.*

Finally he pulled back, wiping his mouth as he eyed the wound, his brows knit together.

"I've been properly whipped for my bad manners," the young-looking vampire said from the ground. "How about you let me get up now?"

Quinn turned hard eyes on him, meeting a laconic gaze. "I've been needing someone to practice my death touch on. I'm thinking you might do nicely."

No fear leapt into the asshole's eyes, disappointingly. Just more amusement.

"It is best if you do not kill him, *cara*," Arturo said, his voice loud enough for all to hear. "He is the one whose assistance we seek."

Quinn stifled a groan even as she continued to stare down the vampire on the floor. "*You're* Tassard? Centuries and centuries of living and you still haven't learned any manners?" Her voice hardened. "You attack me again, and I *will* kill you."

"Release me," Tassard growled.

When she glanced at Arturo, he nodded, so she did. A moment later Tassard was gone, reappearing at the bar in the corner where he proceeded to pour himself another brandy.

Quinn took a deep breath and released it slowly, breathing through the diminishing pain.

Arturo peered again at her neck. "The bleeding has stopped."

"Good." Her clothes were not only soaked with rain, but now with blood. And she was, once more, beginning to shiver.

"You need a blanket."

"I'll be fine as long as I can stand by the fire."

"Have a seat, Arturo," Sakamoto said, his voice sharper than it had been before. "There will be no more attacking my guests, Tassard."

The ancient vampire shrugged. "I wanted a taste."

Sakamoto turned to Quinn. "My apologies, sorceress. As you say, my guest has poor manners. If he harms you again, I will slay him."

The look Tassard threw the vamp master was laced with a wariness that told Quinn that the threat was not idle.

Sakamoto took his seat and again waved to the cushions across from him. "Sit. Sit."

Arturo met Quinn's gaze and she could see he was torn.

"Go," she said quietly. "Use your wiles to get us what we need."

Amusement flickered in his eyes briefly before he turned and strode back to the low table, taking his seat. Micah and Lukas joined him, one on either side, but Kassius remained standing against the back wall watching everything...and everyone.

"You stated that you know why I am here," Arturo said. "I would hear your explanation."

Sakamoto gave a single slow nod. "I believe...I *know*...that the sorceress's power rivals Phineas Blackstone's. Yet twice she has attempted to renew the magic and twice she has failed." A frown furrowed his brow. "What I do not know is why."

Arturo seemed to consider his words. "She has Levenach blood as well as Blackstone. Her father was descended from one, her mother from the other." He'd yet to use his *persuasion,* his ability to exert low levels of mind control, but so far she supposed it hadn't been needed.

"The Levenach curse," Sakamoto murmured.

"Yes. It strangles her Blackstone magic. The curse must be broken if Vamp City is to survive."

"Does Cristoff know you are here?"

"You know he does not. His…plans…are not in the best interest of Vamp City."

"Cristoff Gonzaga and I have been rivals since Vamp City was first conceived. But I find it hard to believe that you fear he would not act in the best interest of even his own kovena, his own vampires."

"Then you've had few dealings with Cristoff of late."

"I have not."

"He's changed." Arturo's expression tightened.

Sakamoto glanced over his shoulder at the tall male at his back. "My cat wishes to read the sorceress's magic. My cats can do much through mental divination, but even more through touch. I would have him touch the sorceress." His gaze swung to her. "If she will allow it."

Quinn would have loved to refuse. She honestly didn't trust any of them. But if the male really was a seer, he might learn something that could help them break through this curse. "If your cat has decent manners, I'll allow it. But he's going to have to come here. I'm not leaving the warmth of the fire."

The dark-skinned male watched her with warm, sympathetic eyes. "I will not harm you, sorceress. I will only touch you."

Her mouth compressed, then softened as she sensed his sincerity. "All right."

Something resembling a smile crinkled the corners of the cat's eyes and he strode to her without waiting for his master's direction to do so. Arturo rose as well and accompanied him.

The cat glanced at Arturo, but said nothing until he stood before her. "I am Davu." He studied her, his eyes intensely curious.

"Quinn."

"Hello, Quinn. As I said, I won't hurt you. I merely want to understand your magic. To do so, I must touch your head." He glanced once more at Arturo as if making certain her vampire guard dog would allow it.

"Tell me what you sense," Quinn said, studying the male in return—the hard planes of his face, his wide mouth, his dark, intelligent eyes. "If I'm going to save Vamp City, I need every scrap of information I can get."

His head dipped slightly, a hint of a smile lifting one side of his mouth. "Deal."

"Why does he call you his cat?"

"My sister and I are werecats."

Quinn stared at him with surprise. "I didn't know there was such a thing."

"There are few of us in this part of the world. Fewer still in Vamp City."

"You have met one already, *tesoro mio*," Arturo said.

She looked at him with surprise. "Who?"

"Ernesta, my Slava."

Quinn stared at him, a *werecat*? The matronly Latino she'd met at Arturo's house a month ago had told her she was neither human nor vampire, but had declined to fill her in further. Quinn turned back to Davu curiously.

"What kind of cat are you?"

"A leopard." He reached for her, placing his fingertips lightly across the top of her skull, his thumbs on her temples.

Quinn stared at him as he closed his eyes, stunned. Every time she thought she'd finally gotten used to the various supernatural creatures that existed in this world, along came another one.

Behind him, his sister walked back in the room, carrying some kind of fabric, though Quinn couldn't turn her head to get a good look. Finally Davu stepped back and, to Quinn's surprise, bowed low, hands together, in the Japanese tradition. When he rose again, his gaze found hers, a warm smile on his face.

"I am honored, sorceress." He turned and walked back to take his place behind Sakamoto.

The moment he moved away, his sister approached Quinn, her steps slowing, her face turning to a scowl as she stared at the blood now soaking Quinn's chest.

"What happened?" The angry demand in her voice as she turned to the others made it clear she was far more than merely a servant.

"Tassard happened," Davu replied from across the room, his voice oddly resigned.

The woman turned back to Quinn, regret in her eyes. "The bleeding has stopped?"

"It has," Arturo said, remaining at Quinn's side.

The woman watched her a moment more, then apparently decided she was telling the truth. "You could use a bath."

"I'm fine," Quinn said.

"Your wet clothes will act as cloths with which to clean off the blood." Bending down, she laid a small pile of clothes on the floor, away from the blood splatters. Shaking out the blanket, she held it up as a curtain.

"You may change, sorceress, free from prying eyes. There is a towel with the clothes with which you can dry off. The clothes will fit, I assure you."

Quinn hesitated only a moment before sitting to strip off her sodden boots and socks. She glanced up at Arturo. "I've got this, Vampire."

"I shall be happy to help." While his words possessed a trace of the charmer, she saw nothing but an iron protectiveness in his eyes.

"I'm fine, Turo. Go, please?"

He didn't move immediately, but, finally, with a dip of his head, moved out from behind the blanket. Quinn glanced up to find feminine eyes peering at her over the top.

"Thank you…?" Quinn began to peel off her wet clothes.

"Dera."

"Thank you, Dera."

It wasn't easy or comfortable yanking off the sodden clothes, but Quinn managed to divest herself of her things, then wipe off the blood with the back of her soaked shirt. With the towel she found at the bottom of the pile, she dried off thoroughly before donning panties, a pair of drawstring black silk pants, and a soft cotton Henley t-shirt in faded blue. At the bottom of the pile, she found a pair of black ballet slippers in exactly her size, which she quickly slipped on. She felt more dressed for bed than battle, but for the first time since the rain started, she was dry, except for her hair. More importantly, she was almost warm.

Dera dropped the blanket. "Would you like to wrap up in this for a while?"

Quinn smiled. "No, I'll be fine if I can stand in front of the fire for a few more minutes." Leaning over, she wrapped her hair in the towel. When she straightened again, she found Dera still standing there, watching her.

Slowly Dera held out her free hand, a question in eyes as warm as her brother's.

At first Quinn thought she wanted something back, but she was wearing everything Dera had handed her, in one way or another. Suddenly, she understood. The werecats read her through touch.

Quinn placed her hand in Dera's, allowing the woman's warm fingers to curve around hers. Quinn watched as Dera's eyes closed, as a look of confusion crossed her face, then cleared, leaving a small smile in its place.

Dera opened her eyes and grinned broadly then, to Quinn's amazement, leaned forward and gave Quinn a quick peck on the cheek before turning and crossing the room to take her place beside her brother.

Quinn found most of the males in the room watching her with varying degrees of bemusement and curiosity. Arturo's brows were knitted. Tassard, who'd resumed his seat across the room, sipped at his brandy, ignoring them all.

"My cats?" Sakamoto prompted.

"She is the Healer spoken of in legend," Davu said. "It is her magic that battles the darkness of Phineas Blackstone's, that cleanses the tarnished souls of all who reside here."

Sakamoto watched Quinn with interest, and no small confusion. "She has not renewed the magic."

"No. But she has twice made the attempt. In connecting her magic to the city's, she has initiated the dissolution of the poison, and triggered the transformation, the reclaiming of our souls."

Quinn stared at Davu, then turned to Arturo, who was watching her intently, a small smile pulling at the corner of his mouth.

"It's *my* doing?" she asked. When she turned back, she found Sakamoto watching her.

"You are our salvation, sorceress. But you must renew the magic or all is for naught." He glanced behind him. "My cats?"

"It is as the Gonzaga vamps say," Dera replied. "The Healer's Blackstone magic is being strangled by the Levenach curse. She requests Tassard's assistance in breaking the curse."

"And how in the bloody hell am I supposed to break a curse?" Tassard scowled.

Arturo turned to him. "It is our understanding that you possess a form of glamour that might change the sorceress into the Black Wizard long enough for her to break the curse herself."

Tassard gave a grunt of disbelief and took another sip of his drink. But his eyes turned to her, filling with speculation. "She has the blood of the Black Wizard within her."

Arturo nodded. "And a considerable amount of it, if the strength of her magic is any measure."

Setting his brandy snifter on the floor beside his chair, Tassard rose. Everyone in the room tensed, guards reaching for their sword hilts.

"No sudden moves, my friends," Sakamoto said calmly. "Tassard, what is your intent?"

"I need to read her."

"Ripping my throat out wasn't enough?" Quinn asked sarcastically.

The bad mannered vamp watched her with that hint of amusement. "You're the one who did the ripping, sorceress, in throwing me off you. I only took a bite."

"And what's your plan this time?"

"To touch you, as the twins did. And to bite you again. I tasted magic, but now I would search for the Black Wizard's."

"No," Arturo said, moving to her side.

"If you want my help, you're going to have to do it my way, snake," Tassard said.

But Arturo didn't budge. "You will not hurt her again."

"I'm a pain feeder. Of course I'll hurt her. But I won't injure her unless she pushes me away. It's her choice."

Quinn's jaw tightened. The last thing she wanted was to let that jerk anywhere near her again. She knew from experience that some, maybe all, pain feeders caused pain with their bite, whether they wanted to or not. But she didn't see a way out of this one.

She met Tassard's amused gaze. "Do what you have to, but go slow and warn me before everything you do, or I'll save Sakamoto the trouble of slaying you."

His eyes turned hard. "Is that a threat?"

"What do you think?"

For a couple of moments, he just stared at her. She didn't have to read his mind to know how tempted he was to spite her. Finally, he gave an annoyed sigh, walked over to her. Slowly, he lifted his hand, his palm open as he covered her face, his fingertips pressing against her cheekbones and forehead. As he stared at her, his eyes slowly took on a glassy appearance as if his consciousness had left his body and gone elsewhere. Minutes passed. Finally, he blinked and stepped back, releasing her. Slowly, his gaze focused on her once more, this time with a hint of excitement she wasn't sure she liked.

"Now for my taste."

"Wait." Quinn lifted her hand, prepared to push him back with her magic if he made a sudden move. She glanced at Arturo. "You'd better hold my arms to my sides or I'm going to hurt him."

Arturo watched her a moment, then nodded and stepped behind her, wrapping his arms tight around her.

Quinn met Tassard's gaze. "Get it over with."

"Only a taste," Arturo warned. "She has already lost much blood."

The ancient vamp's gaze flicked to Arturo, but he didn't respond. Then he reached for her, pushing her hair aside as he dipped his head to her neck, to the spot that had yet to fully heal.

Quinn tensed, determined not to scream this time, but as his fangs slid into her neck like a pair of red-hot pokers, she was helpless to hold onto the yell that came barreling out of her chest and throat. If her hands had been free, she'd have practiced her death touch on him with pleasure, at least enough to steal his energy and drive him to his knees.

Without warning, Arturo shifted, pinning her against him with only one arm. A moment later, Tassard pulled out of her neck and stumbled back, falling to the floor. As Quinn watched, he tried to rise, then sat heavily, as if he were suddenly too weak to stand.

Quinn stared at him, a chill running over her flesh. It was as if her thoughts had become real.

Tassard stared up at Arturo with disbelief. "What the *fuck* did you do to me?"

Arturo shook his head. "Nothing."

"You touched me."

"I did nothing," Arturo insisted.

Tassard tried a second time to rise and this time managed it, though he swayed as if he was the one who'd lost blood, instead of her. The ancient vampire's gaze swung between her and Arturo a moment more, then he turned and made his way slowly toward

Sakamoto. When he reached the vamp master, he paused, as if catching his breath.

"She is indeed the Black Wizard's heir," Tassard said. "I can prepare a ritual."

"What kind of ritual?" Quinn asked warily.

Tassard turned back to her with a shrug. "Fire, magic words...the usual. With the magic that rises, I'll call the Black Wizard forth for an hour or two."

Call him forth. "Will I become him...totally? Or will I still know who I am?"

Tassard waved a hand carelessly. "You will retain your own mind. You will look like him, of course, and may acquire some of his knowledge in the process. But it's unlikely you'll feel his consciousness as anything more than a whisper in your mind."

"So how am I going to break the curse?"

"Intent, sorceress," Dera said from behind Sakamoto. "You must hold the intent fully within your mind, let your will infuse it—the will to dismiss the curse. Then imagine it disintegrating."

Tassard shrugged. "It might work, it might not. Curses are tricky things. Since you have no way of knowing what was in his mind when he created the curse, breaking it could be difficult."

Quinn had a feeling she knew some of what was going through the Black Wizard's mind, if the legends of that event were correct. He'd been dying, stabbed by a blade created by his arch nemesis for just such a purpose. He'd have been in pain, furious, and probably scared. Hatred would have been coursing through him, burning him alive.

"How soon can we get started?" Quinn asked.

"A day. Perhaps two," Tassard said. "It will take time to learn the nuances of your blood and to recreate what I must."

The house began to shake violently. Outside the room, something crashed to the ground and shattered. Within the room, a crack ran the length of one of the walls.

"Vamp City doesn't have a day or two," Quinn said. And even if it did, in all likelihood, Zack did not.

CHAPTER TWENTY-FOUR

"Two hours, Tassard," Sakamoto said to the ancient vampire. "No more."

"These things take time."

"Two hours!"

Tassard's expression turned to one of annoyance, but he bowed low then exited the room without a backward glance.

Arturo exchanged a glance with Kassius. Kassius rose as if to follow Tassard, but Sakamoto motioned him back at the same time two of the samurais moved to block the door.

"You will remain here," their host said. "Tassard will do as promised, you needn't fear. In the meantime, I shall provide you with both food and entertainment."

Quinn always hated this part—the entertainment—because that usually meant blood. And sex. In the house of Cristoff, a pain feeder, she'd witnessed an 'entertainment' so vicious, she'd have nightmares about it for as long as she lived. In Fabian's, a pleasure feeder, the vampires had entertained themselves, and their master, with an orgy to top all orgies. What kind of entertainment would a fear feeder offer his guests? Quinn truly didn't want to know.

She turned to Arturo. "What happened to Tassard back there?"

I did not use the mind blast, cara, if that is what you are thinking. I grabbed the top of his head, ready to pull him away from you if I needed to. And the next thing I knew, he was falling.

A rap at the door had them turning. The guards opened the doors and in walked a small parade of Slavas—three males carrying large platters of food and drink, and four very naked females.

"Have a seat, my friends, while I serve you a four-course meal,"

Sakamoto said, motioning once more to the cushions in front of his low table. "Sorceress, you will dine with my cats at the far table."

It was then that Quinn noticed a second low table in the far corner of the room, the table at which the three male Slavas deposited the meals, setting the table with three elaborate place settings and arraying the dishes in the middle. Glasses were set out and filled from a pitcher of what appeared to be water, while two bottles of wine were uncorked and set in the midst of three wine glasses.

"I'm impressed," Quinn murmured.

Arturo curved his hand around the back of her neck. "Enjoy your meal, *tesoro*. I do not believe you are in danger."

She hoped to hell he was right. As she watched, a curvy blonde lay on her back in the middle of Sakamoto's table.

"What's she, the appetizer?" Quinn asked, not thrilled with the idea of Arturo's mouth on the woman.

Arturo smiled. "She is, indeed."

Quinn noticed the fourth woman looked a little intoxicated and was holding what appeared to be a martini. Raising her blood alcohol? "Don't get drunk on the last one." Her words were meant to be dry, but came out sounding a little jealous.

Curving his hand around the back of her neck, Arturo leaned in and kissed her thoroughly. When he pulled back, he met her gaze, his eyes alive with tenderness. "You are the only one whose taste I crave, *amore mio*. But I would not feed from you. Not today. Not like that." He kissed her again, then pulled back with a smile. "Only like this, drinking of your sunshine."

With a smile, she cupped his cheeks in her hands. "Go eat your dinner."

Dera and Davu were heading toward the table with the food and Dera motioned her to join them. Quinn took a seat on the cushion on the side opposite the brother and sister and surveyed the offerings— half a dozen platters filled with everything from shrimp tempura to chocolate éclairs.

"Wine?" Davu asked her.

"White, please."

While Davu poured, Quinn and Dera served themselves from the various platters.

"Take what you want while you have the chance, Quinn," Dera warned. "Davu will inhale everything else."

Her brother threw her a look of mock disgust. "Says the one who can eat me under that table."

Dera gasped and laughed. "Only the chocolate. You win at everything else."

Quinn smiled at the sibling banter and the last of her tension drained away. She felt unaccountably at ease now that Tassard had left. "My brother's the same. We lived together for a few years and at least half of my paycheck went to feeding him."

Dera nodded sagely. "I couldn't wait until Davu outgrew that phase, but we turned immortal in the midst of it and he never did."

"Turned immortal? So you weren't originally?"

"No." Davu stabbed a large piece of shrimp with his fork. "All weres are mortal, just like humans. Only in Vamp City do we turn immortal." He frowned. "We had no idea that was going to happen, or that we'd become stuck here for life." He shoved the shrimp into his mouth and Dera took over the story.

"Most in our pride are seers, though twins are almost always twice as powerful, and Davu and I were that. We were sold by our pride master to a powerful vampire when we were but children."

"Not Sakamoto?"

"No. Another. When we were nineteen, our master's kovena attacked Sakamoto's. Our master was killed and we became a prize of war and passed into Sakamoto's hands, thankfully. He has, for the most part, been a fair and good master."

"So you must have moved to Vamp City soon after that war. How long ago was that?"

Dera shrugged. "The early 1870's. Just a year later, Sakamoto bought a section of Vamp City and moved a contingent here. We were brought along, of course. Two years later, we turned immortal and now can never leave."

"It's one of the reasons Sakamoto stayed," Davu told her. "All the Slavas he brought with him became trapped by the magic, too. He chose not to abandon us to the mercy of another vampire master and declared he would remain in Vamp City until the last of us died. It's becoming increasingly apparent that could take a very long time."

Dera's eyebrows rose. "Or a very short one now, if the magic fails."

Quinn frowned. "If you're such powerful seers, why didn't you foresee this, the magic failing?"

Dera made a face. "I wish it worked that way."

"We see what we see," Davu explained. "We don't control it. And what we see is almost always out of context. It either doesn't make any sense or it appears useless."

"We never saw the danger," Dera said. "Not the first time Phineas Blackstone sprung the trap back in 1877, nor this time. We were as surprised as everyone else."

Davu scraped the remaining shrimp onto his plate. "I think it has something to do with the nature of Blackstone's magic. There's a darkness around it that our gift doesn't penetrate."

"What about mine?" Quinn asked. "Do you have any idea if I'll succeed?"

As one, brother and sister shook their heads. "Since the magic began to fail, we've been unable to see anything more than a day or two into the future," Davu said. "Lately, we barely see an hour into the future, if we see anything at all. The dying magic has all but shut down our abilities."

The three of them fell into silence as Quinn turned her attention to the delicious meal. As many complaints as she has had about Vamp City, the food has never been one of them. There was a lot to be said for having decades, sometimes centuries, to perfect a recipe. And the immortals within V.C. had done just that, raising cooking to an art form.

A glance at the other table told her that her companions were enjoying their meal every bit as much as she was hers. All had taken a limb and were now drinking from wrists or thighs, or the back of a knee. Sakamoto had his fangs buried in the woman's breast.

Arturo met her gaze over the wrist he held to his mouth.

I sense no threat, tesoro. *Be calm and eat. You will need your strength for what is to come.*

She couldn't deny that. But his words had raised an interesting question. She looked at her table companions. "You don't appear to be afraid."

Davu raised an eyebrow. "Should we be?"

"Not from me." Quinn smiled. "I haven't heard a single scream since I entered this castle. Yet your master has a reputation for being one of the most dangerous vampires in Vamp City."

Dera smiled. "Most dangerous, yes. If you cross him, you'll understand. But he's not cruel." Her eyes contracted briefly. "Not anymore."

"All the vampires were affected by the poison of Blackstone's magic for a time," her brother clarified.

Quinn snorted. "Trust me, I'm aware."

"We saw it happening," Dera told her. "The darkness in the magic corroding their souls. We warned our master, but he could not see it, or chose to ignore it thanks to that poison. When the trap sprung two years ago, he became enraged. And cruel. We'd never seen him like that."

"Everything changed the first time you tried to renew the magic," Davu said. "We saw it, saw your light infusing the darkness, slowly dissolving the poison. We've waited, and watched as it has done just that, more quickly than we thought possible. Within a few weeks, Sakamoto was once again himself. Most of his vampires followed shortly after."

"Unfortunately, not all are reclaiming their souls," Quinn said.

"Not all had them to begin with," Davu said darkly. "And a few of Sakamoto's who did, have failed to reclaim theirs. Sakamoto kicked them out a couple of days ago."

Quinn frowned. "They're probably with Cristoff now. That's where all the soulless seem to be congregating these days."

The wall beside Quinn began to slide back suddenly and she went still until she saw that there was no one behind it. The large, empty room looked like a martial arts dojo, very much like the one at Fabian's palace, though this one retained its Japanese flare with the low beamed ceiling, black mats, and Kabuki masks lining the walls, interspersed with ceremonial swords.

In Fabian's, the mats had been used for orgies and she suspected she was about to have to watch something similar.

"We shall enjoy a bit of exercise," Sakamoto exclaimed, rising to his feet with vampiric grace, confirming Quinn's suspicions. She'd almost gotten used to all the sex and nudity in the vampire world and could tolerate it well enough as long as there was no violence mixed in. It never failed to surprise her that vampires came away from a meal more active and energized than at any other time, whereas humans generally were just the opposite, in need of rest to digest their meal.

Sakamoto clapped his hands three times in quick succession and the doors at the far end of the dojo opened. In strode at least two dozen naked people, mostly males, none with the glowing hair of a Slava, which meant they were either mortal humans, vampires, or something else.

One of the men flashed her a smile that revealed slightly elongated fangs, answering that question. Vampires, apparently.

"Begin..." Sakamoto said as he stripped off his kimono and joined his latest guests in the middle of the mat.

A gong sounded. And suddenly, the room exploded into a vampire free-for-all. Bodies flew vampire-fast, flipping, kicking, turning, slamming onto the mats. They were wrestling, she realized. Honest-to-goodness wrestling. Laughter rang through the room, interspersed by grunts and groans and crows of triumph.

"They do this after every meal," Davu said, topping off Quinn's wine glass.

"Do you ever join them?" Quinn asked.

Dera laughed. "Occasionally, but we prefer to run."

"Run." Quinn cocked her head. "In human form or leopard?"

Davu smiled with a flick of his eyebrows. "What do you think?"

"Definitely cat, then. Why run on two legs when you have four?"

"Exactly." He lifted his glass to her and took a sip, watching her over the rim with smiling eyes.

Dera nudged him. "Watch the flirting, brother. In case you haven't noticed, the sorceress is taken. And her vampire is watching you with fire in his eyes."

Quinn turned to find Arturo standing beside Kassius, his arms crossed, his eyes as hard as flint. She smiled and held out her hand to him, pleased when he immediately strode to her and took it.

"How was your dinner?" she asked him, then tugged on his hand. "Join us. I'm making friends and I'd appreciate it if you wouldn't look at them as if you wanted to kill them."

Arturo's gaze cut to Davu. "Only the one." But he lowered himself onto the cushion beside Quinn with vampire grace, and pulled her back against his chest, one arm curving around her waist in a blatantly possessive manner, one she didn't mind at all since she'd invited it.

"A glass of wine, Arturo?" Dera asked.

"Red, thank you."

Quinn covered his hand where it rested on her hipbone. "You and your friends don't want to play with the other vampires?" Sakamoto was in the middle of the floor, wrestling with the others, his body surprisingly fit.

"No." *When in an enemy castle, even one as seemingly calm as this one, it's never wise to engage in combat unless absolutely necessary. Especially when one is so thoroughly outnumbered.*

"I understand," she said quietly, and squeezed his hand. She noticed a pair of the vampires getting it on in one of the corners, but the rest were still wrestling. "This place isn't what I expected."

"This is how it used to be in all vampire strongholds, *tesoro mio*. The laughter, the pleasure. The Emoras were a fine race, all things considered. I am sorry you've seen little evidence of that."

"There are cruel individuals of any race," Dera said. "Our first master was one. But Sakamoto has never been, except for that short period when he was affected by the poison. But that's over, thankfully, and, by and large, your vampire is correct. The Emoras, at least the males, are more moral and honorable than many humans."

"Why not the females? Why do there seem to be so many more male vampires than female?" Quinn only counted three females in the wrestling group. Four if she counted the one having sex with a male in the corner. It occurred to her that she'd never seen a female vampire at Neo's.

"They do not turn well, *cara*. Far fewer survive the turning than the males and many of those who do lose touch with their humanity. Many become Rippers even though they were turned by an Emora."

And Rippers, she knew, had no souls, no consciences, at all.

"There are only four female vampires within Sakamoto's kovena," Dera told her. "Good ones are exceedingly rare."

She found herself watching the three women who were wrestling. "They're as strong as the males."

"Yes, *cara*," Arturo said. "The vampire sexes are equally strong."

The gong rang and the vampires pulled apart, many collapsing onto their backs on the mats, winded, laughing. One by one they rose, some helping their fellows up, others leaping to their feet as if ready for another round. The pair in the corner continued to rut, drawing ribald comments from the others. But though the copulating pair laughed, they took their time in completing the act.

A happy group of vampires. Who would have thought?

Quinn caressed Arturo's hand. "Was Cristoff's really like this?"

"We were more likely to be found around billiards tables and chess boards than wrestling mats, but, yes, we would spend time together, talking, telling stories, playing chess. It was not like it has become, Quinn. I cannot begin to explain how different things are now."

"I'm beginning to understand."

The vampires rose, finally, and headed for the door, chatting amiably among themselves as they filed from the large room.

"Brandy?" Sakamoto asked as he put on his kimono and tied the sash.

Arturo rose, pulling Quinn up with him. Together they joined Sakamoto at the primary table as Dera and Davu poured each of them a snifter.

"No, thanks," Quinn said. Two glasses of wine had been plenty.

The men had only taken a few sips of their brandy when Tassard strode in. "I'm ready."

Had it really been two hours? Quinn supposed that it had.

Sakamoto nodded. "You will explain what will happen ahead of time and take everything slowly. No more surprises." He glanced at Arturo. "For any of us."

Tassard smiled, but his eyes remained cold. "It's going to hurt, sorceress."

Quinn really did not like this vampire. "You're going to bite me again?"

"No. I will do nothing but touch you. Still, the transformation is going to hurt."

Wonderful.

Arturo rose, pulling her up beside him. "Minimize her pain."

Tassard's smile turned chilly. "The more she fights the change, the more it will hurt. The level of pain is up to her. I do not create a simple illusion. She will be changing. Ask the cats. A change like that is not done without some discomfort."

Quinn glanced at Arturo. "You'd better hold me down again, or I'm likely to make him a wall ornament."

Arturo stepped behind her and pinned her carefully against him once again. *I would like to rip his throat out, but we need his help.*

She snorted. "I'm right there with you."

Tassard's brows flicked together. "Excuse me?"

"Private conversation," she told him. "Let's get it over with, shall we?" She wondered, briefly, how many ways this could go wrong, but knew they didn't have an option.

Micah and Kassius stood just behind Tassard, one on either side, their jaws hard, their eyes telling her she wouldn't suffer alone.

And then her vision was blocked as Tassard lifted a hand to her face. Like before, his fingers splayed, four fingertips pressing against her skin.

Quinn tensed, bracing herself. But there was no preparing for what came next.

Pain sliced through her skull as if six-inch blades had suddenly erupted from Tassard's fingertips and slid right through her head. She screamed, unable to do anything else, then couldn't breathe, could barely stand. Her mind went blank, her world spinning down to a single, blazing agony.

It will be over soon, amore. It will be over soon. Arturo's voice reached her as if from a distance, muffled through the shattering pain.

"End this quickly or it will be your head split asunder," Arturo growled to her tormentor.

"I'm working as fast as I can." But even through the pain, she could hear the pleasure in Tassard's voice.

"I doubt that," Micah muttered from behind them.

Suddenly, blessedly, the pain began to lessen, then subside. Moments later, it had disappeared altogether.

Quinn sank back against Arturo. Slowly, she opened her eyes and blinked. "Did it work?" The voice that emerged from her throat was not her own. Startled, she straightened, looking at the faces of those around her, faces wreathed in amazement and triumph.

Pulling out of Arturo's hold, she turned and found him, too, looking at her with shock.

"It worked," he said quietly.

Suddenly, another pain shot across her skull and she gripped her head, doubling over.

"Tassard," Arturo growled.

"That one wasn't my doing. It's probably just an aftershock."

Arturo grabbed hold of her, helping her stand.

Her head felt as if it were filling, the thoughts too much, too many, until her skull felt ready to explode. Thoughts, memories, *emotions*, that weren't hers. Fury roared up from deep inside her like a volcano about to erupt, catching her in its storm.

Erasing all that was Quinn.

The Black Wizard straightened, pushing away from the one who dared try to hold him. In a quickly receding part of his mind, he knew the vampire's name to be Arturo, remembered him as friend. But the Black Wizard needed no friend.

With a flick of his wrist, the vampire, Arturo, sailed across the room, landing, with a crash, atop one of the tables. The Black Wizard turned and surveyed the others that surrounded him—vampires all? None of them were known to him.

Where was he? How had he gotten here? It was of no matter. He would figure it out soon enough.

He turned on the lot of them.

"Submit to me. Or die."

CHAPTER TWENTY-FIVE

Arturo shook off the head-ringing attack and pushed himself up, staring at the old man dressed in a threadbare brown robe of the type worn millennia ago. *The Black Wizard.* His back was bent, if only a little, his hands covered in age spots and misshapen with arthritis. Little hair grew from the top of his head, but a long gray fringe draped his shoulders and a surprisingly bushy gray beard covered most of his face. He might look rather harmless if not for the power and malevolence radiating from those faded blue eyes.

Tesoro, *are you still in there?*

The wizard's face contorted with surprise and fury. "Who dares to speak to me thus?"

Arturo had his answer. Tassard has assured them Quinn would remain in control, that the Black Wizard's consciousness would be nothing more than a shadow in her mind. Damn Tassard to hell.

She should, at least, be safe enough as long as no one deemed it necessary to kill the wizard. And as long as she was eventually able to break free again.

Thinking quickly, calling on centuries as a diplomat, Arturo rose to his feet and bowed deeply. "Forgive us, great wizard, but we seek your assistance in a grave matter."

As the ancient wizard swung toward him, Arturo rose slowly, waiting for leave to speak. The Black Wizard was like a dangerous animal, cornered and confused. And utterly, horrifyingly, fascinating.

"Why have you called me here?" the sorcerer demanded. "Answer me!"

Arturo glanced at his friends and Sakamoto. All of their eyes were wide with disbelief and uncertainty. How did you inform the most powerful wizard ever to live that he wasn't really alive at all, but long dead, killed by his greatest enemy? Damn but they'd never expected this. Quinn was to have retained her consciousness. How were they possibly going to talk the real Black Wizard into lifting the curse on his enemy? And all to save a few hundred vampires?

He wasn't. This was not the time for truth except what was absolutely necessary.

"We are in the land of Washington, great wizard." Arturo spread his hands wide. "Far in the future from the time in which you lived."

Faded blue eyes speared him with a mix of confusion and fear. "How did I get here?"

"A sorceress of your own bloodline, one of your heirs, has need of your assistance."

"Where is she?" the wizard snapped.

Where is she, where is she? Arturo could think of no plausible lie, so went with the truth. "She is within you. She summoned you and now hosts you."

The Black Wizard scowled as he glanced down. "I do not reside in a female body!"

"Not precisely, no. Still, she is within you and seeks your help."

A withered hand flicked his way and slammed Arturo against the wall, just as Quinn might have done. "She will send me back at once!"

Dio. Arturo hung, pinned, feet dangling above the floor. "And you will return to the dead when she does," he snapped.

The Black Wizard stilled. "I cannot die."

"You did." Micah stepped forward, drawing the Black Wizard's attention. "Nearly two millennia ago. With your dying breath, you cursed your enemy Levenach, and all his heirs. But he was not the one who killed you, and in cursing his heirs, you've unleashed a powerful storm of magic that has all but wiped out your own lineage. Few survive. If your curse is not removed immediately, none will survive."

Arturo was impressed. Micah had twisted the truth, if only a little. Levenach had created Escalla in order to kill the Black Wizard, but he hadn't actually struck the killing blow. The vampire Nerian had.

"And why should I care?" the old wizard growled.

Micah shrugged. "You may care or you may not. Your progeny need your help. Remove the curse against Levenach and they will live. Do not and your line ends here. It is up to you."

"The spell that called you forth is only temporary," Arturo said, drawing the ancient male's attention once more. "You cannot remain here. Save your progeny or let them perish. It is your choice. But you cannot save yourself."

The Black Wizard's face contorted with fury. "You would threaten me, bloodsucker?" His hand lifted, his fingers pointed at Arturo.

And suddenly Arturo felt a band close around his throat, growing tighter and tighter by the second. It was choking him, which was of minor concern since he could live without air. Of far greater concern was the fact that the band was tightening at an alarming rate and might soon be tight enough to take off his head.

Tesoro, *if you are able, I am in need of your assistance.* He greatly hoped she was still in there, that her consciousness hadn't been completely overwhelmed.

Suddenly he felt the urge to whip his hand up. As he did, the wizard went flying and crashed on his back on the floor. Arturo landed on his feet, no longer pinned to the wall. A blast of emotion hit him, suddenly, Quinn's emotion. Triumph, as if she were the one who'd sent the wizard flying. How was that possible?

The wizard struggled awkwardly to his feet. "You will pay for that, vampire."

"It was not I, great wizard, but the sorceress within you who acted thus. She would not have me harmed. We mean much to one another."

The old wizard scowled. "Then she has poor taste."

"She is a fighter. And she deserves to live. The curse must be broken."

The wizard scowled. "Explain this curse."

Arturo stepped forward, coming to stand beside Micah. "You proclaimed that Levenach and his heirs would never again be able to access their magic."

A smirk formed on the old man's mouth. "And I was successful."

"You were," Arturo said.

"But he was not the one who killed you," Micah pressed. "Though you blamed him for your death, it was a vampire who attacked you, who betrayed you both. He stole your power."

Faded blue eyes narrowed. "And who is this traitor?"

"A vampire long dead. Nerian."

A wrinkled brow furrowed. "Nerian was the only vampire I trusted. Why would he turn against me?"

"Power," Arturo said simply, though he had no way of knowing if that was true. All he knew was that Levenach had used the Black Wizard's trust in Nerian against him.

The wizard's gaze found Arturo. His expression changed, a dozen emotions flying across his face at once—confusion, anger, determination, dismay. Some were the wizard's. Some of the emotions he felt as well as saw, and knew to be Quinn's.

"I would see this world of yours," the wizard said, suddenly. He looked around the room. "Where is the land of Washington? In what part of the Roman Empire?"

Arturo exchanged glances with Micah, then had to stifle a groan as the ancient one caught sight of the door and started toward it.

Sakamoto turned on Tassard. "She was not to have lost control."

Tassard just shrugged, a smile playing around his mouth that told Arturo he was enjoying the situation immensely. Had he known this would happen? Or did he simply not care one way or the other? His life was in the balance as much as anyone else's in Vamp City. But perhaps after millennia, it no longer mattered much to him.

The Black Wizard strode down the hall, trailed by the six vampires. In each doorway, he stopped and stared, then continued on to the next. Somewhere nearby a television played.

They had to get him back to the task at hand. This transformation wouldn't last forever. It had better not.

"He's following the sound of the T.V.," Kassius murmured. "Star Trek, Next Generation, if I'm not mistaken."

Micah groaned. "That's going to be fun to explain."

As the wizard stopped in yet another doorway, Arturo peered over his shoulder to find half a dozen vampires and Slavas gathered around a small battery-powered television.

"What magic is this?" the Black Wizard demanded, but the slight unevenness of his voice revealed that he was getting overwhelmed.

Arturo almost felt sorry for the male.

One of the vampires started to rise, but Sakamoto motioned him to sit. "Our guest is not from the current time and has never seen anything like this. Give him a moment to study it."

"Things have changed, great wizard," Arturo said, using his most even tone. "This was not created by magic but by human ingenuity."

With a fling of his hand, the Black Wizard slammed the television against the nearest wall, shattering it. Three of the vampires leaped to their feet and found themselves slammed against the same wall.

"Are you hungry, great wizard?" Sakamoto asked calmly.

The wizard swung to face him then, to Arturo's surprise, nodded. "I am."

"Release my people and come with me, please."

With another flick of his wrist, the wizard did. Sakamoto led them to a small room blessedly free of all technology, then called to one of his Slavas to bring stew, bread, and ale. Arturo approved of the simple fare. Anything the least bit unusual was likely to just get splattered against the wall.

The wizard sat. As they waited, he turned a gimlet eye on Arturo. "Why do vampires care if my line is extinguished after all these years?"

Arturo briefly considered his possible answers and went with one that was the truth. "Because our world will die with them."

The wizard lifted his chin with understanding, the light in his eyes flaring with renewed interest.

The food came and the wizard ate with surprising gusto.

Micah met Arturo's gaze, his finger tapping his wrist as if he wore a watch. Time was of the essence. Tassard had warned them that the glamour wouldn't last more than an hour or two.

But it was a more nagging worry that throbbed in the back of Arturo's head—a worry that a male as powerful as the Black Wizard could find a way to hold on. That he might be able to hijack Tassard's limited magic and remain. That Quinn might never return.

The wizard pushed to his feet suddenly. "Show me to my bedchambers," he demanded.

Arturo exchanged alarmed glances with his friends. Thinking fast, he said, "Great wizard, you cannot sleep, for you will return to death when you do."

The Black Wizard frowned. "Sleep has become my nemesis?"

"Yes."

"Then I would see more of this world—the land, the sky. Where is the door to the outside?"

Again, the vampires exchanged glances.

"We would be happy to take you outside, great wizard, but first we would have you lift the curse."

But the old wizard started for the doorway as if he hadn't heard.

Suddenly, the house began to shake.

The Black Wizard pressed his hand to the nearest wall. "Show me the way out!"

With widened eyes, Sakamoto motioned the wizard to follow him.

Since sunrise was not yet upon the real world, and there was no danger of sunbeams, the vampires led the wizard outside. The rain had stopped, but the ground surrounding the potted plants was saturated, little more than mud.

The wizard halted at the base of the stairs, staring into the darkness, then strode determinedly forward.

And disappeared.

"What the hell?" Micah shouted as they all raced for the spot the wizard had stood a moment before.

Arturo grabbed Sakamoto's arm. "Have any sunbeams broken through this area?"

"Yes. This very spot."

Arturo shouted his frustration. "I should have thought, I should have realized that, like Quinn, he'd be able see the breaks between the worlds, and to walk through them."

Sakamoto stared at him. "Are you saying…?"

"The Black Wizard is now in twenty-first century Washington, D.C., yes."

Worse, much worse, the ancient wizard had escaped through a door through which none of them could follow.

CHAPTER TWENTY-SIX

"*Dio.*" Arturo flew into the space where the Black Wizard had disappeared, but, unlike Quinn, he had no ability to walk between the worlds through the sunbeams—no vampires did. He and Micah were the only two left that he knew of who could still leave Vamp City at all, but only through the Boundary Circle that rimmed the city.

Arturo glanced at Micah. "We can find her...him." He'd put a magical tracer on Quinn weeks ago. He could always find her, but it wouldn't be quick. They had to reach the Boundary Circle first, then make their way back to this spot in the real world.

"Dawn is less than half an hour away," Sakamoto warned.

"Then we're going to have to hurry."

"Two mounts!" Sakamoto called and almost immediately, two horses were being led to the gates.

Arturo turned to Kassius. "If he finds his way back here on his own..."

"I'll protect her." Kassius answered the only question Arturo really asked.

Didn't I tell you not to walk toward the pretty lights?

Quinn sighed with exasperation. The Black Wizard was the most stubborn, most infuriating old man she'd ever come across. He'd taken over the moment he arrived, pushing her up against the nearest wall and pinning her there, mentally-speaking. At first she'd been completely muzzled. But then he'd tried to kill Arturo and she'd managed to fight her way free for a few precious moments, enough to help her vampire. The wizard had never regained complete control over her, yet neither had she been able to get control over him.

If she had, they wouldn't have walked through the damned sunbeam!

At least she was able to talk to him, now, and she'd been giving him an earful.

You're going to get us killed, you idiot. You're in way over your head.

"What is this place?" he murmured.

The capital of a great country across the ocean from where you lived. Two thousand years later. And I'm serious about your getting us killed. Do exactly as I say, or we're both going to die.

That was no exaggeration. The best she could tell, they were standing in the middle of 16th Street, NW. The good news was that it was barely daybreak and there were few cars on the road, but that would change soon enough.

Turn around, she told him. *Turn all the way around.* She needed to know if the worlds were still connected so she could coax him back into Vamp City. The only way she was going to know was if she could look. Unfortunately, he was the one controlling their movements.

But the man was frozen in shock.

As his gaze shifted slightly left, she caught sight of headlights out of the corner of her eye, coming their way.

Wizard, we're about to get run down by a…chariot. One that goes so fast, and is so strong, it will crush us. I need you to turn around. I can get us back to safety.

To her ever-loving relief, he slowly did as she commanded, shuffling back around, his body teetering one direction, then the other. As he looked forward, she saw that the dark column was still there, no more than three feet in front of them. Within those dark shadows, illuminated by the flickering torchlight of Sakamoto's castle, she saw Kassius, Sakamoto, and the twins eyeing one another worriedly.

Step forward, Wizard. As the sound of the car engine drew closer, she began to get frantic. *Move!*

He did, shuffling one small step.

Not enough! More, more. Keep moving.

The sound of the engine grew louder. The car was not slowing and she doubted the driver even saw them.

Wizard!

As she stared at the spot where the worlds bled together, at the door she could so easily walk through if she had the slightest bit of control of this body, it disappeared. The dark column winked out.

The break between the worlds had closed with Quinn and the Black Wizard stuck on the wrong side.

Zack clung to the kitchen counter with one hand, steadying himself as he peered into the fridge. He wasn't feeling right. Hell, he was feeling seriously wrong, kind of the way he had when the magic sickness first attacked him, back in D.C., his body cold despite the sky-high fever, and kind of wobbly. Not all the time, thank goodness. Not even most of the time. But every now and then, like now.

He'd decided maybe he just needed something to eat. But he knew that wasn't really the case. The truth had to do with magic and curses and crap he couldn't control.

He was dying. He could feel stuff happening inside of him just like before. As if his organs were getting ready to turn to stone.

It wasn't like he cared, except that Quinn would be so torn up about it for a while. The worst part was that with him gone, who would rescue Lily? Yeah, the vampires said they were looking for her. And he knew Quinn wanted to find her, too. But Quinn was so focused on saving *him* that she couldn't...or wouldn't...think about anything or anyone else. And maybe if he died, she'd finally turn all her attention to finding Lily.

Latching onto a bowl of leftover potato salad, he closed the fridge, and was pulling a fork out of the drawer when the back door opened and Rinaldo walked in, a stranger behind him.

Zack eyed the skinny, pale-skinned youth with interest. He was young, or appeared to be. No more than early teens. But Zack knew from experience that apparent age had nothing whatsoever to do with real age, not when it came to vampires. And though he couldn't be certain, his gut told him vampire.

"Wait here. I'll get..." Rinaldo saw Zack and stopped in his tracks. "Neo!" he called, instead of going after him as he'd obviously planned.

Why? Because Zack was the *little brother* and heaven forbid they not protect him 24-7. Fuck. That. With a grunt of disgust, he turned and left the kitchen, but was only a few steps away when he heard Neo greet the stranger.

"Alesius," Neo said warmly. "To what do we owe this honor?"

Zack stilled. Yeah, definitely a vampire. Who named their kid Alesius these days? Curious, he moved into the shadows just outside the kitchen doorway.

"I seek Kassius. I bring word on the human he's had me looking for."

Zack felt the fork in his hand begin to bend beneath the force of his sudden grip because, *fuck*, it was Lily Kassius had sent someone looking for.

"Kassius isn't here," Neo replied. "But he should return soon. Will you stay? Or would you prefer I convey the message?"

"I can't stay. Please tell him the female is believed to be hiding somewhere in the Anacostia Forest."

Zack's pulse began to pound.

"How did she get there?" Neo asked.

"It's believed she hid in a Trader's wagon, then slipped out of it before the Traders even knew she was there."

"How long ago did this escape take place?" Neo asked carefully.

"Three days. Two and a half. It's possible she's still alive."

Possible. Zack's gut clenched.

"But unlikely. That forest is no place for humans. The last I heard it was a popular haunt of a splinter faction of the Herewood wolf pack."

Zack's breath lodged in his lungs.

"I'll pass your report on to Kassius, Alesius," Neo said.

"Sorry I couldn't have brought better news."

"You brought the information we sought. That's all we could ask."

Zack waited until the back door clicked shut before striding into the kitchen. "We have to go after her."

Neo turned around, eying him with dismay.

"We have to go now. She's in danger, Neo."

"Zack."

It was all Zack could do to keep his temper in check at the placating tone of Neo's voice.

"Your sister will be back soon. Wait until she gets here, then discuss it with her."

He was fucking *sick* of everyone treating him like he was twelve! Lily was out there in a forest somewhere. Alone. *With werewolves.* But Neo wasn't going to be pushed. Zack knew that about the male.

He was nice for a vampire, and had a crap ton of compassion for humans, but he was no pushover. If Neo suspected he might take off on his own, Zack would find himself enthralled or locked up until Quinn got back. For his own safety, of course. He was too *precious* to be allowed to leave on his own, which was dog shit. He was nothing.

Setting the bowl of potato salad and fork on the counter with more force than necessary, he turned and stalked away, descending the stairs to the sprawling underground. Moments later, he pounded on Jason's bedroom door.

"Come in," a voice called groggily.

Zack strode into the tiny room, lit the bedside lamp, then closed the door, crossed his arms, and stared at his friend, who'd clearly been sleeping.

"I'm going after Lily. You can come or not. Your choice."

Jason peered at him with groggy confusion. "What?" He ran a sleepy hand through his hair and struggled to sit up. "They found Lily?"

"They know where she is. Somewhere in the Anacostia Forest." The panic he'd been struggling to keep at bay tore through his lungs. "It's full of wolves, Jase."

"How long has she been there?"

"Two and a half days."

"Zack…"

"Don't say it! She's smart. Too smart to get herself eaten." His jaw tensed. "I'm going after her."

Jason swung his legs over the side of his bed. "Quinn and the others will be…"

"Fuck them. I'm tired of everyone thinking I need my sister to protect me. Besides, you know what will happen. She'll tell me to wait here, like she has every other time I've tried to go with her. *Wait here, stay safe.* Fuck. That." Zack turned and reached for the door handle. "Come with me or not, Jase, but don't say anything. They'll figure out I've gone as soon as Quinn gets home. You can tell them then."

"Zack, wait, man. You passed out earlier."

Zack whirled back, turning on him. "So what? I'm *dying*. Don't you think I know that? But hanging around here doing nothing isn't saving me. All it's doing is wasting what time I have left when maybe I could be saving Lily."

Jason met his gaze, his own somber, but thoughtful. "You're right."

Zack stared at him. He was?

The ex-Marine grabbed his jeans off the foot of the bed and started to pull them on. "I've been itching to get back out there for days to hunt for my wife."

"Then why didn't you leave before this?"

Jason glanced up, meeting his gaze. "And miss watching you morph into Superman?" He stood, fastening his jeans, then grabbed his boots. "I've been telling you all along that when you were ready, we'd leave together—you to find Lily, me to find my wife. It looks like that time has come." A smile flickered across his face. "Let's see what kind of vampire ass you can really kick."

Despite the bold words and the disappearing smile, Jason's eyes were as serious as the grave. Trying to kick vampire ass usually got a human killed. Zack had seen that during his own days as a captive. He and Jason stood an excellent chance of dying out there. But staying safe in here was no life, not when the women they cared about were missing. Or in danger of being eaten by wolves.

The blast of the car horn startled the Black Wizard, nearly making him stumble. It infuriated Quinn. The asshole driver clearly saw the old man in the middle of the street, but instead of slowing down and going carefully around him, he let his own annoyance at being ever-so-slightly inconvenienced scare the crap out of the ancient male.

She felt the Black Wizard's arm shoot straight out at the car, a small Lexus, and suddenly the car stopped. Just...stopped...as if it had hit a brick wall, its airbag erupting.

The moment Quinn saw the driver move, and knew he was basically unharmed, she smiled, mentally. *Nice job, grandfather.*

"I stopped the dragon. I will kill it."

No, no, don't kill it. It's not a dragon, just a human driving a...horseless carriage. You stopped him and he's uninjured. Let's leave it at that. They needed to get out of the street. *Do you see that building to the right? Walk over to it. Quickly.*

"But the dragon..."

Is disabled. It won't hurt us. Move, grandfather.

Finally, he did, shuffling at the speed of a tortoise. Not bad for a male she now knew to have been over seven hundred years old when he died, although he *was*, technically, using her body. At least she thought he was. It was hard to tell exactly how they'd merged. All she knew for certain was that she was no longer in charge, and had been flooded with his memories from the moment she got here. He'd had surprising honor in his younger years, had loved deeply numerous times, and raised several families. But in his later years, he'd lost all patience with humans. And while that might be understandable, he'd used his abilities unconscionably.

A grumpy old man with infinite power was not a good thing, as it turned out.

Finally, he reached the curb and climbed it. Quinn breathed a small sigh of relief, though only a small one. She still had to get them back to Vamp City.

"Why do you call me grandfather?" he muttered.

Because that's what you are, generations and generations back. I have the same ability to throw vampires against the wall as you have. And I've learned how to create bubbles in which to trap vampires and werewolves. Unfortunately, that's about all I can do since, while my mother was one of your heirs, my father was of Levenach.

"That could never be," he spat.

The feud between you died with you. None of Levenach's progeny were ever sorcerers, thanks to your curse. And your line has almost entirely died out. They're calling me the last sorceress. And I may be that. But the Levenach curse is strangling most of the magic I inherited from you. I cannot be what I am meant to be, the Black Wizard's heir, until that curse is lifted. And you're the only one who can lift it.

He was silent for several minutes as he studied the houses lining the street and ran his hand along a black metal fence. "If I lift the curse, all those of Levenach's blood will suddenly come into a magic they did not know they possessed. The world will be filled with wizards again, *Levenach* wizards."

Hell. Was it possible he was right?

As she tried to come up with a counterargument, he continued down the sidewalk, seemingly fascinated by the porch lights and streetlights. When his gaze moved to the sky, she was half-afraid he was going to lose his balance and fall backward.

"Where are the stars?" he asked.

There are too many lights to see them.

"Then how will we find our way home?"

For a moment she felt sorry for him. *This is all a bit overwhelming to you, isn't it?*

"Overwhelming is an inadequate word. This is the world that will die?"

Not this one, no. The other one. The quiet, safe one. This is the real world now.

"A pity."

A lot of people who live here would probably agree with you.

He turned the corner onto a side street.

Grandfather, where are you going? We need to stay close to where we came in. Let's go back, shall we? She might be able to find another sunbeam, but it could drop them anywhere in V.C.—in the middle of a contingent of Cristoff's guards or a pack of hungry wolves who wouldn't recognize her in the ancient male. *Grandfather, stop!*

But the stubborn old male just continued to walk father and farther away from their safest path home, in his unsteady, shuffling gait.

CHAPTER TWENTY-SEVEN

"**A**x! We're out of time. Unless you want to get stuck here for the day, we've got to go back."

The sky was beginning to lighten in the east with approaching dawn, purple clouds smudging a lavender sky over the Washington, D.C. skyline. They'd reached the neighborhood on the east side of Rock Creek Park which he believed to be the location of Sakamoto's castle in Vamp City, but though they'd been racing up one street and down another, they'd found no sign of the dangerous old man.

"He has to be around here somewhere," Arturo growled.

Micah shrugged. "Where? For all we know, she's already back in V.C."

And it was possible. The magical tracker he'd put on Quinn weeks ago wasn't working. He couldn't even feel her emotions. From the moment Tassard changed her into the Black Wizard, Arturo had been unable to get any sense of her at all. It was as if she no longer existed, which was driving him insane.

"We're already starting to smoke, Ax. We'll be lucky to make it back to the Boundary Circle before we burn, as it is. Any more delay and we'll have no choice but to go to ground. We'll be stuck in D.C. for the entire day."

Which was the last thing they could afford to do.

"All right." The words stuck in his throat, but they had no choice and he knew it.

Together, they ran for the Boundary Circle, which was not, unfortunately, close by. It was going to be tight, and they'd be hurting by the time they reached it.

"Sooner or later that glamour will wear off, and when it does, Quinn will find her way back to Sakamoto's," Micah said.

Arturo glanced at him. "Assuming she has any idea where she is when she snaps out of it. I don't know if she's even aware of what's happening. She might accidentally come through a sunbeam in a bad place."

"A hundred things could go wrong and we both know it, Ax. But Quinn is smart. And she's strong. She'll make her way back to us one way or another."

As long as that bastard wizard didn't do something stupid while he was still in charge. Something that would get her killed.

Zack strode into the kitchen with Jason, dismayed to find Mukdalla standing at the counter, stirring something in a mixing bowl. She smiled when she saw them. "I'll have pancakes ready in a few minutes."

"I'm just going to make a sandwich," Zack said. "I want to sit outside and watch the sky lighten. I still have trouble telling night from day around here. Jason said it's because I'm spending too much time inside." He hoped to hell the explanation made sense and that he wasn't rambling. And that Mukdalla didn't notice he was beginning to sweat.

With the need to reach Lily burning a hole in his gut, he grabbed the bread and ham and made himself two huge sandwiches, while Jason made himself one and filled a couple of water bottles. Getting away from Neo's without someone stopping them was going to take a miracle. His pulse hammered at the certainty they were going to get caught, which of course they were if any of the fear feeding vampires came anywhere near him in this state. They'd know right off that something was up.

He handed the sandwiches to Jason who stuffed them in the leather satchel that hung across his body.

"How far are you going?" Mukdalla asked, a touch of suspicion in her voice. Or maybe not. Maybe he was just imagining it.

"Out by the stables," Jason said. "We'll get the best view out there."

"Rinaldo's on watch."

Zack nodded. They might have to wait until the sun was all the way up and the vampires back inside before this could work. But he'd wait as long as he had to.

He led the way outside, the night air cold on his heated flesh. It was strange. Although he knew he was running a fever that should have long ago baked him alive, he didn't really feel hot unless he was working out. He didn't usually perspire, though he was doing it now, thanks to the nerves that were eating him alive.

Zack headed for the stables, trying to keep his stride to an ambling gait when all he really wanted to do was run. Beside him, Jason played it super cool, as if they really were just out to watch the sky lighten. Then again, a Marine ought to be good under pressure.

"Heading somewhere?" Rinaldo asked good-naturedly, appearing out of nowhere as vampires had the habit of doing. "Is something wrong, Zack?"

Dammit. It figured that Rinaldo would pick up on his nerves. Thinking fast, he said, "I'm not feeling great, Rinaldo. I don't think I have much longer." They kept treating him like some poor, pathetic dying martyr. He might as well use it to his advantage. "I'm tired of spending so much time inside. I wanted to see the sunrise and maybe just spend the morning out here."

Rinaldo made a sound of sympathy that told him that maybe he hadn't overplayed that too much. The vampire clasped his shoulder. "Let us know if you need anything. Either of you. I'm heading back in soon, but Sam's on watch next."

"Thanks, Rinaldo," Zack said quietly, coughing for good measure. He watched the vampire slowly make his way around the house, then turned to Jason. "I should get an Oscar for that performance."

Jason's only response was to grunt.

"Let's get the horses ready, Jase."

"I'd rather wait until the sun comes up. Neither one of us will be able to see shit until the sky lightens."

Zack's limbs were about to go crazy with the need to get this over with, to get on the horses and go. But he knew Jason was right. They sat on the ground on the side of the barn away from the house, where they wouldn't be seen...or their disappearance noticed. Zack thought about eating one of the sandwiches, but his stomach was in knots.

His foot tapped the ground, his hands keeping up a steady tattoo on his knees.

"Keep it together, Zack," Jason said quietly. "Watch the sky. You do need to learn to tell when the sun comes up in the real world, especially now, when it makes such a difference to the vamps.

There's a slight glow when the sun first appears. You have to be watching to notice it." Several minutes later he said, "There. Do you see that?"

Zack shook his head. "Let's go."

Jason snorted. "Fine. We need to get a bead on Sam first so that we can stay under his radar."

Out of nowhere, the terrible, heavy lethargy swept through Zack again, wiping him out. He collapsed back against the wall, banging his head.

"Zack!" And then Jason was in his face. "I'm going to get help."

"No." Zack didn't know where he found the strength, but he grabbed Jason's wrist and held him fast. "No. Nothing's changed."

Jason stared at him, none of the thoughts flying through his head registering on his face. Probably because he already knew what Zack would say.

"If this happens when you're riding, you're going to fall off the horse."

Zack shrugged. "Then I fall off the horse. Give me five minutes and I'll be stronger than you, again. These...events...have been happening for the past couple of days. I just haven't told anyone. I'll be fine in a few minutes." And then for how long? Because they were coming more and more often. He wouldn't admit that to anyone else, but he couldn't lie to himself. "I'll be fine."

He could tell it cost Jason to sit back down, but his friend did. And within a few minutes, thankfully, Zack felt as if his full strength had returned.

All of a sudden, the ground began to shake, violently.

Zack's gaze swung to Jason. "Let's go. They'll never hear the horses over the rumbling."

But Jason didn't move.

"I feel fine, Jase." As if to prove his point, he leaped to his feet, took Jason's hand, and hauled him to his.

Zack held his breath, worried that Jason was going to refuse.

But finally his friend nodded. "Wait here while I find Sam." Moments later, he returned. "He's on the other side of the house, but won't be for long. Can you ride bareback?"

"I'd ride a werewolf if it would get me to Lily."

Jason threw him a look that was half amusement, half respect, and nodded. As one, they slipped into the stables, then swiftly led two horses out again. As they mounted and took off, Zack glanced back at Neo's, at the sunbeam illuminating a small circle in the backyard that would keep the vampires in hiding. The ground continued to rumble, effectively disguising their hoofbeats. Until someone thought to check on them, they wouldn't be missed.

They'd done it! A clean getaway.

But as Zack turned front again, and headed into the now light-dotted, vampire and werewolf infested darkness of Vamp City, he was slammed with a memory of his enslavement, of the beatings he'd taken, of the casual cruelty and murder he'd witnessed.

For a moment, he wondered if he should be celebrating this escape from safety. Because even if Lily was still alive, the chances that he and Jason would be able to find her, and get the three of them back to Neo's in one piece, were slim to none.

For a brief moment, he wondered what in the hell he was thinking embarking on this mission without Quinn and her vampires at his back. Except they would never be at his back, that was the problem. They'd leave him behind.

No, he was doing the right thing. When he thought of Lily, of the shine of laughing intelligence in her beautiful eyes and the sweetness of her bright smile, he knew he'd happily take on every vampire in Vamp City if it meant the slightest chance of seeing her again.

CHAPTER TWENTY-EIGHT

Look, grandfather, if you lift the curse it's possible that a few Levenach heirs may come into their magic... if they have any. But it's unlikely that many of Levenach's bloodline have survived two millennia.

Quinn felt like she'd been arguing with a brick wall for the past half hour, to no avail. As dawn had broken, as the landscape had become fully visible to eyes that she suspected hadn't seen very well in the dark, the ancient male had become more and more agitated. He'd finally stumbled into the backyard of a residential home and lowered himself to the ground beneath a huge maple tree.

Now he refused to budge. She wasn't certain he could get himself back up if he wanted to.

Sooner or later, the transformation was going to wear off—she hoped. He'd be gone and she'd be free to walk back into Sakamoto's garden the next time the sunbeams broke through. But if she didn't get him to lift the curse before that happened, all of this would be for nothing.

She'd been trying to cajole him into lifting the curse since they got here, but he just sat beneath the tree, trembling, his heart pounding. If she hadn't seen some of the truly vile things he'd done in his later years—like sending a thousand poisonous snakes to wipe out a village simply because the villagers had made too much noise during their midsummer's revelry—she might actually feel sorry for him.

A few minutes ago, when the sun came up, her heart sank, because she knew Arturo had tried to find them. And failed. Hopefully he'd made it back to V.C. before dawn and wasn't stuck on this side, waiting out the daylight.

They were running out of time and she was lacking ideas on how to motivate the old man.

The wizard lifted his arms suddenly and Quinn could see that the hair on his hands and wrists were standing on end.

You're cold, she said.

No. I feel energy covering my skin.

Mentally, Quinn's eyes went wide. That always happened to her in the real world when the sunbeams broke through. Which meant...

The worlds are opening again, grandfather. Praying for patience, she tried one more time, keeping her tone as quiet and gentle as she could. *Do you want to go home?*

To her surprise, he answered without hesitation. "Yes. Send me home."

I can do that. But you have to do exactly as I say.

"Anything."

Thank God. *First, you must break the curse.*

"No."

Damned stubborn old coot.

Fine. If you won't help me, I'm not helping you. I'm going to return to my own body. You're on your own here.

It was a bluff, of course. But maybe it would work.

"The vampires told me I had taken your body."

She managed a laugh. *Do you look like a woman? Feel like one?*

When he didn't reply, she wasn't certain what he was thinking. Had she confused him? Scared him, if only a little bit?

"You will not leave me here," he said suddenly, his voice all command. But she heard the thread of fear. He was terrified.

Lift the curse. That was the only thing that mattered at this point.

Again, silence descended upon them, but this time she had the upper hand. Because he'd admitted he wanted to go home.

"All right," he said quietly, grudgingly.

Quinn did mental back flips, but kept her mind quiet, not wanting to lose any ground with him.

Sitting beneath the maple tree in the back yard of a residence in one of Washington, D.C.'s northwest neighborhoods, the Black Wizard—a male who'd lived millennia ago—began to chant a powerful spell. Quinn could feel the words wrapping around her mind, words in a language long extinct, yet words she nonetheless understood perfectly thanks to the links between their minds. Words of magic and power and the earth and sun. She saw herself in his mind's eye as if he knew exactly what she looked like. And perhaps he did. He was definitely concentrating on her.

Somewhere in her own mind, she felt something fly free and give a great sigh of relief.

"It is done," he murmured. "Now send me home."

Happily. Excitement raced through her at the thought that, even now, Zack might be healing, his temperature dropping. *You have to get back on your feet, grandfather. Quickly. We haven't much time.*

The ancient male struggled and huffed, finally managing to stand, though he held onto the maple as if it were a lifeline.

I'm going to lead you home, but you must listen to what I say and follow my directions. We need to return the way we came. Do you remember?

He said nothing, but released the tree and began to shuffle through the grass, toward the sidewalk, with an air of purpose that had her wondering if they might actually accomplish this. But he didn't stop at the sidewalk.

Grandfather, turn right.

He did, but not until he was in the middle of the freaking street. Fortunately, this one was purely residential and there were no cars on it, at the moment. A situation that could change in a heartbeat.

If she'd had a head, it would be pounding.

When they reached 16th Street this time, it was busy with traffic, though the speed limit was low through here and the cars weren't going fast. When she realized the wizard was raising his hand as if to slay more dragons, she stopped him.

Put your arm down! There are people in every one of them. Moms and dads with their children. They won't hurt you, if you do what I say. And she hoped to hell that was true. Getting him into the middle of 16th Street without getting hit wasn't going to be easy.

Do you see that dark column about twenty yards to your left? she asked. In V.C., the sunbeams broke through as light in the darkness. In D.C., it was the reverse, a column of dark in the light, but one only she could apparently see. She hoped the wizard, too, had that ability.

"Is that home?" he asked.

Excellent. He could see it. *Yes, it's the way home.*

Picking up his stride, the old man marched right into the middle of 16th, right into oncoming traffic. Quinn wanted to squeeze her eyes closed, and could only pray no one would intentionally run down an old man. Thankfully, the cars stopped and the Black Wizard walked between them with concentrated focus.

One woman got out. "Sir? Let me help you."

The wizard lifted his hand.

Grandfather, put your arm down! Don't you dare hurt her or I won't help you get home.

To her relief, he did, and continued forward, straight toward the break between the worlds. Now, if the sunbeams would only last this time. If she'd had any control of her lungs, she'd have been holding her breath.

Another ten steps and they'd be there. Eight. Six. Four. Two.

A firm male hand gripped the wizard's arm. "Sir, you're going to have to come with me."

The wizard jerked around to stare into the face of a cop.

Quinn nearly screamed her frustration. *Push him away. Only about six feet. Don't hurt him.*

"You told me if I hurt anyone, you wouldn't send me home."

"Excuse me?" the young cop said.

These are extenuating circumstances. Do it! Now!

He did.

Quinn watched with a mix of regret and relief as the young cop landed on his butt half a dozen feet away, his eyes suddenly too big for his head. And, dammit, if he wasn't pulling his taser.

Into the shadows, grandfather, quickly!

The wizard turned to the front and pushed himself forward the two remaining steps. Reaching out, he touched the dark shadows. And then it was the Black Wizard falling to his knees within a sunbeam in Sakamoto's garden.

Quinn gave a huge mental sigh of relief.

"They're back!" Dera shouted.

As the wizard looked up, Quinn saw that the werecat twins were the only ones waiting for them, but then again, the vampires couldn't be outside with the sunbeams shining through.

Ask them to help you inside, grandfather. Tassard, the vampire, is the one who will send you home, and he cannot be in the light.

"A vampire," he grumbled.

He's the one who brought you here. He's the one who will send you home. Be nice.

"Show me to Tassard," he commanded. "You may assist me to my feet. My daughter has ordered me not to harm you."

His daughter. Quinn gave a mental laugh, relief surging through her mind that the curse was broken at last, and that they'd made it back in one piece.

Dera took the old man's arm and helped him to his feet, then led him up the stairs and into the castle. When they reached the room with the hearth where Quinn had been before, she saw Sakamoto, Kassius, Lukas, and Tassard staring at her...or staring at the wizard...with varying degrees of relief and wariness. Arturo and Micah weren't back, yet, clearly. She just hoped they were somewhere in V.C.

"Where is Tassard?" the Black Wizard demanded. When Tassard lifted his glass of brandy, the wizard said, "Send me home! My daughter says you are the one who brought me here and you are the one who will return me. Immediately!"

The vampires exchanged glances.

"Your daughter?" Sakamoto asked carefully.

"The one in my head!" he lifted his hand and tapped his skull with his knuckles. "She speaks to me incessantly, harangues an old man into doing things he'd prefer not to do. But I did as she commanded and you will send me home."

Sakamoto looked to Dera. "Can you tell?"

She shook her head. "I don't sense Quinn, only him."

Tassard turned to Sakamoto. "It's your call."

"Now!" the Black Wizard ordered, lifting both hands. "Or I will tear down this palace around you!"

Without waiting for more discussion, Tassard shoved his brandy snifter into Dera's hands and stepped forward cautiously. "I am Tassard. I must touch your face to send you home. Will you allow it?"

"Yes."

With a nod, Tassard closed the distance between them and lifted his hands in front of the Black Wizard's face. Locked inside the head of the ancient male, Quinn began to scream.

CHAPTER TWENTY-NINE

Quinn felt firm hands grip her arms, felt herself being lifted, carried, and lowered again to a soft cushion.

The pain that had split her head in two was beginning to fade, her mind starting to clear of the thoughts, the dark memories, that were not hers.

Blinking, she opened her eyes slowly to find faces staring at her from every direction—Kassius, Sakamoto, Lukas, Davu, Dera. Tassard stood to one side, lighting a cigar.

"Welcome back, sorceress," Kassius said gently.

Quinn pushed herself up and swung her feet over the edge of the chase, immensely relieved to have a body again. "The wizard's gone."

"Yes," Sakamoto replied.

She looked down at herself, at her hands. "So is Micah's glamour." She looked at Kassius. "Where are they?"

"Looking for you in the real world," Kassius replied, giving her the answer she'd already suspected.

"Will you allow me to read your magic?" Davu asked. "We would know if he lifted the curse as he says he did."

"He'd better have," she muttered darkly. "Go ahead, Davu."

The werecat stepped forward, then squatted in front of her, his dark eyes smiling. "It's a pleasure to see your true face. A beautiful face."

"I travel with glamour, as I'm sure you've guessed. It keeps me alive."

"Very wise." He placed his fingertips across the top of her skull, as he had before, his thumbs on her temples. "We're glad to have you back. That wizard of yours was one bad-tempered elder."

"You have no idea."

Davu began to frown.

Quinn stared at him, her body going cold. "Don't you dare tell me he lied."

The werecat began to smile. "It's all right. He didn't lift the curse, not precisely, but he's fully freed your Blackstone magic of it." His smile turned to a grin. "Your magic glows brilliantly, Quinn. I believe you'll have no longer have any difficulty renewing the magic of Vamp City."

Sakamoto grinned. Lukas hooted and Tassard let out a victorious shout, utterly surprising her. She hadn't thought the ancient vamp really cared one way or the other. Dera hugged her brother.

Quinn turned and walked to the hearth, staring into the fire as crushing disappointment tore through her chest. If the curse had been broken, Zack would already be healing. But that wasn't the case. That son of a bitch wizard had figured out a way to strengthen her magic without helping the Levenach heirs. Without helping Zack.

"Sorceress?" Kassius asked, his hand cupping her shoulder.

Quinn took a deep breath, and turned to face him. "I have the magic to save you, now. To save you all. We need to get to the Focus."

Kassius nodded, his eyes sparkling with relief and thanksgiving.

"How quickly do you think Arturo will be here?"

"It depends how far into D.C. he got before he had to turn back. Clearly he didn't find you."

"No. The Black Wizard hid under a tree behind a house."

"He expected to be able to sense you. The tracker…"

"He hasn't said a word to me since I merged with the Black Wizard. I don't think he could connect to me."

"If he searched for you until the last minute and still made it back to Vamp City before sunrise, he should be here soon, as long as he doesn't run into any trouble. Fifteen minutes, I would think, at most."

"Good. Let's get ready to go, then."

Sakamoto lifted a hand to one of his guards. "Prepare a score to accompany the sorceress and her companions to the Focus where she will save our world." He turned to her. "You will not go unprotected."

"Thank you, Sakamoto, but the sun's out. I'm worried about putting your vampires in danger."

"They are in far more danger if you fail to reach your destination and fulfill your mission. The magic must be renewed."

Quinn nodded. "True. Thank you." She glanced down at her clothes. "I need to change."

"Your own were washed and laid out," Dera said. "But they will not have dried. I'll pack them up so you can take them with you. And I'll find you something more suitable for riding. Are jeans, okay?"

"Perfect." As she watched Dera stride out of the room, a wonderfully familiar voice floated through her head.

You are back, tesoro. *I am glad.*

Quinn smiled, then jerked, startled by the funny flutter of joy that tickled her mind with his words. A joy that felt like his.

She looked at Kassius with surprise. "Arturo just spoke to me, just to say he's glad I'm back. But I think...I'm pretty sure...I just felt his joy." She began to smile with bemusement. "I've never felt his emotions before, though he often feels mine."

"The two of you share a soul cord," Davu said. "Perhaps you couldn't feel it before."

Quinn looked at him curiously. "What's a soul cord?"

"A deep connection between two souls, as the name implies. Shallow cords are fairly common among humans with strong emotional bonds, but a cord strong enough to sense one another's emotions is quite rare. Then again, this is a soul cord with a sorceress. I suspect they might have interesting possibilities."

"Like what?" Quinn asked.

"Soon after you and the wizard became joined," Davu said, "the wizard tried to strangle Arturo."

Quinn nodded. "I made him stop."

Davu's mouth spread into a grin. "Arturo's hand lifted. The power came from him. Through him. I saw your vampire's expression and he was shocked."

Quinn nodded slowly, her eyes widening as they swung to Tassard. "Earlier, when you were hurting me... Arturo was holding me from behind, but all of a sudden, you fell down. What exactly happened?"

The youthful-looking vampire scowled. "The bastard touched my head and stole my strength."

Quinn's eyes widened. If they were right, she'd begun to steal his life with her death touch. Through Arturo. She remembered badly wanting to hurt him as he was hurting her. Good grief, she was going to have to talk to Turo about this.

Dera returned with a bundle in one hand, Quinn's boots in the other, and a pair of jeans and leather jacket. "I tucked dry socks in the boots. The jacket is my favorite, but you need it tonight and I want you to have it."

"Thank you, Dera. I'll get these back to you when I can." Quinn slipped out of the ballet slippers and the silk pants, and pulled on the jeans, unconcerned that the males watched her. The Henley was long enough to cover everything important.

Dressed, she took the bundle of wet clothes, making a mental note to hang them up when she got back to Neo's, and the jacket. But before she could reach for the boots, Dera dropped them on the floor beside her.

Quinn looked at her in surprise, then froze as she saw the strange look on the woman's face, almost as if she was no longer there. Like an automaton, Dera turned toward her brother, who looked very much the same. Closing the distance between them, they grabbed one another's hands, then turned rigid as boards, their eyes rolling back up in their heads until all that was visible were the milky whites.

"They are seeing the future," Sakamoto said calmly.

Quinn's pulse began to pound as she prayed they were glimpsing the city saved.

One interminable minute passed, then another until, finally, the twins' eyes rolled back down and they blinked and dropped hands. Dera turned to look at Quinn worriedly, but it was Davu who spoke.

"We saw your brother—red hair, yes?"

Quinn's breath caught. "Where did you see him? What—?"

"He set out to save his woman, traveling with one other, a human male. They were...or will be...set upon by vampires."

Quinn's eyes widened. She didn't realize she'd swayed until Kassius grabbed her arm and righted her.

"They are seers, sorceress. What they have seen has not yet come to pass," Kassius said quietly.

"But it may happen soon," Dera warned them. "I'm sorry, Quinn, but our visions now are almost always immediate. Never more than an hour anymore."

Quinn's heart begun to race and she swung to Kassius. "Zack's going to leave Neo's. I have to stop him." If only cell phones worked in this place! She grabbed her boots and pulled them on quickly. "I can't wait for Arturo and Micah."

"Quinn." Kassius frowned. "You have no glamour. And Gonzaga troops could be anywhere."

She rose, her desperation to reach Zack a tidal wave inside of her. "I can't wait." She headed for the door.

Dera joined her. "I'll find a scarf for you to wear around your head to hide your hair. It won't be much of a disguise, but it will be better than nothing."

"Have the men ready to leave immediately!" Sakamoto called. "And prepare..." He turned to Lukas. "Two horses? Three?"

"Three," Lukas said.

Within minutes, they were in the courtyard and Dera was pulling the scarf tight around Quinn's hair. When she was done, Quinn surprised herself by giving the woman a hug. "Thank you."

Dera smiled, but the smile was strained. "Good luck, sorceress. We're counting on you."

The reminder pierced her heart. If she failed to renew the magic in time, they would all die. "I'll renew the magic as soon as I stop Zack from leaving. I won't fail you."

Quinn started toward the small door in the castle's wall, Kassius by her side, Sakamoto, Lukas, and Davu close behind. When she reached the door, Quinn turned to Sakamoto and held out her hand.

"I never thought I'd say this to a vampire master, but it was a pleasure, Sakamoto. I hope to see you again."

The vampire bowed over her hand, then straightened with a grin. "My guards will take their orders from you, sorceress. Use them as you see fit. And when you have saved our world we will hold a feast in your honor, Quinn Lennox. Then you will reveal your heart's desire and it shall be yours."

"Thank you. When Arturo and Micah return, send them after us, please."

"Of course."

They filed through the small door into the steel gray of day. The three horses were already saddled and waiting, the men lining up, vampire-fast, as she watched.

Quinn swung into her saddle, lifted her hand in farewell and took off, Kassius, Lukas, and twenty Sakamoto vampires close behind her.

Zack hadn't been attacked, yet. It would happen in the future. But he might have already left Neo's. For all she knew, her race to stop him, to save him, might already be too late.

Arturo would catch up to her soon, and Micah with his glamour, though the glamouring would have to wait until she reached Zack. She wasn't stopping for anything.

We are in Vamp City, cara mia, *making our way to Sakamoto's. But there is going to be a delay.*

He didn't say more, but she felt it in the fluttering in her mind. Anger. Dismay. He and Micah were in danger, she was certain. Not only from the sunbeams that were breaking through more and more, but from something else. As far as she knew, that could only mean one of two things now that she'd aligned with both wolf packs. Either enemy soldiers.

Or Rippers.

CHAPTER THIRTY

Quinn called to Kassius as their horses galloped over the muddy ground. "Arturo says they're going to be delayed. They've run into trouble, though I don't know of what kind." Cell phones would be so much easier than one-way telepathic communication, but she was glad they at least had that.

She called to the head of the guards Sakamoto had sent with her. "I need you to send half your number to give aid to my companions, Arturo and Micah. They should be somewhere in a direct line between Sakamoto's castle and the Boundary Circle. Hurry!"

The male hesitated only a moment before nodding and giving the order. Ten men peeled off and raced back the way they'd come.

Perspiration rolled down the back of her neck as Quinn turned her full concentration back to reaching Zack, driving her mount faster, frantic to reach Neo's in time. If only she could communicate with Zack as Arturo did her. If only she had a way to tell him to stay put! But would he even listen to her?

He'd been more of a kid than a man when they'd first arrived in Vamp City just a month ago, but that wasn't true anymore. If he chose to go after Lily, there would be no stopping him short of convincing one of the vampires to enthrall him, and even that wouldn't happen without a heck of a fight. And Zack would never forgive her.

No, if he'd finally decided to go after Lily, her only hope was to reach him in time to go with him and, hopefully, keep him from getting killed. Except, she couldn't. Not yet. Not until she renewed the magic and saved V.C. But she could certainly make sure a contingent of vampires accompanied him.

What in the hell was he thinking, taking off with only Jason?

But she knew. If he asked Neo or Rinaldo to go with him, they'd insist he wait for his sister. And he'd obviously decided he was through doing that.

She'd never forgive herself if something happened to him. It was bad enough that she'd gotten him stuck in this place to begin with, bad enough that it was her magic that had somehow triggered V.C.'s demise, tangling him in the magic sickness that was trying to kill him. But if Cristoff got a hold of him, death would be the least of his worries.

"We've reached the Crux, sorceress," Kassius said.

"Savin!" Quinn called.

Before she could warn Sakamoto's guards, nearly a dozen wolves appeared in the distance.

She heard the metallic swish of the guards drawing their swords and lifted her hand. "Put your weapons away. They're allies."

One of the wolves approached, shifting into a man who she recognized as one of Savin's top lieutenants. He eyed Sakamoto's soldiers with hostility. "Can we help you dispel them, sorceress?"

"They're friends escorting us home."

"If they enter the Crux, there will be war. I cannot prevent it."

Dammit, dammit, dammit. She didn't have time for this! And she sure as hell didn't have time to broker a truce between the two factions. Not today. But she was crossing dangerous ground without glamour.

"If I send them away, can you and your pack escort me and my two companions home? It's critically important."

He looked at her, then the samurai, then her again. Finally, he nodded. "But they must leave. Immediately."

"Fine." She turned to the guards. "Send my thanks to Sakamoto, but I am no longer in need of your escort."

"Quinn," Kassius said. "I'm not sure that's wise."

"Sorceress...," the head samurai said quietly. "They are *wolves.*"

"They won't hurt me. Unfortunately, I can't say the same for what they'll do to you. I'll work on that, but not today." She kicked her horse into gear and headed straight into the Crux with a farewell wave to the soldiers. She didn't have time for more.

Within moments, Quinn, Kassius, and Lukas were surrounded by a wolf escort of two dozen running along on either side of them. It amazed her that the horses were as calm about the wolves as they were, but she supposed Vamp City horses were used to just about anything by now.

Arturo, where are you? Are you okay? I wish you'd speak to me! He'd never been able to hear her thoughts, but maybe he'd feel the questions, feel her concern, and reply.

Up ahead, she caught sight of the colorful, sparkling lights of the Focus and was swept with a feeling of terrible urgency to run to it and save this world, and Zack, before it was all too late. To renew the magic before Kassius died, and Sakamoto and the werecat twins, and most of the people she'd come to know and care about in this place.

"Quinn?" Kassius asked, pulling up beside her.

Without realizing it, she'd slowed her mount to a walk. "I need to renew the magic." She turned to him. "Kass, I want you to ride ahead and keep Zack from leaving."

"No, sorceress. Neither Lukas nor I will leave your side until Ax and Micah catch up with us. Let us travel together to Neo's, then we'll accompany you back here."

Never had she been so torn, so desperate to do two things at once. Finally, she nodded, kicked her horse into a full gallop, and continued her race across the Crux. When they reached the edge, the wolves began to pull back, but Kassius called to them.

"She is in need of your continued protection."

The wolf leader howled, giving his own order and the pack raced to catch up with them.

"I'm not sure Neo's going to be happy about us bringing a wolf pack home," Quinn muttered.

"You will be protected," Kassius stated. "That's all that matters."

Quinn nodded. As they continued at breakneck speed, her mind bounced between worry for Zack, and Arturo and Micah. If only Arturo would say *something*, just so that she knew he was all right. If only she'd feel another fluttering in her head, some clue to his emotions. Some reassurance that he was still alive. But she heard nothing, felt nothing, and his silence had a vibrating knot, the size of her fist, forming beneath her breastbone.

Finally the familiar lights of Neo's house became visible ahead and Quinn pulled up, turning to the wolves. "We'll say goodbye here. Thank you!"

As the wolves turned back, Quinn started forward again, riding up to the back door and dismounting. Leaving the horse for someone else to care for, she burst into the kitchen where Mukdalla was washing dishes, Amanda reading at the kitchen table.

"Where's Zack?" Quinn demanded.

Mukdalla looked at her in surprise. "You should have ridden right past them. They were out by the barn watching the sky lighten with sunrise."

"I think he's left. I need to know."

Kassius strode into the kitchen behind her. "There's no sign of them in the yard. Two horses are missing."

"Dammit!" Quinn cried. "Search the house, please?"

As Kassius disappeared, Neo strode in. "What's happened?"

"I think Zack and Jason left to go after Lily."

Neo stared at her, his eyes widening slightly. "I told him to wait for you. They may still be here."

"Kassius checked outside. He's looking downstairs, now."

"I'll look up here."

"I hear Zack's missing?" Rinaldo said, joining them.

Quinn nodded. "Sakamoto's seers saw Zack and Jason going after Lily and being attacked by vampires."

Amanda gasped.

Mukdalla paled. "Where's Arturo? And Micah?"

"I'm not certain. It's a long story. We got separated and they ran into trouble, but I don't know of what kind. I can't wait for them." She whirled toward the back door, wishing she hadn't let the wolves leave. They might have been able to track her brother.

Neo and Kassius returned at almost the same moment.

"I know where they're headed," Neo told her. "Lily escaped a Trader's wagon in the Anacostia Forest three days ago. Word came just a short while ago. Zack overheard and demanded we head out immediately. I told him to wait for you." His face fell. "I'm sorry, Quinn."

"It's not your fault, Neo. He should know better. He has no business out there! He knows what this world is like."

"He is a man, Quinn," Mukdalla said quietly.

"He's my brother."

"Yes, but he is a man, first."

Quinn looked at her, understanding. "I keep trying to protect him. He's been getting tired of it."

"Yes. You love him. But he loves Lily."

Quinn sighed. "I know." She turned to Kassius. "I can't let him die. I have to go after him."

The tall vampire shook his head. "Wait for Arturo and Micah. Please? You have no glamour."

"I can't wait, Kass. I don't know how long they'll be." If they were dead, they wouldn't be coming at all.

The thought gut-punched her and her breath caught on a gasp. She started for the back door.

Lukas was walking in as she crossed the kitchen. "I've saddled three fresh mounts."

Bless Lukas.

"We'll need a fourth," Rinaldo said. "I'm coming as well."

Quinn stopped in her tracks and turned, shooting Mukdalla a worried look. But Mukdalla only slid her arm through her husband's. "He is a fine warrior, my Rinaldo. He's always made me proud. And I am most proud that he rides with the sorceress today, Quinn."

In her head, Quinn heard the echo of Mukdalla's words about Zack. *He is a man.* And men, it seemed, did not take well to being coddled and protected. Dammit, she knew that—logically, at least— even if her heart cried out for the need to protect those they loved, at all costs.

As she looked at Mukdalla and Rinaldo, she was filled with uneasiness. It was daytime, sunbeams breaking through right and left. And while Rinaldo might be a vampire, she'd gotten the impression that he wasn't necessarily a warrior. But it moved her that he insisted on coming to protect her.

She met his gaze. "Thank you, Rinaldo." Then she turned and opened the back door. "Let's go."

CHAPTER THIRTY-ONE

"Rippers," Jason said, his voice low and even.

Zack felt a thrill of excitement go through him even as his body broke out in a cold sweat. He'd been building his strength like a mad man for days. Now it was finally time to see what he could do.

They'd ridden the long way to the forest, avoiding the downtown buildings that Jason said were more likely to hide vampires and other things they'd rather avoid. If they went that way, they'd have to go on foot, and Zack figured riding around the town would be faster than walking through the middle of it. And safer.

But there was nowhere safe in Vamp City, he ought to know that by now. A sentiment proved by the six vampires currently facing them on foot with glowing red eyes. Rippers. They were a different race of vampires than the Emoras. While Emoras supposedly kept their souls when they were changed, Rippers didn't. They'd go after anything that moved, damn the consequences.

Jason pulled a handful of wooden stakes out of his satchel and tossed Zack two. He'd searched Quinn's room for her gun before they left, but she'd apparently taken it with her. Hopefully, he wouldn't need much more than his fists.

One of the vamps blurred, leaping vampire-fast. And suddenly Jason flew backwards off his horse.

Zack's heart seized. But before he could dismount to try to help his friend, he was hit by what felt like a battering ram and the next thing he knew he, too, was sailing through the air and landing hard on his back. The wind was knocked out of him, and as he struggled to breathe, his confidence collapsed, his mind exploding with a barrage of doubts and recriminations.

Why the fuck had he thought he could take on vampires? God, he was such a moron. He was strong, now, sure. In a gym. Against weights, and humans, not fucking vampires! *What the hell was I thinking?* He was going to get himself killed out here, which maybe wasn't such a bad thing. At least Quinn would stop sacrificing herself for him. But damn his sorry ass if he got Jason killed, too.

As the vampire who'd knocked him off his horse grinned down at him with those glowing red eyes, and bared his teeth, revealing long, sharp fangs, Zack reacted with instinct, and anger. Grabbing the vamp's head in both hands, Zack twisted hard, spinning the bloodsucker off him and following, until suddenly he was the one on top. Beside his knee lay one of the stakes that had fallen out of his hand when he hit the ground. Without thinking, he reached for it and shoved it deep into the Ripper's chest.

Red eyes opened wide with shock a moment before the red winked out.

Holy fuck. He'd killed the bastard.

Before he could fully relish the moment, another hit him from behind. But Zack was in the zone, now. He grabbed the head that was already lowering to bite him and flipped this vampire onto his back, too, staking him in one swift, clean move.

The ease with which he was killing the suckers stunned him. He was a freaking vampire slayer!

"Jase?" he called. He tried to see where Jason was, but suddenly the Rippers were coming at him from all directions and it took all of his concentration to focus. Whenever one got near, he slammed his fist into its face or his stake through its heart. Over and over, the bloodsuckers slammed him to the ground. But, over and over, he got up again, ignoring the cuts in his flesh from the fangs that caught on his hands, his arm, and once, his neck.

Dammit, where was Jason? *Don't be dead, Jase. Don't be dead.*

Finally, there were only two Rippers left, but they were a wily pair, circling him with grins on their faces. They didn't seem to care that he'd killed their friends. But then he didn't think Rippers cared about anything but the kill.

Without warning, a wave of strength-stealing lethargy rushed through him. *Oh, hell, no.* Not now, not now.

He stumbled. "Jase?"

Both Rippers hit him at once. He tried to throw them off, and managed to keep them from attaching to his neck, but his muscles were fast turning to putty. He was out of time! If he collapsed like he had before, he'd be dead before he snapped out of it. Killed by Rippers.

Two faces swam in front of his, both with glowing red eyes, both with sharp, lethal fangs. He tried to reach for them, to fight them, but his arms refused to cooperate.

And suddenly, the two were flying backwards, as if someone had stopped the film and played it in reverse.

Before Zack could figure out what happened, his legs gave way and he collapsed onto the ground, the gray sky spinning dizzily above his head. *Shit, shit, shit.* He didn't pass all the way out this time, at least, but pushing himself up took every ounce of strength he had. When his vision finally cleared, he saw that three more people had joined the fray. Two males—vampires, but the speed of them—who were even now killing the final two Rippers. And, on horseback behind them, a woman with a dark braid, a rifle strapped across her back.

Zack struggled to sit up, needing to stand, to be ready to fight, because he had no idea if they were actually there to help him, or just to kill him themselves. But when they turned to him, their opponents dead, he realized that none of the three had the red eyes of Rippers. Which was a mark in their favor, as was the fact that none of them wore the black uniforms of Gonzaga guards. Both males wore jeans, one with long hair and a small hoop in one ear, the other a close-cropped beard. But they might still mean to kill him.

"Who are you?" Zack demanded, pushing to his feet, relieved to feel his strength rushing back in. But even as he asked the question, the bearded one turned and strode away. Not away, Zack realized. Toward something lying in the dirt. A body. But...vampires disintegrated.

Understanding hit him with the force of a sledgehammer. *Jason.*

"Stay away from him!" Zack started running toward the vamp that was kneeling beside Jason's prone form. God, there was blood everywhere, a huge pool of it. And then he saw why. His friend's neck had been ripped wide open.

Zack almost stumbled again, almost sank to his knees because this was his fault. He shouldn't have snuck away from Neo's like a teenager breaking curfew. He should have asked for the help of the vamps. But he'd been so certain they'd pat him on the head and tell him to let them handle it. And, God, he should have. He should have!

The vamp barely gave him a glance. "He's still alive, but barely." His gaze turned to his companions. "He's one of hers, too. We've got to get him to her. Fast."

"Go," said the other male. "We'll be right behind you."

A split second later, the bearded vamp and Jason were gone.

Zack turned on the other male, the shock reverberating through him. "Where's he taking him?" He didn't trust them, not at all. And yet...they sounded like they wanted to save Jason.

"Where he might survive." The male tugged on his earring, eying him with interest. "You're Zack. The sorceress's brother. We've been looking for you."

Fuck. "I don't know what you're talking about."

"Your picture is all over Vamp City."

Zack's eyes widened. There was only one person who would be looking for him, and for only one reason. Cristoff Gonzaga, looking for bait to catch Quinn. Damn him for a stupid, *stupid*, fool! He'd wanted Quinn to quit treating him like a kid, yet he'd acted just like one, running off without the help and protection of the vampires, not only endangering Jason, but his sister.

Stupid, stupid, stupid.

"Are you bounty hunters or something?" he asked sourly.

"No. I am William de Montbray." The vampire to the woman. "My wife, Ana Lucia. You are in no danger from us, Zack. As soon as your friend is delivered to the healer, we'll take you where you'll be safe."

Zack wanted to tell him to take him back to Neo's. But he knew Neo's operation was a secret and he was through being stupid. He wouldn't lead anyone there, or tell anyone who'd been helping him, unless he was positive they could be trusted.

"I want to see Jason."

The male gave a brief nod, then whistled. Two horses came running, one of them the horse Zack had been riding before. Zack mounted one, William the other, and the three of them took off at a gallop.

Lily was out here somewhere. Or she had been. Between the Rippers and the wolves, she wouldn't have stood a chance.

The knowledge sliced through his heart and mind, the pain almost more than he could bear. He was too late. He'd never had a chance to save her. All he could do now was stick with Jason and pray his friend didn't die, too.

CHAPTER THIRTY-TWO

As Quinn, Kassius, Lukas, and Rinaldo raced across the open ground of Vamp City, Quinn realized the sky was becoming lighter than usual. A *lot* lighter. Normally, she had a hard time distinguishing day from night in this place, though she could usually see *something* during the day and, unless there was a moon, almost nothing at night. But, at the moment, the sky resembled a mere stormy day. Not bright, by any means. But *light*.

Her companions eyed the sky worriedly.

"Are you going to be okay?" she asked them.

"We can survive this much light," Lukas said. "But not much more."

"If you start smoking, I'll pull a bubble over us."

The big Swede nodded. "Thank you, sorceress. The magic's breaking down."

"Look at the sky," Rinaldo said.

Quinn followed his gaze to the eastern sky where bright cracks were beginning to appear. Thin, sky-blue lines across the gray sky. A fine panic had begun to spread through her, a desperation tearing at her, pulling her in three different directions—toward Zack, back to Arturo, and to the Focus to save this world and all within it before it tumbled down around their ears.

Her insides had become a quivering mass, her head pounding. The only thing that kept her from splintering completely was the knowledge that she'd sent ten of Sakamoto's soldiers to help Arturo. He'd be fine...assuming they'd reached him in time. And if they hadn't, it was already far too late.

Arturo, if you can hear me, if you can feel me, let me know you're alive. Please? I need to know you're alive. But her mind remained silent but for her own spiraling thoughts.

As she glanced again at the crackling sky, she knew she couldn't wait much longer to return to the Focus. If they didn't come upon Zack soon...

No, fate couldn't be so cruel as to demand that choice from her, that sacrifice. Her brother for the rest of this world, for the vampires and others who'd inexplicably become the best friends she'd ever had.

She'd find him soon, she had to believe that. And she'd find him alive, because the alternative was more than she could deal with.

Kassius pulled up suddenly.

Quinn did the same. "What's the matter, Kass?"

He pointed to the ground, then swung off his horse. "Something happened here. Very recently."

She wasn't sure what he meant until she saw the torn-up earth and the splatters of vampire goo and blood. Then she knew. "A battle." Her hands tightened on the reins until her fingernails dug into her palms. "We're too late."

"It might not be them," Lukas said kindly. "And there are no bodies."

Which meant they might have been captured instead of killed. There might still be hope.

Her head pounded as Lukas and Rinaldo both dismounted, scouring the ground around them.

Rinaldo squatted in front of a dark puddle, reached out and pressed his finger to it, then lifted his finger to his mouth.

Sudden understanding had her going light-headed. The dark puddle was blood. Gripping the reins with nerveless fingers, she urged her mount forward until she could see for herself the huge amount. Dear God.

"It is Zack's?" She barely managed to get the words through the constriction in her throat.

Rinaldo rose, his eyes sad. "No, Quinn. It's not. It's Jason's."

"Heads up!" Lukas called with a quiet urgency that had all of them whirling.

Vampires surrounded them, suddenly, nearly two dozen Gonzaga vamps. By the cruel expressions on their faces, she was pretty sure none of these males were going to suddenly decide to help them.

As if reading her mind, Kassius confirmed, "Cristoff's mercenaries. Several never had souls. The rest are new to Gonzaga, drawn by the depravity. This lot will go for the kill and the sorceress."

"We'll see about that," Quinn muttered. Adrenaline surged through her, and with it, a feeling of power unlike anything she'd ever felt. Always before, pulling up her magic had taken concentration and effort, but thanks to whatever the Black Wizard had done to her...*for* her...my God, it was just *there* in her palms, as if it lived there, now.

She thought of the power, imagined it as a fireball in her hand, and saw it glowing there. Holy cow. She'd played softball in high school for a while and had always had a good arm. And while vampires were fast, she'd developed a sixth sense for which direction they were going to move.

But before she could send her fireball flying, the vampires disappeared in one massive blur. Her heart seized because she knew they were flying at her and her friends from every direction. And without her glamour, they knew exactly who she was. They would try to snatch her and deliver her to Cristoff.

Like hell.

Quinn threw her fireball, somehow hitting one of the Gonzaga guards, then threw up her hands, sending out a powerful blast. No fewer than a dozen vampires flew backward to land on the ground. Unfortunately, her friends among them. She needed to pull the bad vamps off to the side, as she'd seen Arturo do centuries ago through Kassius's memories.

The trouble was, she wasn't nearly as fast as they were. Nor was she a great rider. She kicked her horse, trying to get it to run, but the vampires were all around her and the horse was starting to panic.

Heart thudding, she pulled out her stakes as battle raged all around her, and told herself she could do this. She could track their movements. She knew how to fight them, and she was strong! But there were so damn many of them.

As they closed in on her, she took a stab at one, and missed. And suddenly they were grabbing her, a dozen pairs of hands trying to pull her off her horse in different directions.

With a roar of anger, she sent her magic flying out in all directions and the groping hands fell away, vampires once more flying.

Sweat beaded her brow, her breath coming in short, desperate pulls. Still she heard the sound of battle all around her and knew there would be no rescue from her friends. Not yet. She was going to have to handle a dozen vampires on her own.

I can do this.

Forcing herself to calm down, she pulled fireballs into both palms and threw them, watching with immense satisfaction as one of the vampires went up in flames. Unfortunately, she needed to work on her aim with her left hand. That fireball fell short, snuffing out on the ground.

Two males grabbed her suddenly, one on either side of her mount, both snaring her wrists. Dammit! She kicked out at one, then called up that fury, that power, and sent it flying out in all directions again. Once more, the vampires flew back. If she could keep sending out power blasts, she could hold them off indefinitely. But she wasn't at all sure she could keep it up. She was already breathing hard, sweat drenching her shirt.

Three more times, they came at her. Three more times, she pushed them back. But each time took more out of her. After the third blast, she had to grab the pommel as her head began to spin.

The vampires continued to circle her, watching with greedy, excited eyes and she could only guess at the reward that awaited the man who brought her in and laid her at Cristoff's feet.

A quick glance told her that her friends were still fighting their own battles, taking out their opponents one and two at a time. Each time they dispatched a vamp, more would fly at them.

Her own attackers were now down to five. But the five rushed her again and though she tried, she couldn't call up another blast of power to throw them back. One got a hold of her wrist and pulled her down off her horse and she hit the ground hard.

Quinn managed to wrench away from him and scramble to her feet as they circled her, smiling like cats playing with their prey. But this prey didn't intend to lose.

They rushed her, one grabbing her wrist and wrenching it hard behind her back. She cried out even as she kicked him, twisting out of his hold, but as she tried to lift her hands, both arms were grabbed.

Dammit! Twisting loose, she yanked herself free of them, then kicked out at the first one who flew at her again, knocking him to the ground.

She hazarded a glance at her friends, then wished she hadn't.

Lukas and Kassius, both large, powerful males, were still holding their own with apparent ease, but Rinaldo appeared to be struggling badly. As she watched, one of his opponents knocked the sword out of his hand. Rinaldo dove at the male. But as he did, the other Gonzaga guard he'd been fighting swung his sword hard, catching Rinaldo in the neck.

Rinaldo's head went flying.

"*No!*" Quinn screamed.

Something slammed into the back of her skull. And the lights went out.

CHAPTER THIRTY-THREE

Quinn regained consciousness, screaming.

In an instant, she knew where she was—on her back on the cold marble floor of Cristoff's throne room. Cristoff stood over her, his eyes bright orbs of glowing power and madness, his hand holding the jeweled hilt of the sword buried deep within her abdomen.

Escalla.

Vaguely, through the shattering glare of pain, she saw guards standing at attention around her, though she could barely make out more than their uniforms.

She coughed and her mouth flooded with the warm metallic taste of blood.

Her mind went blank with shock, with disbelief. After all she'd been through, it would end here. Cristoff's prisoner. Once more at Cristoff's mercy. He would kill her without even letting her save Vamp City first.

She tried to lift her hands, needing to push him away, but her arms wouldn't budge. She was paralyzed with weakness, with pain. And when she coughed again, she gagged on the river of blood filling her mouth.

Quinn!

Arturo's voice rang in her mind, filling her with relief that he was alive. And despair because she would never see him again.

A terrible sound began to fill the room, a horrible screech that somehow wailed of triumph and horror, and echoed a madman's cackling glee. The sword. It was Escalla itself making that keening wail.

Her vision spun and she feared she was spiraling down into death.

Then suddenly she was kneeling on the ground beside a boiling lake, the sky overhead dark with storm clouds raked by bolts of lightning. She stared at her hands...no, not hers. *The Black Wizard's.* For one moment she thought she'd somehow become him again, but as she saw what those gnarled old hands gripped—the jeweled hilt of Escalla, which had been plunged deep inside of him—she realized what was happening. She was experiencing his death millennia ago. *Through his eyes.*

She looked up to find another old male hobbling toward her with the help of a cane, a male with few teeth and no hair.

"Levenach," the Black Wizard said, choking on the name of his nemesis even as his slayer, his loyal Nerian, stepped away from him.

"We used to be friends, Remus," Levenach said conversationally. "But with each passing year, your actions have become less and less conscionable until I had no choice but to stop you."

"With murder?" The Black Wizard...*Remus?*...spit out a cup's worth of blood.

"I had hoped it would not come to this."

The Black Wizard struggled to find the strength to form words. "They are fools!"

"They are human." Levenach shook his head sadly. "Fools, yes. Some. But not all. And that does not justify your actions."

"Curse you, Levenach. Curse you!" Even with the blood gathering in his throat and mouth, Remus began to whisper fast and hard, a curse that would strip Levenach of his magic. And while he was at it, strip his heirs of their magic as well.

Levenach shot out his hand, attempting to strangle the words from his throat, but even moments from death, the Black Wizard's power was formidable, and the final words were said. The curse was cast.

The Black Wizard smiled the smile of the damned and spit the blood out of his mouth. "It is done."

Fury turned Levenach's face red. "Then let it be known that any vampire who uses Escalla to stab a wizard with your blood will acquire your power. Your heirs will be hunted to extinction!"

Quinn's vantage point changed, as if she lifted out of the Black Wizard's dying body to stand between the dueling and ancient wizards. From here she got a better view of Nerian, a young-looking, lanky vampire with long, stringy hair and a look of amazement on his face. His eyes were beginning to glow, just like Cristoff's had.

"Neither curse will be broken until the sword is destroyed!" Levenach proclaimed.

The Black Wizard visibly struggled to remain upright. "Only happen...by drinking of power." His voice was barely audible, but Quinn heard him clearly. "And the heart blood of the one..."

Quinn wasn't sure what he meant. But Levenach nodded. "And the one will know."

The Black Wizard fell, collapsing onto his side as the blood ran freely from his mouth onto the ground. "The curse...will never be...broken." His body went still, his eyes remaining open in death.

Levenach stepped forward until he stood over him. "Time will tell, old friend. Time will tell." Slowly, Levenach turned to Nerian. "My curse was added in anger, and I fear it was a terrible mistake. You will greatly abuse the power you've just received."

Vampire-fast, Nerian pulled Escalla from the Black Wizard's body and impaled Levenach on the sword that had just killed his enemy.

Nerian smiled. "I certainly hope so."

Quinn's sight swam and once more she was looking up at Cristoff who was no longer staring at her with mad glee, but with surprise. And confusion. As if he'd witnessed the same scene she just had.

"The one will know," he murmured, confirming her suspicion. His gaze dropped to where his hand gripped the sword that still buried inside of her, pinning her to the floor, then rose back to hers.

She had to be hallucinating, because she could swear his eyes filled with regret.

"*What have I done?*" he asked so quietly that she was certain she was the only one who heard. "I was entrusted with the protection of this sword, so that it would never again be used thus."

She was glimpsing the man Arturo had loved, a vampire who might, perhaps, have been worthy of the love of his son.

But even as she felt the pull of pity, madness rushed back into those still-glowing eyes. The Cristoff she'd come to know and hate began to laugh. "The power is mine!" Still laughing, he pulled the sword out of her with rough indifference that would have had her screaming if she wasn't already choking on her own blood.

Lifting the sword, he made as if to shove it into a scabbard at his waist. He didn't have one. And then, just as suddenly, he did. Out of nowhere, a jeweled scabbard appeared. Cristoff laughed again, shoved the sword home, and strode toward the door of the throne room.

"Come!"

His guards hurried after him, leaving her alone in a warm pool of her own blood, without the strength to move. As she stared up at the high, blood-splattered ceiling, fearing it would be the last thing she saw, Arturo's precious voice caressed her mind, wrapping around her heart, sending tears sliding down into her hair.

Hold onto life, amore mio. *Don't leave me. Hold on.*

But what was there left to hold onto? All those she'd tried to save would die unless

Cristoff had the power...and the will...to renew Vamp City's magic. Perhaps it was better this way. Perhaps Cristoff would succeed where she never had.

The darkness rushed in to claim her, scooping her into its arms and carrying her away, leaving behind the taunting litany of all the ways in which she'd failed.

CHAPTER THIRTY-FOUR

Zack pulled up beside William and Ana Lucia in front of one of the old houses that dotted the landscape of Vamp City, the doppelganger of what had probably been a farmhouse in the nineteenth century.

As William tied up the horses, Ana Lucia motioned for Zack to follow her. "You're safe," she told him, her tone brisk, yet not unkind.

"Are you a vampire?" he asked. He'd seen very few female vamps.

"Human. I've spent the past two years hunting Rippers with William."

"Shouldn't you be a Slava by now?"

"I spent a few months in the real world last year to keep from turning immortal. William and Max are stuck here, but one of William's friends isn't. Micah helps me come and go."

"William and Micah are friends?" Maybe he wasn't in as much danger as he'd feared.

"Yes. You know Micah?"

"Yeah. He's..." Zack clamped his mouth shut, realizing that admitting that Micah was in league with Quinn, the sorceress, could compromise everything if these vamps weren't really who they said they were. "I've heard of him," he said lamely.

Ana Lucia nodded and led him through the front door of the house. There were people everywhere, at least a dozen of them. A couple were Slavas, but the rest looked like mortal humans, freshies, though there may have been a vampire or two scattered among them, including the bearded male, Max.

On a blood-soaked blanket in the middle of the floor, lay Jason, a woman kneeling on either side of him.

The curly-haired blonde in jeans had her back to Zack and appeared to be holding Jason's hand. The other looked like she'd just walked in off the nearest wagon train, her colorless dress long and old fashioned, her hair pulled back tight. When she glanced up at him, he saw that the pupils of her eyes were a stark white, her fangs elongating even as he watched.

"She's a vampire," Zack growled, starting forward.

Ana Lucia stopped him with a hand to the arm. "She's also a talented healer. If anyone can save him, Octavia can."

Zack heard the unspoken stress on the word 'if'. He wanted to hit something, preferably one of the vampires. But this one was on him. Jason's chances were bad and it was all his fault.

As Zack watched, the lady vamp dipped her head to the site of Jason's terrible wound. Zack tensed because how could taking more blood possibly be good for him? Unless she was trying to turn him? Oh, *fuck*, no.

He started forward again, but William grabbed his shoulder. "Let her work," he said quietly.

"Is she trying to turn him?" Zack demanded.

"No."

That was apparently all the answer he was going to get. But even as Zack watched, the lady vamp straightened, replacing her mouth with her hand, pressing her palm to Jason's wound as she closed her eyes. Zack wasn't sure, but he thought he could see light beneath her hand. No, he *was* sure. It *was* light, like her palm had suddenly lit up. What the hell?

None of the people in the room moved. All watched, half of the women with their hands pressed against their mouths or hearts as if they gave a shit whether Jason lived or died. And maybe they did. Jason had lived in enough places in Vamp City over the past year and a half that he probably did know people wherever he went.

The minutes ticked by, but nothing happened. Zack felt sick to his stomach. The back of his head was beginning to pound.

Suddenly, Jason's arm spasmed. All the women and half the men in the room gasped. And then Jason did the impossible...he opened his eyes. Chills skated over Zack's skin and it was all he could do not to let loose a crow of relief.

Jason turned to the blonde kneeling beside him, the one with her back to Zack. His eyes widened, a look of disbelief, of…*wonder*…transforming his usually stoic face. And then the Marine's eyes filled with tears.

"*Heather?*" he croaked.

Zack stared. *Fuck. Oh, fuck,* she was his wife! He felt his own eyes burn all of a sudden and had to look down until he got it under control.

"Am I dead or dreaming?" Jason asked, his voice raw.

"Neither." Heather's voice was thick with tears. "You're safe. We both are."

Zack looked up again just in time to see Jason reach up and pull her down on top of him, tears running down the side of his face into his ears. Zack had to wipe another damn tear from his own eye, but no longer felt like such a wuss for doing so.

As Jason squeezed the bejeezus out of his wife, most of the women laughed, teary-eyed. Half of the males in the room coughed, the other half turning away to wipe something out of their eyes or off their cheeks.

Finally, Jason let Heather go. "Help me up."

Heather looked to Octavia, whose eyes were as damp as every human's in the room.

The lady vamp nodded. "He will be tired for a day or two, but he is healed." And damn if she wasn't right. Zack got a glimpse of Jason's neck and the wound wasn't even visible anymore beneath all the blood.

Heather rose, gripped Jason's hand, and helped him sit up.

Jason looked at her. "What happened?" he demanded, sounding like a Marine again. "Where's Zack?"

"I'm here."

All eyes turned his way. Jason's expression went from hard demand to raw relief when he saw him. But Zack noticed that Octavia was looking at him with surprise and Heather was staring at him with her mouth open.

A chill traveled down his spine. Then again, hadn't William just said that everyone in Vamp City was now looking for him? Hell.

Admiration filled Jason's eyes. "You took down six Rippers?"

Zack snorted. "Four. We'd both be dead if not for William and…" He looked at the bearded male. "Max."

Both males dipped their heads in acknowledgement.

Zack stepped forward, then squatted beside Jason and his wife.

Heather moved back, making room for him. He liked the look on her face, one part joy, one part welcome, and ten parts fierce protectiveness.

"You're Heather," Zack said. "Jason's been going crazy trying to find you."

She smiled, swiping the last of the tears off her cheeks. "I've been going just as crazy trying to find him." She slugged Jason's shoulder lightly. "How many kovenas did you escape from? Three? Four? Every time Octavia and I got a bead on you, you'd left."

Jason gazed at his wife with incredulity, his face breaking into a wide grin. "God, I love you." Right in front of the entire room, he pulled Heather into his arms and gave her a way-too-passionate kiss. Zack shot to his feet, not needing a front row seat for that, and found himself facing the lady vamp, who had also risen.

She was watching him with an odd look on her face. "You are one of mine, Zack."

Oh, fuck, no. His brows drew down. She was claiming him as her slave now?

As if reading his mind, her expression softened. "Not my slave. You have power buried deep within you."

He looked at her curiously. "Levenach."

She smiled with delight. "Yes! Yes, indeed. Before I was a vampire, I was a powerful sorceress. Now I'm a very weak one, but for my healing skills."

"He can't stay here, Octavia," William said, coming to stand beside him. "Cristoff's looking for him."

Zack met William's gaze. "I'm not going anywhere without Jason."

"Jason will be safe here." William paused, his voice lowering. "I would take you to—"

"No!" Octavia cried out suddenly, doubling over as if in pain, as if someone had just stabbed her in the stomach.

Jason and Heather pulled apart and Heather shot to her feet to grab hold of Octavia.

Jason tried rising, too, and began to sway. Zack grabbed him, steadying his friend.

"Octavia?" Heather asked.

"Escalla has just ordained a new king," the lady vamp gasped.

Both William and Max swore. Everyone else appeared as confused as Zack by that comment. A new king?

"Cristoff?" William asked, his voice as brittle as glass.

"Yes." Octavia's sorrowful gaze swung to Zack, sucker punching him. "Cristoff caught the sorceress. The sword has feasted on her blood."

Zack stared at her, not understanding. What sword? Damn Quinn for telling him *nothing*. But the lady vamp's words finally penetrated his skull. *The sword has feasted on her blood.*

"She's not dead." The words shot from his mouth. But the look on the woman's face had his heart suddenly pounding in his chest.

"She dies." Octavia's expression hardened suddenly as she turned to William. "The war begins. To arms!"

William's hand landed on Zack's shoulder. "You'll be safe enough here. Cristoff has what he wants."

Zack barely heard him. His mind had gone blank, like a white board freshly cleaned. "Quinn," he whispered.

Vaguely, he was aware that it was Jason who was holding him up now.

CHAPTER THIRTY-FIVE

Arturo raced across Vamp City on horseback, Micah at his side. His vampire heartbeats, slow as they were, thudded in his chest as his mind roared. Deep inside his head, he followed the magical tracer he'd put on Quinn back when he'd first released her and Zack to the real world, knowing he'd someday come to retrieve her. Back when he'd still thought he might hand her over to Cristoff. Before he'd reclaimed his soul. Before he'd lost his heart.

A lifetime ago. His only need since had been to protect her.

And now he was too late.

If only they hadn't run headlong into Rippers as they'd tried to return to her. The battle had been fierce and he and Micah had come close to losing, but ultimately they'd prevailed, thanks to the timely arrival of Sakamoto's troops.

It was during those last minutes of the battle that he'd felt Quinn's anguish. Then nothing. His own heart had nearly ceased beating altogether in that moment, and might have, if not for the tracer that told him she was still alive.

He'd wondered if she'd been attacked by Rippers, or rogue wolves. But the tracer was leading them straight for Gonzaga Castle and he could no longer deny the increasingly obvious.

Cristoff had her.

Beneath him, the ground began to rumble, the land shaking violently. Even the sky began to vibrate, the tiny cracks of blue shattering the slate gray sky widening.

Dio. The magic was failing fast.

Sunbeams broke through, suddenly, all around them, one not ten feet directly in front. Arturo leaped from his mount, knowing there was no way to stop the horse's stride before it carried Arturo to his death. Even now, pain exploded on every inch of his skin as his flesh began to smoke. He raced back out of the way, but he was unable to go far. The sunbeams bore down like trees in a forest, dozens of them, as far as the eye could see.

"Micah!"

"Here." His friend had escaped as he had. Barely. "I'm smoking."

"As am I." But Arturo could see no path through. There was nothing for it but to wait until the sunbeams winked out, and pray he didn't catch fire in the meantime. Minutes passed, the agony from the searing heat of the light miniscule compared to the pain in his heart. Finally, the light doused and he ran for his mount, standing a few yards away. While he could run faster than a horse, no vampire could maintain that speed for any distance. And he had to get to Quinn.

"Another one like that and it might all crumble," Micah said as they took off again.

Arturo nodded. The two of them might not be stuck in Vamp City, but if the magic failed during daylight, they might well find themselves standing in sunlight. And dead a moment later.

As they reached the edges of Gonzaga territory, Arturo felt Quinn's emotions suddenly, a blast of pain followed by a scream of the soul that was almost more than he could bear. And he knew.

"He's stabbed her with Escalla."

The look Micah turned on him was one of grim horror. But when Arturo would have raced straight to the castle, Micah stopped him.

"The tunnels," Micah said.

"There's no time!"

"Ax! You have no idea what you'll run into. Let's go through the tunnels first. We can assess the situation, then do what we need to in order to maximize our chances of getting her out of there alive."

Everything inside Arturo demanded he go to her without delay, but Micah was right. Arturo changed directions, kicked his mount forward, and raced for the stables. If they drew attention to themselves with such breakneck speed, so be it. He would not compromise speed for anything, not now.

Within seconds of reaching the stables, he was leaping down into the tunnel, hoping to hell Grant had disabled his booby trap. He was dying inside. Never had he felt this kind of pain before. Quinn was his sunshine, his heart, his life. And the knowledge that he was losing her felt like his heart was being ripped from his chest with red-hot pliers.

"Ax." Kassius appeared suddenly in the tunnel ahead. "We have her. Bram's trying to save her, but…"

Arturo's mind seized. "Where?"

Kassius led him to the cave where they'd had their private discussion with Grant…was it just yesterday? Lukas was there, standing to one side, his expression grave. But it was the woman on the pallet on the ground that drew all of his attention.

Quinn.

Arturo flew to her side, watching as Bram worked frantically within her abdomen. *Mio Dio.* He'd stripped her down and opened her up. Arturo could see her internal organs. His friend was performing surgery, having somehow managed to smuggle in what appeared to be a hospital's worth of surgical supplies.

Arturo knelt beside her and took her hand in his, her flesh paler than any vampire's. Her skin felt cool to his touch.

"Bram?" The question caught in his throat.

"I'm doing the best I can, Ax." But when Bram glanced up, his eyes were bleak. "I'm losing her."

Lily woke to the soft sound of crying.

She opened her eyes only a slit, careful not to move, hoping for some advanced warning of where she was and what was going on before she made it known she was awake.

From what she could see, she was in a tiny bedroom. On a stool at the foot of the bed sat a Trader, a woman, by the looks of her. And a heartbroken one, by the sound. Standing behind her, arms wrapped around the Trader's shoulders, was another woman, a petite woman with long, dark, wavy Slava hair.

Lily sat up slowly, aching at the mournful sound of the woman's crying.

Both women looked up, the Trader catching her breath on a sob, then brushing away her tears to find a watery smile.

"Hello, Lily. You're safe here."

Lily watched her a moment, feeling for the truth, and sensing she'd just heard it. "Where am I?"

"Neo's. Neo and I run a safe house for escaped slaves. I'm Mukdalla."

"And I'm Amanda," the Slava said. "Dr. Amanda Morris. I've been treating a friend of yours, I believe. Zack Lennox."

Lily blinked, then gaped at her. "He's not dead?"

Both women looked away, but Dr. Morris's gaze returned to hers quickly, an unhappy expression in her eyes. "He was here just hours ago. Quinn went to find him, but..." She swallowed. "None of them have returned."

Mukdalla's tears once more began to roll. "Forgive me," she said with a wave of her hand. "My husband was with Quinn." She couldn't continue and once more dissolved into sobbing.

Dr. Morris held the other woman tight. "She felt him die," she told Lily.

"Oh, no." Lily's heart began to pound. "The others?"

"We have no way of knowing," Amanda said. "All I can tell you is that *you* are safe, Lily."

"Are Zack and Quinn...were they okay? The last time you saw them?"

Dr. Morris's expression turned professional as she launched into a description of magic sickness and high fevers and Zack's unaccountable muscle gain. "You'll barely recognize him when...when you see him again."

"If I see him again."

Dr. Morris nodded. "Yes."

How was it possible he'd survived? It wasn't fair. For the past weeks, she'd been mourning his death. But he'd been alive all this time, only to go missing hours before she arrived. Hours!

"Why did he leave?" she asked. Had he hated it here?

"Word came about you," Dr. Morris said gently. "He went to find you, Lily. From the day he arrived here, he's been frantic to find you."

Oh, Zack.

"Amanda!" A man's deep voice echoed from somewhere in the building.

"Back here, Sam," Dr. Morris called.

A moment later, a man appeared in the doorway, a nice-looking Slava. "It's happened. Word just came. Cristoff Gonzaga has killed the sorceress."

Lily gaped at him. "Quinn? He killed *Quinn*?"

Sam looked at her with apology. "I shouldn't have blurted that out."

Amanda turned into his arms and buried her face against his shoulder. "No, you shouldn't have."

Mukdalla's hand rose to cover her mouth. "This is a terrible, terrible day."

Sam let out a sorrowful sigh. "I'm afraid it's only going to get worse. There had to have been a hundred sunbeams with the last breakthrough. Blue cracks are erupting all over the sky. It's not going to last much longer."

"Do you think Cristoff will save Vamp City?" Amanda asked. "Do you think he can?"

Sam frowned. "That's the question, isn't it?"

Mukdalla rose suddenly and held out her hand to Lily. "Well, I'm not going to sit around and watch this world and everyone I love die. I can't do anything to stop any of this, but I can take this young woman home." Mukdalla met Lily's gaze. "I can take you back to the real world. Zack will be able to find you there, yes?"

Lily's hands remained in her lap. "I'm not leaving. Not until I know what's happened to Zack." She looked at the three of them. "And even if he's..." She couldn't finish that particular sentence. Her breath caught in her throat, her heart all but shattering at the thought that she'd almost found him only to lose him again, for good this time. "I've heard there's a war coming. A war against Cristoff Gonzaga. I was told that I might be needed to help fight it." The words sounded ridiculous coming out of her mouth, given her petite size and complete lack of fighting skills. But she was only repeating what Octavia had told her. "I'm staying."

Sam and Amanda looked at one another, then turned to her with admiration in their eyes.

Mukdalla's smile bloomed wide, despite the depth of sadness in her eyes. "I like you, Lily Wang. But given how much Quinn and Zack think of you, I knew I would. You're right. There is undeniably a war coming. And if I can't take you home, then I'll be fighting at your side."

CHAPTER THIRTY-SIX

"Have you bitten her?" Arturo demanded. His heart was breaking, his hand stroking Quinn's lovely face, as still and pale as death.

"Twice. Both Kassius and I tried to initiate healing through our bites," Bram said. "Both times her body went into cardiac arrest. I've tried everything, Ax. I think the shock of what was done to her—not just the stabbing, but the ripping away of her magic—was too much. Decide now if you want to try to turn her. She doesn't have much time."

"No. She wouldn't want that." Not if it meant risking her humanity.

Arturo turned to Kassius. "Did you find Zack?"

"No. There was sign of a struggle. A pool of Jason's blood. Too much for him to have lived." Kassius's usually stoic demeanor shattered. "We were ambushed by Gonzaga mercenaries. More than two dozen of them. By the time I could fight my way through, Rinaldo and Quinn were gone."

"Rinaldo, too." Arturo bent his head, his heart shattering for Mukdalla.

"We knew they'd bring Quinn here, but Cristoff wasted no time. By the time we arrived, it was too late."

"Talk to her, Ax," Bram said. "She's a fighter—I can feel her trying to hang on—but she's losing the battle. Help her."

Arturo met his friend's gaze, then turned to cradle Quinn's cold hand between his. That her hand felt cold to his touch was a very bad sign. "Fight, *amore*. Zack is missing. We must find him. He needs you, *cara mia*." His voice broke. "I need you."

He switched to telepathic communication. *You are everything to me, Quinn Lennox. You've given me back my soul, my heart, my purpose. You've given me back the sunshine. Do not leave me,* amore mio. *I beg of you. Do not leave Zack. He needs you. We all do.*

Bram cursed under his breath. "The bastard did everything but twist the knife inside of her."

"Ax, I think you need to bite her," Micah urged. "Or kiss her. *Something.*"

"Not bite," Bram said quickly. "She won't survive it."

"Maybe, maybe not. They're connected, Bram, in ways I can't even begin to understand."

"They're connected..." Lukas stepped forward suddenly, turning to Kassius. "What was it Sakamoto's werecat told Quinn? Something about a soul cord."

Kassius nodded, his expression growing suddenly intent. "Do you remember when you threw the wizard, Ax, then again when you touched Tassard and he fell? The werecats believe Quinn did both of those through you. They believe you've become so connected that she can actually work through you."

Arturo's eyes narrowed. "Tassard? All I did was touch him."

"He said you stole his strength."

His strength. His life? Had Quinn somehow used her death touch through him, enough to weaken Tassard?

His mind leaped. If she could use it through him to attack, maybe he could help her use it to save her own life.

Turning to her, he gripped her hand tightly. "I'm going to try something," he told his friends.

"You can't do any worse than I'm doing," Bram said unhappily.

Arturo stared at her fragile hand in his, wondering how to proceed, where to start. He had no idea what he was doing, all he knew was he had little time.

Releasing Quinn's hand, he proceeded to grip her cold cheeks between his palms. She'd pushed her power through him. Now he needed to coax her power to him. Specifically, her death touch. He needed to share with her his own life force if she was going to continue to live.

The question was how?

Closing his eyes, he found her in his mind, her quiet presence, her silent emotions. A soul cord, his friends had called it. A soul cord. But how to coax her to use her power on him?

He thought of his own gift of *persuasion*, his ability to use low-level mind control on others. He was certain it wouldn't work on Quinn. Not with her sorcerer's gifts. But, then again, it was possible that her magic was gone. Perhaps, if he tried, he could reach her and gain her cooperation even in her unconscious state.

I share my strength with you, amore mio, *but you must take it. You will take it now, Quinn. Feel it flowing into you, strengthening you. Feel the life I would share with you seeping into your body, into your blood and your bones. You will pull that force to you, Quinn. You wish to, for you are hungry for sustenance and it will feed you well.*

He felt nothing. No change, no pull on his energy.

Opening his eyes, he peered at her, desperate for some sign that she was hearing him, that his words were beginning to reach her. But she remained as still as ever. And a quick glance at Bram's closed face confirmed he was making no progress.

Draw, Quinn. Draw on me! You must take what I have to offer. I beg of you, tesoro. *I plead with you to do so.*

But still nothing happened. Crushing despair swept through him, the desolation of certainty that he had no way to save her. His sunshine. For centuries he'd lived without her, believing himself alive, but without being able to see that his existence was cold, bleak. Now that he'd experienced the unbridled joy of love, how was he ever to return to that bleakness? How was he to live without her?

He leaned forward, pressing his mouth to her cool lips, his forehead to her still flesh.

Live for me, Quinn. Take what I offer. Let me share my life with you. My life force.

But still nothing happened. Devastated, he released her precious face and sat back on his heels, taking hold of her hand once more. He looked at his friends and shook his head.

"I don't know how to save her," he said brokenly. But even as he said the words, a strange sensation traveled across his chest. An odd sensation of weakening.

His pulse lifted with hope. A wave of exhaustion swept through him. She was doing it!

"Bella! That's is, *amore*. Drink from me." *Swiftly, fill your depleted body with the sustenance I freely share.*

"Something's happening, Ax," Bram said excitedly. "Her color's coming back. Whatever you're doing, don't stop."

He wouldn't dream of it. *That's it,* bella, *that's it. Drink from me.*

A tingling sensation swept down his torso and limbs. A wave of dizziness washed through his head.

"Ax?"

Drink, tesoro. *That's it,* cara. *That's it, Quinn. Drink from me.*

It was becoming a struggle to hold his head up. Vaguely, he was aware that he was beginning to shake.

"Ax, that's enough." He felt hands on his shoulders. Micah's voice in his ear. "She's looking better by the moment. You're looking worse."

But when those same hands tried to pull him away, he fought like a madman.

Suddenly, his head began to float free of his body. His thoughts disconnected. And black rushed in.

For the second time in one day, Quinn awakened screaming, voices darting all around her.

"She's coming to without anesthesia. Enthrall her!"

"She can't be enthralled."

Still she screamed, the fire in her belly ungodly.

"Kass," Bram said. "Quiet her before she has the whole castle down here. Micah, bite her!"

A belt was gently shoved into her mouth. "Bite down, sorceress." Kassius's face swam in front of hers, indistinct through the raw, slashing pain.

Micah briefly entered her field of vision.

"Dammit, Ax, what did you do?" Bram's voice. "That's it, Micah. She's starting to heal on her own. Shit, I've got to get my clamps out of there before she heals around them."

"Lukas?"

"Arturo's still alive. But barely."

Quinn bit down on the leather until she thought her teeth would crack, the scream strangled, but still pouring up out of her throat.

Slowly, the terrible pain began to drop to a level she could almost survive.

"Uro." The T got trapped by the belt. "Uro!"

Micah reappeared in her field of vision, his countenance clear this time, his eyes terrified as he removed the belt from her mouth. "He's passed out. Quinn, what happened? Something happened. He held your hand and told you to drink from him. Then he collapsed."

The fire in her gut continued to recede, little by little. Her mind was still spinning in a blaze of pain. But she searched for the answer, and a memory whispered.

"My death touch. He called it."

"He gave you his own life force," Micah breathed.

"And I can't give it back! Dammit, Turo." She tried to roll over, to reach him, and screamed.

Micah pressed her back. "You've been badly injured Quinn. You're healing, but it's going to take a little while. Tell us what to do to help him."

"I don't know." Oh my God, he'd given her his life force, his *life*. *Oh, Turo. Forgive me for ever doubting you.*

"Quinn." Micah stared at her, his brows hard together. "At Sakamoto's, when Tassard collapsed, you stole his strength through Ax, but not Ax's. Could you do that again, but give it to Ax, instead?"

She frowned at him. "I don't understand."

"I want you to steal my strength and give it to Ax. Could you do that?"

Kassius moved into her line of vision beside Micah. "Just a little from him, a little from me."

"And me," someone else said. Lukas.

She stared up at Micah through eyes blurred with pain. "I could kill you all."

"No. We won't let you do that. Will you try?"

If it might save Turo? "Yes, of course."

Micah nodded. "Take all you need. Just tell me what to do."

She had no idea. "Give me his hand, then take his other."

Micah looked away, reached for something, and a moment later, Arturo's cold hand pressed against hers. Quinn grabbed hold of his lifeless fingers, her heart squeezing.

Turo, what were you thinking?

Fear swept through her. "I don't know what to do, Micah. I don't know how to save him!"

"Shh, sweetheart. Let's think about this, shall we? Think back to Sakamoto's. Tassard was hurting you. Do you remember that?"

"Yes." She'd wanted that asshole on his knees, and badly.

The trouble was, she didn't want Micah on his. Maybe if she concentrated on what she did want...Arturo saved...

Closing her eyes, she did just that, willing Micah's life force into Arturo. "Let go of his hand the moment you start feeling anything, Micah. I can't be certain how fast it will come."

Seconds later, she heard Micah's, "Whoa."

"My turn," Kassius said.

Quinn struggled to shut out the pain, concentrating only on saving Turo. She continued to pull. "Micah?"

"I'm okay, just…hungry."

"I'm ready, sorceress," Kassius said.

As before, she willed life force to fill Arturo. The hand Quinn held twitched and she gasped. "I think it's working."

"Not enough," Bram replied. "My turn."

"No." Lukas's voice. "You're still wielding scalpels. Let me go first."

Suddenly, Arturo's hand gripped hers in return.

Quinn gasped. "It's working!"

"Ax? Dammit, man," Bram exclaimed. "You scared the shit out of us."

Quinn released Arturo's hand and turned her head to watch as Arturo slowly sat up. His gaze swiveled to her, his dazed eyes clearing as he stared at her, filling with joy.

"*Tesoro.*" He lifted his hand slowly. Cool fingers stroked her cheek. "You live."

"So do you." Tears filled her own eyes. "What did you think you were doing, giving your life for mine?"

He bent over her, covering her lips in the most tender of kisses. "Loving you," he said quietly. "Just that."

Lifting her arms, she curled them around his neck and held him close, deepening the kiss. As his hands stroked her hair, his tongue sweeping against her own, the last of her pain washed away, strength sweeping through her in its place.

"I would say both procedures were a success," Kassius said dryly.

Micah began to laugh. "Hell, yeah."

Arturo pulled away, smiling down at her with such tenderness, sparking such a rush of tenderness in return, that she feared her chest couldn't contain it all. He held out his hand to her and slowly helped her sit up. Belatedly, she realized she was stark naked but for the blood coating her abdomen.

"Any pain, Quinn?" Bram asked, all brisk doctor.

"No. I feel good." She grimaced. "Though clearly I could use a wash cloth and some clothes."

Bram smiled. "That's what post op is for. Even I can't perform surgery through clothing. Lay back down, Quinn, and I'll clean you up, then we can get you out of here."

Bram's words had her noting, for the first time, where she was. The cave beneath Gonzaga. Memory slammed into her with blunt force, making her gasp. Cristoff had stabbed her with Escalla, stealing her power, Zack and Jason were missing, possibly both dead. And Rinaldo.

"Quinn?" Bram asked worriedly.

"*Amore?*"

"Rinaldo." Tears stung her eyes as she met Arturo's gaze. "They beheaded him."

Arturo pulled her against him and held her tight, stroking her hair. "We knew he'd not survived." Kissing her temple he pulled away.

Quinn met her friends' gazes, saw the grief in their eyes. And the hunger.

"He died a warrior's death," Kassius said. The pupils in his eyes had gone white. "It was what he'd always wanted."

"Poor Mukdalla." She ached at the pain her friend would suffer.

Micah's eyes were white-centered with hunger as well, and suddenly she understood. In saving Arturo, they'd depleted themselves. "You need to feed. All of you."

"Not from you," Arturo growled.

"No, not from me. Go. I'm okay."

"Ask any of the Slavas in the tunnels," Bram said. "Lukas, have Deb bring clean clothes and food for Quinn."

Without argument, Kassius, Micah, and Lukas filed out. But she knew Arturo must need blood, too.

"Go," she told him. "Eat. I'm fine."

He hesitated only a moment, then squeezed her hand. "I will not be far."

"Go."

He did.

"Lie down, Quinn," Bram said with cool professionalism once Arturo had ducked out. "Let's get you cleaned up."

She did as directed and he pulled a damp towelette from a plastic package and began wiping the blood off her abdomen. It always twisted her mind to see modern convenience items in this place. Then again, she'd heard him talk of clamps and scalpels, so he'd clearly had surgical supplies brought in at some point.

She tried to keep her mind on innocuous things, but quickly failed, and the thoughts and memories that threatened to cripple her rushed back in. Rinaldo. *Zack.*

"Are you okay?" Bram asked.

"I don't know," she said honestly, tears filling her eyes. "I feel like my emotions are going to crush me."

"You're worried about your brother."

"Yes. And Jason. And Mukdalla." Her chest felt as if it would cave in beneath the weight. How did people live like this?

"Try to think of something else. If you're interested, I have some excellent whiskey upstairs. Alcohol isn't the best answer to most problems, but it's an excellent one in a case like this."

He was right. She had to find a way to put her worry and grief behind a strong wall of denial and leave it there or she wouldn't be able to function.

"Were you the one who stole me out of Cristoff's throne room?" she asked Bram as he continued to clean her up.

"Yes. Once he'd stabbed you, Cristoff left, along with his entire contingent of guards. Those of us whose loyalty has faded slipped away. I grabbed you, brought you down here, and began sewing you up."

"Where did Cristoff go?"

Bram tossed the wipe aside and grabbed another. "I have no idea."

Deb came in carrying clean clothes in one hand and a bag in the other. "I made you a sandwich, sorceress. I hope that's okay."

Quinn looked to Bram. "Doc?"

"As far as I can tell, you've healed, Quinn. Between the magic, the bites Kassius and I gave you, and your own sorcerer's strength..." He shrugged. "If you're hungry, eat."

She turned to the Slava woman. "Thanks, Deb."

The woman smiled warmly, then turned and left.

When Bram was finished, Quinn rose and dressed, then dug into the food. As she ate, she lifted her hand and tried to call one of the discarded towelettes to her, but it wouldn't come. Cold dread trickled through her veins. She closed her eyes and tried to form a bubble around herself, and failed that, too. *Had he taken it all?* No, not all. She still had her death touch.

If only she'd renewed the magic when she had the chance, during that short time she'd had her full Blackstone power. Maybe she still could.

She forced herself to finish the sandwich even though she could barely taste it. When she was almost done, Arturo returned, looking his dashing self once more. He sat beside her, pulling her against him, as his friends returned, one after the other.

When they were all back, Quinn rose to her feet. "I'm riding for the Focus."

"Now?" Micah asked.

Kassius frowned.

Arturo shook his head in quick denial. "No, *tesoro.*"

But she wouldn't be swayed. "I need to renew the magic."

"You don't know if you can, *cara.*"

"Cristoff has probably already headed there to do just that," Bram added.

"We don't know," she told them, her gaze moving from one vampire to the next. "I had a chance to renew the magic earlier and chose to go after Zack instead. Rinaldo is dead as a result. I owe this to him, if nothing else. If Cristoff has already renewed the magic, then I won't be needed. But if he hasn't...or he can't...then I intend to try."

"Quinn..."

The ache in Arturo's voice had her turning to him. "I have to save the ones I can."

"Let's find Zack," he said quietly.

"No. Not now, not yet. The magic is failing and I won't forsake everything, and everyone, for him. Not again."

CHAPTER THIRTY-SEVEN

They rode back to Neo's, Micah in the lead, Kassius and Lukas bringing up the rear. Arturo and Quinn rode in the middle, sharing one mount. Arturo had not been willing to release her, even to ride.

He brushed his jaw against her silken hair, the scent of sunshine filling his senses. Glamoured again, she didn't look like herself, but she smelled as she always did and felt as perfect as always in his arms as she leaned bonelessly against him.

She was tired, exhausted. But he knew she fought sleep, her mind and heart in turmoil. Her emotions pummeled him—the terrible grief, the fear for her brother, the crippling anger at her own failures. Worse, by far, were the moments when her emotions eased off, moments that were growing longer and longer. Because he knew what she was doing—slowly, brutally, trying to lock away her heart once more. She didn't want to feel the terrible pain, he sensed that clearly, and he understood. But the only way she knew to escape it was to retreat back behind her walls, to stop caring. And that was the last thing he wanted for her, because behind those walls she would find only isolation and loneliness and a place where love would never reach. A place he could not go.

"What do you think Cristoff will do with his newfound power?" Lukas asked. "Nerian was said to have subjugated a large part of the human world, but that was millennia ago. I'm not sure any vampire could manage that, not with the firepower humans possess these days."

None of them answered, for none of them had any idea. Cristoff had been the most powerful vampire in Vamp City before he came into the Black Wizard's magic. The thought of what he might become had the ability to terrify.

"Levenach is actually the one who gave Nerian all that power," Quinn said sleepily. "And, Cristoff, for that matter."

Arturo slid his hand up and down her arm. "By creating Escalla?"

"No." Her fingers rested on his forearm. "The sword didn't automatically convey the power to the wielder. Levenach added that tidbit out of spite."

Micah glanced back. "Did you learn that from the Black Wizard's memories?"

"No. At least, not when he and I shared a body. When Cristoff stabbed me, I was briefly transported back to the day Nerian stabbed the Black Wizard. I don't know if it was memory or vision, but Levenach was there."

Arturo met Micah's startled gaze. "We would hear this story, *cara.*"

"Sure. Oddly enough, the two old wizards used to be friends. Levenach and Remus. But in his latter years, Remus, the Black Wizard, lost all patience with the human race, and much of his conscience. Some of the things that he did out of spite and annoyance were truly horrific. Levenach lost patience with Remus and decided he had to die. He enlisted the aid of Nerian, the Black Wizard's trusted vampire friend, to stab him with the enchanted sword. The Black Wizard was furious, of course, especially when he realized it was Levenach who'd put Nerian up to it. Impaled on Escalla and dying, the Black Wizard cursed Levenach and his heirs, stripping them of all their magic. That so enraged Levenach that he uttered the counter curse that any vampire who stabbed Remus or one of his heirs with Escalla would acquire his incredible power. He guaranteed that any vampires who came into possession of Escalla would immediately begin searching for sorcerers to stab, hoping to steal that power."

"He wanted the Black Wizard's line hunted to extinction," Micah murmured. "And he's come close to succeeding."

Quinn nodded, her hair brushing his chin. "They were just a couple of angry old men with far too much power."

Arturo looked at her curiously. "Did either of them reveal how to break the curse?"

"Yes...I think? I remember Levenach saying that neither curse would break until Escalla was destroyed. The Black Wizard added that it would only happen by drinking the heart blood...and power, I think...of the one. I'm not sure what that means."

"Who's the one?" Micah asked.

"I don't know," Quinn said. "I hope to hell it's not me. I don't think it is. Levenach's last words were, *And the one will know.*"

Arturo's hold on her tightened even as his brows drew together. The meaning was no more clear to him than it was to Quinn.

They were almost to Neo's when the ground began to shake, though not quite close enough to make it in time. As one, they pulled up. Arturo held his breath, praying none of them stood within a sunbeam when the light broke through.

Quinn straightened in her seat, partly pulling away from him. "I'm trying to call up a bubble," she said with frustration. "But I can't do it!"

Light suddenly exploded all around them. Arturo's flesh began to sting, but, thankfully, none of the sunbeams stood within ten feet of their little group.

"Damn," Micah muttered. "They're everywhere."

As far as the eye could see.

"Hold on," Arturo told Quinn, then dismounted to stand in the shadow of his mount. His friends did the same, leaving Quinn, alone, in the saddle. Without warning, she cried out, bending over as if she'd been stabbed all over again.

Arturo lunged for her, fearing she'd been shot, or that her injury hadn't healed. But before he could pull her off the horse, Lukas groaned, lifted his hands to his head and doubled over as if he, too, were in excruciating pain.

In the next second, chaos erupted all around them. Vamp City all but disappeared. Arturo stared, stunned at finding himself suddenly standing in the lobby of a modern D.C. hotel, his companions and their mounts around him. The horses were quickly losing their nerve and he grabbed the reins of two of them as, all around him, humans screamed, falling to their knees, writhing on the floor, in as much pain as Quinn and Lukas.

Mio Dio! Had the magic failed? Was Vamp City gone? But, no, neither Kassius nor Lukas was dead, though when he turned, he saw, with horror, that Kassius was trapped within the frame of a leather armchair as if he'd been welded *inside* of it.

"Kass!" Micah had grabbed the reins of the other two mounts and had been struggling to calm them. Now his horrified gaze turned to Arturo. "He's part of the chair."

"We have merged," Kassius said through gritted teeth. "I can't move."

As the horses became increasingly agitated, Arturo plucked Quinn off her mount and held her close against him. In his arms she was tense as iron, her suffering pummeling his mind and heart. Of all within his sight, only he and Micah appeared to be in no pain.

Belatedly, it occurred to him that it was dark. Though it was still the middle of the day, there was no daylight filtering in from the windows, and no electricity lighting the hotel lobby. To a human's eyes it would appear pitch dark.

"Turo," Quinn gasped. "He's doing this. Cristoff."

And suddenly it was over. Without warning, they were back in Vamp City, the hotel, humans, and sunbeams gone.

"What the *hell*?" Lukas gasped, straightening.

In Arturo's arms, Quinn went soft, the terrible tension leaving her body in a rush. The horses settled. Kassius fell to the ground, his lower body...crushed. Absolutely flattened.

"Kass." Micah ran for their friend.

Quinn pulled from Arturo's hold. "He needs blood."

"*Cara.*" She was not long recovered herself. But she went to Kassius, kneeling beside him and offered him her wrist.

Kassius's pained gaze met Arturo's as he took Quinn's proffered arm. "Don't let me take too much." Then he sank his fangs into her flesh.

"I thought the magic had failed," Micah said as they waited for Kassius to feed. "For a moment, I thought we were in the real world. But it was dark, and it shouldn't have been."

"So what happened?" Lukas asked.

"The two worlds merged," Quinn told them from where she knelt beside Kassius, her wrist fastened to Kassius's mouth. "This was Cristoff's doing. I felt him, I felt his glee in the suffering." She shook her head as if uncertain if her words made any sense.

Arturo was all too afraid they did. He looked at Micah. "You didn't feel any pain."

His friend's eyes narrowed. "Neither did you."

"No. And unless I'm mistaken, neither did Kass, at least not until he merged with that chair. Somehow Cristoff protected his own."

Kassius's body healed, quickly returning to its natural form.

"Kass, that's enough," Arturo said, laying a hand on his friend's arm. "We'll get you back to Neo's and find you more blood there."

His friend released Quinn's wrist and tipped his head back with a shuddering sigh. "I won't need more for awhile. The sorceress's blood replenishes unlike any other." His gaze found Quinn's and he smiled. "Thank you."

Quinn returned the smile. "Any time."

Micah started to help Kassius to his feet, but Kass held him back and rose without assistance, if slowly. "You were correct. I felt no pain until the chair and I suddenly shared space."

"I sure as hell did," Lukas muttered. "I haven't felt anything like that since I was human."

Arturo reeled as the ramifications hit him. "If Cristoff can cause even a vampire agony, he'll demand fealty from every single one. And he'll get it."

Quinn's gaze met his, her expression ominous. "He's only been a sorcerer for a couple of hours and he's already figured out how to pull the real D.C. into his world. Not just a copy, as Blackstone did. He's more powerful than we can even begin to conceive. And far, far more dangerous."

CHAPTER THIRTY-EIGHT

Quinn gave a sigh of relief as they rode into Neo's yard a short while later. She wanted her vampires safely inside where the sunbeams couldn't hurt them. The beams had broken through once more on the way home, but not nearly as close as the first time. Her nerves wouldn't take much more of this. Arturo and the others were taking their lives in their hands every time they walked outside during daytime, now.

Of course, the magic could fail at any moment, and then most of them would be dead.

As they neared the house, Quinn frowned at the sight of Sam and Neo in the yard, each aiming a gun at a naked man. A very tall, very buff, naked man. A male she recognized from Savin's werewolf pack.

She glanced at Arturo. "I need to talk to him."

"Caution," Arturo said quietly. Then he dismounted and waited for her to do the same.

"What's going on?" Quinn asked as she approached the small, tense group, Arturo and Micah close behind her.

To her surprise, the werewolf bowed to her. When he lifted his head, he was smiling. "We believed you dead, sorceress. Not even the Black Wizard survived Escalla. I am very glad we were wrong."

"How...?" She shook her head, clueless how news could have traveled so quickly in a land without cell phones. "It was close, but I made it through." She turned to Sam and Neo. "Please drop your weapons. He's one of Savin's."

Neo met her gaze, his eyes wary. But, slowly he did as she asked and Sam followed.

Quinn turned back to the werewolf. "If you thought me dead, why are you here?"

"Savin bade me bring word to Arturo. Cristoff Gonzaga stands in the Focus, more than a hundred vampires guarding him. We have overheard the talk of his guards and believe that he is not attempting to renew the magic of Vamp City, but to create a new world of his own. One in which all will know pain."

Quinn's mind swam with horror.

"*Dio,*" Arturo breathed.

Neo swore. "So that's what happened. I felt like I'd been cleaved in two."

"Cristoff has acquired the magic of the Black Wizard," she told them. "He has more power than we can conceive of, including the ability to create worlds."

They all fell silent as the ramifications of that hit them.

"A world of pain," Sam said, clearly stunned.

"He'll enslave thousands," Neo muttered. "And every one of us, mortals and immortals alike, will serve him either with our loyalty or our agony." He turned to the werewolf. "How close is he to succeeding?"

"He has assured his faithful that when the midnight hour comes, so too shall his new world." The male's gaze turned to Quinn, then Arturo. "He must be stopped. He cannot be allowed to succeed. But the wolves cannot stop him alone."

"You will not have to," Arturo assured him. "Though your help would be welcome."

The werewolf nodded. "The sorceress has the loyalty of both Savin's pack and the Herewood." He turned to her, that genuine smile lighting his eyes again. "All will rejoice at your survival."

"Thank you," Quinn said.

Arturo began to outline a plan. "We'll need every possible fighter, but the vampires will be at risk until dusk. Watch for the armies amassing at the edges of the Crux a couple of hours before midnight. I'll make sure all know you are allied with us."

The wolf nodded, then turned back to Quinn with a quick grin before he shifted back into wolf form and took off.

Almost immediately, Quinn found herself enveloped in Neo's hug. "We thought he'd killed you," he breathed, pressing his cheek to hers.

"I'm okay," she assured him, returning the hug.

As he released her, Sam took his place, hugging her tight. Finally, she faced them both, her chest aching. "I'm afraid I have terrible news." But even as she said the words, she noticed the grief still thick in their eyes, a grief that couldn't be for her, now that they knew she was all right.

"Zack and Jason?" Sam asked tightly as if waiting for another blow.

"We didn't find them." And clearly they hadn't miraculously turned up back here. Her heart twisted. She hadn't realized how much she'd hoped that might be true until that hope was dashed. "No. It's Rinaldo."

"We know," Sam told her. "Mukdalla felt his passing the moment it happened."

Quinn sighed, unaccountably relieved that she didn't have to be the one to break the news to the woman she'd begun to consider a good friend. "I have to speak to her."

Arturo squeezed her shoulder and she let him pull her against his side. "I must go. We'll round up all the warriors we can from the other kovenas, and it will take time."

Quinn turned in his arms, cupped his face with her hands, and kissed him soundly. "Be careful."

Arturo kissed her temple. "Sleep. You must sleep, *amore mio*. Neo, make certain she does." With a last kiss, he turned and strode back to the horses, Micah beside him. Kassius and Lukas were still mounted.

Quinn lifted her hand in a wave as the four took off, then walked with Neo back to the house while Sam remained on watch. She *was* exhausted, made even more tired by the thought of facing Mukdalla and her terrible grief. Quinn's heart ached for her friend.

"How's Mukdalla doing?" she asked Neo.

But before he could answer, the back door flew open revealing Mukdalla's distinctive, broad shouldered form silhouetted by the light. The Trader woman rushed down the stairs and enveloped Quinn in a hug that nearly stole her breath.

"Thank goodness, thank goodness, thank goodness," she crooned. "Oh my, Quinn. We thought you'd perished. One of Neo's fae acquaintances stopped by only a short while ago with the terrible news that Cristoff had stabbed the sorceress." She suddenly pushed

Quinn to arm's length, studying her. "You're not even injured?"

"I was. Bram performed surgery. And Arturo..." She didn't want to get into all of it. "Arturo refused to let me die."

Mukdalla's eyebrows shot up. "Did he turn you?"

Quinn gaped at her. "Into a *vampire?*" She shot an apologetic look at Neo. "No offense."

He grinned at her. "None taken."

Quinn turned back to Mukdalla. "I'm still human, still a sorceress, though it appears that Cristoff stole most of my magic." She grabbed the other woman's shoulders. "Mukdalla... We were ambushed, completely outnumbered. Rinaldo fought valiantly, but..." Her voice caught. "He shouldn't have been there. None of us should have been. If I'd renewed the magic when I had the chance..."

Mukdalla gripped her hard in return. "Don't ever blame yourself for this, Quinn Lennox. Never, ever. In war, there are always choices, often none of them good. My Rinaldo died in battle, protecting the sorceress. That you were captured anyway doesn't take away an ounce of my pride in him. He died fighting for what he believed in, Quinn. That was always his wish." Releasing Quinn's shoulders, Mukdalla took her hand and pulled her toward the house. "Now, come. I'm not the only one who will be thrilled to see you alive."

As Quinn followed her into the kitchen, she noticed someone sitting at the small table, a petite dark-haired woman who even now was rising and flying around the table toward her.

Lily.

CHAPTER THIRTY-NINE

Quinn felt the tears running down her face as she fell into Lily's arms, as much joy that the girl was here as bitter sorrow that Zack wasn't. They clung to one another, both in tears, each unwilling to let the other go. Finally, Quinn pulled back, brushing away the moisture on her face with both hands.

"I can't believe this," Quinn said, wiping her tear-stained hands on her jeans before gripping the younger woman's hands. "How did you find Neo's?"

"A vampire brought me here." She shook her head. "It's a long story."

"I know. Aren't they all?"

"Is Zack really alive?" Lily's eyes welled up all over again. "At least...he was? I thought... I know he was chosen for the Games."

"He was rescued from the Games. We were both set free, but he insisted on coming back to find you." That might not be the whole truth—Zack had been ill from magic sickness. But at the time he'd believed he was going to die either way and had insisted on returning to Vamp City to see Lily one more time. He hadn't believed himself capable of saving her. Not then.

Lily pulled her hands free to swipe the tears off her own cheeks. "And now he's missing." She swallowed. "I couldn't believe it when I got here and they said you'd both been here just yesterday. Then someone came and told us the sorceress was dead. I'd just found out you *were* the sorceress. Oh, Quinn. That is *so* cool."

Quinn began to laugh because that had been Zack's response when he'd first learned she had power, after she'd spent her entire life hiding her weirdness from him.

"I don't know how cool it is," Quinn said, pulling Lily back into her arms. "I'm not sure I'm even still a sorceress. But I am so glad to see you."

Lily hugged her until she almost couldn't breathe. "How did all this happen, Quinn?"

"Long, *long*, story."

"Which she will tell you later, once she's slept," Neo announced. "Arturo's orders."

Lily pulled back, understanding in her eyes. "Once we find Zack, and are safe, and have had time to grieve and process everything, we'll talk. About everything."

With a sigh, Quinn nodded. "Agreed. Now, I really do need to sleep."

"Go," Lily said. "I'm fine here."

Quinn smiled and turned to leave, but as she reached the doorway, she nearly ran into Amanda.

"Quinn!"

Once more she was enveloped in a breath-stealing hug. She laughed. "I'm okay. I'm okay!"

"*Thank God.*"

"Let her sleep, Amanda," Neo said. "She can fill us in on what happened later."

"Of course." Amanda grinned at her, squeezed her hand, then let her go.

After four hours of solid sleep and a quick shower, Quinn made her way back upstairs to find Mukdalla, Amanda, and Lily at the kitchen table, an empty bottle of red wine sitting between them.

Mukdalla, it was clear, had been crying. But when she saw Quinn, she motioned her to join them.

Amanda pushed a full glass of wine her way. "This one's yours. Drink. Doctor's orders."

Quinn smiled, gave Lily a quick hug as she passed, then took the empty chair and picked up the glass.

"I want to hear everything, Quinn." Mukdalla's puffy eyes were as strong as any Quinn had ever seen. "If it's not too hard for you to tell, it won't be too hard for me to hear. Traders process emotions differently than humans. We don't love any less, at least not some of us. But, let's just say, we're better able to compartmentalize. And right now I need to *know*."

Quinn considered that, then nodded. Taking a sip, she began her tale, leaving nothing out. She told them about finding Jason's blood, about the ambush. She glanced at Mukdalla before she continued, but that steely determination to know everything remained, so Quinn recounted every detail of Mukdalla's beloved husband's final battle.

They were all crying by the time she got to the end of the story.

Amanda lifted her glass. "To Rinaldo. To all the men we love, and to the courage to love them despite all risks."

"Hear, hear," Mukdalla said quietly as she lifted her own glass and took a sip.

Quinn merely played with the stem of hers as she stared into the rich red depths of the liquid. "How do you do it?" She looked at Amanda. "You could have escaped Vamp City, returned to the real world, to your practice. Instead you gave up everything, you gave up your *life*...for Sam."

Amanda's smile was quiet and sure. "Sam *is* my life."

Quinn frowned and turned to Mukdalla, the words tumbling out. "Why did you let Rinaldo go with me?" If only she hadn't. If only Rinaldo had stayed here.

Mukdalla's smile was sad. "I didn't let him go, Quinn. I simply loved and supported the man he needed to be. His accompanying you, protecting you, was a gift of the heart that he needed to give."

"All any of us can do is what we think is right," Amanda added. "Zack—"

"Had no business leaving," Quinn said heatedly. "He didn't stand a chance."

"He did what he thought was right." Amanda's hand curved around Quinn's forearm. "He's young, Quinn. He's in love and impulsive. He'd been told a hundred times that he needed to wait until he was strong enough before he tried to find Lily. Well, he's now as strong or stronger than any human alive. He had to do this, don't you see? He had to try to save her even if, as it turned out, she didn't need saving."

At the sound Lily made, Quinn turned to find the girl watching them with confusion and an aching hope in her eyes. "Zack and I are just friends. At least...that's all I've ever been to him. He's not in love with me."

Mukdalla patted the young woman's arm. "Whatever the emotions behind his actions, he's been desperate to find you since he first got here, Lily."

"Quinn," Amanda said, drawing her attention once more. "Your brother is a man, now. He couldn't sit on his hands forever, letting you risk your life over and over to save and protect him. It's remarkable he waited as long as he did. To his credit, he waited until he had a good idea where to look for her. Love drove him to risk all for her. Just as you've risked all for him many, many times."

She was right. As hard as it was to hear, she knew Amanda was right.

"Love means taking risks," Mukdalla said. "It's what life is all about." She set down her wine glass and leaned forward, her eyes earnest as her gaze met Quinn's. "Sometimes we risk for the ones we love. Sometimes it's the loving them in the first place that's the gamble."

"Zack's my brother."

"It's not Zack I'm talking about. Arturo loves you, Quinn. You must know that. And I think you're hesitant to love him back. Yes, you'll eventually lose him, either to his death or your own someday. It is the nature of life for all creatures. So we live and love as if every day is the only one we'll ever have. And when you live that way, when you love that way, there is no room for regrets."

Quinn didn't reply. She didn't have a reply because she wasn't at all certain Mukdalla was right about Arturo loving her. Except, what did he say in the caves when she demanded what he thought he was doing, giving his life for hers? *Loving you. Just that.*

She'd heard him, but in that moment, his meaning hadn't registered. And now...

She shoved to her feet. It was more than she could deal with right now.

"Where are you going?" Mukdalla asked.

"I need to get to work and figure out what kind of magic I still possess. I'll be in the storeroom. When Arturo returns, send him down, please. We're going to need every advantage we can get tonight."

CHAPTER FORTY

Sweat dampened her brow, frustration boiled in her gut as Quinn focused on the single can of beef stew sitting on the floor of the storeroom deep below Neo's. Once more, she tried to call it to her with her mind. Once more, just like every other one of the hundred times she'd tried this in the past two hours, she managed to lift it into the air only to watch it hover six inches off the ground for half a dozen seconds, then drop with a clatter to the cement. It refused to come to her! And regardless of how angry she got, she couldn't throw it against the wall. At least not with her mind alone. Her arm was another matter. Six cans now lay broken, their contents splattered across the bricks. If there was any good news, it was that she still had the physical strength she'd acquired with her power. She hadn't lost everything. Just almost everything.

She was about to pick up a seventh can and slam it against the wall when Arturo appeared in the doorway.

Her heart gave a kick of joy at the sight of him, her body warming in the way it always did at the sight of him. And he was a vision to behold, with his lean, athletic body, and those dark eyes watching her with softness and hunger.

"Is it safe to enter?" he asked, his mouth kicking up into the charmer's smile she'd seen far too little of lately.

Quinn gave a huff. "About the most damage I can do right now is chuck a can at you. Although, at two hundred miles an hour, you'll want to duck."

His smile broke into a grin, then quickly died as he seemed to sense her unhappiness. He walked to her. "The magic is gone?"

"Not all of it, obviously. I apparently still have my death touch. But, when it comes to the rest…" She demonstrated by raising one of the cans six inches. "That's it." The can clattered to the floor. "I've managed to form a couple of small bubbles, but they pop almost as quickly as I create them." Desolation engulfed her. "It's gone, Turo."

He stepped close, cupping his cool palm against her cheek. "Several times you've managed to work magic through me."

"The soul cord." She eyed him curiously, then turned and pointed to the can that had fallen to the floor a moment ago. "Let's see if you can lift that."

"Tell me how."

"Just stand there. I want to see if I can do it through you."

His expression turned to one of bemusement. "Do you not have to be touching me?"

"I don't know." Her gaze met his. "Let's try it this way first."

Arturo nodded and turned to the can in question. A moment later, it lifted, as before, and suddenly began to float calmly to his hand. His delighted gaze flew to hers, making her laugh.

"You did that?" he demanded.

"Through you. We both did it. We've developed a soul cord, a powerful connection."

"We have, *tesoro*. I can speak in your head, and feel your emotions."

"I'm starting to feel your emotions, too."

His eyebrows lifted in surprise. Then excitement lit his eyes. "Try something else."

Quinn smiled. "All right." Closing her own eyes, she concentrated on a bubble forming around the two of them. Then concentrated some more, but not even a fragment appeared. "This is going to be more complicated. I think we're going to have to do this together."

He took her hands in his. Long, cool fingers wrapped around her own. "Tell me what to do."

Quinn met his gaze. "I need you to help me concentrate. Focus on creating a bubble around just the two of us."

"One I can enter and exit at will," he added with a lift of the brow.

Quinn snorted. "Your bubble, your specifications. Ready?"

With a brief nod, he closed his eyes and Quinn did the same. Almost at once, she could feel something happening. "It's working," she said excitedly. And suddenly she was enclosed in a dark space. Together, they'd called it as easily as she had yesterday. Unfortunately, her perfect bubble was also perfectly dark.

She released Arturo's hands and attempted to call a light into her palm, but nothing happened.

"Turo, let me see if I can form a light in your hand."

"That might not be a good idea, *amore*. Vampires and fire do not mix."

"It's not a real fire…I don't think. Actually, I have no idea. Okay, no flame."

She felt Arturo's hands on her hips, pulling her closer. "We are very good together," he said, his voice husky and very, very pleased.

Quinn chuckled. "Apparently so. Now let's…"

Arturo bumped into her. "Quinn?"

"What's the matter?"

But she felt the brush of the rubbery surface against her shoulder and understood. Oh…shit. "The bubble's collapsing." Just as it had that first time, when she'd accidentally trapped Savin. Reaching out, her hand sank into the wall but refused to penetrate. "You forgot to specify that I can lead us out. I hope *you* can."

But a moment later, Arturo's words confirmed her fears. "I cannot. Quinn…" He pulled her close against him.

"I know, I know." That other time she'd nearly suffocated before she'd figured out how to break free. And she still had no idea how she'd done it.

The bubble pressed at her back and the top of her head. She knew it was collapsing, but after all the two of them had been through these past hours, she refused to believe they'd die like this.

"Quinn!"

"Let me think."

"I'm trying to make it bigger," Arturo growled. "Tell me what to do. You will not be able to breathe!"

"Okay, stop and clear your mind."

"*Cara*…"

"I know! We have to work together." She'd learned a lot about how to manipulate bubbles since that first one. She just had to figure out how to do it through Arturo this time.

"Turo, listen to me. Clear your mind and listen to my voice."

His hands pressed at her back. "I am listening," he said tersely.

"Imagine the bubble is made of dust. Nothing substantial. On the count of three we're going to imagine it dissipating. Both of us together. One, two…three."

She imagined the bubble bursting into nothingness. And suddenly they were free, once more standing in the storeroom, an oil lamp flickering in the corner.

Quinn stepped back, needing some distance, some air. She stared at Arturo, wide-eyed. "No more bubbles."

He reached for her hand, pulling her into his arms, and kissed her thoroughly, as if he'd been terrified he might lose her. That he still was. And it was a fear she shared, that tonight's battle might well end in disaster for one or both of them. She found herself wrapping her arms around his neck, clinging to him. She never wanted to let him go.

He gathered her even closer, reading her emotions, knowing them. Her senses swam in the feel of his strong body against hers, in his rich scent of almonds, and in his unique taste, one that always made her think of dark liqueur and darker nights, lush and crystal clear. His strong hands roamed her back, and lower, one pressing her against the thickness of his arousal. Those clever hands found the hem of her shirt and quickly removed it, then unfastened her bra and dispensed with that, too. And then his mouth was on her breast and she was gasping, her fingers digging into his hair at the exquisite feel. She wanted this, *needed* this. She needed him.

"Turo," she breathed when he tugged on her nipple, laving it with his tongue.

Even as his mouth remained locked on her flesh, his gaze rose to hers, his pupils white with hunger. She felt the prick of fangs against her flesh.

Her fingers ran through his hair, tracing the strong lines of his skull. "I want to know what it feels like if you bite me there."

Shall I show you?

"Yes."

I would like nothing more.

He pulled back. As his gaze found hers, she saw that his fangs had almost entirely elongated.

"I'll take only a little blood," he assured her, but she wasn't the least bit worried. His bite wouldn't hurt. He would, quite literally, die before he hurt her. Odd to think that, to *know* it.

With his gaze locked on hers, he pulled back his lips and sunk his fangs into her breast, one on either side of her nipple.

At first, the sensation felt a little strange, a little ticklish. Then he closed his mouth around her breast and took a small pull of her blood.

Quinn gasped, then moaned as heat roared into a living flame deep within her core. She began to pulse low inside.

Did you enjoy that?

"Do it again."

The eyes he turned up to her were nothing short of wicked as he took a second pull of blood from her breast. She cried out this time, the pleasure so intense she could barely breathe.

"I need you," she gasped. Whenever he pulled on her neck, she invariably came. But this was different. Though the feel was every bit as intense, it instead set up a powerful hunger between her legs, a need to be filled that was almost more than she could bear. Her hips began to rock, her legs moving restlessly. "Turo...*now.*" She grabbed him by the upper arms and pulled him to his feet.

For a startled moment, he stared at her, then began to laugh. "I keep forgetting your strength, *amore mio.* I will give you exactly what you want but you will have to wait a moment." He disappeared in a vampire flash, blurring back and forth. Moments later, he was again at her side, sweeping her into his arms. Then he carried her back to another section of the storeroom, one she'd never been in, where there was a stack of more than a dozen blankets and quilts, open wide, one on top of the other.

"Did you just do this?"

"Of course. I would not make love to you on the bare cement floor."

Quinn grinned. "We'll probably sink so deep into it that we'll need help getting out."

To her surprise, Arturo didn't return her smile, but watched her, his eyes achingly serious. Lifting his hand, he stroked her hair. "I would give you a palace if I could, *bella.* A palace in the sun with floor to ceiling windows and a view as far as the eye can see. I'd give you pristine white beaches and I would lay with you in the surf in broad daylight. So many places I would take you if I could. But I am a vampire. And we are about to go to battle for our worlds, if not our lives. A bed of blankets in the storeroom will have to do."

Quinn stroked his cheek, unaccountably moved by his words. "I've seen enough of palaces to last a lifetime. This is perfect."

His lips turned up and he kissed her, long and passionately, tightening the need inside her even more. She grabbed for his belt and began to undress him as he removed the last of her clothes.

Finally, he swept her up and laid her in the center of the stack of blankets, then followed her down, sliding deep inside of her on a thick, powerful, *perfect* stroke.

Quinn cried out, rising to meet him with a hard thrust of her hips. Hunger roared through her and their lovemaking turned hot and frantic, a desperate attempt to claim every scrap of beauty and pleasure they could before the world came crashing down upon their heads.

Arturo lifted just enough to watch her as he drove into her, his eyes once more dark-centered, though just as hungry as before. In those dark depths she saw such tenderness, such adoration, that her eyes began to film and she had to blink back the moisture. Somewhere inside of her, she felt his emotion, a piercing sadness, and she was suddenly filled with the certainty that he was saying goodbye.

Closing her eyes, she pulled away from that well of sorrow, immersing herself instead in the sensation, in the heat, meeting him thrust for thrust until they were both climbing, racing toward the sun, exploding into a million heat-filled pieces each one of which floated slowly back down through the air.

Arturo collapsed on top of her, then rolled slightly until he was only half on her. The blankets rose all around them and she did wonder how they were ever going to fight their way out again. But for now she was content to lie within Arturo's strong arms, against his now-warm body, and pretend they didn't have to worry about whether either of them would survive the night.

After a time, Quinn looked up to find him watching her with deep, fathomless eyes. She stroked his jaw. "Were you successful in enlisting the aid of the kovenas?"

"For the most part. Of the four Kassius and I visited, three have pledged full support. One, Borzilov, is aligned with Cristoff and refuses to move his kovena against him. But I do not believe he'll send troops to fight with Cristoff."

"What about the other four?"

"Micah and Lukas were not yet back when I came to find you." He turned to her, his dark gaze grabbing hold of hers. "I want you to go home, Quinn. Now, before the battle begins."

"What do you mean...home?"

"D.C. Farther than D.C. Perhaps California. Or Japan."

She opened her mouth to argue, but before she could form words, he continued.

"Take Lily. When the battle is over, I will search for Zack. If I find him, if he's well, I'll set him free."

Quinn shook her head. "I'm not leaving."

"You must." His expression was suddenly as intense as she'd ever seen it. "I want you to be happy, *cara*. I want you to find a man you can love, one who will walk with you in the sunlight and give you babies with beautiful green eyes."

"Turo." She stared into his dark, determined gaze, her own emotions a hopeless tangle. "I'm not leaving. This is my battle, too."

"You have lost your power."

"Not all of it. I still have a little, more when we work together."

Frustration ignited in the dark depths of his eyes. "I will have no time to concentrate on your tricks, Quinn, not in the middle of battle. I will be consumed with saving all of our lives. I do not want you there to distract me."

Her *tricks*? She understood he only wanted her safe, but his word choice annoyed her. "Tough." She rolled away from him, fighting her way out of the blankets to stand. As she dressed, she glared at him. "I'm not leaving, Vampire. And you damn well better not try to make me."

He rose from the bed with annoying ease and slid into his own clothes, vampire-fast. She could feel his frustration, see his anger. "You will get yourself killed. For what? In all probability Zack is already dead."

His words were razor sharp, meant to hurt, and they did. Quinn fisted her hands, longing to slug him.

"You want to know what I'm fighting for?" she asked, pulling her shirt on over her head. "Do you want to know?" But before she could tell him, her world exploded in a single mass of excruciating pain. An unseen noose tightened around her throat, cutting off her air.

CHAPTER FORTY-ONE

Arturo leaped to his feet, racing to Quinn. He wasn't sure what was happening until, suddenly, a male in some kind of maintenance uniform appeared in front of them, clutching at his throat much as Quinn clutched at hers.

The worlds were merging again. *Dio.* What was Cristoff doing? Scaring them? *Suffocating* them? He'd kill them all!

"*Tesoro,* open your mouth. Let me see."

Her struggle, her terror, flayed him alive, but she did as he asked even as she struggled for air. But he could see nothing, no blockage, nothing for him to tear away or battle against.

He didn't know what to do! But of a certainty, he couldn't stand here and do nothing. Sweeping her into his arms, he ran through the underground, leaping over half a dozen more humans who'd suddenly appeared, humans all in the throes of strangulation. Racing up the stairs, he found them everywhere. But scattered among them were his friends—Mukdalla, Neo, Lukas, Amanda. The immortals were suffocating just as completely as the humans. And while they would take longer to die, no creature could live indefinitely without air.

Something hit the roof. Then something else. Again and again, as if the sky were falling on top of them. Or humans.

"Ax!" Micah made his way to him, his eyes almost as wild as those struggling to pull in air. "*I don't know how to help them.*"

Around them, the thrashing was beginning to fade as one by one, the victims lost consciousness.

Quinn's eyes were round with terror as she stared into his. Her hands clawed at her throat, then began to slacken as he felt her losing her own hold on consciousness.

"*Cara,* you must hold on. Hold on!"

Suddenly, she gasped and took a deep, lung-filling breath.

Arturo nearly sank to his knees in relief. He pulled her tight against him, cradling her, treasuring her. Belatedly, he realized the humans who'd suddenly appeared had disappeared again, just as quickly.

His friends, too, were again beginning to breathe.

"Lily!" Quinn cried.

Micah turned, then lunged for the girl who had apparently fallen unconscious. But even as he reached her, she began to gasp and cough, slowly opening her eyes.

Quinn sank against him, her arm curved around his neck, her head tilting against his as relief softened her body. "You can put me down."

His chest was still tight from having nearly lost her. Again. "I would rather not."

She pulled back, a smile softening her eyes, and she kissed him lightly. "You would slay all my dragons."

"Always. But one in particular."

Her smile died. "Cristoff. I felt him again."

He set her on her feet, but kept one arm protectively around her. "Explain."

"I'm not sure I can. Just as I'm starting to feel your emotions, I've been feeling his. Ever since he stabbed me. It's almost as if, in taking my magic he formed a connection between us. Heaven knows, I don't want a soul cord with *him.*"

"What did you feel?"

"This time, confusion. Then a rush of elation. He enjoyed our suffocating, but I don't think he meant for it to happen. My guess is that he's not in control of his power, yet. He's learning what he can do, largely by trial and error."

"He's powerful," Mukdalla said brushing off her skirt.

Quinn nodded. "And he's barely scratched the surface."

"God help us all," Neo muttered.

Sam strode in the back door and made a beeline for Amanda, pulling her tight against him.

"Clean up?" Arturo asked.

Quinn looked at him with confusion.

Sam shook his head, his face ashen. "They're gone."

"What are you talking about?" Quinn asked.

Sam's gaze moved from Quinn to Arturo, and back again. "The worlds merged on this side this time. But only the people. Not the buildings they were in."

In his arms, Quinn jerked with shock, swaying. He saw the horror in her eyes, felt it, as she realized that thousands had just lost their lives and hundreds more probably lay broken and dying. When the worlds merged, and their multi-story buildings disappeared beneath them, they'd fallen, many undoubtedly to their deaths.

"We have to help them."

"They're gone, *cara*. They returned to D.C."

She clung to him for several minutes more, one arm wrapped around her middle as if trying to breathe around the blow. Slowly she straightened and turned to face him, her eyes glowing with righteous fire and fury.

"You wanted to know what I'm fighting for, what I would risk my life for. This. Stopping *this*. Stopping *him*."

Deep within that connection they'd formed, within the core of her fury at Cristoff, he felt her courage and protectiveness rearing up like a lioness's to surround all those in Neo's kitchen. And more. Many more. That need to protect and save extended outward to all those in Vamp City. To all those suffering and dying in D.C.

She would protect the world, both worlds, from the monster that was his father. Her heart, so long closed, had opened wide enough to embrace a multitude.

He wondered if it was yet wide enough to embrace him.

"Ax," Kassius said, striding in the back door. "The wolves have arrived."

"How many?"

"Both packs. Most of the wolves in V.C." When every male in the room shot to his feet, Kassius held up his hand. "They've set up a perimeter around Neo's to protect the sorceress."

Arturo frowned. "I told them to wait for us in the Crux."

Kassius's gaze turned to Quinn. "The old legend is spreading through V.C. like wildfire."

"What legend?" Quinn asked warily, hoping he didn't mean the one that claimed that sorcerer's flesh empowered the wolf that ate it. That one had nearly gotten her killed.

But Kassius was referring to another. "The tale of the Healer and the Snake and how, together, you will save the world," he told them. "Savin has informed me that his wolves will follow the two of you and no others. Nor will they follow one of you alone. Legend says that together you will fight. Only together will you win. And wolves are nothing if not superstitious."

Quinn turned to Arturo, flashing green eyes now lit with fire and satisfaction. Her mouth turned up in a savage smile. "I'm not leaving. End of discussion."

And though the thought of her anywhere near that battle, especially with her magic all but gone, turned his blood and bones to ice, he knew she was right. He'd never stop her.

And the truth of those words just made him love her more.

CHAPTER FORTY-TWO

"How are we going to stop Cristoff?" Jean-Luc Oubre, asked. The powerful vamp was one of five vampire masters now sitting around Neo's kitchen table along with Quinn, Arturo, Kassius, Micah, and the werewolf Savin.

Poor Neo, Quinn thought. For decades he'd kept his house and operation a secret. Now half the vampires and virtually all the werewolves in the city were either in his house or prowling the perimeter of his yard.

The vampires had been arriving over the past hour from all over the city—five kovenas, so far. Word had spread quickly that the wolves were the first to pledge fealty to the Healer and the Snake and now none of the vampires wanted to be the last to do the same. Most of the vampires now resided in Neo's basement where they were safe from the sunbeams. Unfortunately, there was nowhere for any of them to hide from Cristoff's attacks of pain and terror.

"Tassard may have an idea," Sakamoto said, glancing back at the youthful-looking vampire who stood against the wall, listening, with half a dozen others including Lukas and the werecat twins. "Tassard was alive in the days of Nerian, the only other vampire to drink of the Black Wizard's power through Escalla."

Tassard stepped forward, a different man from the indolent, brandy-sipping jerk who'd nearly ripped her throat out. Why he'd changed so drastically in a matter of hours, Quinn didn't know, though she suspected the threat Cristoff now posed had shaken a few manners into him. Though only a few.

"I know for a fact that Nerian could not be killed by any of the usual methods," he told them now. "For nearly four centuries we tried. Not until his own queen stabbed him with Escalla did he die."

"And Nerian's queen did not acquire his power, oui?" Jean-Luc Oubre asked.

"She did not," Tassard said, glancing at Quinn, the hint of a smirk in his eyes telling her he hadn't changed much after all. "The only way to acquire the power of the Black Wizard is by thrusting Escalla deep into one of the wizard's heirs."

Quinn glanced at Arturo, saw his mouth hardening, and knew they were both thinking the same thought. The Black Wizard had only been stabbed once, because he'd died from his wound. Quinn had not. And while all of these vampire masters had, presumably, reclaimed their souls, even honorable men were known to succumb to the lure of great power.

On the one hand, as strong as Cristoff now was, the chances of him losing his prized sword—and her being stabbed with it a second time—were exceedingly low. On the other hand...

"We will have to steal Escalla and wield it against Cristoff if we wish to stop him," Arturo said, clearly attempting to turn all thoughts back to the conversation at hand and away from the potential of any of them claiming that power for himself.

The back door opened and Sam stuck his head in. "Fabian Neptune's kovena has arrived."

Quinn met Arturo's gaze with dismay. After their last experience with Fabian, she'd be happy never to see him again.

"I can't fit another sixty vampires in my house," Neo said, standing in the doorway, his eyes a little wild.

"Of course we can fit them," Mukdalla said, patting his shoulder. "We'll pack them in like sardines, if we have to. The sunbeams are breaking through too often now to let any of the vampires remain outside. Thank the heavens most of the basement exists in both worlds."

They'd discovered a half an hour ago, during the third convergence of the two worlds, that one wing of the basement was solid dirt in the D.C. world. Fortunately, only vampires had been in that space—about a dozen of Sakamoto's contingent—when the worlds converged. For nearly five minutes, they'd been buried alive, but they'd survived, though not without a thoroughly renewed sense that Cristoff must be stopped at all cost.

"There's still room in the stables," Micah said. "They're light tight. There's also the safe house. It's not far."

"The safe house," Neo said with relief. "That's where we'll put them. The windows have all been blacked out. They'll be all right there."

"I'm happy to lead them," Sam said. "But they're insisting on seeing the sorceress, first, like everyone else."

Though at first it bemused her that the vampires all insisted on offering her fealty, Quinn was beginning to realize that her surviving Escalla, as well as being one of the main players in the legend of the Healer and the Snake, had turned her into something of a miracle to the inhabitants of Vamp City.

Quinn rose. As she headed for the back door, Arturo, Micah, and Savin fell into step behind her. They were her constant shadows, now. Neither Arturo nor Micah fully trusted the other vampires, fae, or wolves, including Savin, though they did seem to appreciate his show of support.

Arturo opened the back door before Quinn could reach for the handle, and she stepped out beneath a sky that had the hair rising on her arms. The cracks that had, at first, appeared blue had turned bright red, as if the sky were beginning to bleed, turning the daylight reddish-orange, making her think of the End of Days. It was as if the fires of Hell pressed in from the other side, threatening to break through at any minute.

As they started across the yard, Quinn found herself tensing, not because of the vampires—or wolves, for that matter—but because of the constant threat that the earth might rumble again. If it did, she might be able to form a bubble big enough to at least save Arturo and Micah, but only if Arturo was within reach.

The sunbeams had been breaking through far less than before she was stabbed—only one since the last pain world appearance. Whatever Cristoff was doing, seemed to be having an effect on the crumbling of Vamp City. But no one knew if that was a good thing or bad.

Far to the back of the house, a group of some sixty vampires stood stiffly, held at bay by dozens of wolves. At the front of this latest group to arrive stood an unassuming male of average height, his body past its prime, his head bald but for a thin salt and pepper fringe that hung nearly to his shoulders.

Fabian Neptune, one of the most powerful and dangerous vampires in Vamp City, watched her wolves with a wariness that almost made her smile. That pleasure-feeding bastard had come damn close to raping her while she and Arturo were 'guests' in his palace.

Quinn turned to Arturo, keeping her voice low. "Do we really trust him?"

"Presumably, he, too, has reclaimed his soul, *cara.*" Which, she noticed, was neither a yes nor a no.

As she and her companions neared the wolves, the animals parted, making way for them. Savin was the only one of the wolves who'd remained in human form and he now wore jeans, at her request. His second-in-command, still in wolf form, fell into step beside Micah. This show of alliance had become ritual as each of the kovenas arrived.

A rumble of voices slid through Fabian's group, drawing the attention of their master. Fabian's gaze turned to her, his expression softening with a mix of gratitude, admiration, and a startling, aching, regret.

"Sorceress." Fabian sank to one knee as she approached, dipping his balding head. Behind him, every one of his vampires did the same. Slowly, Fabian looked up, and in his eyes, she saw a stranger. Gone was the brittle sharpness of a dangerous cunning. In its place, she saw a warmth and compassion she could hardly credit. While he had, at first, looked like the same man she'd met before, he didn't now. Not at all.

"Forgive me," he said. "I am most ashamed for the way you were treated in my palace. The vampires you met there, myself included, were not ourselves." In his eyes, she saw a pain she would never have thought he could feel. "The things I did…" He shook his head slowly, that pain becoming so acute that she found herself hurting for him. "I only thank the gods that I did not harm you unduly while you faced the danger that was my kovena at that time. I do not expect you to forgive the Fabian you met that day. I certainly will not. But I hope you will open your mind and heart to the friendship and loyalty *this* male would offer."

He held out his hand to her, his eyes hopeful that she would take it. Yet in those surprisingly compassionate depths, she saw only gentle understanding should she rebuff his offer. How could this be the male who'd callously drained a Slava of all her blood before tossing her empty body to the floor?

Five times before this today, she'd welcomed vampire masters—

all wise, all powerful, all showing her a surprising honor, warmth, and occasionally, humor. Sakamoto, she'd met before. The others—Jean-Luc Oubre, Raoul von Essen, Zegher Geert, and Phillip York—she'd been introduced to only today. But this was the first time she'd met one whom she'd known previously to be a bastard.

Was it possible that Cristoff, too, could make such a transformation? She knew Arturo deeply hoped so, or at least he had before Cristoff had gleefully stabbed her and become as terrifyingly powerful as Nerian.

Quinn took the vampire master's outstretched hand. "It's a pleasure to make your acquaintance, Fabian."

Warm eyes filled with relief as he pressed his lips to the back of her hand. "You have my unswerving loyalty, Healer. And my undying gratitude." In his eyes, she saw an emotion that welled up from deep within his heart and he said quietly, "You gave us back our souls."

Giving in to impulse, she squeezed his hand. "Stand before me, Fabian. You and your vampires."

Still holding her hand, Fabian did, rising with vampire grace, but human speed. They stood eye to eye, she and Fabian. Leaning forward, she kissed his cheek.

"Friends," she said. The unspoken qualifier hung in the air between them. *Unless you prove otherwise.*

Fabian grinned, leaned forward and kissed her on both cheeks in return. "My queen."

Quinn laughed. "Just call me, Quinn. Sam will show you to the farmhouse where you'll be safe from the sunbeams until dusk. It's not far."

Fabian dipped his head with a smile. "Healer...Quinn."

As Fabian and his vampires turned to follow Sam, Arturo's hand slid beneath her hair to cup the back of her neck. "Well done," he said, for her ears only.

She cut him a glance. "I'm becoming a diplomat after all."

He grinned at her, his eyes were infinitely soft. "You acted from your heart, *cara*. And you took measure of his. You saw past the face of a man you had reason to hate, to the truth of who he is now. And you responded to *that* person instead, to that soul. More, far more, you felt the pain of his regret and opened your heart to him, easing his pain, and in doing so, likely formed an alliance that will never break."

"All that?" Though her words teased, her heart swelled from his praise.

"All that and more, I suspect." He pulled her against his side.

As they walked back to the house, Quinn marveled anew at the situation she found herself in. They called her the Healer. They revered her for giving them back their souls. Yet all she'd really done was set in motion the crumbling of their world when she'd moved into D.C., accidentally triggering the destruction of the magic of Vamp City when her own cursed magic became tangled in it.

Then, again accidentally, she'd begun to initiate the healing of the vampires' souls by attempting to renew the magic, the first time at Cristoff's demand, the second time to save her brother. She felt as much Destroyer as Healer. Fortunately, they saw only the latter.

How was she either? She felt as if she were once more wearing glamour and they were all paying homage to a person who didn't actually exist. The real woman, Quinn Lennox, was just a lab tech at the National Institutes of Health in Bethesda, Maryland, just a normal woman, if a bit weird at times. She liked to run, was a halfway decent cook and a better baker, and enjoyed sports. Now they were calling her sorceress and Healer, treating her as if she were their savior.

"Another group arriving," Sam called.

Arturo turned, then nodded, his hand on her shoulder.

"Who is it?" she asked. His vampire eyesight was so much better than her own, though she could see far better than usual thanks to the added light.

"Bram and his group." He made a sound of surprise. "Grant and Sheridan Blackstone are with him."

Quinn groaned.

Arturo squeezed her shoulder. "They've surely seen what Cristoff has in mind. No one wishes to live in a world of constant pain, even if they've been spared the actual suffering. And Cristoff may or may not have spared the Blackstone brothers." He turned to her, his gaze as deep as the oceans and as turbulent as a storm-tossed sea. "I wish you would stay here, at Neo's, when we go to war. The wolves will protect you."

"You know I can't do that. We're going to need the packs on the front lines. And however little magic I possess now, I may still be able to help. If nothing else, they seem to believe that only you and I together will prevail. They need to know I'm behind you."

Resignation and pride filled his eyes in equal measure as he took her hand and tucked it against his heart. "Not behind me, *tesoro*. Beside me. The Healer and the Snake, though perhaps we can come up with a better name for me? I find myself less than delighted with the term."

Quinn smiled. "What shall we call you then? The Lion? The Bear?"

"Perhaps just the Healer and her vampire?"

"*My* vampire?"

His eyes ignited with a fervent fire and an emotion that nearly took her breath away. "Always."

An answering emotion bloomed inside of her so strong, so overpowering, that she felt as if her chest might burst from the strength of it. She hadn't wanted this, had struggled against it, but she knew now that the battle for her heart was lost.

She'd fallen head over heels in love with a vampire.

CHAPTER FORTY-THREE

"Let's get inside before the sunbeams break through again," Quinn said to Arturo. Micah had walked out to meet Bram and she was confident the wolves would let them through without any trouble.

But as she turned back toward the house, her hands exploded in a burst of pain. Damn Cristoff for creating a pain world! If he succeeded in making it stick, she might suffer like this for the rest of her life. They all might, except for Cristoff's chosen few.

All around her, the others—vampires, wolves, and Slavas, alike—began shouting, crying out, dropping whatever they'd been holding.

Arturo grabbed her hand and she screamed, his touch like fire.

Snatching his hand back, he apologized profusely. "I thought I might be able to help you carry the pain."

"No," she gasped.

"I am sorry, *bella*. So very sorry."

"It won't last." She hoped.

Suddenly the real world flashed in and out, then in again and stayed. Once more, the worlds had merged on the D.C. side. A street suddenly appeared right where they were standing and if not for Arturo's vampiric speed, they'd have been crushed as two vehicles, two ambulances, slammed together in a horrendous crunch that was echoed elsewhere, over and over and over.

The street looked like a war zone, or the aftermath of a massive genocide. In the grass, all around, lay shroud-covered bodies. *The victims that had fallen from the upper stories earlier.*

Dear God.

Now those who attempted to help were dying, too, the drivers of the rescue vehicles suddenly unable to touch their steering wheels and losing control. Across the street, in front of a line of row houses, a group of close to a dozen people stood screaming, holding their hands out from their sides. As Quinn watched, a car suddenly jumped the curb and plowed right into them.

"Oh, God." Quinn lifted her burning hands in front of her face, not wanting to see. There had been children among them!

Arturo lifted Quinn and deposited her in the entryway of an apartment building, relatively safe from runaway cars. "I have to try to help those I can."

"Yes. Go."

Micah joined him and a moment later they were lifting away the car as if it were made of cardboard. Kassius, Bram, and some of the other vampires were pulling people from vehicles, trying to save them.

The screams of hundreds, of thousands, pummeled Quinn's ears and tore at her heart. This had to end! Cristoff had to be stopped.

With a sudden, dizzying flash, the worlds separated again and Quinn found herself standing near Neo's back door, the pain in her hands quickly fading to nothing.

Back by the stables, Bram gave a frustrated yell. "I almost had him breathing again!"

Suddenly the ground began to rumble, an earthquake worse than any they'd felt before. Instantly, vampires flashed past her, into the house, seeking safety.

Quinn remained outside, Grant coming to stand beside her on one side, Mukdalla and Lily on the other as sunbeams erupted *everywhere*. Quinn felt herself pulled through one, back into the real world, back into the scene of chaos and carnage she'd just left, though one now lit by the afternoon sun in a sky once more blue. It was somehow worse seeing it this way. From the Vamp City side, she'd almost been able to believe the real world hadn't been affected. That it was all just Cristoff's malevolent magic. But seeing the blood and bodies in the bright sunshine, she could no longer doubt that both worlds were suffering, now. The real world by far the most.

Stunned, she turned stiffly toward the nearest column of shadows and walked back into the red twilight world of Vamp City. This time she was careful to dodge the sunbeams, though it was difficult to do. Rarely could she find a path three feet wide between them and often the path became blocked altogether. Finally, she gave up and stood still until the sunbeams disappeared again, praying Vamp City didn't disappear with them.

Finally, it was over, but Quinn remained where she was, in shock.

Lily came to stand beside her. "Are you all right, Quinn? Do you want to sit down?"

"No. To both questions." Slowly she turned to Lily. "I knew it was real. I knew it was happening on both sides, but..."

Lily took her hand and squeezed it. Quinn clung to her friend's hand, the woman whom she'd once thought of as her future sister-in-law.

Vampires began to join them—Arturo and Micah, Kassius, Bram, Lukas, and Neo. A strong arm went around her waist, but she barely noticed.

"Look at the sky," someone said.

"It's getting worse."

Above them, the red lines ran every which way, three times as many as there had been before.

"His attempts to form his world are hastening the destruction of Vamp City," Kassius murmured. "If he fails, most of us will die. If he succeeds, most of us will long for death."

"He's close to forming it," Quinn told them.

Arturo's hand gently squeezed her waist. "Are you inferring this from the growing length of time the worlds are remaining together? Or do you know in some other way?"

"I felt his euphoria, his satisfaction, then his frustration when the worlds parted again. But his frustration wasn't deep." She turned and met his gaze, though it was an effort to move. She felt...heavy, as if everything she'd just seen weighed on her shoulders, pressing her into the ground. "I think he knows what went wrong and knows how to fix it so that the worlds never part again."

"We have to concur, sorceress." Davu and Dera, Sakamoto's werecat twins, strode into their midst, joining their discussion. "We just had a vision. The next time Cristoff merges the two worlds, they will not part again. His pain world will be complete and we will all be trapped within it—humans, vampires, mortals and immortals alike. D.C. and V.C. joined, at last, in misery."

Quinn stared at the two of them, her pulse accelerating. "You told me you never see visions more than an hour before they happen."

Davu's mouth compressed, his eyes tightening with unhappiness. "That is correct."

Shit. Quinn whirled toward Arturo. "We have less than an hour to stop him. We can't wait until dusk."

Bram gaped at them. "We can't mobilize in daylight! If the sunbeams breakthrough again, we're all dead."

Micah shrugged. "Better dead than slave to a madman."

Lukas nodded. "I agree."

Arturo met her gaze, his eyes as grave as she'd ever seen them. "We leave at once."

"Another group arrives!" Sam yelled.

"More vampires?" Quinn asked. Maybe one of the two kovenas who'd declined to mobilize against Cristoff had changed their minds.

Arturo's hand gripped her shoulder, suddenly, flexing, as the rest of his body turned strangely still. She couldn't see that far, so glanced at him worriedly until she saw the small smile begin to lift the corners of his mouth.

The wolves parted suddenly to reveal a small group of people, men and women alike, dressed more like western settlers than warriors, except for the two males and one female on horseback bringing up the rear. At their head, strode a woman of confident bearing. Beside her a powerful-looking man with a crimson face and a shock of shaggy red hair.

CHAPTER FORTY-FOUR

"Zack." Quinn stared at him, relief that he was whole, and alive, making her legs weak.

Beside her, Lily moved first, racing forward.

Zack froze in his tracks. "Lily?"

Even from a distance, Quinn heard his voice and the wonder that thickened it. The incoming group stopped. The entire yard went silent, all apparently aware they watched a miracle unfolding.

Tears burned Quinn's eyes. Arturo's arm went around her shoulders as he pulled her close, understanding.

Zack stared at the woman running toward him, unable to move. His feet turned to lead. His heart began to thud, his mind stunned as he watched the tears running down her cheeks, as if she were almost as glad to see him as he was to see her. His arms opened of their own accord even as he told himself he was reading too much into her enthusiasm. She'd probably just stop in front of him and smile at him. But even if that was all she did, his world would be complete. She was alive, alive, alive! The word thudded in his head with the pounding rhythm of his heart.

Lily was safe.

To his surprise, his joy, she didn't stop in front of him. Instead, she ran right into his arms, her slender body plowing into his, her arms reaching up to encircle his neck, and before he knew what he was doing, he'd lifted her like she weighed nothing and was twirling her around, his cheek pressed against her damp one. She smelled so good, felt so damn right in his arms. Alive. *Alive.* Without a doubt, this was the most perfect moment of his life.

"You're okay," she breathed against his ear. He should probably let her go, but he didn't want to, he didn't want this moment to end.

"I was going to rescue you," he whispered. "But you didn't need me."

She pulled back and he set her down, thinking she wanted to move away, that being in his arms must feel kind of awkward to her.

But instead of stepping back, she kept her arms hooked around his neck, forcing him to lean forward a little, which was more than okay with him. She stared at him and she was so damn beautiful with tears spiking her lashes and her eyes sparkling and glowing like the prettiest gems.

"You goof," she said with a laugh that sent bubbles fizzing all through his chest. "I've always needed you. You're the only one I've ever wanted."

Zack stilled, staring at her with confusion. "*Me?* Why would the most beautiful girl in the world want me?"

"Oh, Zack. Don't you know how much I love you? How much I've always loved you?"

He just stared at her, because he couldn't have heard her right. Or maybe he had, but she didn't mean…

He felt a nudge at his shoulder.

"This would be the time to kiss her, man," Jason said quietly behind him.

Zack stared down into that shining face and knew that was all he wanted to do…all he'd ever wanted. Still stunned that this was happening, he bent even lower as Lily raised up on tiptoe. As their lips touched, as Lily's fingers slid into his hair and tears ran down her cheeks, as his heart flipped end over end, he knew *this* was the most perfect moment in his life.

Quinn stepped forward slowly, not wanting to break the spell, but needing her own reunion with her beloved brother.

She came to a stop a dozen feet behind Lily, Arturo at her side, as she waited for her brother and his girlfriend to come up for air. Finally, Zack lifted his head and glanced up. The moment he saw her, she knew from his shock that he'd thought her dead. He stared at her for a full four seconds, utterly stunned. Then he released Lily and strode forward, pulling Quinn into his arms and hugging her almost too tight.

When he finally pulled back, his gaze searched her face, his eyes joyous and confused, the shadows of grief still lingering. "I thought he'd killed you." His voice broke on the last and she heard the same devastation she'd felt when she thought he was dead. How could she have ever believed he didn't love her as much as she loved him?

Pain lanced his eyes. "I fucked up, Quinn. I shouldn't have gone after her with just Jason. He almost died. You almost died." His eyes tightened. "I heard Cristoff stole your power."

Quinn shrugged. "You did what you had to do." She gripped her brothers rock-hard shoulders. "We've both made rash decisions based on emotion. I could have saved Vamp City—I had the chance—but I put you first again and now Rinaldo is dead."

Zack's face fell. "Rinaldo, too?"

Quinn pressed her hand to his blazing hot cheek. "Not your fault. That one was on me." She wrapped her arms around his neck and he pulled her against him a second time, hugging her tight.

"I needed to save her," he said against her hair. "I needed to not be a fuck-up."

"You've never been a fuck-up. And I do understand the tendency to act first and think second. It apparently runs in the family."

"Being fuck-ups?"

Quinn pulled back with a laugh. "I prefer to call it being devastatingly loyal to the ones we love."

Zack's mouth twisted ruefully, then he turned back and held out his hand to Lily who took it without hesitation. Zack pulled her close against him and faced Quinn. "Do we stand a chance of taking that asshole Cristoff down?"

"We might." Quinn's gaze moved between the two of them then locked on her brother. "Our goal is to kill Cristoff, of course." Though they hadn't discussed this with the other vampire masters, phase two of the plan was still to find a way to destroy Escalla and break the Levenach curse. And if that happened... "It's possible you could come into some kind of...power."

"Magic," Zack corrected. "I'm a sorcerer."

"We both are," Lily said with a look of bemusement.

Quinn stared at her. "You, too? How...?"

"Octavia, the vampire who saved me and took me in after I escaped Castle Smithson, used to be a powerful sorceress before she was turned."

Zack nodded. "Did you know that only a sorcerer can enter Vamp City on a sunbeam? So all those humans who have…"

Quinn gaped at him. "There must be dozens of them."

"You're the only Blackstone sorcerer left, Quinn," Lily clarified. "The rest of us are all Levenach heirs, without any magic."

But if Escalla were destroyed… Goosebumps raced the length of Quinn's body.

"Octavia and a couple of her vampire friends—William and Maxwell—are able to spot the heirs, Sis. They've been collecting us. Octavia's been building an army, teaching us what to do if our magic comes back, if you manage to free us from the curse."

It was Quinn's turn to feel stunned. "So the group you just arrived with. You're *all* sorcerers?"

"Yup," Zack said. "Even Jason and his wife. Heather, is Octavia's best friend."

Quinn's gaze jerked to where Jason stood a couple of yards away, his arm hooked around the waist of an attractive woman with curly blonde hair. How he'd survived, she didn't know, but she was so thankful he had. And… "He found his wife."

Zack grinned. "Yeah. It was pretty epic."

Quinn shook her head, trying to take it all in. "You're both sorcerers, too." All those years of feeling so strange, so *alone*. With a laugh, she hugged Zack and Lily and they hugged her in return.

"It's time to go," Arturo said, dragging her back to reality. "We don't have much time."

Quinn nodded then turned back to her brother. "I'd love to ask you to stay out of the battle."

Zack smiled a man's smile. "And I'd love to ask you and Lily to do the same."

Quinn's mouth twisted ruefully. "I guess none of us are going to get our wish, are we?"

Zack squeezed her shoulder. "We'll be careful."

She supposed that was all the assurance she was going to get. Quinn turned to Arturo who was holding her horse, and mounted. She met his gaze and saw his own joy for her in his eyes. His pride in her.

But in those dark depths, she saw, too, a stoic courage and the knowledge that death rode with them into battle. They would not come out of this without losses. Possibly losses too terrible to bear.

But Cristoff must be stopped.

The Healer and the Snake led the resistance together into a battle none of them really believed they could win.

CHAPTER FORTY-FIVE

Quinn rode beside Arturo toward the Focus where Cristoff worked his vile magic. The sky was veined in blood, the world holding its collective breath.

On either side of them, and close behind, rode Savin and the six vampire masters who'd now aligned with them. As they neared the Crux, in the very center of which was the small domed Focus, Arturo continued the discussion of battle plans begun in Neo's kitchen.

"What if he's still in the Focus?" Fabian asked. "None of us, but the sorceress, can breach those walls."

"Driving him out of the Focus is our first task," Arturo agreed. "And it might be the most difficult one we face. Geert, when you're in range of Cristoff, attempt to exert your mind control to draw him out." Arturo had told her a little about each of the vamp masters earlier and Quinn recalled that Geert's mind control was far stronger than Arturo's own power of persuasion. There were few of any race, including vampire, who could resist it.

"Von Essen, we'll need you to attempt to pull Cristoff's power."

"Will do, Mazza," the powerfully built male said. Apparently both Sakamoto and Von Essen possessed the ability to steal another vampire's power, much as a silver noose might. But while Sakamoto had to be touching his victim, von Essen didn't. And that was a powerful advantage since the only vampire in Vamp City who could walk into that Focus was Sheridan, one of Phineas Blackstone's sons. Whether von Essen would be able to hold onto Cristoff's great power when he did steal it, was a question they did not know the answer to. They'd have to be careful that they didn't trade one tyrannical monster for another.

As Arturo laid out the plan and led the discussion, Quinn watched him with pride. Kassius had once told her that Arturo didn't see himself as a leader, and didn't really care to be one, but his friends had always known it was a mantle he'd been born to. She had to agree.

A whiff of diesel teased her nose, a scent breaking through from the real world.

As they reached the edge of the Crux, Arturo held up his hand and pulled up. While the others stopped, he rode forward a few steps, then turned his mount to face his army.

"Sakamoto will lead you into battle. Protect the Healer and drive Cristoff from the Focus, if he's still there. Kassius, Micah, and I will pretend to join Cristoff's forces. Fight us, do not kill us, and we will not kill you. When the time is right, we will strike together."

It was a terrible risk, letting an entire army know of the subterfuge, but there was no choice, given that the three would be openly fighting beside Cristoff. All must understand that the only betrayal was to Cristoff.

Arturo turned to her, his expression fiercely tender. "We will prevail, amore." Then he turned and galloped off to join Cristoff's army, Micah and Kassius close on his heels.

Quinn watched him go, hating that they would fight this battle separated. Up until this moment, she'd comforted herself with the thought that if the ground began to rumble, she'd pull a massive bubble through Arturo and protect them all. But he was no longer in reach, and soon wouldn't even be in sight. For all she knew, his cover had already been blown and Cristoff would slay him the moment he rode up. Anything might happen.

But she couldn't think like that. She had to stay focused on the task at hand which, for her, meant rallying the troops around Sakamoto now that Arturo was gone. Sakamoto motioned for her to proceed. To lead them.

How had she come to this, leading an army of vampires and werewolves? With a bemused shake of her head, Quinn started off. Sakamoto followed, his mount a half a length behind hers, the others trailing them both.

In the distance she caught sight of the colors of the Focus and knew immediately that something had drastically changed. She'd often thought the Focus looked like a landed aurora borealis, its colors swirling in a confined dome about the size of a two-car garage. But what stood in the middle of the Crux now was something entirely different. Green, gold, and black lights shot out in every direction, like lightning bolts shot from the earth.

"Is Cristoff in the middle of that?" Quinn asked. They were still too far away for her human eyesight to make out those kinds of details.

"He is," Sakamoto confirmed. "The lights are coming from him now."

Quinn glanced at the vamp master. "Why does he stand in the Focus to create his world? The Focus was the center of Blackstone's. He could stand anywhere to create his own, couldn't he?"

"I do not know the answer to that, sorceress. All I can surmise is that the one who has now drunk of the power of the Black Wizard's heir finds more of that power in the dense magic of that space, a magic created by another of the Black Wizard's heirs—Phineas Blackstone."

As they drew closer, Quinn could see the dozens of Gonzaga guards circling the Focus, defending their master. Only about a dozen were mounted, the rest on foot.

"Do you see Arturo, Micah, and Kassius?" she asked.

"Yes, sorceress. They've been enfolded into the heart of evil. We need but to draw Cristoff out of his protective dome and they will fall on him."

It sounded so simple when put like that.

Suddenly, beneath them, the ground began to shake.

CHAPTER FORTY-SIX

Quinn's eyes went wide as the earth rumbled violently and a warm, stinging breeze whipped up out of nowhere, ominous and unnatural. The sky, shot through with red cracks, almost appeared to glow. Her heart seized, terror drilling down deep inside of her, because she was all but certain the sunbeams were about to break through again. And she no longer had the magic to protect any of them. The vampires...*Turo*...were all going to die.

Pushing away the fear, locking down her emotions, Quinn stilled, closed her eyes, and fought to find the magic to call up a bubble. But it wasn't there!

Instead, she struggled to reach for her connection to Arturo. Perhaps, even from a distance, she could pull the magic through him. But her senses connected, not with Arturo, but with something else, a strong, pulsing, powerful warmth, like a glowing ball of light. Energy shot through her, latching onto her and Quinn's pulse leaped, but not with fear. There was something about the energy that felt...benevolent.

Suddenly she was aware of someone striding toward her, the woman Zack had accompanied to Neo's. The sorceress-turned-vampire, Octavia.

"Quickly, sorceress, take my hand," Octavia said, reaching for her. "We can protect them together."

Quinn stared at her for only a moment before grabbing the outstretched hand. The second their fingers touched, that same energy poured up into Quinn's arm, flowing through her body in a tingling, almost pleasant, buzz. Suddenly, the others who'd accompanied Zack swarmed around Quinn's horse, joining hands like some new age prayer circle.

"Quinn."

At the sound of Zack's voice on her other side, she turned and found him reaching for her other hand, Lily at his side. Quinn took her brother's hand, completing the circle that flowed out around the front of her surprisingly accepting mount.

Quinn glanced at her brother, catching his bemused expression, one she suspected matched her own.

"Now what?" she asked, turning back to Octavia.

But at that moment, she felt the sunbeams breaking through and all she could think about was protecting the vampires. Her will flew outward, wishing for a bubble to enclose them all.

No bubble formed. But suddenly, darkness blanketed the Crux, blotting out the red sky and all the sunbeams.

"It's like some kind of giant umbrella," Zack said quietly, his voice filled with awe.

Quinn turned to Octavia with wonder. "You did this."

"*We* did this, Quinn."

"But…"

Octavia smiled softly. "You are a magnifier. You may have lost much of your own power, but you are able to magnify the little I have left."

It was similar to what Arturo was able to do for her. "What about Zack and the others?"

"I'm connected to them, as are you, now. Their power is untapped, yet it is there, lying dormant within them. Between your ability to magnify my power and my own to connect with the power within others of Levenach's line, we were able to form the shield that now protects our comrades."

"How long will it hold?" Zack asked.

"Long enough."

Quinn peered at her, stunned, excited. "What else can you do?"

Octavia once more smiled that small smile. "We shall see, shall we not?"

Behind Quinn, vampires and others murmured and exclaimed. When she glanced back at them, many bowed their heads to her in gratitude.

Quinn nodded back, then turned to Octavia. "Are you really a Levenach sorceress?"

"In a way. He was my brother."

Quinn gaped at her. "You've been around a long time."

Octavia chuckled. "I have indeed, little sister."

Quinn blinked at the term, then gave a small laugh. She'd been so focused on her ties to the Black Wizard that she'd almost forgotten she was descended from Levenach, too.

"Disband and fall back into line," Octavia said, then turned to Quinn. "I suggest we start this war."

Quinn nodded and turned to Sakamoto. "Ready?"

The vampire grinned, then gave a piercing war cry, kicked his horse into gear, and galloped forward, lifting his samurai sword high. The wolves snarled and followed. Vampires blurred all around her, leaving only the humans, fae, and Traders to catch up at their own, slower, speed.

From atop her horse, she had a good view of Cristoff's troops and frowned as they made no move to meet the oncoming attack. Moments later, she understood why as vampires and werewolves began to hit some kind of invisible wall...and began to scream. The rest of her troops pulled up short, uncertain what had just happened.

Cristoff's soldiers began to laugh.

In her head, she heard Arturo's voice. *He has infused the force field that encircles us with dragon fire, tesoro mio. I did not realize it until just now or I would have warned you.*

"Stay back!" she yelled. "The force field is made of dragon fire!"

Those who hadn't already, now backed up, making Cristoff's guards laugh even harder. But at the sound of her shout, Cristoff whirled within the Focus to stare at her. Apparently, he hadn't realized...until now...that she'd survived his attack.

Quinn waved at her nemesis, getting great pleasure from his knowing he hadn't actually killed her. He was too far away for her to see his expression, but she felt his surprise and a disquiet that contained a small thread of something that felt like fear. While the thought might be misplaced, it pleased her tremendously to think that the terrible, all-powerful, Cristoff Gonzaga was just a tiny bit afraid of her.

But that hardly did her, or her team, any good. Not when they couldn't even reach Cristoff's forces, let alone Cristoff himself. Her gaze moved to Arturo who stood with his back to the Focus, along with Micah and Kassius. Cristoff's personal guards. She was terrified Arturo would decide he was their only chance, and decide to attack

Cristoff on his own. He'd been unable to beat his master even before Cristoff had come into his power. As it stood now, he didn't have a chance.

But that didn't mean he wouldn't try.

As she watched, one of Cristoff's guards strode forward and cut off the heads of three of the vampires and one of the werewolves writhing in pain on the ground. She heard the crack of gunfire and saw the big vampire jerk back once, then twice, then a third time. She'd handed her gun to Jason before the battle, after he'd admitted to being an expert shot.

"Jason got him," Zack said. "Right through the heart, yet the sucker's not going down."

"You can't see that far," Quinn countered.

"Actually, I can." Together, brother and sister watched the guard turn with a sneer and walk back within the protective force field to stand beside his mercenary brothers. "We're fucked."

And they were that. They'd been concerned about getting Cristoff out of the Focus. Now they had two barriers they had to find a way to break through in order to reach him.

Quinn turned to Octavia. "You don't have any force field-zapping powers, do you?"

The ancient sorceress looked at her thoughtfully. "No. But you might."

"What do you mean?"

Octavia reached for Quinn's hand. "I felt something within your magic." As her cool fingers closed around Quinn's warm ones, the woman closed her eyes. When she opened them again, moments later, satisfaction lit their depths. "You possess the ability to draw the life force from a person."

"Yes. My death touch."

"It is useful for more than killing. You can draw the life out of that field of energy."

Quinn's eyes widened with alarm. "Draw the dragon fire into me?"

"No, you won't have to touch it, just get close enough to consciously draw it to you. Those of us connected to you, now, will help you. As you pull that tainted power, I will send it deep into the ground where it can harm no one."

"How close do I have to get?" How much did she really trust this woman? Then again, Octavia had used Quinn's power to create the shield. And did she really have any choice but to trust? They had to disable that force field.

"Close. Within six feet, I believe. You'll have to be careful not to touch it. And be forewarned, Cristoff's guards will come after you."

"Of course they will." Nothing was ever easy. Quinn dismounted and strode to where Sakamoto's werecats stood. She looked at Davu and Dera. "Any words of wisdom?"

Eyes grave, they shook their heads. "No visions."

"Maybe that's a good thing." She turned to Fabian. "I might be able to disable that force field, but I'm going to have to get close to it, and stay there for probably several minutes. Can you put together a team to defend me?"

"Of course, sorceress. Can anyone be between you and the field?"

"It shouldn't matter," Octavia said, joining her. "She does not need an unimpeded path, simply close and sustained proximity."

Fabian nodded. "Let's go."

Quinn followed him through the throng of fighters. At one point, he stopped and said quietly to those around him, "The sorceress has a plan, but will need protection."

All those who heard followed, swelling her heart. She clung to the belief that she would succeed, hoping that Arturo would feel it and release any thought of attacking Cristoff just yet.

As Quinn feared, the moment she and her band approached the edge of the force field, Cristoff's soldiers moved toward them. Swords were drawn on both sides. But this time, her side stopped short, forcing Cristoff's mercenaries to leave their protective dome to reach them.

Closing her eyes, Quinn lifted her hands and felt for that wall of dragon fire-laced energy. At first she felt nothing. Then suddenly, that odd connection stirred within her again, her connection with Octavia and the Levenach heirs. And suddenly the wall tingled against her senses. It appeared in her mind's eye as bright orange fire and she marveled at its terrible beauty for several moments before finally gathering the courage to call it to her. Her body tensed for the possibility of pain, but as the energy rushed into her hands, she felt nothing but a prickling, tingling flow of electricity.

Briefly she wondered if she could, either accidentally or on purpose, steal life forces in this way. But even as she wondered, she knew the answer somehow. To steal the energy from a body, she had to be touching it. She couldn't accidentally harm anyone around her, whether she wanted to or not.

"Stop her!" Cristoff's voice rang out. "*Kill* her!"

Quinn's eyes flew open and the sight that met her gaze sent a cold shaft of fear right through the middle of her heart. Cristoff's entire guard force was turning toward her, death in their eyes.

Hell.

No, nothing was ever easy.

CHAPTER FORTY-SEVEN

The sounds of battle exploded all around her, the clash of swords, the growl of wolves, the tearing of flesh. Quinn forced herself to keep her eyes closed even as her flesh crawled and her muscles bunched with tension. There was nothing to be gained by seeing the battle when she couldn't run, couldn't protect herself. When all were counting on her to disable the foul energy of that force field.

A spray of warm blood hit her face and she flinched, struggling to hold back the primal scream that tried to claw its way up her throat. Which of her friends had just died?

Easy, cara. *Concentrate on what you must.*

Arturo's voice, his presence in her mind, helped to ground her. Breathe. She must breathe. Everyone was depending on her.

Shaking, she forced herself to focus on the energy flowing into her hands. Slowly, she felt Octavia's strength and power merging with her own, and felt the life-signature of others in the mix, both individually and as a group. Zack's was there. And Lily's. It terrified her to think they were close to this battle. In her hurry to reach the front lines, she hadn't bothered to ask Octavia if they'd have to be close, too.

With effort, she shoved that fear away, just as she had the others, and forced herself to block out everything but the energy flowing swiftly into her hands. Little by little, the energy flow became less until it was barely more than a trickle.

"It is done!" Octavia's voice rang clearly over the field of battle. "The barrier is down!"

"Come, sorceress." With no further warning, Quinn felt herself swept into strong arms and then she was moving vampire-fast, the rush of air blowing the hair into her face.

By the time she could see where she was, she felt herself being set her on her feet beside Octavia, far behind the line of battle. Fabian's quick grin flashed before he once more disappeared into the fray.

A strong hand clamped around her arm, steadying her, and she looked into the face of her brother.

"Good job, Sis."

Lily smiled beside him.

"Yes, well done, Quinn." At the sound of Octavia's voice, Quinn turned and met the other woman's gaze. She'd spent enough time with vampires, now, that she was becoming used to seeing ancient eyes in young faces. But in Octavia's eyes she saw so much more than years and experience. She saw the wisdom of the ages and a gentleness almost too perfect to comprehend.

"I couldn't have done it without you," Quinn told her.

Octavia smiled. "That is true. You were in need of my power. But there are few I've ever known with the kind of courage you just displayed. As I said, well done."

Quinn smiled, then turned back to the battle. As she watched, her army swarmed Cristoff's guards who, she noticed with satisfaction, were no longer laughing. Too many stood between her and the Focus for her to easily find Arturo, but she could feel occasional blasts of his emotions and knew he was battling those he had no desire to kill. Unfortunately, in the heat of battle, anything could happen.

A fire arrow arced through the sky and bounced off the Focus to be snuffed out in the dirt. The crack of gunfire erupted in the midst of the battle from time to time. But those deadly arcs of green and gold light continued to shoot out of the small dome, uninterrupted.

"They're not dying," Zack muttered.

Quinn retrieved her horse and mounted, needing a higher vantage point from which to see what was going on. Zack was right. Cristoff's forces weren't dying. Dead wolves littered the ground, as did Slavas and fae. Vampire after vampire exploded, but never Cristoff's.

"Cristoff must have acquired some kind of indestructibility spell from the Black Wizard," she muttered. "Something he was able to cast over his entire army."

"Then we're fucked."

She glanced at her brother and had to agree. The only upside was that perhaps Arturo, Micah, and Kassius were protected by it as well.

Unfortunately, with each failure to strike a blow at Cristoff from the outside, the likelihood of Arturo having to do it from the inside increased exponentially. And if he did, he was going to need her help. She tried to connect to him, tried to feel the connection forming, but he was still too far away.

Do not attempt to call up your bubble through me, amore mio, *I implore you. I do not dare do magic or Cristoff will become suspicious.*

Quinn stopped immediately, but the need to find a way to protect him against Cristoff's retaliation, should it come to that, burned a hole in her.

She continued to watch the battle. Having heard the plan ahead of time, she understood what she was seeing when, one after another, Fabian's opponents—Gonzaga guards—turned away from him to attack their own. He apparently had a powerful ability to enthrall other vampires when he needed to, when cajoling and ordering didn't work. Unfortunately, his enthrallment wasn't lasting. Of the three so far who'd turned on their own, only one had actually killed one of Cristoff's. All three had quickly recovered. Too quickly.

Now she turned her attention to the vampire master Geert who was standing away from the battle, focused on Cristoff. The plan, she knew, was for Geert to try to mentally manipulate Cristoff out of the Focus. But even as she watched, Geert began to scream, his hands clutching his head. A moment later, his head exploded.

Dear God. Was that what would happen if Arturo attempted to mind blast Cristoff? He'd told her Cristoff could not attack anyone he wasn't touching, at least he couldn't before he came into the Black Wizard's terrible power. But he *could* counterattack from a distance. And maybe that was what he'd done with Geert, counterattacked with devastating results.

Searching, she found von Essen battling with his sword not far from where Geert had just died. The plan had been for von Essen to attempt to steal Cristoff's power remotely, but she wondered now if he'd aborted that plan after watching what happened to Geert. She couldn't say she blamed him.

A sudden movement caught her eye, a blur slamming through the walls of the Focus. Startled, she watched as the blur turned into Sheridan. He lifted a sword as if to strike, but a moment later, his head flew back out of the Focus to land in the dirt, face up.

Oh, Sheridan. He'd used his ability to breach the Focus to go after

Cristoff himself. Vampire-fast, he might have stood a chance before Cristoff became so powerful. Today, he'd stood none.

Without warning, Quinn felt a fire go through her middle. For one terrible moment, she thought she'd taken a bullet until she realized that everyone around her was suddenly yelling and doubling over in exactly the same way. It could mean only one thing. Cristoff had once more managed to call forth his new world, his world of pain. And if the werecat twins were to be believed, this one wouldn't fail.

CHAPTER FORTY-EIGHT

Arturo battled three of Fabian's loyal soldiers, careful to fight hard but not go for the kill. The roar of a helicopter erupted overhead and he glanced up to find a police chopper hovering above them. Structures began to pop up out of nowhere—not entire streets of them, just random buildings. In some cases only parts of buildings. One erupted close enough to the battle that the vampires and werewolves who'd been standing on the spot were sent flying. Half a dozen moving cars appeared far to his right, but not the roads they'd been driving on.

Quinn's army—most of the citizens of Vamp City—suddenly doubled over. Humans began to appear all over the battlefield, screaming not only from pain but from the blows of swords already in motion when they'd appeared.

The two worlds were merging, but in an even more macabre way than before.

As Arturo watched with horror, Cristoff's guards waded into the pained throng, kicking and flinging the humans out of the way as they attacked the vampires and werewolves, most of whom were in so much pain they were unable to fight effectively. What exactly Cristoff had done to empower his mercenaries, Arturo didn't know. He didn't feel any different himself.

Quinn's agony blasted him suddenly, her fear that it was all over, that they'd lost.

Tesoro. It tore at him that he couldn't go to her, but the only way to help her was to end this. And it was time to do just that.

"I want Sakamoto," he growled. Anyone listening—anyone who didn't know better—would think he was gunning for the vampire's blood. But Fabian's vamps did know better. One of them disappeared. Moments later, Sakamoto moved in to battle him.

"I can't wait," he told the male. "He's never coming out."

"And what will you do?" Sakamoto asked, his face a mask of agony even as he parried Arturo's blows as if fighting to kill him.

Arturo didn't respond and Sakamoto's expression said he knew a secret when he saw one. "You'll fail."

"Probably."

"Then wait," the vamp master gasped, one arm tight around his middle.

"I already have."

"Wait a little bit longer. Once he believes he's won, he'll come out of there."

"You may all be dead by then. And this world will be locked in."

The need to keep Cristoff from hurting Quinn burned through his blood. But he knew Sakamoto was right. Their only real chance of success lay in acting together...if Cristoff ever left the Focus to give them that chance. Sakamoto was one of the most powerful vampires in Vamp City for a reason. If they could get Cristoff out of the Focus, they had a plan. With his abilities to phase and to deaden another's powers with a touch, Sakamoto would grab hold of Cristoff without the latter seeing him approach, and deaden his power long enough for Arturo to attack him with his mind blast.

They would get, at best, only one shot. And while there was an excellent chance one or both of them would die, the hope was that they'd be able to disable Cristoff long enough for Kassius or Micah to snatch Escalla and stab Cristoff.

The thought that they'd be killing his father barely registered anymore. The male causing so much destruction, so much agony, bore no resemblance whatsoever to the man Arturo had once been so faithful to. The Cristoff he knew was gone.

"He leaves," Sakamoto said suddenly, then yelled out as if he'd taken a deadly blow. Arturo watched, bemused, as his opponent fell, and to all the world, disappeared.

Arturo turned to find that Cristoff had, indeed, walked out of the Focus. *Finally.* The power radiated from him, the bolts of green and gold fire leaping out of him in a wing-like arc, giving him the look of some kind of angel from Hell.

Cristoff wore an expression of such triumphant cruelty, of such madness, that it made Arturo sick to his stomach. Swallowing his revulsion, he strode forward to meet his master, then fell into step beside him as he'd always done as Cristoff's most loyal.

"My world will soon be complete," Cristoff told him with a grin. He slapped Arturo on the back. "Our world. A world of pain and terror. I shall have to work on feeding my pleasure feeders, for I suspect the only pleasure for some time will be ours."

Arturo struggled to keep his expression devoid of the horror he was feeling. "Will the real D.C. continue to exist, my liege? I am fascinated by this world you create."

Cristoff's chest expanded. "Both worlds are mine now. Or will be once the transformation is complete. Those who did not flee, or die, during my creation attempts will be trapped within the ever-increasing boundaries of my worlds. The two will no longer be entirely distinct from one another, merging at odd times and in odd ways, eliciting constant disquiet, constant fear. And of course, constant pain to all but the vampires who pledge undying loyalty to me." He looked at Arturo, madness glittering in his eyes. "Are you not pleased, my loyal one?"

"Most pleased." Most revolted. "How long will it take to form this intriguing world?"

"As long as it takes. Minutes, perhaps. An hour? It is impossible to say and matters not at all. For it is done!"

Micah and Kassius strode forward to join their master in his moment of victory. Cristoff nodded as if having the three of them by his side at this moment was the most natural thing in the world.

Despite a lifetime of diplomatic acting, this was his most challenging role as he fought to hide his fury, his horror, at the slaughter going on all around them, the vicious murder of Quinn's army. He felt her within him, her desperation for him to take down their foe a powerful force flowing through his body.

His muscles shook as he kept his hands fisted behind his back and waited for Sakamoto to make his move, praying the male did not lose his nerve at the last minute.

In the distance, a small cloud of humans tumbled out of the sky over the Potomac. With horror, he realized they'd undoubtedly been inside an airplane that had not accompanied them into this world.

"God's wounds."

Arturo jerked at the ancient expression uttered by the voice of the male he'd once revered as both master and father. He turned to find Cristoff staring at the battlefield, at what he'd wrought, with an expression of dismay.

Arturo's heart gave a hard thump, his mind leaping, as he realized that, even now, the real Cristoff fought to break through. If only Arturo dared to try to enlist the aid of *this* male before the other returned. But it was a terrible risk, for he'd be giving himself away, and the monster could return at any moment.

Cristoff turned to Arturo, his eyes shattered. *"What have I done?"* But even as Arturo struggled to find words, Cristoff's expression changed, hardening, his eyes once more glittering with cruelty and triumph. "Soon it will be over, my loyal one. Then I will reign supreme and you will stand at my side and all that you want will be yours."

Arturo stared at him, then turned away, his body cold, his heart beating at twice its usual pace. He risked a glance at his friends and saw the sympathy in their gazes, the regret. But no doubt. They knew he would do everything he could to kill his own father, even knowing the male he'd once loved still existed somewhere behind the mask of the monster. *Because he had no choice.*

And suddenly that moment was upon him. Out of the corner of his eye, he saw Sakamoto appear behind Cristoff and a split second later, Cristoff roared. Then Sakamoto roared. And died just as Geert had.

Arturo seized the opportunity, leaped out of Cristoff's reach, and slammed him with his own mind blast. At the same time, he threw up shields, desperate to hold Cristoff's counterattack at bay, or he would die as quickly and devastatingly as Sakamoto and Geert had.

Cristoff roared for a second time, this time in agony as he clutched his head. Kassius and Micah acted, Kassius grabbing for Escalla as Micah attempted to slide a noose of silver around their master's neck. But before either of them could succeed, they were soaring backward with a force that would have them landing at least a quarter of a mile away.

Cristoff rounded on Arturo, his hands clutching his head, his face a mask of disbelief. He'd yet to counterattack, yet he was holding up to Arturo's deadly blast with disastrous ease, as if the master had become as indestructible as his guards.

His expression shifted to one of confusion as his eyes once more filled with the soul of the male Arturo had once worshiped. "You betray me."

"You, never. I do not betray the master to whom I long ago pledged fealty, the master I loved. I betray only the monster who now wears his face."

Fury flooded Cristoff's countenance. And, a moment later, a blast hit Arturo's mind shields, shattering them.

CHAPTER FORTY-NINE

Quinn leaped off her horse and ran, despite the pain burning through her gut. She'd seen Cristoff exit the Focus and knew the time had come for Arturo to attack his father...if he could bring himself to do it. And Cristoff would almost certainly counterattack with enough force to kill the man she loved.

All around her, the fighting continued, her allies in terrible pain, Cristoff's mercenaries taking swift and deadly advantage.

"I need protection!" she yelled. Almost instantly, eight vampires surrounded her. And then half a dozen wolves. She was stealing them from other battles, and she was sorry for it, but she had to get closer to Arturo or everything was lost.

The helicopter she'd seen appear out of nowhere had begun a death spiral, the terrified pilot probably in too much pain to fly it any longer. Out of the corner of her eye, she saw it career downward. At the exact moment it hit the ground, a row of buildings appeared suddenly on top of it, and the resulting explosion burst out the windows.

Every minute, more people materialized out of nowhere, more cars and vehicles, more buildings. It was a world in chaos, a world of madness.

A Quinn ran, her protectors, all of them debilitated by pain, battled back Cristoff's vamps, some succeeding, some dying. As vampires and wolves fell, others slid in to take their place, clearing a path for her. She struggled to concentrate on Arturo, to connect with him, but he was still too far away. With horror, she saw Sakamoto die. Then suddenly Cristoff roared and turned on Arturo. And then she felt it, the blast to Arturo's mind that would kill him.

Her heart pounded, her breath tearing in and out of her lungs. Her own mind went white as she desperately fought to connect with him, to push power through him. Dimly, she began to feel him, but she was still too far away, so she continued to run, pushing through battle in the wake of her persona guard.

Slowly the connection with Arturo strengthened until, finally, she felt that door open in her mind, felt her connection to Arturo click into place.

Quinn stopped in her tracks, trusting the vamps and wolves to protect her, and closed her eyes. She imagined pushing her power through him, imagined throwing up a brick wall to keep Cristoff's blast from reaching Arturo, but almost at once she felt the wall shatter. Cristoff was too strong!

She tried to help Arturo battle back the ungodly force of Cristoff's counter blast, and while she felt Arturo's own power strengthened, it wasn't enough. Not nearly enough. She needed help.

Turning her thoughts to Octavia, she felt that connection once more stir, felt a powerful wave of energy flow into her through it, and without hesitation, flung every bit of it at Cristoff.

But even that wasn't enough.

Arturo was going to lose.

In some part of his mind, a mind now awash in flame, Arturo knew he'd never stood a chance. Though he'd attacked his master with every ounce of strength he possessed, sending his mind blast at him hard and fast, Cristoff had counterattacked with a strength at least three times stronger. Arturo knew his head should have exploded by now. Yet somehow he managed to continue to fight.

Because of Quinn. Her power infused his own. Her strength was slowing Cristoff's ability to pulverize his brain. Slowing, but not stopping. His head was on fire. His brain was turning to mud. Yet still he felt Quinn's steely, protective energy pouring through him, trying to help. But there was no defeating Cristoff. His strength was just too great.

"*You* are my traitor?" Cristoff roared, his face contorting until he was barely recognizable to his own son.

Arturo felt the pressure building in his skull, in his eyes. His eyesight was beginning to fail again.

"After all these years, you still don't know who I am." Arturo had nothing left to lose by telling the truth. "I was...your first born. My mother, Valentina, named me...Little Cristoff."

He felt rather than saw Cristoff's jaw drop. The counterblast fell away. For a second, Arturo was too surprised to take advantage. Then he slammed his shields into place, praying that Quinn could help him keep them up this time, and he hit Cristoff with his own mind blast, using every ounce of power he still possessed.

Cristoff stumbled back, falling to one knee. For one bright, terrible moment, Arturo thought he might actually have a chance of destroying his father. But through the darkness stalking his sight, he saw Cristoff rise, fury on his face as he reached for him with his hand.

Arturo pulled his sword and drove his master back, knowing that if Cristoff touched him, it was over. If Cristoff's counterattack was this powerful, his frontal attack would kill him instantly.

Cristoff pulled Escalla and Arturo fought him with sword and mind power, Quinn's energy weaving through his, helping him. He fought bitterly even as his brain felt as if it were being squeezed in an iron fist. Blood began to run from his ears and nose. His sight faded. And though Quinn attempted to help, her power was no longer strong enough.

He was going to die. And there wasn't a damn thing he could do to stop it.

The world had gone to Hell.

As Quinn fought to help Arturo, fought to push away the brutal force of Cristoff's mind blast, death and horror swirled all around her. Though she tried to keep her eyes closed in order to concentrate, it was impossible when she suddenly heard vehicles tearing in from the other world, crashing into one another, into vampires and wolves. And when those who protected her kept being struck down, kept dying. She was covered in blood, covered in vampire splatter, but it was her heart that bled.

She needed to stop this! But her power was gone. And the energy she managed to borrow from Octavia wasn't enough.

Her gaze swung to where she'd last seen Zack and Lily. Octavia and her group were still far to the back, out of the fray, though they appeared to be staring at something on the ground close by. Zack and Lily were no longer with them.

As combatants parted, Quinn got a glimpse of the ground in that area and realized that it was Zack on the ground, Lily kneeling at his side.

The need to race to her brother barreled through her, but she tamped it down. Arturo and his battle were her only concern. She turned back and found her vampire with her gaze, watching his sword flash with superhuman strength and speed. He was a glorious warrior forever in the prime of life. Except that blood trickled from his ear, more from his nose, and she feared she was watching him die.

The thought hit her with the force of a sledgehammer, nearly driving her to her knees.

Vampire, you can't die!

Squeezing her eyes closed, she concentrated hard, pushing every ounce of power she possessed through him and against Cristoff. It felt as if the two vampires were aiming fire hoses at one another, the force of one stopping the force of the other. But Cristoff held the bigger of the two hoses, by far, and Arturo's power was slowly losing ground. And when it failed altogether, his head would go the way of Geert's and Sakamoto's. And her heart along with it.

The ground beneath her began to rumble again, as violently as before. Her eyes flew open and she watched a subway train explode out of the ground and race across the open field, passengers staring out the windows with terrified faces. But the rumbling beneath the ground didn't cease and Quinn knew the sunbeams were about to burst through again. She was much too far from Octavia and the others to join hands and help them form the shield a second time.

Despair rushed up, threatening to strangle her. She was helping no one! She was going to lose them all.

Do not fret, little sister. Octavia's soft voice in her mind startled her for only a moment. *I can connect to you even from this distance. I can form the shield without your help. Worry not.*

With a nod, Quinn turned her full attention back to Arturo, back to his fight. She could feel his emotions breaking through. Agony. Devastation. A despair to match her own. He knew he was losing. He knew he was going to die.

As she watched him fight, his face a mask of determination, she wished she'd told him how she felt. She wished he could hear her as she could him.

You can't die, Vampire! I can't lose you. I won't.

Pressure built inside her chest and head, a terrible grief, a furious love, swirling, thick and painful. And it was growing, building, until she was shaking, until she felt as if she would explode from the force of it.

Release your power through him, little sister. Do not hold back.

I'm trying! It's not enough.

You have all the power you need inside of you, but you're holding back.

Quinn blinked with the realization that Octavia had heard her. *I'm giving him everything.*

You are not. Do you not feel it ready to burst free of you? He needs that energy, little sister! Do not be afraid.

Quinn scrambled to make sense of this conversation. *I'm not afraid. I mean...are you telling me I need to calm down?*

No! It is not fear of the physical danger that hampers you now. I suspect it has never been.

What are you saying, then?

You love him.

There was no denying it. *Yes.*

And that scares you.

No. I mean... God, yes, it terrified her, the thought of opening herself up like that. How many times had Turo told her she had to open herself to others, to friendship, to love? And she had, or she was trying. But...

The block is your fear, Quinn. It is the dragon you must slay before you can slay any other.

I don't know how! She was willing to do *anything* to help Arturo, to save him. But how was she supposed to suddenly turn into someone she was not?

Love is power, Quinn. It is the single most powerful element in the universe. And that power is building inside of you, but you hold onto it and refuse to set it free. It's backing up on you and will soon weaken you.

Quinn wanted to scream because she didn't know how to do what Octavia was demanding. Yet she could feel the energy building inside of her, pounding against the walls of her chest and skull.

Let it go, little sister.

Such simple, unhelpful words.

Release it. Or the man you love is going to die.

No. In her mind's eye, she saw Arturo's beloved face, his dark gaze burrowing into her very soul. The tenderness, the fierceness of the emotion within her rose on a tidal wave until she knew it would split her open if she didn't let it out. If she didn't let it go.

Mukdalla's words echoed in her head. *Love means taking risks. It's what life is all about.*

Let it go, Octavia said.

As tears ran down Quinn's cheeks, she quit holding back and let the emotion swamp her, the fear, the *love*. The dam broke. The energy burst free to rush through that connection between them.

Deep within her mind she felt Arturo's surprise, his wonder, his joy, bittersweet, but shining, crystal clear. And deeper still, she felt something more.

A small flicker of hope.

CHAPTER FIFTY

Arturo's sight was nearly gone, his physical strength waning, his mind on fire from the pain of Cristoff's blast. He was losing, dying. Yet it was joy that kept him fighting. Joy that strengthened him, keeping him upright when Cristoff toyed with him, dragging out his death.

Quinn's emotion...never had he felt its like. Love, *for him*, more powerful than anything he'd believed existed. Except, perhaps, his love for her.

Without warning, energy shot through him, merging with his mind blast, strengthening him until the two blasts were, once more, equally matched. But he was barely hanging on. With his sight almost gone, he traced the arc of Cristoff's deadly blade by the barest glint of the steel as they hacked at one another.

Bella, he told Quinn telepathically. *You are my life. My love.*

"You're my son. In truth?" Cristoff asked. Though his twin attacks—sword and mind—did not ease off at all, his voice was once more that of the father Arturo had loved. A voice filled with confusion.

"Yes," Arturo replied, parrying every deadly thrust and swing of his father's sword even as a glimmer of hope flared that the good man might finally conquer the monster. "Your loyal son. Always."

Cristoff didn't question that statement. Instead, his voice changed, a thread of wonder weaving through the words. "You knew who I was."

"Always, my liege. You were my father. I was warned to keep the truth of my parentage to myself, and I did. But my love and loyalty were always yours."

The deadly thrusts intensified, as if Cristoff the Monster sought to end the discussion even if he couldn't regain control of the voice he now shared with the male he used to be, an identity he had no more use for.

"I've lost my soul." The words felt torn from a heart that no longer bled.

And still the battle intensified. Arturo could feel his brain being crushed. But the chance to speak, once more, with the man he'd revered was a rare and precious joy.

"Blackstone's magic poisoned most within Vamp City," he told his sire. "You most of all. He wanted the vampires to die from the inside out, from the souls out. And he almost succeeded. But most have now been healed."

"By the light," Cristoff said with wonder. "A sun that does not burn."

Arturo's brows rose in surprise even as he fought for his life. Quinn's healing energy must be burrowing down, slowly freeing Cristoff's soul.

"The Healer's magic heals us all. I had feared you lost."

"I am lost, my son."

"No. You're healing." But even as he said the words, the pain in his head became almost unbearable.

"For so many years, I imagined I saw Little Cristoff in you," his father said. "I think that's why you have always been my favorite. I've never forgotten him, and often I hoped that he'd grown to be as fine a man as you."

Arturo heard the words, felt them soak into his heart, filling him with a rare and precious gladness even as he knew his own end was near. He was battling through instinct alone, unable even to see the glint of sword, now. The moment the monster reclaimed Cristoff, Arturo would be dead, he knew that. His strength was giving out. Even the power Quinn continued to blast through him, the power of her love, was not enough.

He felt her desperation, her anguish, and though his strength was nearly gone, though the pressure squeezing his brain threatened to crush his mind any second now, he struggled to continue the fight.

Without warning, the pressure on his brain ceased. With surprise, his vision returned just enough that he could see Cristoff stepping back, his face a mask of struggle.

His father was giving him a chance to slay the monster!

But before Arturo could swing at the neck of his sire, Cristoff turned Escalla on himself, driving it deep into his own heart.

Arturo froze. "My liege!"

Cristoff looked up, meeting his gaze with the eyes of the father he'd loved, eyes now filled with both pain and triumph. "I end this now. And the one does know."

As Arturo stared in stunned horror, Cristoff exploded, and with him, Escalla. In the same instant, all signs of the real world disappeared as if they had never been, all evidence of Cristoff's pain world. Across the battlefield, the vampires and wolves roared with relief, finally able to renew their attacks on Cristoff's mercenaries, free of pain.

But the sky above was beginning to bleed, the ground rending, opening great fissures in the earth. Cristoff's world had hastened the destruction of Vamp City, or perhaps only masked it. But it was all too apparent that Vamp City was in its death throes.

Most of those on the battlefield, those who'd fought so valiantly to defeat evil, were still going to die.

CHAPTER FIFTY-ONE

Quinn watched, stunned, as Cristoff turned his sword on himself and exploded, taking Escalla with him.

She'd certainly never seen *that* coming.

And suddenly, something swept through her, a release, as if all her life she'd lived with a band tight around her chest, a constriction she hadn't even known was there. And now it was gone. And she could breathe.

Elation swept through her, a relief of the soul, and with it a burst of energy, of *power*. With wonder, she understood. She'd just come into her Levenach magic. In dying, in destroying Escalla, Cristoff had broken the curse.

Exclamations of surprise and delight burst quietly beneath the sounds of raging battle and she knew the other Levenach heirs must be feeling their own power for the very first time. Zack. Lily.

She looked for her brother where she'd last seen him and he was gone. Searching, she quickly found that mass of curly red hair. Her heart nearly stopped when she saw him battling two of Cristoff's guards. With a sword! Good grief, when had he learned to use a sword?

Dear God, Zack. Must you be the hero? Now?

Her muscles tensed with the need to race to his side, a need born of an instinct and love that had driven her for twenty-two years. But as she watched him wield the sword with skill, slicing off one of Cristoff's guards' heads, she checked that instinct once more. Zack had become a man. A warrior.

Goosebumps lifted on her skin, a rush of pride.

Turning her attention back to Arturo, she took off running. As if reading her mind, the wolves and vampires who'd been her protectors cleared a path for her, then created a barrier between her and the quickly falling remnants of Cristoff's army as she ran straight at the man who'd, relentlessly and completely, claimed her heart.

He turned toward her as she approached, his eyes shining, but his face as pale as she'd ever seen it. Before she could reach him, he sank to his knees and she knew he'd given all he had in that fight. Reaching him, she knelt before him sliding her hand around the back of his neck as she thrust her wrist against his mouth.

"Drink."

"Amore." Dark eyes stared at her with such wonder, blazed with such love, that she felt as if her heart would swell to bursting all over again. But he shook his head. "You are needed elsewhere. The world fails."

Damn, but he was right. She gripped his face in both hands and kissed him hard and fast. Pulling back, she met his gaze. "I love you."

"And I you. More than you know. Now, save them."

She nodded and jumped up, yelling, "Arturo needs blood!"

The ground began to shake suddenly and so violently that she almost lost her footing. With a keening wail, the earth split apart, right through the middle of the battlefield, leaving a deep, black fissure in the ground.

Quinn stared at it. "Someone get me to the Focus!"

She didn't see the vampire who swept her up, then two seconds later, deposited her on the ground just outside the dome of magic from which Phineas Blackstone had once created his vampire utopia, his vampire death trap. But the magic within had been badly corrupted by Cristoff's. She'd hoped the dome would have returned to its more placid state once Cristoff left it, but instead, the violent green, gold, and black lightning bolts continued to fly every which way. And they were tearing the dome apart. It was beginning to shrivel!

"Are you really going to walk into that?" Micah asked, apparently the one who'd carried her there.

She glanced back at him. "I'm glad you made it," she said with heartfelt relief. "Kass?"

"He's fine." He glanced worriedly at that dome. "For the moment."

"I wonder if it will let me in now that I've come into my Levenach magic. I guess there's one way to find out."

"Be careful, Quinn."

She threw him a rueful smile. "Since when have I ever been careful? Make sure Turo's getting blood, please?" With that, she strode forward, her steps slowing as the dome's energy reached out to her, stinging her flesh, which was nothing new. The Focus had never liked her. She was certain that once more it wouldn't let her renew the magic without a fight. She just hoped it recognized her as a Blackstone heir, or at least a sorceress, and let her in at all.

She needn't have worried. The moment she touched the energy of the dome, it grabbed her and yanked her into the heart of its power, right into the middle of a lightning storm. A bolt tore through her like a knife. As a second did the same, Quinn screamed. She couldn't move! She couldn't dodge them.

Tesoro! Arturo shouted in her mind.

"Quinn!" Micah exclaimed. "Quinn, you've got to come out."

But she couldn't. The energy had immobilized her so completely she couldn't even draw breath.

Even her heart had stopped beating.

Arturo tore himself from Sam's wrist, the blood coursing through his veins once more as he leaped to his feet.

"*Quinn!*" He raced to the dome and tried to dive inside to save her, but the Focus threw him back so fast, so hard, he landed in the middle of one of the last of the battles, between one of Cristoff's guards and three werewolves. Two, now, since he'd just landed on the third.

"Apologies," he muttered, pushing himself off the wolf and out of that particular skirmish. There was only one person he knew who might be able to enter the Focus unassaulted.

"Where's Grant Blackstone?" he yelled.

"Ax!" Micah called.

Arturo turned toward his friend's voice and saw Grant already carrying Quinn out of the Focus's lethal dome. By the time Arturo reached them, Quinn was beginning to rouse. Arturo's heart began to beat again.

"I could have told you that would happen, Quinn," Grant muttered. "The Focus hated you even before your Levenach magic was free."

"I had to try."

Arturo took her from Grant, holding her tight against his heart. The gaze she turned on him was pained, but not from the physical discomfort she'd known far too much of in the past days.

"How can I save them?" she asked, her voice an aching whisper.

Grant scratched his beard, a touch of regret in his voice, for once, as he turned to look out over the battlefield. "You can't. It's too late."

Arturo helped Quinn to her feet, then pulled her against his side. Together they turned and followed Grant's gaze to where several wolves lay on the ground, breathing heavily, as if unable to pull in enough air. A handful of vampires had already collapsed. Even as he watched, one exploded.

They were dying. The Vamp City world was ending.

And they had no way to stop it.

CHAPTER FIFTY-TWO

Quinn watched with shock as the battlefield went deathly silent, as the combatants, one by one, started to collapse. She saw Neo sink to his knees, watched Sam fall unconscious. The wolves, too, were crumpling, one by one, into boneless heaps on the ground.

Not five feet away, one of the Slavas suddenly began to age drastically, his dark hair turning gray, then white, his skin wrinkling, his bones curving in on themselves. When the aging ceased, he'd be dead.

Quinn stared, her mind blazing with the need to do something.

"Octavia." She whirled on Arturo. "Find me Octavia!"

Arturo simply swept her up and deposited her, seconds later, before the ancient sorceress who, like many of the other vampires trapped by the magic, was already on her knees, her fledgling sorcerers gathered worriedly around her. The only ones unaffected by the dying magic were Arturo and Micah, those humans who were still fully mortal, and the handful of Traders and fae who'd joined the fight.

"Put me down, Turo."

As he set her on her feet, Zack strode over to her and gave her a quick hug. She squeezed his arm in return, but her gaze was riveted on Octavia.

"How do I save you?" Quinn demanded, kneeling before the ancient woman. "The Focus won't let me save this world."

"Create...another."

Quinn stared at her. "Another world?" Her heart began to thud. "How?" She looked around her. It was like forming a bubble, right? Good grief. No, it wasn't. Not at all. It was so much more.

"I don't think I have that kind of power."

Octavia's fingers curled around her wrist weakly. "Then harness the others'. You're connected. Quickly!" Weak fingers slid away. Zack and Jason moved, catching the woman as she collapsed, lowering her to the ground.

Desperate faces turned to Quinn from all directions—the Levenach heirs, Micah, Arturo, a handful of Traders. A few of the vampires and wolves were still conscious, but the rest all lay on the ground now, dead and dying.

"Save them, Sis," Zack said, voicing the words all were thinking, she could see it in their eyes.

Save them.

Oh, shit. "Okay."

If Cristoff could create a brand new world, if Octavia believed she could, too, then that was what she had to do. There was no time for doubts, though she was drowning in them.

Taking a deep breath, she started issuing orders. "Form a circle around me."

"Quinn." One of the women—Jason's wife—stepped forward. "Octavia's been teaching us how to pull power. For just this purpose, I suspect."

Quinn nodded. "Good. Do that. Follow…"

"Heather."

"Follow Heather." Panic threatened to choke Quinn, a performance anxiety that put all others to shame. But she closed her eyes and almost at once sensed connections flying out from her to all those around her, energetic cords she'd either never had before, or never noticed. Two of them were stronger, by far, than the others, and she immediately recognized them as her connections to Arturo and Zack. Interestingly, of all of the energetic powers she sensed around her, Zack's was by far the strongest. A Levenach sorcerer, indeed, little brother.

"Make Zack your focal point," Quinn told them. "Him alone. He's the strongest of you, by far, and the one best connected to me." As she said the words, she opened her eyes and met Zack's gaze. She hadn't taken a good look at him until that moment and realized, with a bit of shock, that his face had returned to its natural color. His fever was gone! In the steady gaze of green eyes the same shade as her own, in the small smile that lifted his mouth, she saw a confidence she'd never seen before. Belatedly, she realized he was splattered with blood. He'd fought today, and won. And while he might have become a sorcerer, in battle he'd claimed the most potent power of all, that of a confident man.

She glanced outside the circle to where the smattering of others stood. "Join us please. Anyone who can still stand. Micah, you too."

The Traders and fae threw her surprised or questioning looks, but all did as she asked. She was running on instinct, now, uncertain where any of this was leading.

Above, the sky cracked open. As the golden light of sunset poured down, Quinn threw up a powerful shield to protect those within her charge. And knew it worked.

They're mine, dammit! You're not taking them.

She found Arturo with her gaze and held out her hand to him. "I need you."

The look he gave her melted her heart all over again. "I am yours, *amore mio*. Tell me what to do."

"I'm going to focus my power through you again."

"You have power of your own now."

"Yes, as do you. But just as I magnified your power, I need you to magnify mine. Don't ask me how I know that, I just do."

"Don't we all need to hold hands or something?" one of the young sorceresses asked.

"Only if you want to." Arturo's hand was the only one she needed. As she reached for him, as his strong fingers curled around hers, she closed her eyes and opened her heart and mind to the power swirling through her, a power now infused with Arturo's love and the sunlight and warmth that always bloomed when they came together. It filled her heart with joy and might have made her smile if not for the keening cry of the earth as another crack tore through the ground.

She felt, rather than saw, one of the downed vampires explode. And another.

Terror that she was going to be too late to save any of them tore through her heart and mind even as words began to flow from her lips, words she'd never heard before. Power raced into her from two sources—Zack and Arturo, funneling the energy of all those gathered, all still standing. The power welled up inside of her, an energy pulsing with life, with love, and with a brilliant, glowing sunlight. A thrumming, swelling pressure filled her chest, brimming with hope, with joy, amidst the despair.

She continued to whisper the words, focusing only on that glowing light, growing, pressing against the walls of her chest, demanding to be set free just as her feelings for Arturo had. Demanding to be born.

The pressure grew and grew, but there was no pain, only an indescribable joy. Arturo's hand gripped hers hard as if he felt it, too, as if he experienced this same excruciating anticipation.

She thought of what Octavia had said before. *Let it go.*

And what would happen if she did?

It didn't matter. There was no alternative.

With her will alone, she set that energy free, expelling it in a powerful, raw, immensely satisfying explosion that felt as if it came right out of her heart.

As she watched in horror, the red sky above her shattered, disintegrating the shield she'd formed to protect her vampires. Golden sunlight poured, unimpeded over all those she'd claimed as her own.

Deadly, deadly sunlight.

CHAPTER FIFTY-THREE

Arturo froze as the sky shattered, as raw sunlight blanketed them all.

A few voices cried out, but most who were still conscious merely stared in stunned silence, meeting their deaths with stoic acceptance. They'd done all they could.

Arturo waited in agonizing dread for the burn of sunlight on his flesh, for his body to erupt into flame. For death.

But seconds passed. Nothing happened.

A couple of vampires sat up, looking at one another in confusion.

Arturo's own brows drew down. He felt no fire, no burn. Just warmth. Quinn's loving warmth.

His eyes widened and he turned to her, his gaze slamming into hers. He saw the moment she, too, understood—the leap of joy, the catch of her breath.

"I did it." Her words were little more than a whisper followed by a gasp. "I did it!"

Still, the others looked at one another and Quinn, utterly perplexed.

With a laugh that erupted from deep in his belly, a euphoric shout, Arturo swept her into his arms and twirled her around, then caught her mouth with his. As her arms caught around his neck, he kissed her, thanking her, rejoicing with her, loving her.

All around them, voices began to murmur.

"What happened?"

"What does this mean?"

"Are we safe?"

"Did she renew Blackstone's magic?"

"No, of course not. Look around you. This is not Blackstone's world. This is the Healer's."

"But...*the sun?*"

Arturo pulled away, kissing Quinn's hair. "We must see how many we can save."

Her euphoria immediately doused, Quinn nodded, worry flooding her eyes. But as Arturo released her and looked around, he found the wolves pushing to their feet. And most of the vampires, Slavas, and fae, as well—Kassius and Neo. Lukas and Sam. Fabian and Grant.

Many had died, he knew that, both in the battle and the failing magic. But from a quick scan, he would guess more than half of their army had survived.

Fabian strode forward, then turned to address the others. "Blackstone gave us a world of darkness," he shouted, quieting the throng. "The Healer has given us back the light!"

Silence blanketed the crowd.

"How?" someone asked.

Fabian laughed. "How do you think? Magic!"

Micah came to stand beside Arturo and Quinn. "Cristoff stabbed himself," he said with wonder.

Arturo nodded, not quite sure how to process the loss. "He knew." Arturo turned to Quinn. "He said, just before he died, 'And the one does know'."

Finely arched brows knit. "The curse could only be broken by Escalla drinking the heart blood and the power of the one."

"The one who stole the power in the first place," Arturo said. "Cristoff. It was a diabolical provision, for what were the chances of the same vampire stabbing a sorcerer for power, then sacrificing himself?"

"Yet the two minds of Cristoff managed just that," Quinn said. "When he stabbed me, I'm pretty certain that we both saw that vision, the two wizards uttering the curse. Cristoff knew what it took to break the curse and to destroy Escalla. When the good Cristoff finally broke free, he used that knowledge to end it."

Kassius joined them and Quinn hugged him. "I'm so glad you're okay."

"Ax," Micah said quietly, and nodded behind him.

Arturo turned to find every vampire, every wolf, every Slava, and fae, on one knee watching them. Quinn glanced at him in confusion. A confusion which cleared when Fabian, directly in front of them, called out loudly, "I pledge fealty to the Healer and her Snake."

"The Healer and her Vampire, please," Quinn replied with a laugh. "Or better yet, just Quinn and Arturo."

Fabian grinned. "To Quinn and Arturo!"

All throughout the gathering, the shout went up. "To Quinn and Arturo!"

As Quinn turned to him, her eyes filled with wonder, Arturo felt a pride in her he could barely contain and a love that filled him beyond imagining. As their gazes met, she smiled at him, a smile that had him almost lifting off his feet.

Do you have any idea how much I love you? he asked her.

Almost as much as I love you?

He stared at her, startled by the sound of her voice in his head. *Marry me.*

Now it was her turn to stare.

His heart tightened with chagrin. "That was too soon."

But to his amazement, she took his face in her hands. "Not too soon." She searched his eyes, her own filled with wonder. "Marriage? Are you sure? As a potentially powerful sorceress, there's no telling how long you might be stuck with me."

His hands gripped her waist. "*Potentially* powerful? You just created a *world*." His arms slid around her and he pulled her close. "I pray you live forever." It was his turn to search her face, her expression, for sign of her answer. "You don't have to stay here. It wasn't fair of me to ask you to live the life of a vampire, unable to walk in real sunshine."

Her smile, filled with such tenderness, sent his heart soaring. "I once asked Amanda why she'd given up her life for Sam. She said, 'He is my life.' At the time, I didn't understand. But I do, now, perfectly. Where I live doesn't matter, Turo. Whether it's in real sunshine or my magical sun, D.C. or V.C., all that matters is that I live my life with you." Quinn lifted an eyebrow. "For now, though, we're staying right here. This is *my* world, now." Her smile turned wickedly mischievous. "And I'm making some changes."

Joy surged through him, a joy he'd never believed possible. And he began to laugh.

EPILOGUE

"**W**e should be up and running by the end of the week," Amanda told Quinn and Arturo as she showed them around the brand new Vamp City Hospital, previously known as Neo's basement. "Bram's insisting we can't open without a decent supply of antibiotics and pain killers, though I really think the antibiotics will be unnecessary with healers and vampires working here. I've yet to find a bacteria that can't be quickly overcome by a vampire bite. The pain killers are a different matter since we may run across other Levenachs who can't be enthralled."

Quinn poked her head into one of the newly appointed examining rooms, impressed by how much it looked like any doctor's office in the real world, complete with overhead fluorescent lights. Neo's now had a number of generators.

It had been two months since the sun rose on Vamp City and the changes wrought in that short time Quinn found nothing short of astounding. Then again, when vampires put their minds to something, they could accomplish it amazingly fast. And to her immense gratitude and delight, they'd set their sights on making her world exactly what she wanted it to be—a utopia not just for the vampires who lived here, and those who were arriving by the legions, but also for the wolves and Slavas, the Traders and fae, most of whom had no way to leave. Only the Rippers continued to be problematic.

As Amanda walked them down the hallway, showing them examining rooms and surgery centers, one after the other, Arturo began to frown.

"I thought we'd agreed on no new mortals for the time being. All this for Octavia's dozen Levenach sorcerers?"

Quinn smiled. "Are you forgetting about her school?"

He looked at her warily. "Her school for the dozen."

Quinn's smile turned into a laugh. "That's just phase one, training the trainers." She slid her arm through his. "Oh, Vampire, you have no idea the plans she's making."

Amanda nodded sagely. "When you consider how many Levenachs accidentally walked in on sunbeams in D.C. alone, there must be thousands worldwide. All of them are coming into their power, all without a clue what's happening to them."

"Thousands of wild sorcerers. That's a disaster waiting to happen," Arturo muttered.

Quinn had to agree. Fortunately, there were those who possessed the ability to see the magic in others. A team of vampires and sorcerers had been assembled to start hunting them down, to try to coax them into studying with Octavia.

"How did your call for staff go?" Quinn asked Amanda. She and Arturo had spent most of the past week traveling between the real world and Sakamoto's, where they would live, for now. Though Arturo could have claimed Cristoff's castle for his own, he'd agreed that the memories there were too horrific. For both of them.

"I have nine vampires and three fae who've committed to helping staff the hospital," Amanda told her. "All but one have healing skills. The last is Bram who, while not technically a healer, has mad surgical skills and tremendous hospital experience. He'll continue to work nights at G.W. Hospital in D.C., but he'll spend his days with us."

"I notice you still haven't convinced Neo to add more electricity upstairs."

Amanda smiled ruefully. "No. Despite growing up in the late twentieth century, he's taken a liking to what he calls the more natural way of life of the nineteenth. Mukdalla and Sam both prefer it, as well, so the generators will remain hooked up to the kitchen and hospital only."

"Most of the vampires agree with Neo," Arturo said. "Micah and I are exceptions."

Amanda smiled. "From what I hear, you two always have been."

As his dark eyes, as warm as the sun, crinkled at the corners, Quinn kissed his cheek. "Truth."

He met her gaze, his own filled with such love that her heart swelled almost beyond bearing.

With a smile, Quinn turned back to Amanda and gave her a quick hug. "We need to get going, but come visit us, please? We're installing a media room at Sakamoto's complete with a small theater-sized screen. We'll be holding monthly movie nights for the Slavas and wolves, and anyone else who wants to attend."

The smile that bloomed across Amanda's face was one of pure delight. "With popcorn and soda?"

Quinn laughed. "I was thinking appetizers and wine, but sure. We'll serve whatever you want."

They said goodbye to Amanda and headed upstairs where the sun shone brightly through the windows. In the kitchen, they found Neo and Mukdalla chatting with Zack and Lily.

Quinn smiled when she saw her brother and his fiancée. "I didn't know you two were here."

Zack gave Quinn a quick hug. "We just stopped by."

"Actually, we didn't *just* stop by," Lily admitted. She turned to Mukdalla with a smile. "Octavia would like for you to consider running her school for Levenach sorcerers."

Mukdalla's mouth dropped. "*Running* it?" Her hand went to her chest. "Me?"

Lily reached for her. "You don't have to say yes. But you'd be wonderful. You could hire whomever you want to do the work, but we're going to need someone with organizational skills, someone used to dealing with scared humans. We expect a lot of the students coming to us to be pretty dazed and confused at first."

"Wait," Quinn said, turning to Lily. "You're using a lot of *us'es* and *we's*. Are you telling me that you and Zack are going to stay and help run the school, too? I thought you were going to program computer games."

Zack grinned, for a moment looking twenty-two again for the first time since they'd stumbled into Vamp City. "Anyone can be a programmer, Sis. We have a chance to help build *Hogwarts*. For real."

All she'd ever wanted was for him to be safe. And happy. Part of her wished he'd find that happiness in California, a continent away from anything to do with vampires, though she was learning that vampires, in particular Rippers, could be anywhere. There was no place that was truly safe. It was here that Zack had found his strength, both physical and emotional. It was here, he'd come into his sorcerer's power, helped defeat a monster, and discovered that the girl he'd loved for years had loved him in return. For years.

He was happy, in love, and he appeared to have found a calling. For now.

"Will you be teaching?" she asked her brother.

"Who knows? We have to be students first. Octavia still has a ton to teach us. But we'll help her set up the school and find her students." To no one's great surprise, the Levenachs were the only humans who could enter and leave the new V.C. at will.

Lily nodded. "I can see their energy—the faint glow of a Levenach. I can help William and Maxwell identify them."

Quinn hadn't met William, Maxwell, and William's wife, Ana Lucia, until after the Great Battle, as it was coming to be called. But they, too, had become instant friends, especially Ana Lucia.

"The new sorcerers are probably everywhere," Zack said. "And terrified. You know how that feels, Sis, when weird stuff happens and everyone looks at you like you're a freak. We don't want anyone to suffer who doesn't have to. People, especially in D.C., have already suffered too much."

There were still hundreds missing, hundreds more dead from what officials were calling a terrorist attack. It amazed Quinn how adept humans were at seeing only what they wanted to see. She read the occasional speculation on-line that aliens were to blame, but for the most part, chemical weapons and hallucinogenics were being blamed for the strange things people claimed to have seen, and the numbers who'd 'jumped' to their deaths.

"I'm glad you want to help," Quinn told her brother sincerely.

Davu strode into the kitchen, Dera close behind. "The same band of Rippers who pillaged the market two days ago will attempt to hit it again tonight."

Dera nodded. "They'll be stopped by Emoras again, led by Neo and Micah."

Neo gave a resigned sigh. "I guess we'll be staking out the market again tonight."

"Yes you will," Mukdalla said. "The market's grand opening is tomorrow and every Slava in the city will probably be there. I've heard *everything* they've asked for will be available for sale, and at reasonable Vamp City prices." Which meant a fraction of what they cost in the real world. Most of the Slavas had been in V.C. for decades, some more than a hundred years. Real world prices would give them a heart attack.

Quinn's first proclamation, after creating her world, was to officially emancipate all slaves. There would be no slavery in *her* Vamp City. Of course, in reality, the Slavas were ideally suited to being the primary food source and household labor for the vampires. And they couldn't leave for fear of suffering sudden death when their immortal bodies became mortal again. But now, instead of mere chattel, they'd become valuable, and empowered. Because now the Slavas could work for and/or feed, whomever they chose. And if they weren't being treated or paid well enough, they were free to leave and find other employment.

So far, the vampires had been bending over backward to please them. She suspected that many, if not most, of the Emoras were ashamed of the way the Slavas had suffered and were more than happy to find ways to make it up to them, including building and furnishing brand new Slava cottages complete with soaking tubs and hot water.

Micah walked in the back door followed by Lukas and his fiancée, Elizabeth. The first thing Lukas had apparently done after Quinn saved V.C. was leave to find Elizabeth and talk her into spending the rest of her life with him, now that he could walk with her in the sun in at least one world. Quinn liked the woman, a school teacher, immensely and had learned that Micah had been keeping an eye on her while Lukas was trapped in V.C.

Quinn smiled. Her list of genuine friends was growing nicely. It was hard not to be open, and happy with the world, when she was so much in love.

"Savin's pack and the Herewoods are feuding again," Micah announced.

"Not that we expected that truce to last," Lukas muttered.

"Hi, Quinn," Elizabeth said with a smile and handed her a small bunch of wildflowers.

Quinn gave her a quick hug at the thoughtful gift. Elizabeth, too, was one of the Levenachs, another who'd accidentally wandered in on a sunbeam before Cristoff's defeat. Elizabeth had told her yesterday that she planned to try to find and help the youngest sorcerers.

"In other news," Micah announced, "we've had two more kovenas—one from Croatia, another from the Philippines—query us about moving here. That makes more than a thousand new vampires with the other five kovenas who've already contacted us. They all want to live under Quinn's sun."

Quinn met Arturo's rueful gaze and smiled. "Why do I feel like the politics of this place are going to make my head spin?"

Arturo slid his hand beneath her hair to cup her neck. "That would be because you're as wise as you are beautiful."

She snorted. "It's a good thing you're such a skilled diplomat."

He grinned, his eyes as deep as the oceans, and kissed her. "Vamp City will never be an easy place to live, *amore mio*. If the politics and the feuding become too much, we will leave. I will live wherever you choose, you know that."

She smiled. "I do know that, my vampire. For now, though, this is where I choose." *We've made a difference here, Turo,* she added for his ears only.

An understatement, tesoro mio. *You've changed the lives of everyone here, all very much for the better. Many owe you their lives, many our souls.* As he spoke the words, he stared into her eyes, his thumb stroking the side of her neck with the most tender of touches until her heart melted and her body warmed.

Quinn reached for him in return, gripping his lean waist with her free hand, the one not holding wildflowers. *And I owe you...everything. You've changed me, Vampire. You helped me find and appreciate my strength.* He'd taught her the power of friendship. And love.

Behind them Micah cleared his throat. "Earth to Ax and Quinn."

Laughing, Arturo pulled her against his side and they turned to face the others, her family, her friends.

"You didn't get the significance of Elizabeth's gift," Micah said, a funny look on his face.

Quinn glanced down at the small bunch of wildflowers. Then back at Micah.

A huge grin spread across his face. "We found those growing in the Crux."

She stilled, her mouth dropping open. "The *Crux?*"

"Right by the new Focus. Grass is beginning to grow. Leaves are starting to bud on the trees."

Her brows slammed down. "It's November." Which, under the circumstances, was completely irrelevant.

Most of them apparently agreed and laughed.

"Your magic has brought more than light, *amore mio*." Arturo hugged her closer. "It has brought life."

And it had, she knew that. In the heart of a vampire otherworld, she'd found her life. Her heart.

Most of all, she'd found herself.

Don't miss the first two books in the Vamp City *series!*

A BLOOD SEDUCTION
Vamp City Book 1

Quinn Lennox is searching for a missing friend when she stumbles into a dark otherworld that only she can see—and finds herself at the mercy of Arturo Mazza, a dangerously handsome vampire whose wicked kiss will save her, enslave her, bewitch her, and betray her.

A KISS OF BLOOD
Vamp City Book 2

One of the few humans who managed to escape the deadly twilight world of Vamp City, Quinn Lennox vows to never return. But the vampires want her back, for only she has the power to renew the magic of their crumbling world—and free the vampires trapped within.

ACKNOWLEDGMENTS

Thanks, as always, to Laurin Wittig and Anne Shaw Moran who make every journey a pleasure. Thanks also to my wonderful team: Amy Atwell, Patricia Schmitt, Joan Turner, and Kelly Poulsen. I couldn't have done it without you.

To my readers, I offer my endless and heartfelt appreciation. It is because of you that writing is such a joy. It's your imagination and enthusiasm that truly bring my worlds to life.

ABOUT THE AUTHOR

Pamela Palmer is the *New York Times*, *USA Today*, and international bestselling author of nineteen paranormal romance and urban fantasy novels. When Pamela's initial career goal of captaining starships failed to pan out, she turned to engineering, satisfying her desire for adventure with books and daydreams until finally succumbing to the need to create worlds of her own. Pamela lives and writes in the suburbs of Washington, D.C.

For more information on Vamp City, or to read excerpts, connect with Pamela, or sign up for her newsletter, please visit her website, www.pamelapalmer.net. Pamela can also be reached via Facebook at www.facebook.com/PamelaPalmer and on Twitter at www.twitter.com/Pamela_Palmer.

Made in the USA
Middletown, DE
22 October 2015